PRAISE FOR B. MICHELAARD AND *THE PEGASUS PROJECT*!

"*The Pegasus Project* is an ultra-high-tech yarn that starts with a bang and ends with a bigger one, with enough plot twists in between to satisfy the most demanding of readers."
—S. K. Wolf, author of *Mackinnon's Machine*

"Michelaard puts finely-drawn characters on a world-wide stage of intrigue beneath skies roaring with mach-2 fighters and exciting air-to-air combat. A must!"
—Col. Jimmy Butler USAF (ret.),
author of *The Iskra Incident*

"Disguised as a page-turning thriller, B. Michelaard's *The Pegasus Project* is a riveting account of the terrifying shape of things to come. A first-rate read."
—Loren D. Estleman, author of *White Desert*

"HEADS UP, ALPHA LEAD! ONE OF THESE BANDITS JUST FIRED A HEAT-SEEKER!"

Gus rolled, corkscrewing into a 30-degree dive, plugged in the afterburners. "Stay clear, Alpha Two."

Michelle was aboard that Antonov, and the missile's infra-red sensor was homing on one of its three operating turbo-props. He had to decoy that missile with something even hotter—the F-24's afterburners.

He dipped in behind the Antonov, then pulled up to the left. "Alpha Lead, that heater's chasing you now!" Gus was too busy to reply. He killed both burners, pulled the throttles back to idle, and toggled a thermite flare. It was an infra-red source a heat-seeking missile couldn't ignore.

Twisting his neck, he looked back, saw the smoke trail of the missile diverging where the Scimitar had turned. It had taken the bait and was chasing the flare.

An instant's brilliant flash enveloped him. He felt a jolt. The heater had sensed a miss and self-detonated.

His first clue that something was wrong was smoke in the cockpit. Then red lights on the panel and a warning screech in his earphones.

Looking back, he saw a smoke trail.

He was hit.

THE PEGASUS PROJECT

B. MICHELAARD

LEISURE BOOKS   NEW YORK CITY

*To the memory of my 431st 'Red Devil' squadron mate,
the late General Charles L. 'Chuck' Donnelly
USAF—1929-1994.*

A LEISURE BOOK®

May 2000

Published by

Dorchester Publishing Co., Inc.
276 Fifth Avenue
New York, NY 10001

ISBN 0-8439-4707-1

The name "Leisure Books" and the stylized "L" with design are trademarks of Dorchester Publishing Co., Inc.

Printed in the United States of America.

SPECIAL ACKNOWLEDGMENT

I wish to recognize the valuable technical support by the Rasheed family and their staff at Computers and Concepts in Keego Harbor, Michigan, without whom this story may never have found its way from computer to screen to printed page.

—B. Michelaard

This is a work of pure fiction, meaning it is entirely the product of the author's somewhat fevered imagination. Anyone who thinks he recognizes himself or his friends or enemies or indeed any actual person in these pages is mistaken. As far as I know, none of this ever happened. But then, who's to say…?

THE PEGASUS PROJECT

Prologue

North Vietnam
May 1972

Thunder-wasps out to deliver a sting, the strike force came in low and fast off the water. Crossing the coast, they flew under both enemy radar and the blue-black bellies of towering CBs lined up like sentinels, shoulder-to-shoulder.

They skimmed up the Red River Valley. Ahead, the cotton-boll cumulus floated in congealed serenity.

Out of them swarmed the defender-wasps, the MiGs.

Gus Halstrom, still a first lieutenant but on his second combat tour and leading a flight of four, called for afterburners. They were assigned to counterair and flak suppression, so he took them on a deliberate detour around one of those cauliflower heads and in behind a pair of MiG-21's, the delta-wing Soviet hot rods that spearheaded Ho Chi Minh's air force. Gus's squadron and their 104's had been assigned here because they had the performance to counter the MiG-21.

Closing from six o'clock low—the ideal blind spot—he maxed the audio growl from a Sidewinder missile on the number-two MiG's tailpipe, and pressed the stick button. The missile roared off its launch rails, squirting him with its acrid tail smoke.

That corkscrewing smoke-trace led right up the enemy's ass. The MiG dissolved in a greasy fireball that sent blazing shards in all directions.

The leader lit his afterburner and wracked into a hard turn. But Gus had overtake. He lit his own burner, then centered the glowing rings of the gunsight reticle on the delta. A half-second burst, and its left side flamed and folded. The MiG gyrated a trail of black, oily smoke.

Meanwhile, the strike pilots, leaving smoke and destruction, began withdrawing.

None of this was without cost. It added to the dead and broken American bodies and expensive made-in-USA junk that littered the landscape between Hanoi and Haiphong.

Among the withdrawing strike aircraft were the usual cripples. And as always the route back to the coast was a gauntlet of flak. Bursts from the big 80mm shells generated a mud-umber pall, like sediment stirred up from the bottom of a pond. A not-very-near miss from one of those could shred an airplane, yet they were not the major threat. They were meant to frighten and funnel the attackers into the fields of fire of the radar-controlled quad forties and twin fifty-sevens.

Gus and his flight took over escorting a damaged A-7, strafing gun positions that lay in its path.

Turning for rejoin after a firing pass on one flak battery, Gus flew directly over another he never saw.

From the heavy jolt of high explosive, he recognized the twin 57's.

Smoke filled the cockpit. Blue, oxygen-fed flames bit at his flesh.

Trained automation plus survival instinct took over.

Before he had time to think, he had hit the wind-blast and was trying to "beat the gizmo"—separate from the seat and open the chute before the automatic device did it for him. If he could arm the seat and blow off the canopy, then the hard kick in the butt from the ejection seat would register only as memory.

But the gizmo was quicker. It was designed to be. Trying to beat it was backup in case it failed.

Well before his first combat mission, he had tried to prepare himself mentally for this event, bailing out over hostile territory.

The reality overwhelmed all of it.

One moment, he was in the cockpit, secure and dominating; the next, he was dangling in a parachute. And waiting below were Vietnamese eager to have his guts for garters.

The descent was brief, and the moment his feet touched, he popped the quick-releases. The light breeze carried the shrouds and canopy clear. Still in automatic function, he undid the chest and groin buckles, freed himself from the harness, threw off the helmet and oxygen mask.

Then, with his first considered act, reaching for the pistol holstered near his left armpit, he discovered his forearms were scorched and blistered. In the humid heat of Southeast Asia, pilots wore their sleeves rolled up. He had neglected to roll his down before launch.

Another rude shock—the sight of large bloodstained patches.

Then deep stabs of pain, the feeling of metal imbedded in his flesh. Finally, weakness and nausea.

He had hoped to clear the area, get outside any search cordon, then cover the twenty miles or so to the coast during darkness. Now he found the prospect of going twenty feet rather daunting.

It was no use anyway. Vietnamese emerged from the brush all around. Wherever he looked, he faced militiamen with leveled rifles. Raw hatred on taut Asian faces.

13

At once, he was surrounded and set upon—pummeled with farm implements and rifle butts. Something struck him in the head, and the ground swayed beneath him.

His last conscious sensation was of having his face in the dirt while they still kicked and beat him.

When he came around again, three men in the uniform of the NVA, holding Kalashnikov automatic rifles, were standing over him, shouting and pushing the others back. The last one to be shoved away, a mere tot wearing sandals made from segments of auto tires, was industriously kicking him in the head.

Gus was hauled to his feet, his arms bound behind him. The rough hemp scraped the burned skin. He was marched a mile or so across the landscape of brush, rice paddies, and clongs to a small group of buildings around a dusty square. There he was shoved onto an open stake-bed truck with four self-serious young militiamen to menace him with guns, bayonets, and hostile scowls.

The next hour or so was a kaleidoscope of pain, fear, and exhaustion. He was hauled from place to place with his wounds untreated and no attempt made to handle him gently.

Finally they arrived at a large, two-story masonry structure he judged must date from the French colonial era. Small clusters of NVA troops idled in the courtyard. He was prodded off the truck by the adolescent militiamen, who clearly enjoyed the chance to perform like real soldiers.

With his six-two frame, he felt a bit like Gulliver among the Lilliputians. The eyes that followed him took in the flying boots and G-suit. The hostility grew thicker than Los Angeles smog.

They entered a large room where men and women in uniform worked at desks. From here on, he was entirely in the hands of the NVA. Two guards marched him down a corridor and into another nearly bare room floored with pale terrazzo squares. There was a heavy wooden table with three straight chairs. He was not invited to sit.

Shortly, an officer with captain's insignia came striding in. Even in his fog of pain and fatigue, Gus felt a certain amusement at the man's posturing in cavalry boots and breeches with a riding crop in his hand.

The captain was short but more thickset than the average Tonkinese. Brandishing the crop under Gus's nose, he said, "I am Captain Trang, and you will cooperate with me completely. You understand?" He had to tilt his head far back to look up into Gus's face. When Gus remained silent, Trang leaned closer and shouted, "You understand!"

"And I'm Gustavus Halstrom, first lieutenant, U.S. Air Force." He gave his serial number.

"Oh, you one o' duh brave ones, huh?" Trang's tone carried a thick sneer. Abruptly, he lashed Halstrom across the face with the crop. It was sudden and vicious. Gus was caught entirely off guard, but said nothing. When Gus did not react, Trang again swung the riding crop. "Okay, I give you chance to be plenty brave. Real big hero." The laugh that followed was ugly, ominous.

He started down the corridor. The two guards prodded Halstrom along with their rifle muzzles. They came to what appeared to be a supply receiving point. Large overhead doors closed off what had to be a cargo platform. Flatbed handcarts stood against one wall. On an overhead track was a hand-operated chain hoist for heavy items. There was also a rack of meat hooks for handling dressed animal carcasses.

Trang grabbed one of the hooks and slipped it onto the chain that hung from the hoist. He spoke to the guards, who shoved Halstrom forward. One of them jerked his head back. With an abrupt, vicious movement, Trang drove the point of the hook into the underside of Gus's jaw. It penetrated the soft tissue in the V of the mandible and emerged in his mouth just beneath his tongue.

His first reaction was a sort of disbelief. As with most severe wounds, the pain was not immediate. It came in waves, building to a crescendo.

He had an almost overpowering reaction to pull away, struggle to free himself. But that would only aggravate the injury and feed Trang's sadism. By an effort of will he could not himself comprehend, he retained control, forced reason to prevail over animal panic.

"You hooked like a fish now," said Trang with another snorting, humorless laugh. He began pulling on the operating chain of the hoist, drawing the hook upward. Amid the throbbing pain that radiated from his mouth, Halstrom felt the hook pulling his jaw. To relieve it, he tilted his head and then raised himself on his toes.

Incredibly, he felt himself being slowly lifted by his jaw. "You still feeling brave?" Once more Trang uttered that gruesome, nasal laugh while he kept pulling on the revolving chain. When Gus could extend his toes no farther, his weight began to bear on the hinges of his jaw. Trang kept raising the hook till the limit of muscle and sinew was exceeded. Unable to support his 220 pounds, his jaw popped out of its sockets. The pain screamed through his nervous system like a siren. It even had a red, flashing quality about it, like the warning lights in a fighter cockpit.

His lower teeth dug into his upper lip at the philtrum. Then came the nausea. He had to fight down the impulse to vomit, knowing it could block his airway and suffocate him.

He continued conscious and aware of each excruciating moment. Which shattered another comforting misconception—that extreme pain would pop circuit-breakers in the nervous system and release the victim into unconsciousness.

Madness threatened. Halstrom felt it edging up on him like an ominous black storm cloud, more frightening than the pain itself. Once it closed in and the delicate neuron circuits of the master control burned out, they could not be fully restored. He had known men whose minds had been pushed beyond the limit, and they were never really themselves again. Therapy and rest let them function within the limits of normality, but the bedrock of their psyches had been shattered and, like glass or porcelain, could not be fully mended.

So when Trang again cackled, "You still feeling brave?" Halstrom scarcely heard. He was defending a tight inner citadel against the onslaught of madness, where no further stimuli could penetrate. How long this waking nightmare lasted he could not know. Somewhere in the midst of this battle he was waging inside himself, he finally passed out.

He awoke in a small hospital ward. Like nearly all of Indochina, it was oppressively hot and humid. It was also dismal and noisome, buzzing with flies and fetid with the losing struggle of too little antiseptic against too much bacterial corruption. Yet even stronger than the organic stink was the aura of hate.

He still wore his flying suit, with its mud spots and bloodstains. His jaw, back in its sockets, radiated a deep, throbbing ache, along with the wound from the meat hook. Attempts to move the jaw brought shooting pain. The whole area was swollen and discolored. He could not see the black and blue, but knew it was there.

His burned forearms, cleaned now and treated with some lavender-tinted substance, felt as if they were still in the fire. The shrapnel wounds had also been tended. Some bits had been removed and the holes stitched up. Each one transmitted its own pain on its own frequency.

He lay like that through uncounted days and nights. Gradually, he was able to chew and was fed the standard diet of rice with bits of fish and vegetables, which at first he had some trouble keeping down. When he had to relieve himself, an armed militiamen went along.

As soon as he could stand and walk reliably, he was

taken under guard to a cell in a brick and concrete prison. He surmised this too had been built by the French.

Gradually the pain diminished. His wounds healed as his rugged constitution asserted itself. He began a routine of daily exercise. The diet was skimpy, and he did not recover his normal weight and strength. Twice a day, he was allowed out for fresh air in a small, paved compound. He was able to hand-wash his clothing in a sink.

He still wore his flying suit and boots; his captors simply had nothing large enough to fit him. His G-suit with everything he had carried in the pockets—aerial charts, airplane checklist, escape kit with several hundred dollars worth of gold coins—was long gone. His captors seemed amused that an American flag was included to help him escape, and made him sew it on the back of his flying suit.

There was something else in the suit they missed. If they found it, they might take extreme exception. Yet he drew a certain comfort knowing it was there.

Then one day, he was moved to a new location where for the first time he met other American prisoners. More than a dozen, they were housed in a two-story masonry compound, another facility from French colonial rule. It had steel bars or gratings over the windows, and the single door was well guarded. This was not the notorious Hanoi Hilton, but from the sound of nearby air strikes, they could tell Hanoi was not far.

Most of the men here were aircrew—Air Force, Navy, or Marine pilots. The senior man was an Army lieutenant colonel named Donaldson, an ordnance expert caught when the unit he was working with was surrounded in what was supposed to be a pacified area. He was primarily a technician and struggled with his role as senior officer—maintaining morale and discipline and fostering escape plans.

"So what's your degree?" he asked Gus soon after they met.

"MS, aero engineering. Why?"

Donaldson bobbed his head. "Fits the pattern. We're a special group here. All advanced scientific or technical degrees. Carson over there's physics. Close to finishing his Ph.D., I understand. Milsop's chemistry. Sanborn mathematics. Dumont's one of your Air Force weather types. Ph.D. in meteorology. Poor bastard went on a flight to gather first-hand weather data. Strayed off course and wound up practically over Haiphong."

"So how do the North Viets know all this?" After what it had cost him to stick to the Code of Conduct, Gus was in no mood to hear that others had been passing out details like business cards.

Donaldson sagged in his chair and showed a deeply troubled look. "We don't know. Every man here claims he gave nothing but name, rank, and serial number. Some were barely interrogated. But these Viets have all kinds of personal data on us. Families, schooling, career. Stuff that can only come from the States."

Over the next few weeks, Gus came to know all his fellow inmates, none very well. The shock of discovering the enemy knew so much had caused most of them to withdraw inside a shell of privacy.

They were well fed here, and with exercise, Gus finally regained his normal weight and strength. There was a great deal of plotting for escape, but the opportunity was rare as ice cubes. They amused each other by devising or recalling mathematical games and puzzles and interesting scientific problems.

Later yet, after Gus had made the adjustment and was confident he could endure, he was again moved and this time installed in fairly comfortable quarters. He could shower and shave. A barber cut his hair, which had grown shaggy. He had always worn it in a typically short military cut. Now a look in a mirror showed it styled to a kind of theatrical luxuriance. They shot several photos of him, from various angles.

Next, he was taken before a Viet officer who introduced himself as Major Minh. Gus at once noted Minh's casually efficient air and perfect Midwestern American English. His complexion was similar to most Tonkinese, but he was much taller. His build was lean and sinewy, his features larger and coarser. "It may interest you," he said, "that I was deemed to qualify for this job because I went to university in your country. Here." He slipped a class ring off his finger and showed it to Gus: Ohio University, 1960. Minh lit a cigarette, blew out smoke, and offered the pack—Gauloise, made in France. Gus declined.

"I regret that Captain Trang exercised his patriotic and Marxist zeal on you so pointlessly," he went on. "You actually have little or no information of value to us." He leaned back and laced his fingers behind his head. "This whole war is in fact regrettable and quite pointless. Of course, you're only a tool of the Pentagon, which is in turn a tool of powerful interests. Not merely on Wall Street but in London, Paris, the Vatican, and elsewhere."

"And I can't believe," Gus responded, "that your country's interests lie in acting as surrogate for a small and power-obsessed coterie in the Kremlin. Or a similar one in Peking."

Minh showed a faint, off-center smile. "You're closer to the truth than even you might guess," he said. "In the long run, the small, tropical nations will have to confederate in some way to avoid domination by the temperate powers. Even those that are nominally Marxist."

Despite this outwardly reasonable attitude, Minh was more menacing than Trang. He was clearly one who would bring both patience and ingenuity to the task of destroying his enemies. And consider it a lifetime commitment. He fixed Gus with a hard, direct stare. "I don't know what the arrangements may be for prisoner exchange once these hostilities end. Whatever they are, I have the feeling you and I will face each other as enemies for a long time to come."

The interview ended, and Gus was returned to his quarters, but it left him puzzled. "Interview" was indeed an apt word, as if he were being considered for a job. He had the feeling that Minh wanted not so much to question as to examine him.

Two days later, he was again summoned. As soon as he entered the large, classroomlike enclosure, he recognized what had to be a delegation of antiwar Americans, a dozen or so. They ranged from disgusting, hairy young radicals to sober, worried-looking elders. And just as he expected, they were there to persuade him to denounce the U.S. role in Indochina. The young radicals snarled obscenities, called him "pig," "murderer," "baby-killer," and "Wall Street lackey." The older people spoke earnestly, in gentle tones, with frowns of concern. He supposed they might be Quakers. There was a third group, in age about thirty-five to fifty, career Marxists, who had almost nothing to say. With them, he had at least a basis for understanding with no words spoken—a solid pact of mutual hatred.

He could forgive the Quakers and elders their foibles. The rest he'd gladly napalm.

He sat there impassive, ignoring gentle plea and invective alike, appearing relaxed, but coiled, ready. His opportunity came when one of the hairy young radicals advanced to shout into his face. Hallstrom's fist made solid contact. Feeling the satisfying crunch, he was on his feet in an instant, pummeling his enemy. In his cold rage, he was going for the kill, and might have managed it had the Viet guards not rushed in.

He was sure this was both the culmination and termination of his stay in these more gentle surroundings. With their last hope of "turning" him frustrated, the enemy would now send him to rejoin those other prisoners with technical degrees, for whatever purpose they had in mind.

The moment he got back to his quarters, he discovered how wrong he was. Entering the room was like Alice's step through the looking-glass.

21

B. Michelaard

In the most bizarre experience of his life, he came face to face with himself.

Whoever this other man was, the two of them shared an amazing resemblance, whether natural or artificial—the result of plastic surgery—he could not discern.

While he stared in both dread and fascination, his double gave a small, relaxed smile, one very much like his own, and said, "Well, what do you think?"

Even the voice seemed a good match.

Chapter One

April 2002

The missile came at them out of the mist.

Anvil Bravo was on station at thirty-three thousand. Below, the coastline of Colombia lay shrouded in sinister mystery and ocean vapor.

They were on somebody's radar. Routine. Captain Thorne, the ECM officer, put it on audio and let them all hear the soft "z-z-t" generated by the beam as it swept over them. That was routine too.

But that signal was suddenly replaced by the strident, pulsing signature of missile-guidance radar. Definitely not routine. "Ho-ly Christ, Skipper! We've got an incoming SAM! For real! Bearing one-three-zero. Seventy seconds to impact." He activated the chaff and flare dispensers. Bundles of radar-reflecting foil strips were vented from the belly. Magnesium flares to decoy a heat-seeker drifted away on small parachutes. Jamming signals jarred the electronic spectrum.

B. Michelaard

"Don't I hear it!" said Major Gil Austen, the aircraft commander. "Go figure." He cranked the wheel hard over. The long, silvery swept wings of the RC-141 AWACS tilted hard port. With stiff back-pressure on the yoke, Austen kept the horizon slicing by at sixty degrees, a tighter turn than ever demanded of most 141's. The crew was reacting with varying degrees of shock at having their butts jammed down by two-and-a-half Gs. Some had served in Desert Storm but had never actually been fired on.

Pencil-like, covering nearly two thousand feet per second, the missile was at twenty miles and passing through 25,000 when it showed as a faint blip on the screens. "Thirty seconds to impact!" Thorne continued the countermeasures along with his doomsday countdown.

Heading directly into an oncoming missile was standard evasion technique. It turned the hot tailpipes away from any IR sensor, minimized the radar silhouette, and maxed the rate of closure. Forced the missile's electronic brain into quicker decisions, amplified its errors.

"Twenty seconds to impact!"

With the missile head-on, Austen began jinking— small, quick turns combined with short dives and zooms. Behind them now was a vast, spreading plume of chaff and a trail of flares.

"Ten seconds to impact!"

Confused by the jamming signals and getting a strong return from the chaff, the SAM became indecisive. Its corrections grew large and erratic. As it sensed the miss, an alternate loop in its control algorithm took over and triggered the detonators.

The warhead was made like a baseball, a core of torpex wrapped with heavy-gauge steel wire and enclosed in a metal casing. Fragments spread in a spherical pattern from the epicenter, like Fourth of July fireworks. The sphere expanded at some five thousand feet per second to enclose Anvil Bravo.

The blast of shrapnel cut through sheet metal, wire bundles, microchips, flesh, and bone. Circuits shorted; scopes went dark. Control panels crackled and smoked. "O-h-h, shee-it!" came a voice with an East Coast accent. "This is gonna ruin the whole day."

Tech Sergeant Bert Holley died at his console between eye-blinks. One of those fragments passed through his neck, severed the spine and carotid artery. Airman First Class Cynthia Naybors, the only female aboard, started to say "That was scary!" What came out was, "That was . . . Oh, my god! Bert's . . ." Seeing the torn flesh and spreading blood, she covered her face with her hands and stifled a scream.

"Ho-ly shit!" said Staff Sergeant Kyle Bean. He looked at the haggled exit wound at the back of Holley's neck, pulled the torso upright, felt the other, still-intact carotid artery, shook his head. The faces around the compartment were almost as pale as the late Sergeant Holley.

Ragged shards had ripped through the number-three and-four engines, broke off pieces of rotor and stator blades. Each piece was sucked aft and broke off at least two more. The compressor stages self-destructed in geometric progression. Airflow dropped and temperatures rose. Burner cans and turbine blades began to distort and then melt. Out of balance, the engines vibrated. Fuel lines cracked and sprayed jet fuel.

It all happened in seconds. Before Austen could pull the two starboard throttles to idle, both engine pods were in flames. And before the copilot could close the fuel cut-off valves, the number-four engine exploded. The flames died, but smoke still streamed from number-three.

Out of balance in both mass and aerodynamics, Anvil Bravo skidded and rolled. The skipper managed something resembling controlled flight, but knew it would never carry them back to Panama. "Prepare to abandon aircraft!" he ordered, then transmitted: "Mayday! Mayday! Mayday! This is Anvil Bravo. We've been hit by a

SAM. Lost both starboard engines and have marginal control." To ease the effects of asymmetrical thrust, he retarded the throttles for the number-one and -two engines, and found the nearest thing to a stable flight condition was a descending spiral.

"Anvil Bravo, this is Arena. We have you on radar. Scrambling rescue at this time. Say your angles and your intentions."

"Descending through angles three-one. We'll try to reach angles fifteen or below before bailout." Though they were only some seven degrees north of the equator, bailing out at thirty thousand feet still meant frostbite and hypoxia. When he could spare a moment, the skipper got on the intercom to Thorne in the main compartment: "We've had our hands full. What's it like back there? Can you handle things?"

"Bad, but under control. The scopes are all knocked out, and Sergeant Holley was killed outright. Duda and Micheals were hit too, but we're patching 'em up. I've got everyone in life vests and chutes. We're losing cabin pressure, but we've broken out the oxygen bottles."

"Roger. We'll continue descent to fifteen or below for bailout. Get the life rafts in position."

"Roger, Skipper. You get us down to fifteen, we'll manage."

There was plenty to be done, and assigning tasks kept them from thinking about the danger. "Sergeant Bean," said Thorne, "take two men and get those life-raft packs positioned near the cargo doors. And make sure you hook up the static lines.

"Brock, Martini." He motioned to the two who were tending Duda and Micheals. Brock was a lean, bespectacled, sober-faced black man. Martini had dark, movie-actor looks and a smart mouth. That "ruin the whole day" remark had come from him. Some thought he might smart-mouth his way into Hell some day, but right now, that mouth could help keep the crew from thinking how scared they were. "Those two guys are going to need help when we bail out. Here's what you do. Walk your man off the edge and hold onto his D-ring. As soon as you're clear, pull the ring. After his chute opens, free-fall for at least a count of four before you pop your own."

Sergeant Bean—a wiry, toothy towhead from Arkansas—reported the life rafts ready. "You've done this before?" said Thorne. "Bailed out, I mean." When the sergeant affirmed it, Thorne said, "Listen up, everyone. Sergeant Bean here's had experience at this. A few words from him might help us all."

With an awkward grin, Bean hooked his thumbs in his belt. "Ain't nothin' to it. Pull yer D-ring soon's you hit the airstream. And remember, inflate just one side o' your vest afore you hit the water. Else'n it might make you sing sopraner. And don't pop those risers till your feet are wet."

"When the time comes," Thorne said, "Sergeant Bean will lead us out."

Meanwhile, Fate was not yet finished with Anvil Bravo. The controls were losing effect. The hydraulic gauge showed the pressure near the bottom red line. Activating the auxiliary pumps brought no change. The problem was loss of fluid. Too many holes in the airplane.

They passed through twenty thousand. "Time to let George do it," said Austen, and engaged the autopilot. Instantly, he found himself fighting to keep the aircraft from going inverted. He overpowered the Lear, disengaged it, and brought the 141 back to its downward spiral.

With the continuing drop in hydraulic pressure, he wondered if the bird could reach fifteen thousand before it lost flight controls altogether. "Better get the doors open," he told the copilot.

"Better hope they work," the copilot said, and passed the order back to Thorne. In this AWACS conversion, the side doors used for dropping paratroops had been sealed off and the space taken up with electronic gear. The clamshell cargo doors offered the best in-flight exit.

With the diminished cabin pressure, there was no sudden drop as the doors opened. The two pilots already wore oxygen masks.

"They won't open all the way, Skipper." It was the voice of Master Sergeant Willis, the crew chief.

"How far?"

"About eight . . . ten feet."

"That'll be okay once we level out and slow down." With the doors only partly open there could be a strong reverse airflow in through the gap. Anyone trying to go out could simply be blown back in.

"*If* we get leveled out," the copilot muttered. It was the kind of remark you kept to yourself.

"Coming down on fifteen thousand," Austen said to Thorne. "As soon as we're level, shove the life-raft packs out and then start with the crew." The hydraulic pressure seemed to stabilize, and he still had some control. The lower the bailout, the less the crew and the life rafts would scatter before they hit the water.

Reaction to the flight controls had become very sluggish. He got the wings level at ten thousand. They actually stopped the descent at eight thousand. "Okay, Harry," he said to the copilot. "Time for you to go. Nothing you can do here." He was trimming for a straight-ahead glide.

"I'll stick with you till—"

"That's an order, Captain!" The skipper jerked a thumb. "Get your ass aft and bail out! You've got about thirty seconds."

Thorne had the rest of the crew lined up on the cargo deck. When he saw Harry, the copilot, coming aft, he gave the signal. They pushed the survival kits out, then stepped off one by one. The chutes blossomed about a hundred feet aft. Against the misty, blue-green backdrop, the turgid canopies with their alternate white and orange panels were like psychedelic mushrooms. Thorne took a deep breath, shivered, and edged up to the lip of the deck.

"Hey, get going!" said Harry. He gave Thorne a small shove, and they both tumbled out into the airstream.

Even with full aft trim, the nose wanted to drop. The skipper applied a little power on the two good engines. That helped, but made the bird both yaw and roll to starboard. He compensated with rudder and aileron trim, but neither was quite enough. Face it. This badly wounded bird had no stable, hands-off flight condition. And the autopilot was useless. He'd have to trim the best he could, then dash for the exit.

Like most multi-engine pilots, he seldom wore a chute on the flight deck. He had put on his life vest, but the chute hung on a rack in the companionway. When he lifted it off, he saw both the pack and harness had been pierced by missile fragments.

There were spare chutes in a locker. As he got one out, the airplane was already beginning to nose down. He was a big man and had to loosen the harness before he could get into it. It was still a poor fit and hampered his movement.

Struggling aft against the increasing tilt of the deck, he noted a strange, frightening sense of desertion that weighed on his spirit. All he wanted now was to get out of the damn thing.

By the time he reached the cargo door, the nose was down some fifteen degrees.

If the 141 had been twenty feet shorter, he could have made it.

In the seconds it took him to cover that distance, the tilt of the cargo deck, the airspeed, and the reverse flow all combined to exceed the angle at which the friction of his shoe soles would hold. He began slipping back.

His legs worked frantically as he saw the lip of that cargo deck begin to recede. He bruised and tore his fingers against the rivet-heads on the floor as he found himself sliding down the deck toward the nose.

He almost sobbed with both fear and frustration. How could this happen to him? What would it be like getting killed in a crash? Would he be wiped out by the impact, or would he be conscious as the sinking fuselage carried him with it to the bottom?

And his family. He had helped tuck the kids into bed last night, kissed his wife this morning. Would they never see each other again?

His best hope now was to try to ditch in a way he might hope to survive. All but falling down the steepening slope of the deck, he almost hit his head on the instrument panel, took hold of the wheel, and pulled back on the control column.

No effect. The hydraulic gauge needle was hovering near zero. The control system with all its multiple redundancies had been overwhelmed by those holes that let the fluid escape.

His panic gave way to anger. What bastards thought they could get away with shooting down one of Uncle Sam's airplanes over international waters? If it took him ten years, he'd get those bastards and kick their balls up to their Adam's apples. And right now, he'd goddam well get out of this high-tech aluminum can if he had to kick his way out. He swung his foot at the nearest windscreen panel.

Meanwhile, the crew was well grouped as they neared the water. The chutes with the large, inflatable life-raft kits were clearly visible, and the sea showed a reassuring calm.

But the siren wail of flying surfaces battling the atmosphere and each other pursued them like doomsday. Amid the scattered clouds and the misty atmosphere, the 141 emerged, rolling and spiraling slowly but descending faster than they were.

The sound of the impact was like a locomotive overturning plus all the whales in the world broaching at once. A huge fireball with seams of oily-black smoke billowed, and a dull boom reverberated across the water. The flame died quickly as the sea bubbled and frothed before it closed over the final resting place of Anvil Bravo.

They had no way of knowing if the skipper had made it. All their eyes scanned the airspace in search of a parachute. It was obvious he had stayed at the controls so they could get out.

Chapter Two

Broken, multilayered stratus spread over the Gulf Coast from Houston to Tampa. Near the western end of the Florida Panhandle, it covered the huge complex of airfields and weapons ranges that made up the U.S. Air Force Air Proving Ground, centered on Eglin Air Force Base.

Returning from a test flight out over the Gulf, Colonel Gus Halstrom was following a flight path among the shelving cloud layers like the descent of a pachinko ball.

The aircraft had both an unconventional form and a synthetic pearlescent surface that was all but invisible against the cloudy backdrop. He switched on the strobe light. The brilliant flash showed up for miles on even the brightest day.

At ten thousand feet, he cleared the lowest of the heavy cloud layers. Ahead, lacy surf lapped gently against alabaster sand.

The Mach number was .94 and rising. Knowing how easily this super-slick bird could go supersonic and jolt the coastal inhabitants with a shock wave, Halstrom further retarded the twin throttles and thumbed the speed-brake switch. Deceleration pressed him against the safety harness, and the sensation of flight was transformed from whipped-cream smoothness to a mild, high-frequency shudder.

East and west, the gentle curvature of the coastline stretched into the murky distance. In places, the smooth sweep was broken by sand-spits and small inlets. Inland, the dense Southern pine forest merged with the cloud and haze over the interior. Patches of bare earth, the Eglin bombing and gunnery ranges, looked like outbreaks of mange on the deep evergreen shag. Between the Gulf and the interior lay the almost glassy calm of Choctawhatchee Bay. The strip separating the bay from the Gulf was a gaudy chain of resort developments.

With the shoreline just over the nose, Gus retracted the speed brakes and shallowed the descent. "Eglin, Potluck Alpha, Point Zulu, entering approach corridor Charlie for landing at Broadway."

"Potluck Alpha, you're cleared through approach corridor. Contact Broadway after passing point X-ray."

In the tower, one of the operators pointed out the distant flash of Alpha's strobe, then trained a pair of binoculars toward point Zulu. "That's Colonel Halstrom and his mysterious toy airplane," he said. "What's it called? The XFL?"

"Right. Experimental fighter, lightweight," said the tech sergeant who was shift chief.

"See anything?" asked the weather observer.

"Barely a glimpse. Little bugger's hard enough to see right overhead. That plastic blends with the clouds."

"Synthetics," the tech sergeant corrected. "They say it's the thing of the future." Voices came from the speakers and required responses. The crew mixed conversation with directing air traffic.

"It hardly shows up on radar, I can tell you that," said

the red-haired Sergeant seated at the scope. "Without the transponder, forget it."

"That Colonel Halstrom," said the airman on ground control, "he was a test pilot, right? And an ace in Vietnam. All kinds of medals and citations."

"In the Gulf War too," said the tech sergeant. "He was hit by ground fire up on the Red River and captured. One of the damn few who ever escaped. Just how he did it's never been told." He turned his gaze on the approach end of the runway and frowned. "Watch your spacing. Those FA-18's are a little close to that Charlie-five."

The redhead looked up from the scope and said, "Wasn't he married to a movie actress?"

The tech sergeant observed the surrounding airspace with cool detachment. "Valerie Aubin, a real sweetheart."

"Kind of an odd pair," said the weather observer. "The way she was into demonstrating for peace and disarmament."

"That's how she got to be an ex."

Meanwhile, Halstrom had leveled at three thousand feet and four hundred knots over the calm surface of the bay. "Broadway, Potluck Alpha to land one."

"Potluck Alpha, runway zero-two. Winds light and variable. Altimeter niner-eight-niner. Call turning initial."

"Broadway" was the designator for one of the many auxiliary airfields in the Eglin complex. From the air, it looked like a wound in the pine forest that had festered mud and sand and then had a two-mile concrete Band-Aid stuck over it. The facilities were bare-bones. Right now they shared it with only two other test projects, and the ramp was almost empty.

For all its startling performance, this airplane was fairly docile. Despite a wing area that looked more suited to a bumblebee, it came down final at a mere 150 knots. This miracle was achieved with an airframe of light-weight materials plus high-pressure air off the compressors to blow away stagnation in the boundary-layer.

There were four of them on the test project, which was actually a transition from experimental status and the designation XFL into the production fighter, the F-24. It had proved itself as an aircraft; here it was undergoing the rigors of becoming an aerial weapons system. Gus and his team were working out weapons-delivery parameters and techniques plus the complete figures on the performance envelope required for the pilot's manual.

Halstrom noted their ramp space was empty; so the afternoon flights had all gone as scheduled. He braked to a halt, stop-cocked the throttles, then removed the helmet with its oxygen mask and rested it on the bow of the windscreen.

"So how's our toy airplane, Colonel?" Technical Sergeant Joe Sakata, called "Honolulu Joe," leaned over and peered into the cockpit while the other two men chocked the wheels.

Halstrom gave a thumbs-up, then disconnected the radio and oxygen leads and handed the helmet to the sergeant. He stood up, sat on the canopy rail, pivoted, and dropped to the ground.

Out of long habit, he started to fill out the 781-1 using the wing, but the ground crew was already putting the cover on. Sergeant Sakata grinned. "Sorry Colonel, gotta keep that showroom finish. Protect the resale value."

Halstrom stepped back and waited. Each XFL came with a coverall of polypropylene fabric—"snoods" to the pilots and ground crews. To allow maintenance without walking, standing, or sitting on the aircraft skin, the snoods had openings for access to various removable panels. The talk around Eglin was that the covers were to hide the unconventional shape. The real intent was to preserve the precise synthetic finish, one of the features that helped give the aircraft its amazingly low drag and high performance.

Which didn't prevent sneers about the "toy airplane," or the "plastic pursuit." To Halstrom and his men, it was the "lighter fighter" or "boron bird"—from the boron fiber used in much of the airframe. Boron was lighter than aluminum, high in tensile strength. Fully loaded, the XFL weighed about 8500 pounds, and each of its two pocket-sized engines developed some 5100 pounds dry thrust. Over seven thousand with afterburner.

Hostility to the whole XFL concept was widespread and no joking matter. Gus had seen Pentagon generals turn livid at the mere mention. It symbolized the cutbacks of the nineties and the pared-down staff.

In the thirties, truss frames had given way to light alloys and the monocoque fuselage, with dramatic reductions in weight. War II brought jet propulsion. By the fifties, this had combined with studies in compressible flow and brought flight speeds exceeding mach 2. Now a third revolution was under way: Synthetic materials, first developed for home-built aircraft, were replacing metal in many parts of commercial and military airframes.

Waring Aircraft Engineering, of Traverse City, Michigan, designers of the XFL, had gotten its start making kits for private builders. And because synthetics were easier for home builders to work with than duralumin, they became the industry pioneers in synthetic airframes.

Halstrom closed up the form, and Sergeant Sakata handed him the tape capsule from the onboard data recorder. Gus thanked the crew for a good airplane, took the tape into ops, and stuck it into the hybrid computer. The readout was pen traces in different colors on a broad strip of pale green graph paper. He was sipping vending-machine coffee and watching the paper emerge like a huge tapeworm when the phone rang.

"Ninety-Nine Delta-Bravo." That was the project designator, the year of its origin plus a letter code. "Colonel Halstrom."

"Gus, Barney here. How're they hanging?"

"Barney! Where the hell are you?"

"At the shop in the puzzle-palace. The boss wants to

talk to you, so straighten your tie." Colonel Barney Boulding had been a squadron mate in Desert Storm and was now General Pete Cassidy's aide. They kept in touch because they had once shared mortal danger and trusted their lives to each other.

Most colonels who got a call direct from the chief of staff would tend to choke up. But Halstrom had known Pete Cassidy for over twenty years. Pete had been his flight commander and ops officer, had recommended him for early promotion. Going up fast himself, Pete had carried Gus along on his coattails, gotten him some juicy assignments—a tour with the Thunderbirds, the flight-test school at Edwards, a NASA research fellowship at Wright-Patterson.

"You on, Gus?"

"I'm on, sir."

"We've gotta talk. How soon can you get here?"

"Well, I've got test data to reduce. And I'll have to revise the flight schedule for the time I'm away. Then I'll have to see what's going to Andrews. I could be there in a couple days."

"Gus, you're in the wrong time frame. I meant hours, not days. I want you in my office bright-eyed and bushy-tailed by tomorrow morning. So saddle up an air-chine and get your Viking ass up here."

"Christ, sir! I can't take myself out of the test schedule just like that. Too much chance of getting behind. And you know what can happen to the weather down here this time of year. Besides, what am I going to use for an airplane?"

"Eglin's full of 'em." Gus could picture Pete talking around a super-corona clamped in his teeth.

"And they're all on some test project."

Pete let out a huff, and Gus knew he was off the hook. "Okay. I'll give you thirty-six hours. Then get a commercial flight or climb aboard a missile. But be here not later than oh-nine-hundred day after tomorrow. Or I'll disconnect your buns from your bifurcation. Do you read me, Gus?"

Gus gave his own small sigh. "I read you, sir."

"*Ciao*. See you soon."

Gus hung up, curious as hell about what Pete wanted. Could be the situation in Eritrea. With the recent discovery of mega oil deposits along the Red Sea, a devil's coalition calling itself the Islamic Front had massed forces in Sudan and was threatening to invade. Perhaps the Administration had decided to block this oil grab, just as Saddam's had been blocked in Kuwait. Which could mean a chance to wind up his career with a flourish—and a few more MiG scalps on his belt.

Anvil Bravo and its companions, Alpha and Charlie, were part of Operation Shadowbox, out of Albrook Air Base in what was once the Canal Zone. The treaty that handed the canal over to Panama already contained the 'DiConcini clause,' a provision under which the U.S. could intervene militarily in case of any threat to the steady and secure operation of the canal. In view of the drug trade and rising terrorism—plus the increasing Chinese presence—the current administration had negotiated a further codicil which allowed U.S. forces to operate 'as necessary' from former American bases. The result was Operation Shadowbox. Colonel Damon Salter, on-site commander, sat in GCI—the radar control center—listening to the radio exchange with Red Flight, four F-16's covering the rescue helicopters. GCI was handling both on a common tac channel. With Salter was Lieutenant Colonel Max Ehrman, Shadowbox ops officer.

GCI was a large, dimly lit room, most of it taken up by a dais on which stood a six-foot-square plexiglass screen. Radial lines divided the screen into ten-degree sectors. Concentric circles marked fifty-nautical-mile increments. Permanent lines marked the principal features such as the coastline of Panama, the canal, and the runways at Albrook.

Behind the screen, two sergeants, one male, one female, marked it in various pale colors of chinograph. Aircraft tracks were dashed lines with pointers in the direction of flight. The marking glowed with induced fluorescence from the otherwise unseen light source around the edge. Each track was identified by call sign and kept current minute by minute. The two working the board used mirror writing so it could be read naturally from the front.

"Why didn't Gil answer that last transmission?" Salter fretted. He was about five-seven and had the intense, abrasive manner that often goes with shorter stature. He spoke in the dry, flat tones of the Midwest. His class had graduated from the Springs—the AF Academy—eighteen years ago, but his boyish face and sandy, crew-cut hair could easily be mistaken for his yearbook photo.

"No news may be good news," said Ehrman in the accents of upper Manhattan. "Maybe they all got out." He had his own air of intensity, softened a bit by incipient humor. His dark, washboard-wave hair had the beginnings of silvery sidewalls. "You red-flag the Pentagon already?"

Salter nodded. "Had to. Gil said they were hit by a missile. Act of war. President himself has to be informed. God knows what kind of shit-fit certain members of Congress will have." He paused, fiddled with the class ring on his finger. "What's the status on Charlie?"

"We put out the recall . . ." Ehrman checked his watch. "Seventeen minutes ago. Average actual ready time from three-hour status is just over an hour-twenty."

"This time, let's take the whole three hours. I'm recommending we stand down till the situation's clarified. I'm not putting another bird up for somebody to shoot at. Not without direct orders. In writing."

Before Ehrman could respond, a voice from the speaker said, "Arena, Rescue One is getting an emergency beacon signal on two-forty-three-point-zero. Bearing one-seven-zero."

"Roger, Rescue One. Alter course your discretion to home on the beacon. Breaker, breaker. Red Flight, go buster, investigate bogies also bearing one-seven-zero for sixty. That's in the target area. Angels below one. Probably helicopters."

The crew members of Anvil Bravo had all landed safely. Two of the three twelve-man rafts had been inflated and lashed together, and each was under the control of one of the officers, Captains Thorne and McGowan. The third raft had been punctured by shrapnel from the missile.

Still, when the two helicopters in camouflage paint swept in low and came to a hover, the crew members waived and cheered. The choppers carried no national markings, but the operators followed standard rescue procedures, lowering rescue collars on lines from power winches. The officers had the lashings undone, and the rafts were rowed apart so a copter could hover over each.

The two wounded men were sent up first. Then, following standard practice, the crew members were winched up in reverse order of rank. So one of the first was Airman Cynthia Naybors.

She was followed by an airman first class, a staff sergeant then Sergeant Bean. As soon as Bean was inside and got a good look at things, he bolted across the cabin and jumped from the open door on the opposite side. "Captain!" he yelled as soon as he broke water. "Don't—"

A burst of automatic fire from the copter turned his head into a bloody mess. More gunfire poured down. The rafts collapsed inward into bowl-like shapes that settled quickly. And in the hollow of each bowl, inert bodies sloshed in water that turned quickly red.

The two copters turned and headed east, staying close

to the water as they got up speed. Behind them, sharks were already circling the scene.

At 450 knots, Red Flight took only eight minutes to arrive over the site. "Red Leader," said the controller. "We have you over the last known location of Anvil Bravo at this time."

"Roger, Arena. Nothing in sight yet. We'll circle and have a look."

"Lead, I have something in the water down there at about ten o'clock." The voice of Red Two.

"Roger, looks yellow. Could be part of a life raft. I'll go down for a closer look. Hold at fifteen hundred so we don't lose contact."

There was an extended silence, then again the voice of Red Two: "Lead, I have yellow dye marker about a mile west. Could be somebody in a life vest in the middle of it."

Snatches of broken transmissions from Red One came through the speaker. Blood, debris, and sharks were all mentioned.

With a grim set to their faces, the two Shadowbox officers remained in GCI till Rescue arrived on the scene and reported winching Major Gil Austen aboard.

The pair of unmarked choppers had picked up eight Americans. Even before the massacre, they realized they had been captured, not rescued. The crewmen aboard the helicopters wore Castro-style fatigues and carried AK-47's. On the flight eastward, they said nothing, but grinned at each other and stared at Cynthia Naybors.

As the choppers crossed the coast, they began a climb, holding about five hundred feet above the terrain. They passed over the arid coastal zone, cleared the foothills of the Andes, and finally dropped toward a level, grassy plain that held a fair-sized town.

It was typically Latin American—pale stucco beneath roofs of red tile. In the center rose the twin carved-stone towers of a church. On the edge of town was a quadrangle of single-and double-story buildings. The copters circled, headed into the wind, and landed on the paved courtyard. Waiting there were perhaps a dozen men in the same Castro-style fatigues. They carried the same weapons, except for a few who wore holstered pistols.

The captives were hauled out of the aircraft and marched across the flagstone surface into one of the larger buildings. They were handled roughly, but not tied or handcuffed. The two wounded men got no gentler treatment. Inside, in a large, stone-floored room on the ground level, the six were prodded into a rough line before a man who sat at a plain wooden table. He was addressed as *"El Jefe."* There was no other furniture. The smell of unwashed bodies suffused the low-ceilinged room.

Unlike the rest, the seated man was well groomed and wore a plain, dark business suit. His cold gaze swept over the prisoners. In time, it focused on Cynthia Naybors, and his mouth formed a mocking smile. "Well," he said. "Uncle Sam must be getting desperate. He's sending his crack troops against us." A guffaw broke out from those who knew enough English to appreciate his wit. "What's your name, girl?"

Next to her, Staff Sergeant Micheals, one of the wounded men muttered, "You don't have to tell 'em anything. They have no—"

The butt of an AK-47 against his head knocked him to the floor. "Anyone else want to play hero?" asked the man at the table. "Or argue technicalities?" He looked at Cynthia again, then jerked his head. Grinning, the men nearest her began pulling at her clothes. She fought back, struggled to free herself. And between sobs, she screamed they had no right to do this.

Airman first Class Devon "Dev" Jackson, of Lakewood, Ohio, was next to Cynthia. As a high school basketballer, he had been known for his quickness. When he moved, both the quickness and shear audacity took everyone by surprise.

The men holding Cynthia Naybors had their hands full, leaving their holsters unprotected. Jackson grabbed the Colt 45 automatic from one, swung it, and knocked the man senseless. Then he began shooting.

The others followed his example. One took the pistol from the man Jackson had shot. In the low-ceilinged, stone-lined confinement of that room, the gunfire, some of it full-automatic, was head-splitting. When it finally ended, the floor was puddled in blood and littered with dead men. A thick pall of smoke and the acrid smell of cordite hung in the air. *El Jefe* had bolted out the door. He returned with a look as dark as the clouds that gathered over the distant Andes.

Cynthia Naybors, the only American left alive, huddled on the floor with her face in her hands, sobbing.

Chapter Three

The rescue helicopter that fished Major Guilbert Austen out of the Pacific took him directly to the base hospital. He did not pass "Go" or collect any compensation for his ordeal. He expected none.

"I couldn't kick a hole in the windscreen," he told Salter and Ehrman. "So I used the cockpit fire extinguisher. It was still a tight squeeze. Scraped off about a square yard of skin. Then once I got out, I had a brush with the airplane and broke some ribs. Or so they tell me."

Describing what he saw happen to his crew, he had to fight back tears, then broke into shouts of helpless rage.

"Hey, Gil!" said Ehrman. "There was nothing you could do."

"I'm putting you in for an Air Medal," Salter said.

"Thanks. Now how soon can you get me back in the left seat of a One-Forty-One?"

The two exchanged looks. "Replacements take a while," the CO said. "Those birds are all special order.

44

For now, the Pentagon wants to hear this first-hand, just the way you told us."

Two days after his release from medical captivity, Major Gil Austen stepped off a MAC transport at Andrews AFB in Maryland, the military airdrome serving the Capital.

A wry smile formed on Colonel Barney Boulding's face as he read through the TWX just in from Eglin. Then, holding it by the corner like rancid fish-wrapper, he carried it into Cassidy's office. "From Gus, sir."

Cassidy looked up from his desk. Fingers laced behind his head, he gazed at the ceiling and said in a voice loaded with irony, "Read it to me, Barney. I want to get the full flavor of Gus's special humor."

"I think you'll agree he's in top form here." Barney held up the sheet and read aloud: "In obedience to your orders, arriving Mason County airport approximately oh-eight-hundred local. My entrance aboard rare artifact shouldn't be missed. Be there or be square." Barney could no longer keep a straight face, yet above the laughter, a frown crept onto his forehead. "It's signed Leonidas."

Chuckling, Cassidy said, "That's just Gus showing off his education. Leonidas was the Spartan commander at Thermopylae. Reference the phrase 'in obedience to your orders.' " Still grinning, he said, "Makes me want to kick his smart Viking ass. If I could just get my foot up that high."

Mason County airport was not an airport for Mason County but a county airport named after a Stewart Mason who had donated the land. It had three concrete runways, an FAA-operated tower, instrument-approach facilities, and the usual cluster of private flying schools and aircraft dealers. It was also home to a number of corporate and private aircraft.

Those arriving that morning wondered if they might be caught in some kind of time warp: Out of the south and out of the past, the low morning sun turning its spinning prop to a golden halo, an airplane came boring in fast just above the treetops. It bore the battle paint of a war that had faded into legend. And the full-throated howl of its twelve-cylinder Packard-Rolls stirred the hearts of a generation now in its twilight.

Just over the runway, it arced up in a tight left zooming turn. Ropy white trails of condensation streamed from the wing tips, and the engine note dropped to a tiger's purr. At the apex, 180 degrees of turn and one thousand feet above the runway, it rolled level, the gear came out of the wells, and the flaps extended. Then the nose dropped into a steep left bank.

In the cockpit, Gus slid the canopy open and rechecked the essentials—gear and flaps down, hydraulic pressure in the green, prop full-high RPM, mixture auto-rich. He turned to look over his shoulder as the runway came slowly into view.

That pitch-up landing pattern was the same vintage as the aircraft. Final approach was a shallowing turn that let him see past the long nose until the moment of flare-out. The slight left crosswind was a help. Touching down on the left main and tail wheel, he eased the right main down and tapped the binders.

He taxied to the ramp in front of operations and shut down, got out, and removed a garment bag and a small overnight bag from behind the seat. Some bystanders recognized him and asked about the airplane. "I belong to the Old Warbirds, and this is part of our collection. It's a Fifty-One H. The ultimate Mustang. Two thousand horse. Top speed around four-forty. Cruise almost four hundred." He flicked a smile. "That's miles per hour, of course."

Despite that "Be there or be square," Gus knew Pete

Cassidy couldn't spare the time in person. But he had sent a staff car and driver.

It was typical of the Pentagon: After browbeating Gus to be there bright and early, Pete couldn't see him till after lunch. Gus took the extra time to check out the latest at the Air and Space Museum. Some of the aircraft on display were those he had flown. Visitors recognized him and asked him to pose for a snapshot in front of them—or just for his autograph. He ate lunch, then returned to the Pentagon.

The corridor outside the chief of staff's suite had its own historical/PR display, and he took a few minutes to browse over it. There were models and pictures of famous aircraft and photos of the men who had flown them to fame and glory and often into the Great Beyond.

The famous names and faces were there—Chuck Yeager, Pete Everest, et al. A younger Pete Cassidy stood beside the X-15, in which he had set a record. Gus was there twice himself, as an ace and a well-known research pilot. He felt a certain satisfaction that the Gus Halstrom posed over twenty years ago by the needle nose of an F-104 could be easily recognized as the man he was today. The hair was still straw-blond, the face still longish and hollowed, the six-two frame still lean and solid.

In the office, he got a nasty shock: He'd heard about the flare-up of the hepatitis Barney had caught in Kuwait on Desert Storm, but he wasn't prepared for this. From his graying hair to his crisp collar, Barney's skin looked stained with iodine.

They gripped hands and slapped shoulders. "Barney! You don't look a day over a hundred. How long's it been?"

Barney grinned. "Longer'n it is now, that's for sure."

Cassidy stuck his head out. "You two can gossip like old ladies some other time. Get your ass in here, Gus.

And Barney, I'm not available except to the other chiefs and up."

Pete's office had the traditional clean desk and official photos, the U.S. flag and AF standard. As soon as the door was closed, Cassidy looked at Gus and gave a shake of his head. "Tears you up to see Barney like that. I've been doing what I can in the hope he'll respond to treatment, but it doesn't look good. I don't think he'll ever get back on flying status."

He motioned Gus into a seat, settled into his own high-backed swivel chair, took two seven-inch coronas from a humidor, tossed one to Gus, clipped and lit the other. This was just one of the items that made Pete unpopular with the Washington establishment: He refused to go along with the "smoke-free" hysteria. Next he reached into a desk drawer and withdrew a folder with PEGASUS PROJECT in big, red, upper-case letters. He shoved it across the desk. "Here, sign the access roster." He snipped the cigar, lit it, and billowed smoke. Gus noted the roster carried only nine names, including the five members of the Joint Chiefs. This was just for one particular copy of the document, but it was some indication of how restricted it was. Whatever it was.

He signed and handed it back. Cassidy put it in his desk drawer. "Okay, Gus, sit back and hear the ungarbled word. And the first thing to remember is this is all classified burn-before-reading."

He rose and began to pace the thick, dark-blue carpet. The chestnut hair with its slight wave was thick as ever. For the first time, though, Gus noticed a touch of gray at Pete's temples. "Note the fact that even I can't have the actual document here in the office. It's locked away down in the dungeons. I'll give it to you quick and dirty, then you can go down there to read the full text." He paced, trailing smoke from the corona. "Ever hear of something called the Willard Effect?"

"Can't say I have."

"I'll get back to that. Anyway, Pegasus isn't exactly a new idea. It's an old one whose time has finally come. Wasn't much of a success the first time around because we just didn't have the technology. A-a-nd . . . it was done by the Navy." Gus suppressed a smile. Pete was constantly taking verbal potshots at the Navy.

"Back before our time, the Navy, bless their saltwater souls, tried dirigibles as aircraft carriers. They were all wrecked, but the idea wasn't half bad. Now suppose you built one several times as big as the Hindenburg, with all the advantages of today's technology."

Gus frowned. "Seems like we're talking about a mighty big and mighty vulnerable object."

"On the face of it, yes. But this is where things like the Willard Effect come in. To recap what we both know, just for background—a transmitter converts electrical energy into radio waves. Electro-magnetic radiation. Same as light but not visible to the naked eye. And like light, those waves reflect from solid objects. Radar emits radio waves and then measures their reflection to locate an object. This guy Willard found a way to reverse the process. Convert the radiation back into electrical energy with about ninety-nine-point-something-percent efficiency and almost zero reflection. Genuine, ultimate stealth."

"Sounds great. But what about plain old eyeball contact? Anything that big is still going to stand out like the pyramids."

Cassidy checked his pacing a moment. "That did occur to a few others. Long time ago, in fact. Back during War Two, the blimps they used for antisub warfare had a special lighting scheme that made them damn hard to see even in broad daylight. One of the best-kept secrets of War Two. They could appear right out of a clear blue sky and pounce on surfaced subs. Now, do a similar thing with an airship whose skin is imbedded with optical fibers, and it's much more effective. The fibers are molded into sheets with just the right blend of translu-

49

cence and reflectivity and tend to cause the light to follow their curvature.

"Sensors pick up ambient light and feed the results into a computer, which adjusts the back-glow. At any distance, and I mean close as half a mile, it blends into almost any background. Sky, clouds, water, earth. It's been tested with large objects, and it works. I was skeptical as hell at first, but I've seen it myself. Or non-seen it, to be more accurate.

"Then there's another gimmick, which is simply to make the thing look like a cloud whenever it's not in motion." He showed a rueful smile. "Remember the contrail project?"

Gus made his own sour face. The contrail project had sought ways to suppress those telltale white streamers aircraft trail across the stratosphere. "Well," Cassidy went on, "contrails are really just artificial clouds. And part of what we learned was that water and certain chemicals turn readily into condensed vapor. Released through surface outlets, it produces a very natural-looking cloud."

"Hmh. Smoke and mirrors. Literally. Anyway, somebody's done his homework. And it's made to carry airplanes? Like a Navy carrier?"

"An air group of four squadrons. Fighters and attack aircraft. A squadron being twelve in this case. First flight of the XA-17 is next week."

The XA-17 was a lightweight attack aircraft built of synthetics like the XFL, though in more conventional form. Gus frowned harder and shook his head. "I hate to mention such basics, but each of those birds will still burn a few thousand pounds of JP-4 on each mission. That's—"

"That's a gotcha!" Cassidy showed the special grin he kept for the few times he caught Gus off base on a point of technology. "No JP. Hydrogen. Liquid form, same as in booster rockets. Twice the specific energy of petroleum-based fuels and cheap as dirt. Extract it from seawater by electrolysis, reduce it to a cryogenic liquid, and pump it aboard. We'll have vessels for doing this dispersed around the world."

Pete puffed the cigar and paced some more. "Now that the Soviet threat's gone poof, what we can expect is wars like the Persian Gulf thing. A Qaddafi or a Saddam Hussein or some other Third World kook can pop up almost any time. In fact, that situation in Eritrea is shaping up as a case in point. Rapid, stealthy deployment's the key to pissing on this kind of brushfire before it gets out of hand.

"Pegasus will give us the capability of putting airpower on the scene anywhere in the world in not over forty-eight hours. It can also carry missiles and drop paratroops. And the neatest thing of all is it's deniable. No carriers hanging around off shore, no tactical air wings gone from their home bases." Pete turned his palms up with a look of exaggerated innocence. "Air attacks? Us? Nah! Must've been the Lower Slabovians."

Gus couldn't suppress his grin. Then his face turned sober. "I can think of some places where it would've come in very handy over the last ten years or so."

Cassidy turned silent then, his face almost studious. "Development actually started over ten years ago. Under Reagan." Again he paused, drew on his cigar. "But then we had *that* President and his staff who couldn't be trusted with anything so delicate or important, so it was put on hold." He took a few paces in silence. "And I don't have to tell you about the task we face cleaning out the Augean stables that first couple made out of the whole DoD. Beginning with de-Shroederizing."

Gus recognized the name of the "Congressperson" from Colorado who had pushed for female roles in combat. "I left active duty and went to work for NASA right after Jimmy Carter came on the scene. I never knew how good we had it then. Then after Reagan came in, you and some others talked me into coming back aboard and taking a regular commission. So when that pair took over the White House, my only options were resign or grit my teeth."

Cassidy gave him a wry smile. "Worked out okay in the long run."

"Except I wore a lot of enamel off my teeth." Gus pondered: What did it say about the state of the Union when the nation's top military leaders didn't trust the President? "So, just where do I fit into this scheme?" he finally asked.

Pete resumed his pacing. "Pegasus is set up as a joint project. The airship itself will be Navy. Partly because the ships that furnish the liquid hydrogen are theirs. But the air group is ours, and it's independent, not under command of the ship's skipper. The basic principle is that he has the final word on anything involving the safety and security of the airship. Beyond that, he's required to proceed and maneuver in accordance with the mission requirements of the air group commander."

He made a jabbing motion with the cigar. "And that, Gus old buddy, is you. If this first one works out, we'll build some more, and you'll move up. Get you that star you scared off the first time around. And that break in service you had is looking like rosewater. Without it, you'd be up against the thirty-year limit for colonels, and that barrier is a lot tougher to bust than Mach 1. Even I couldn't push you through."

He referred, Gus knew only too well, to the DoD regulation limiting officers in the grade of O-6 to thirty years total service. Only those of general or flag rank could stay beyond thirty. Cassidy said, "If your mouth hadn't ripped your knickers, you'd be wearing at least two, maybe three stars by now."

For reasons they both knew but seldom discussed, Gus had assumed the XFL test project was the final stage of his Air Force career. For some years now, that whole subject had been a sore point between them. Pete had been preparing him for high-level command and had actually gotten him the star of brigadier general. But after that affair in Stockholm, Senate approval was hopeless.

"Well, I'll be damned," was the only response Gus could manage.

"Probably. But for now, you have to stick around and help get Pegasus off the ground."

"Must've had to jump through your own asshole to get me the job."

Pete squinted through cigar smoke. "Not quite." His face turned sour. "Not that there wasn't plenty of opposition right here in DoD. Old Bilgewater near had a shit-hemorrhage when your name came up."

Gus smiled. "Old Bilgewater" was Pete's private term for Admiral Anson G. Broadwater III, CNO.

Cassidy's look turned to a satisfied grin. "I trumped him with his own suit. Your exchange experience flying off carriers in the Persian Gulf. Right from the start, I saw Pegasus and these new lightweight, synthetic airframes going together like beer and limburger. Which is why I put you in charge of that project. You know that airplane better than anyone else. Considering you even had a hand in the design."

Gus straightened abruptly and frowned. "Are you saying the XFL project was your way of setting me up for assignment to Pegasus?"

"You could put it that way."

"Hell, I'm grateful, Pete. I really am."

"Hang onto your ass and your gratitude both. A year from now, Pegasus may have turned into a can of worms we'll both have to eat. But I figure it'll have the best chance in your hands." He tapped cigar ash into a big, crystal ashtray on the desk.

"That's one helluva vote of confidence in somebody who ripped his knickers. By the way, is this thing actually under construction yet?"

"Your professional and technical qualifications have always been recognized as A-one, Gus. It's your grasp of diplomacy which is about like what a grizzly gets on a salmon. And to answer your question, it's almost complete. Be ready for the first test flight sometime this summer. Construction actually began back in ninety. But, as I mentioned, they put it on hold when he was elected."

"Ho-ly! . . . Really? And where is it? I mean anything that big—"

"Construction site's out in Middle-of-Nowhere, North Dakota. One of those closed-down missile sites. Security in the form of electrified chain-link fence and such was already in place. Overflight by civil aircraft was already restricted. Workers from all the shut-down plants in southern California were available." He tapped off some more ash. "Questions?"

Gus got out of his chair. "Only a few hundred. But if you had the answers, you wouldn't need me."

"Very well." Pete strode back to the chair behind his desk and his voice took on a crisp formality. "Effective immediately, you're relieved of current assignment and duty and reassigned to Pegasus. You'll report to me directly. Barney should have your orders on his desk." He wrote on a memo pad, tore off the sheet, and handed it to Gus. "Go to this room, and they'll give you the complete Pegasus file. When you've read it, come back and see me. Barney's arranging office space for you."

Gus winced. "An office? Me? Here, in the Pentagon? Maybe I could just set up a desk in a men's room somewhere. Could be the only place in this whole damn building where everyone knows what he's doing."

Pete showed a smile. "Get your ass out of here, Gus. You've got a week to wind up at Eglin and hand over to your next in line. Then I want you back bright-eyed and bushy-tailed and ready to go to work."

Halstrom straightened, snapped the extended fingers of his right hand up to his brow and his heels smartly together. "Yes, sir."

Pete returned the salute. Gus turned and left.

54

Chapter Four

Arthur Penross, syndicated snoop and self-styled gad-fly—his many detractors used much harsher terms—pressed a button on his fax machine, and his latest column was on its way to the editorial offices.

This was the twelfth floor of a high-rise condo near Bethesda. The view took in part of the course at Burning Tree. Gertrude Stein was supposed to have said she liked to have a view, but to work with her back to it. He would agree. It made a nice reward when he finished a column.

Yet looking at even this de-luxe scenery palled. Normally annoyed at interruption by the telephone, he was glad now to hear it.

"Got a juicy one for you." It was one of those anonymous voices who fed him information.

"I'll be the judge of that. But go ahead."

"Your favorite subject. Or object. The Pentagon. You know they've got radar planes watching the coast down south? Part of the antidrug campaign." It was half question, half statement.

"That's a fairly open secret. And not terribly interesting."

"It's pretty certain they just lost one."

"Small potential embarrassment. Military planes are lost all the time."

"But there's more. Rumor has it the bad guys shot it down with a missile. Probably with all hands lost."

"Hm!" Penross straightened in his chair. "You know I don't print rumors. I'd be out of business in less than a month."

"It's something to go on. The rest of your snoops can follow up. And if it's true, remember you heard it from me first."

"By all means, my dear fellow." Penross's tone mocked the words. "Now where or how did you come by this provisional tidbit?"

"A friend of mine stationed at Albrook, that base in the Canal Zone."

"There is no Canal Zone. Though there are American bases in Panama." He paused, thinking. "Very well. I'll see where this leads. If anything comes of it, you'll see the results just as always."

He hung up, pondered briefly, then picked up the phone and punched a number. "I need you to check out something. For the usual fee."

"Go ahead." The voice was one of those he could connect with a name and a face.

"Did the Pentagon lose a radar aircraft on the drug watch? And if so, was it shot down by a missile?"

"I'll get back. Give me a day or two."

It was 0820, and the Cuban day-laborers had already passed through the gate onto the Naval base at "Gitmo Bay." A truck carrying Cuban soldiers approached the gate. The Marine guards were immediately alert and a little tense.

But the truck made a U-turn some forty feet short, and

soldiers in the rear dumped a large olive-drab rubber sack out on the ground. Laughing and jeering, they also threw out refuse—fruit peels, cigar butts, empty but rancid food tins. Then the truck sped away.

The gunny in charge of the shift had seen and used body bags from Vietnam to the Gulf War. He and a corporal went out and examined it, determined it actually seemed to contain a body. A detail retrieved it, and once it was checked for booby traps, it was taken to the base hospital, where medical personnel were called upon to examine the contents.

They found the nude body of a young woman. She had blond hair and blue eyes, and on a chain around her neck were Air Force ID tags. An Air Force physician flew down from Washington to consult with the Navy doctors who did the autopsy.

"The body must have been kept on ice," said the Naval captain-physician who commanded the hospital. "It was well preserved. Cause of death was strangulation." His face darkened. "But I don't even like to think about what must have been done to her before that. Gang rape was the least of it. Nothing her family should have to know about."

"We'll take care of it," said the major from Washington. So Cynthia Naybors became the only crew member of Anvil Bravo to be buried in her native soil.

Monroe, Indiana, population some eighteen thousand, lay west of Richmond, about halfway to Indianapolis. News of the death of Cynthia Naybors was front-page news in the local weekly. The color photo, taken when she completed basic training, showed an attractive, open face with blue eyes, wheat-blond hair, and a slightly upturned nose.

The story noted she had been a high school cheerleader and homecoming queen. She had joined the Air Force to be with her boyfriend. But their mutual service had actually caused them to grow apart. He'd learned enough electronics during that first hitch to open his own repair shop. She had found a niche in the service and chose to reenlist. And working aboard an aircraft got her extra pay. Her friends mentioned she could not tell them just what she was doing.

Wearing slacks and sport coat but no tie and carrying a whiskey and soda with ice, *El Jefe* descended the short, shallow stone staircase into the *sala grande*. The stairs, quarter circles fanning out from top to bottom, took up a corner of this huge, three-story rectangular room. The stones were mixed in size and shape, with a finish just rough enough to show they were real, not terrazzo or composition.

On the long exterior side, cathedral-like windows between high columns looked out on Lake Curracabamba and the distant Andes. The high roof was supported by heavy, sloping beams. Like most of the interior, they were a rich, natural-toned wood.

Opposite that, thick slabs of plate glass some eight feet square held back a murky green body of water whose boundaries were beyond view, the habitat of various species sensed only as sinister, gliding shadows. Above this aquarium was a mezzanine floor with a wooden balustrade.

A profusion of plants embellished every segment of the room, including the balustrade. Some were in glorious, fragrant bloom; others conveyed a feral, junglelike threat. Bushes in big terra-cotta urns were carefully placed to give the appearance of random location. Still more plants in pots hung from the wall-brackets or the rafters above. The air was gently stirred by three large overhead fans.

The floor was tiled in a Moorish pattern. And despite the profusion of greenery, there was indeed room for dancing. When "Etienne Alvarado," the international socialite and philanthropist, entertained the local gentry and government officials, the orchestra occupied the mezzanine while the guests went gliding and whirling over the tile below.

El Jefe strolled over to a certain segment of the aquarium and peered in. "Alejandro!"

A bony, pale-tan face with a thin mustache emerged from among the potted plants atop the balustrade. It belonged to a man of slender build, dressed in a technician's white smock. *"Sí, Jefe?"*

"Time to feed our little friends here, isn't it?"

"The crew is just bringing it now."

"What are they having today?"

"Rodent, *Jefe*." The tone was casual.

El Jefe took a seat where he could observe the aquarium. Men in work clothes dragged something in a sack across the floor of that upper level. The something was live and made squeaky-grunty noises of protest. The men lifted a section of the flooring, dumped the object into the aquarium with a splash, replaced the section, and left, taking the sack.

El Jefe watched through the glass as the large, furry creature plunged into the water. It resembled a rat but was the size of a small pig. The capybara, the world's largest rodent, was at home in the water and began to swim, exploring its surroundings.

Those swimming movements brought on its doom.

The piranhas swarmed. The capybara was overwhelmed, but struggled and kicked as the biting began all over its body.

The water quickly became blood-clouded, but the roiling, biting frenzy went on. Finally, out of that spreading red miasma, the skeleton of the capybara sank to the bottom. A few of the piranha darted in for a last nip or two at bits of membrane that still clung to the bone, then sped away.

Even the eyes were gone, *El Jefe* noted. All that

remained beyond the skeleton was the claws, bits of the leathery footpads, and a small tuft of fur on the tail.

"Alejandro!"

"*Sí, Jefe, sí.* The filters are already on. The water should clear in a few minutes."

El Jefe smiled. "You anticipate my wishes, Alejandro. You are a gem." He turned then to greet his guests.

They showed a keen interest in the aquarium, and *El Jefe* was pleased to explain it. "I keep specimens of the most fearsome aquatic species native to our continent here. Caymans, piranha. Some have to be separated from others, which is the reason for the internal glass partitions. I study them. They also serve as an inspiration."

Near one end of the room, chairs were drawn up in an arc, facing a lectern. He invited them to sit. Behind him was a projection screen. A still projector and other gear were standing by.

These were men accustomed to giving orders, not sitting and listening. Each was vastly rich, and together they disposed of more wealth than many of the world's nations. They had ordered the deaths of judges, police officials, cabinet officers, legislators, even heads of state.

All this was through the good offices of this Etienne Alvarado, called *El Jefe*. He knew where to find trained mercenaries, skilled assassins, how to recruit disaffected youth. The money came from the profits of the cocaine trade. He fostered the expansion of that trade, making more money.

Having already put out the word it was time for the next phase of their operations, a new expansion, he had summoned them to hear an outline of the plan. Some of the faces showed eagerness: *El Jefe* had always delivered, made them even richer. Others looked apprehensive, worried that going too far could ruin everything.

Yet they sat like school children before this man they called *El Jefe*. None of them knew his name—his real name, the one inscribed on his birth certificate. Some had been heard to mutter he might not have been born of woman at all. Was instead an incarnation of one of the ancient spirits.

These furtive thoughts were reinforced by his subtle differences. He resembled them, yet he didn't.

Whatever the case, they all feared him. His word assured the goodwill of the guerrilla bands that infested the area. Goodwill meant successful harvest and shipment of the coca crop.

But *El Jefe* also commanded both power and huge sums of money in many distant parts of the world. Fanatics in India, the crime lords in the new Russia, guerrilla movements in Africa and Asia all seemed to defer to or at least consult him. From time to time, he had announced that certain events would happen, outbreaks of violence in distant parts of the world. And these things had indeed taken place.

"We have sent the Yanquis a message," he said. "Taken the first step in teaching them they can no longer keep us under scrutiny like laboratory specimens. Our radar stations report that these aircraft which have been watching us are no longer doing so. Our ships and planes can now come and go without interference."

"What we've done is poke a hornets' nest," said one. "And what they will do is come swarming out and sting us. We have a good thing here selling cocaine. So far, the Yanquis have played into our hands. Kept it illegal and our profits high. But once we make them angry and determined enough . . ." He shrugged. "Why can we not just leave well enough alone? Go on as we have?" He shrugged again and glanced around at the others. "I have no desire to end up as another Noriega."

El Jefe's expression shifted to fulgerant scorn. "You are a pig, Emil. A stupid, timid pig." The level tone was the sort he might use for noting a shirttail was out or a shoelace untied. "You are offered the chance to do great things. To change the shape of the world for generations to come. And all you want is to be safe and comfortable in your mud-wallow." Toward the end, the voice sank, emerging as a sinister hiss.

"We've gotten hold of a handful of missiles," said another of the older members. "The Yanquis produce a full range of modern weapons. Including the big ones. And they need only enough provocation to turn them on us. Look what they did to the Iraqis. And Hussein was better armed than we are."

"I tried to warn him that he faced humiliating defeat. That the time was not yet." *El Jefe* paused. "As for weapons, there will be plenty available. Certain former Soviet officials whose privileged status under the old regime has dissolved want to go on living well. For enough money and a new life, they will deliver almost anything we want in the way of missiles. Including the big ones."

Alejandro had set up some maps, the sort once used in classrooms to teach geography. *El Jefe* selected a large, multicolor Mercator projection of the world. From his shirt pocket, he took what looked like a ballpoint pen but telescoped into a pointer with a plastic tip. "Even before the East-West conflict ran its course, a new and more basic one was already taking shape. Call it the North-South conflict. To be more accurate, the Temperate-Tropics conflict."

His pointer touched the map. "Now observe. The Eurocentric states occupy the north temperate zone. With enclaves such as Australia and New Zealand in the southern hemisphere. Most of what the Yanquis are pleased to label the Third World encircles the globe near the middle. For the past two centuries, this Third World has been like a jackal. Could do no more than dash out now and then and snap at some tender, exposed part. But soon it will have teeth and claws like a tiger.

"The traditional nation, defined by territory, soil, language, culture, and history, is becoming obsolete. The nation we are creating is not so much a state as a state of mind. A philosophy of what mankind is and how we should live. And the citizens of this new nation are spread over a territory much larger than any traditional country. So they form a natural fifth column. They influence decisions, reshape public attitudes, impair national cohesion and unity by undermining the culture, eroding belief in the national history and traditions.

"Ultimately, they can cause people to doubt their own nation—its aims, its legal forms, its very legitimacy. And they can surface at the critical moment to carry out subtle forms of sabotage. I'm in personal contact with many enclaves. We have already influenced the policies of certain countries, brought resistance to American aims.

"In the former Soviet Union, we've been fomenting crime and chaos. Russia, having abandoned its role as the Marxist center, is now serving as a blunt but useful instrument, a nest of gang-lords who recognize no law but their own profit. I have influence there, key people among the various factions. Under their guidance, the chaos will be spread westward into Europe. And when the governments there can no longer protect their own citizens or control their own territories, they will no longer pose a threat to our emerging new nation.

"Meanwhile, we are gaining strength, making war by subtle methods, preparing for the day when we shall challenge the *nortes*. I have networks of agents in Europe and North America. Many of them experienced in espionage, sabotage, and subversion. People who worked for the Soviets or the Chinese until each abandoned the cause of World Marxism.

"The future, *compañeros,* lies in a new federation of states in this equatorial band. A federation that will in time unite into the world's first true superstate. It will have both a central position and the bulk of the earth's resources, including most of the oil. It will lay claim not only to the land mass it occupies and the airspace above, but the tropical oceans as well. Ocean trade, so essential to the Euro style of commerce, will cross those waters only at our pleasure and by paying a substantial toll. Which will make you all rich beyond imagining. Incidentally, we have chosen to call this new nation Centralia."

At this point, one of the older ones stood up and interrupted. "You're talking nonsense," he said. "We are simple men here. Farmers really. Just glad to have the wealth that fortune has given us. Perhaps I am only a timid pig, *Jefe*"—he gave the words a mocking tone—"but I have no interest in your grand design for the world. I only care to enjoy the riches I've won and to pass them along to my sons. Let the world shape itself as it will."

El Jefe sighed and looked sad. "In that case, Emil, you are dismissed." He waved an open palm toward the door. "I had hoped to open your eyes to a vision beyond the confines of these mountains, but apparently you are too old and too tied to the past."

Diego, another who had objected earlier, also rose. "I too shall go, *Jefe*. No offense, and I wish you well, but— as you say—I am also too old. I shall not live long enough to see any of the wonders you describe. But I fear we shall all reap the result of the dangers."

The two of them left, and *El Jefe* returned to giving his *lección*.

The seats were set up in an arc, centered on the lectern. So those to his right had the aquarium on the edge of their vision. Some minutes later, as *El Jefe* was explaining how certain banking maneuvers could be used to wage economic warfare, the man in the end seat began staring in horror at the glass of the aquarium. Then he rose and pointed a quivering finger. The others followed it.

From behind the glass, Emil stared at them with wide, sightless eyes. His body moved and revolved gently in the slight current. Then Diego too drifted into view.

El Jefe finally stopped speaking, turned to see what had them all astir. For a moment, he was silent, showing a thoughtful frown. "Tragic," he said, with a small head shake. "Very careless of them both. Wandering in among the electric eels like that."

The faces registered shock as if they too had been among the electric eels. They also registered fright—and understanding.

Chapter Five

Gus rinsed off the razor, dashed cold water on his face, dried and splashed on aftershave. Outside, the wind huffed, and thunder rumbled in the middle distance. A wind-driven layer of dark cloud tore itself on the finial of the Washington Monument. His mood matched the weather.

For most of the summer, he'd been stuck away in a cubbyhole in the Pentagon, busting his butt twelve to fourteen hours a day and getting damn little flying time. In a month or so, Skyhook, the new airship, would begin her shakedown flights. A few months after that, he would take the first F-24 Scimitars aboard.

He had to familiarize himself with all the gear and facilities designed into Skyhook, ensure their compatibility with both the F-24 and A-17, then work out tentative operating and emergency procedures, safety guidelines. In short, he had to foresee a host of unforeseeables.

Meanwhile, as part of his political rehabilitation, Pete Cassidy insisted he also show himself in the right places.

And this evening, the right place was Fiona Freeland's. "There's a network of arbiters in this town," Pete declared. "Not much importance in themselves, but they function like a septic system. Filter shit. You don't have to suck up to them, just let the word seep through that you're not an unexploded bomb."

Gus had just put on a fresh T-shirt when the doorbell rang. Muttering imprecations, he dashed down the steep staircase, along the gleaming parquet in the hallway, and wrenched open the front door.

There he faced the most striking dark-skinned woman he had ever seen. Indeed, she would have turned men's heads in any gathering. He felt qualified to make that judgment after his marriage to Val and the mingling with the Hollywood set it had brought.

She was about five-eleven, slender yet full-bodied, and dressed for a party. The taxi that had dropped her was just leaving. Her look showed surprise, but no ripple in her composure. The scowl on his face dissolved as he made a leap of insight. "Ah! You thought this was Fiona's."

"Yes!" The lively face flashed, then segued into a look of relief.

Her complexion was rich, with a powdery texture. She wore no hat. Her hair—blue-black, like a raven's wing, with a near-metallic sheen—was drawn back tight against her scalp into an artful roll at the back. Her face seemed formed by the mutual effort of a poet and sculptor, each at the peak of creativity. Her eyes were a bright hazel, the eyes of a tigress.

"I'm due there too. If you'd care to wait inside, I'll lead the expedition. Oh, I'm Gus Halstrom." He offered his hand.

There was a pause, brief but definite, while her eyes surveyed and her mind evaluated. Then she put her foot over the doorsill. "Yes, by golly, you are. *The* Gus Halstrom. Fighter ace, record-setting research pilot." Her smile teased. "And Pentagon embarrassment."

"You could've talked all night and not said that last bit."

"Michelle St. Clair." She added a moiety of width to her own smile and extended her hand, palm down. He took it in a gentle grip and gave a faint bow, noting its capable, long-fingered grace. The nails were lightly silvered, trimmed to very short points. Her lips also bore a very light silvery tint. Her face, with its full color, needed little in the way of makeup.

Going upstairs, he turned and said, "Georgetown's a confusing place. Half the cab drivers in town will let you off at the wrong address. Fiona's one street over." He pointed at the wall phone. "Why don't you give her a call. Her number's on that pad."

She picked up the receiver and began touching the buttons on the phone. He continued upstairs, where he began fastening those on his shirt. Her voice carried up the stairwell: "Hi, Fiona? Michelle St. Clair . . . Oh, no. No problem. I'm over here with Gus . . . Gus Halstrom. We're running a little late, but we'll make it soon . . . No, not at all . . . About five minutes, I guess." He heard the receiver go into the cradle.

Despite the threatening skies, the rain was holding off. Still, he threw a folded trench coat over his shoulder. She carried one of those bumbershoots that collapse into a small cylinder. "This way," he said, turning up the brick-paved walk toward the rear of the house.

"You . . . live here then?"

"Just renting. From a guy on foreign assignment with the State Department. It's inconvenient as hell but loaded with charm."

He took the opportunity to sneak glances, appreciate her attractions in more detail. In profile, she made him think of the faces on Egyptian monuments of the Amarna period. The wide, full lips arched like a ship's bow wave on either side of a deep philtrum. The flare of her hips below the slender waist was statuesque. And while women her height were apt to have skinny calves, hers had the fullness of a ballerina's. "So, are you here by Fiona's command?" he asked.

"Oh, no. I'm grateful Fiona invited me. Lets me make contacts and pass out business cards. Here." She flicked one from her purse and stuck it into his shirt pocket. "We entrepreneurs like to keep an eye out for the passing dollar." Her speech was newscast American. The voice was rich—faintly nasal in a very pleasant way. She turned her gaze on him. "You implied you don't much expect to enjoy this. And you don't seem the type to be going where you won't enjoy yourself."

"It's a long story. Fiona's origins are British, you know. Back in the fifties, she married Captain Jack Freeland. In time, he became General Freeland, retired, took a corporate job, and made quite a bundle. You could say his life was a cliché of sorts. Ending with the cliché coronary and leaving her poised to establish herself as a Washington hostess in the pattern set by Perle Mesta. Nowadays, she's also into publishing. Puts out what's either a gossip magazine with a lot of art and culture or a cultural mag that carries a lot of gossip. She calls it *Avanti*."

"That's all very interesting. But it doesn't really answer my question, does it? What brings *you* to her premises?"

He grimaced inside. "Well, Pete Cassidy was a friend of Jack Freeland. And I work for Pete Cassidy. And one of the ways he gets along in this town is to furnish unattached males as grist for Fiona's social mill."

The path led through back gates and along shaded, brick-paved walkways already green with moss when Lincoln was President. They came out onto the sidewalk opposite Fiona's impressive manse. Just then, thunder rumbled close overhead, and the wind gave the trees a hard shake.

This was one of the few houses in Georgetown with a large front yard and a driveway. The drive was gravel, concrete in Georgetown being an affront against history. But gravel underfoot in high-heeled pumps is an affront against anatomy. He offered his hand, and she took it. Twenty feet or so, and they regained the brickwork, but he retained his grip.

From inside came the sounds of urbane revelry. As he was about to touch the button, Fiona herself, in all her overdone elegance, swung the door aside. "W-e-l-l!" Her tone and mien were loaded with *entendre* in several multiples. Just then the rain struck, and they scurried in past her.

He knew from old photos that Fiona had once been quite a beauty. Now she was so thin every bone in her body seemed evident, and only the layers of makeup kept her face from the suggestion of a death's-head.

Her wits had always been sharp, and whatever the ravages of time or illness, she was unimpaired up in the loft. The reporting staff of the magazine she ran did double duty. Any choice bits of scandal they dug up not verifiable enough for print went into her personal file, much of which was in her head. Thus had she worked her way into the thick of the male-female stew in all the postal zones touched or enclosed by the Beltway.

Inside, they separated from Fiona and took cover among the guests. She was too good a hostess for a single-minded pursuit of any one objective. On the other hand, she was too single-minded to lose the trail of any quarry. She'd be lying in ambush somewhere along the course of the evening.

She was known to be a free-lance scout for Sotheby's, and the house was a showcase of her certified good taste. Which injected a certain hazard in these affairs—breaking something expensive. And she was not shy about sending a bill for damages, which might easily run to four figures.

By now he had formed some acquaintance with the others riding this party circuit. Word had spread of his hand-in-hand approach with Michelle, and there was a general assumption she was his date. Questions carefully worded to seem casual he parried with Delphic responses.

Fiona's questions would not be casual. That wasn't her way.

Somehow, he managed to evade Fiona till the first guests began departing. Then there was a sleek, dusky feminine presence beside him and a stirring female voice. "Gus, darling, the rain's let up and it's . . . ah . . . about that time. We've got maybe half an hour." Michelle's hand was on his shoulder and her watch held out for him to see.

He picked up at once. "I guess you're right. I'll get my coat."

Fiona intercepted them at the door. "Lovely party," Gus said, with his finest ring of insincerity. "But we must be running. Prior commitment, you know."

"Very well," she said. "But there will be a next time. And you will tell me everything."

Michelle raised her palms and her eyebrows. "What's to tell?"

"Everything!" Fiona pointed a skeletal finger. Her tone and manner would have done for a Grand Inquisitor.

The rain still pattered lightly, so Michelle unfurled her umbrella. Each threw an arm around the other while they laughed and cavorted like schoolkids over some fabulous prank. "Thanks for going along," she said. "I was getting bored plus a little uncomfortable with all the probing."

Her proximity, the touch of her stirred him in a way he had not felt in a long time. "It got us both an early release. And now, the sixty-four-shekel question: Do you really have anything on for this evening?"

"Depends. Make me an offer." She gave him a teasing smile.

"Dinner and an evening's frolic?"

"Sounds good. As long as the frolic isn't too unrestrained."

71

"Excellent! I shall be the very model of restrained frolic. But come along. My chariot's back at the villa."

The house had a garage in back, unusual in Georgetown. She waited at the sidewalk while he backed the car out. The low, sleek, silvery shape sent her eyebrows up. He opened the door to help her in, and instead of swinging out on hinges, it rose on a single pivot. "It's a Countache!" she said. "Does it come with the house, or are you independently wealthy!"

"Neither," he said as he settled behind the wheel. "New, this car sells for about four hundred big ones. Way out of my league. This one was confiscated by the feds in a drug bust and put up for auction. All that stuff goes for pennies on the dollar, so, as sort of a lark, I put in a bid of twenty gees. I figured somebody would bid at least fifty. But a few days later, they called and said would I please come down to the warehouse with a certified check and pick up my car. I had to sell off a chunk of stock, and the capital-gains bill really hurt. But it was a chance I couldn't pass up."

She drew the kind of breath that serves as a preamble. "Everyone there assumed we were an item." Her eyes cut at him. "And I have a confession: I encouraged it. I couldn't resist when they all started congratulating me."

"So did I. Helped relieve the boredom. But I have to confess to being a little slow. Took a while to realize you're *the* Michelle St. Clair." How many years was it now since she had won a place on the Olympic figure-skating team and been a major hope for a gold medal? He recalled film of her spectacular leaps and twirls. But then she'd been disqualified on a technicality involving unauthorized expense money. The affair became one of the factors in the eventual overhaul of the Olympic rules.

"Seems we're rattling the skeletons in each other's closets."

At the Army-Navy Club there was the usual weekend live orchestra. He wasn't all that much on dancing, but he would have stood on his head to get his arms around her. Whenever the beat was slow enough, he cuddled her close. She seemed to enjoy it.

From the moment they touched, he was aware she was a very solid body. Yet she had a lightness and grace and unity with the music. Every point of contact transmitted some indefinable human energy. He thrilled just to the rhythmic flexing of her spinal muscles beneath his hand.

"You smell great and you dance beautifully," he said. "This is like guiding a fragrant balloon."

Her mouth formed a complex smile. "I've been called a lot of things, but that's a new one. I'll take it as a compliment."

Some minutes later, she suddenly resisted being drawn up close. Her eyes cut swaths through the crowd. Puzzled, he asked, "Have I developed an acute case of halitosis?"

"No, love. But I'm afraid we're drawing stares."

"Oh? Did I split an infinitive or something?"

"It's our color scheme, love. Black and white in our kind of combo makes some people see red."

Stock still, he frowned. "N-o-o! Here in Washington? In the Army-Navy Club? In this day and age? Are you—?"

"Trust me, love. I know about these things."

"Then perhaps we should sit out a while."

They took a seat in the bar and ordered drinks. It gave him the chance to further his study: The curvature of her lips was both sensitive and sensual. The narrow span across her cheekbones gave the eyes a slight feline tilt, adding to the image of the tigress. He also sensed the substance, the fierce response if her deeper feelings were challenged.

Coffee? mahogany? ginger? He could find no exact name for her color. It drew its tints from too rare a mix of the spectrum.

Those tigress eyes gleamed at him over her cocktail glass. She nibbled a few peanuts, then swallowed some of her drink. "Six and a half cents—that's an inflation-adjusted penny—for your thoughts."

He grinned. "You'd be making a bad bargain."

Her lips parted, and her head tilted back in real though nearly silent laughter. In the soft lighting, the whiteness of her teeth stood out against the dark velvet of her skin. The faint pink streaks along the parting of her lips made it seem she had nibbled rose petals instead of peanuts and picked up a delicate stain. She raised her glass to him and slid a little closer till their knees touched. "Okay, I'll raise. Ten cents."

"How are we going to deal with Fiona?" he said. "She's a good soul, but she's the self-anointed match-maker and romance broker of greater Washington. Affairs of the heart, or the lower parts for that matter, are sup-posed to have her imprimatur. And that rubs me the wrong way."

"Let's bug her. Let her think it's been going on for months right under her nose." Again, her face had the look of a schoolgirl playing a prank. It was a face in which intelligence mingled with serenity and good humor, yet beneath these lay a note of tragedy. As if the sufferings of distant ancestors were somehow registered there.

"Agreed." He got to his feet. "And now, since we get looks of disapproval here, we'll take our custom else-where. Come with me."

Handing her into the car, he said, "I guess you realize, if we're going to make Fiona think there's been some-thing between us, then . . ."

"Of course, love." She lowered herself into the seat. When he was settled behind the wheel, she laced her fin-gers over his shoulder and rested her chin there. "As soon as you mentioned your unattached status, I began schem-ing. So Fiona really was a matchmaker. We just won't let her take the credit." She wrinkled her nose at him again.

The place was called the Ristorante Piemontese and sat

right on the edge of Georgetown—four rooms of pale stucco, Roman archways, red-tiled floors, red-checked tablecloths, candles in wine bottles, and waiters in black tie. The voice of Placido Domingo in *Nessun Dorma,* somehow both robust and unobtrusive, issued from unseen speakers.

The place looked full when they walked in, but the proprietor himself, all smiles, hurried over and greeted Gus as "my dear colonel." The man bowed over Michelle's hand, then escorted them to a table in a shadowy corner. Soon a waiter arrived with a bottle of Asti Spumanti in ice. "With the compliments of Signor Capelli." He poured two glasses and departed.

"Well, you must have quite a standing here," she said. They clinked glasses and drank.

"I'm practically an habitué. I found this place my first week or so in Washington, and I eat here often. Easier than cooking dinner and a lot more pleasant than a tray alone in front of the TV set."

"You've been alone since your divorce from Valerie Aubin?"

"Unmarried, if that's what you mean."

"I mean with no one to cook your dinner and cuddle up to at night."

He chuckled. "Val never cooked a dinner in her life. And she wasn't around for much cuddling. You know the life of a movie star."

"Did she make you gun-shy of commitment?"

He shrugged. "Let's just say wiser. More careful."

"But it's what—several years now since you split with her? That's a lot of careful."

"That's military life. Rootless. Outer-directed. Tends to foster the temporary."

For Gus, the evening was a romantic epiphany. The first act in the drama of the youthful first love he had never had in his youth. The thing with Val had been unreal from the start, and marriage to a movie actress was

B. Michelaard

like watching himself in a film. It had taken a while to recognize his own role as the clown.

But something mystic and near-magic made tonight different. The dinner itself was enough to etch a place in his memory. But great as it was, it was only backdrop.

Afterward, he drove her home. Home for her was a townhouse condo on three levels in a development that somehow achieved a warm, federalist ambiance despite a lot of mullioned glass. This was done mainly through the soft glow from pole-mounted carriage lamps that shed their light on winding brick-paved walkways and into cunning alcoves.

She had him put the Countache in the garage beside her Chrysler Laser. "I took a taxi to Fiona's because parking there is such a problem."

On the walk to her door, she said, "Now, let me outline the program for the rest of the evening. While you fix us a nightcap, I'll slip into something more comfortable and put on some romantic music. Then we'll cuddle on the divan, and you can make a restrained pass at me. Remember, the frolic was to be restrained. Jumping into bed when we've only known each other about eight hours just isn't our style. Or at least not mine. So, after a reasonable interval, we'll say good night." Her look was direct. "And I'll expect to hear from you within twenty-four hours."

"Sounds like a winning program."

And so it went—for as far as it went. Sometime during the "restrained" kissing and cuddling, she began pouring herself more brandy, and her half of the restraint began slipping—along with her "something more comfortable," a robe of royal blue with a velvety nap. It kept opening up to reveal more and more of the most marvelous female body he had ever seen.

Finally, her head came to rest on his shoulder. Her arms were around him, and the robe was parted down to her navel. He made to get up, but her grip tightened. She had not passed out, just subsided into a state of immobility.

Well, so be it. Only one thing to do.

He managed to get his arms in position to cradle her. But standing up took a real effort.

There were bedrooms on the upper floors, but she had done her changing here, on the lower level. So he assumed this was where she slept. Beyond a short crook of passage, he entered a typically feminine bedroom with a queen-size bed already turned down. Lowering her onto it without dropping her was another physical feat. He removed her high-heeled satin slippers, pulled the sheet and blanket up over her, turned out the light, and tiptoed out.

The telephone stand was a small *escritoire* with a selection of paper and stationery and several kinds of writing instruments in a dice cup. He chose a plain notepad and a large, felt-tipped marker and wrote in bold script: "Mike, I love you. Gus."

On the way home, distanced from the powerful aura she cast, he began to think about her and the events of the evening. Vague impressions limned into sharper outlines: He had already noted a whiff of covert federal connections among many of those in Fiona's party circle. Could Mike . . . ? No. It didn't make sense. On the other hand, there were things about her, her situation, that felt like a quarter-bubble skid.

As he came to a stop for a traffic light, his hand strayed to his shirt pocket and the card she had placed there. He pulled it out and read:

Dr. Michelle St. Clair, MD PC
General and Thoracic Surgery
President, Med-Tech Enterprises, Inc.

Chapter Six

Standing on the fantail of the airship, Gus felt staggered by both its size and potential future. Through the revival of lighter-than-air, the oldest concept in flight, American airpower would soon be able to arrive on an enemy's doorstep over night and with mystifying stealth.

This was the landing impact zone, where airplanes would alight as they came aboard. The rest of the flight deck was entirely inside. He found the length breathtaking considering the ship was built to fly. Above it was a vast space containing the mylar cells for the millions of cubic feet of helium. Below it were the tanks for the liquid hydrogen fuel.

Overhead loomed the cascade of airfoil shapes that would keep the downward flow off the aft fuselage from slamming a landing aircraft onto the deck. In normal flight, they lowered and joined to form a closed panel.

He went over to the lip of the flight deck, mildly unsettling since there was no railing and the ground was over a hundred feet below. From there, he could look forward and see the two vast deltoid wings that gave the airship a shape like a manta ray.

Unlike the old-style dirigibles, this was actually an LTA airplane, designed to fly on both helium buoyancy and aerodynamic lift. It would turn and maneuver airplane-fashion, by banking. So the controls were like those on large airplanes. Besides helium cells, the wings also contained the eight giant electrogenic propulsion units, each with an intake the size of a highway tunnel. Energy for propulsion came from heating intake air by electric arcs instead of burning fuel. Otherwise they were much like conventional fan-jet engines.

With launch on the maiden flight only hours away, the helium cells were partially inflated, and the ship was slightly buoyant. It moved gently, snubbing and straining against the mooring cables, giving Gus the sensation of being in the middle of a mild earthquake.

Trials would last over a month before he could start bringing the first skeleton air group aboard. After that would come more trials and shakedowns as they worked their way up to operational readiness.

His watch read 1830. Launch was scheduled for 2300 local. Meanwhile, the ship was fully functional. The reactor was on-line, furnishing an abundance of electrical power. The crew had been living aboard for over a week. It took remarkably few men to operate this monster, so they were all officers, handpicked and mostly unmarried. Long separations could strain a marriage, and a crew member with troubles at home could become a risk to security.

Given the airship's dimensions, walking was generally not practical. To reach the forward part of the ship, where the command and control functions were centered, Gus rode an electric-powered trolley, like a bosun's chair, that ran on an overhead rail.

Arriving in the nose, he climbed a spiral staircase the Navy would call a ladder. So far, the Navy and Marine

Corps men used nautical terms for the ship's parts. Those from the Air Force favored aircraft terminology. Terms would have to be standardized soon. In any craft meant for warfare, everyone had to know exactly what everyone else was talking about.

The non-stressed interior partitions were a fireproof material much like Styrofoam. Their sound-deadening qualities made for an eerie silence aboard. The structural members were boron or carbon fiber, like the XFL.

In his cabin, he showered, shaved, and put on a clean uniform. Much of the technology was borrowed from nuclear subs: Solid waste was converted into an innocuous granular substance and jettisoned. Lost water could be replaced either by catching rainfall or siphoning from any large body.

The wardroom, one Naval term fully accepted on board, had a decor much like those on Navy ships. Hank Borland was already seated. He had the blond, blue-eyed, square-jawed good looks the Navy seemed to favor in its officer corps. He had also graduated near the top of his class at Annapolis, was a Naval aviator of long experience, and had a master's degree in nuclear engineering. He had come to the Pegasus Project direct from command of the nuclear supercarrier *Ronald Reagan*.

"Damn, Gus," Borland said with a smile. "Thought you might have fallen overboard. Better get your dinner on the line."

"Right away." The food was like airline meals—precooked, frozen, and reheated in microwaves. Not gourmet but satisfying and guaranteed nutritious. By long-standing Navy policy, there was no alcohol aboard.

"Damn glad we're on our own," said Borland. Security meant they were spared visiting dignitaries. The Pegasus executive committee, a panel of general and flag officers plus civilian technocrats, had guided the project from the start. It was code-named Mother Hen and reported directly to the Joint Chiefs.

"So, you were involved back as far as the construction phase?" Gus said.

"Oh, yeah. I froze my buns in the winter and poured sweat all summer."

"So explain to me how that atomic pile can operate without thick lead walls and still not fry us all," Gus said.

"Well, the basic principle is to surround the core with an electro-magnetic field. It either traps or decelerates escaping particles and allows absorption by much thinner shielding. Gamma rays are focused into a beam and out the upper surface, through a panel like a radome. And the new core technology produces less radiation." Hank paused to squeeze ketchup on his burger. "But the real advance has been direct generation of electrical power without some intermediate mechanical device like a turbine. That's still a mystery even to me."

"I'm still amazed security has been so good."

"Sometimes I am too. The key was to keep the number who know below two hundred, the critical mass that leads to compromise. It's a black program, so we've kept it well below that. No one outside the President, the SecDef and undersecs, the Joint Chiefs, key members of Congress, and those assigned to the project know we're about to launch a colossal new military airship. And incidentally, the biggest thing ever to fly."

Borland chewed his burger, took a swallow of iced tea. "The program actually originated back in the eighties. The funds were all buried in other DoD procurement packages." He paused, and his look and tone turned confidential. "And you know about the hiatus under the recent Administration. Of course, certain key members of Congress had to be sold on it first. And it's compartmented like a beehive. None of the subcontractors knows the ultimate use of whatever they supplied. They had specs and delivery dates and that's all."

"When I saw the propulsion system," Gus said, "I near dropped my teeth. I worked on the design of those electrogenic engines during my NASA fellowship at Wright-Pat."

"Small world," Borland said.

"But somebody had to do the actual airframe design. Structure, flight mechanics and control, aerodynamics. And they had to know what they were designing."

"Team of engineers, some from NASA, some from industry, some from universities. All sworn to secrecy. Did most of it on computers. And even they were never told it would actually be built. It was billed as a feasibility study."

"And what about the work crews? Toward the end, when it was taking shape, they must have had some kind of clue."

Borland shook his head. "The work crews never saw anything but the spot where they were putting new parts in place. Everything was covered by big plastic tarpaulins. The men arrived in buses and came in through covered walkways. And we spread all kinds of talk about what it really was. Because of the isolation, there was high turnover. But it also helped security. No one was there long enough to form an impression."

"What about satellites?" Gus went on. "The Russians have given up Marxism, but not their snooping ways."

"Well, we did the best we could to disguise the shape. Hung tarpaulins where there was nothing underneath. Draped 'em over derricks and what have you."

At 2100, Borland, Gus, and the chief flight surgeon began a final inspection. It was 2233 when they arrived back on the bridge. At 2245, Borland began the final countdown for launch.

In profile, the airship's fuselage sloped down both fore and aft. The nose section resembled the forward half of a gigantic horse's hoof. The focus of command and control was a compartment thirty feet across, located just above the flight deck, near the tip of the nose. Like the nautical equivalent, it was called the bridge. The plexiglass windscreen conformed to the forty-five-degree slope of the nose. Readouts of altitude, airspeed, and vertical speed were displayed in large ruby digits on a panel just above the windscreen. Magnetic heading was by traditional rotating compass card.

The cockpit, the pilot's station containing the flight controls, protruded like a bay window at the center of the bridge. It gave the flight crew a two-hundred-degree field of vision. Decker, the chief pilot, along with the second pilot and a flight engineer, was well into the prelaunch checklist. Decker was an AF colonel and the ship's executive—second in command under Borland.

The only light on the bridge now was the ruby glow of instruments and a few small binnacle-type lamps. The men were shadowy figures. Through the sloping plexiglass windscreen, Gus could see starlit gaps in the cloud cover. A chronometer with an LED-display read 2236 and counted down the seconds. One by one, Decker fired up the eight electrogenic turbines, checked their performance at idle.

At 2257, Borland's voice crackled through the darkness. "All right, gentlemen, everyone strapped in a seat. Silence on the bridge." As 2259 dissolved into 2300, he ordered, "Release mooring lines." Decker pressed a button, and small explosive charges sprung open the latches that secured the tie-down cables. The ship rose slowly and made history as the largest object ever to take the air.

Gus had no real sensation of rising. It was rather like riding a slow elevator. "Okay, Tom," Borland said to Decker. "Pick up the course and altitude." The cockpit crew began further inflating the huge mylar cells. Liquid helium from cryogenic tanks was converted to gas and passed over glowing electric filaments. The temperature inside the cells rose to over two hundred degrees Fahrenheit, giving a large increase in buoyancy.

"Power coming in," said Decker. Again, there was no sense of acceleration, only the steady increase in the airspeed digital readout.

It rose past a hundred knots and the altitude went through a thousand feet. They felt a gentle nose-up tilt, and the vertical speed shot up to 1700 feet per minute.

Interphone voice reports announced the various systems were "go." For Gus, those crisp voices, the sense of precision, the mental intensity among the men on the bridge brought an acute awareness of being part of the warrior fraternity. Since primitive times, men had grouped themselves into fighting units and set out to meet their enemies. It was in their genes. Over the centuries, they had developed ever more sophisticated weapons, but the human element was unchanged. Among all forms of group bonding, that among fighting men was the strongest. More than any other phenomenon, it led men to sacrifice themselves for the unit.

The climb continued through broken clouds. Just above six thousand, they topped the final layer and emerged into a night of crystalline beauty. The tufted surface of the cloud deck caught the slanting rays of a three-quarter moon and turned to silvery iridescence. The welkin was a blue-black crystal that had caught a zillion starry fireworks at the moment of ignition.

The effect rippled among those on the bridge. Even the old flying hands murmured things like, "Good night to be flying." Pilots were often romantics, yet awkward about it. So they tended to hide their feelings for the romance and beauty of flight behind a hard-headed absorption with the techniques and technology of their craft.

As the nose lowered into level flight, Borland released his seat belt and stood up. "I think she's demonstrated enough stability so that we can move around. How does she fly, Tom?"

"Like a cream puff, Skipper. Good precision, good response. Wants to go up and down a little in the vertical currents. But in smooth air, I think you could hold the altimeter within twenty feet with no sweat."

"Sounds like a winner. I'll have to take a turn at the

controls myself before we get back. What do you think, Gus?"

"Looking great so far."

Borland pressed a button on the intercom panel: "Comm section, this is the skipper. Message for Mother Hen: The horse has left the stable. All systems go. Position . . ." He gave the figures on longitude and latitude from the readout on the inertial nav. "Course two-seven-zero. Angels seven. Speed one-seventy. Ready for big-eye check. Wish you were here." The last brought smiles around the bridge. As soon as the message was read back, he pressed another intercom button and said, "ECM, this is the captain. Are we being swept?"

"Affirmative, Skipper. Three separate sources. Two strong and one sort of weak. Instrument readings indicate maximum black. We shouldn't be on any of their scopes."

"We'll know in a minute," Borland said as he clicked off the intercom.

The big-eye check was a test of the stealth system. Radar stations had been alerted to a target passing along the track of Skyhook sometime before midnight. They were given direct phone hookups to Mother Hen and told to report any contact but take no other action.

Within five minutes Mother Hen reported: "Negative contact all stations. See you in the funny papers."

Borland grinned. "Somebody there actually has a sense of humor."

Beyond the flat prairies of the mid-continent loomed the Rockies. They followed the Great Northern Railway through the Marias Pass. The seven-thousand-foot altitude gave them clearance on everything within five miles of the course. The inertial nav system kept them within a few feet of the prescribed track.

They emerged from the Rockies almost over Spokane, crossed the Columbia River basin to join the Yakima River and Northern Pacific Railway. They followed its gap through the Cascades, and crossed Puget Sound about midway between Seattle and Tacoma.

There, less than an hour from the coast, Borland remarked about needing some new weather, and was just reaching for the intercom when a voice came out of it. "Bridge, this is met. Weather map and revised forecast coming over the fax." At the same time, a paper began emerging silently from the fax machine.

The chief forecaster was an Air Force major, with a Navy lieutenant as assistant. The met section could receive fax photos and television pictures from weather satellites and monitor weather station reports from around the world. Data could be fed into the ship's computer to produce any desired weather chart.

Borland tore off the sheet. "Somebody better warn those guys. They're not supposed to make the skipper feel superfluous."

The forecast showed considerable cloud over the cold Japanese current near the coast but nothing hairy. They could expect mostly clear skies beyond and unlimited visibility at flight altitude.

The cockpit had a digital display of the volume and temperature in each helium cell, given as a percent of maximum. From this, the crew could determine the max attainable altitude, the free-floating altitude, and the positive or negative aerodynamic lift needed to maintain any given level.

Much of the next few hours was spent exercising these and other capabilities. Decker flew turns of increasing angle of bank, but was careful to limit the G-load to about 1.5. Engineering theory could predict general behavior, but all the theory in all the books and computers was no substitute for direct linkage between pilot and aircraft.

By the time they had completed the series, the dawn's aurora had smothered the stars over the northeastern sky and turned the rest of the welkin more blue than black. Once more they were treated to a sight that few who do not fly ever experience: the subtle shading of light and color near sunrise, unmarred by the haze or lights on the earth. Borland handed Decker a folded sheet and said, "Steer for these coordinates. Give Flagon a call on 336.6 UHF. When we're in contact, we'll rendezvous."

"Hello, Flagon. How do you read Skyhook?"

"Skyhook, Flagon reading you five-square. How do you read me?"

"Skyhook reading you five-square, Flagon. Give us a tone, and we'll home on you."

"Roger, Skyhook. Five-second tone commencing . . . now."

In the cockpit, a needle swung in response, and Decker pointed the ship toward the source of the signal. "Skyhook has your tone, Flagon. Rendezvous in about forty minutes. Skyhook out."

It was full daylight when they arrived at the rendezvous. Borland had Decker fly a five-mile-square pattern around the location at about a thousand feet. They were in and out of scattered clouds, but they did catch a glimpse of the sail of a nuclear sub.

After some twenty minutes, they took leave of Flagon and climbed away. Sometime later, they had a message from Mother Hen: "Received the following signal from Flagon: 'I saw it, but I didn't, and I don't believe any of it. I think it was done with smoke and mirrors.' "

Arthur Penross was in full momentum. His fingers did a lively gavotte on the keyboard, the cursor sprinting across the screen, the lines of text scrolling steadily upward. So, when the phone rang, he scowled and for some seconds declined to answer. But it was his personal line, the one the secretary didn't have.

He hit the button for the speaker, said, "Yeah," and went on writing, though the cursor slowed its pace to a hesitant walk.

"Yes to both of your questions," said the familiar voice.

"Umm?" Penross searched his memory for connections.

"You wanted to know if the Pentagon is using AWACS aircraft to watch the coast of Colombia and if one was shot down. Yes and yes. Mission call sign was Anvil Bravo. Only one to survive was the aircraft commander, and they gave him an Air Medal. Notification to next of kin said only that each service member had died as a result of a crash."

"Any corroboration?"

"You know better than that."

Penross mulled in silence for a moment. "Ah, well. That's the fun in taking on the Pentagon. They can't really fight back." He paused again. "Very well. The check will go into your account."

He returned to his text, eager to finish while his thoughts were still concentrated. They were already beginning to stray toward his newest verbal offensive— how he would use the loss of Anvil Bravo to achieve maximum embarrassment to the Pentagon.

Chapter Seven

"Can you imagine now, Alejandro, that this is where we once learned to make revolution?" The question was followed by a bitter, derisive snort.

"I see what you mean, *Jefe*. It hardly seems the same place."

The terminal at Sheremetyevo was littered with refuse like a sports arena after a game. Two stolid *babushkas* plied their push-brooms against the tide of grime and refuse.

A man in a well-fitted leather coat, sharply creased trousers, and shiny shoes approached. "Comrades Peña and Maldivo?" He gave a slight bow and tip of his astrakhan. "Kravinskoi. Grigori Mikhailovich. If you would like to come with me. I have a car waiting. I trust you had a pleasant flight in." His English had only a mild accent.

He ushered them past customs and passport control. "You see there is still authority here in this *commonwealth*." He pronounced the word with a derisive sneer.

"And a few of us who can still assert it." He led them outside to a plain black Volga and took the wheel himself.

Conversation was minimal. Kravinskoi made small remarks to the effect that the trip was risky and not really necessary. The drive ended at Tushino, Moscow's older and less active airport, where the pilot of a six-passenger Tupolev turbo twin awaited them for the flight to Odessa. There, another car took them to the port, where they went aboard the SS *Juaquin Salazar*, twelve thousand tons, built in Gdansk, registered in Panama.

The ship lay at one of the piers reserved for dangerous cargo. The interior of the hold was an arms dealer's showcase. Missiles nestled in packing crates. MiG fighters sat on cradles. Kravinskoi sounded a constant note to hurry the inspection.

"Many of these items were supposedly dismantled under the terms of the various disarmament agreements and do not officially exist," said Peña, "I think it's reasonable that we satisfy ourselves."

"But your own representatives have done all this already. Seen to the packing at the points of origin and the loading aboard here."

"Things can happen. Items get switched or go astray between one location and another. Even the largest items. For example, in America, a magician made their Statue of Liberty disappear. Which, I might remind you, is something the Kremlin never managed."

Finally satisfied, the visitors sent a wire to Zürich. Within thirty minutes, Kravinskoi had an answer regarding the transfer of funds, and the *Juaquin Salazar* was cleared to sail. Officially, the visitors had never entered the country. Their exit went equally unrecorded.

Dusk was gathering as the ship cleared the harbor. From the deck, they watched the lights on shore recede. "So, Alejandro, are your doubts appeased?" *El Jefe* took a humorous, chiding tone.

"Some, *Jefe*. I'll admit I wasn't really convinced the

former Soviets would actually sell us major weapons systems. But even these are a long way from making our country the equal of the *norteamericanos*. We have no nuclear warheads."

"Peace, Alejandro. Warheads are being developed. Meanwhile, we maintain the image of a poor, weak people just trying to provide a few amenities for ourselves and opportunities for our children. And keep our level of provocation low."

The pair left the ship at Istanbul. From there, they could get a flight to Madrid, with connections to all the major cities of South America. Alejandro saw the actual destination on his ticket, frowned, and said, "Berlin, *Jefe?*"

It was a typical November day in the restored German capital. Beneath a dark, fustian sky, the air was damp and chilly. On busy streets, slushy snow spattered shoes and hissed beneath auto tires. Along the Kurfürstendamm, traffic and business were brisk. The brilliant colors of electric signs cast shimmering reflections on the wet pavement. Smiling faces reddened by the chill thronged the shops and cafes. Standing amid this bustle and swirl yet apart from it, the jagged truncation of the ruined Gedächtniskirche reared its somber message against the louring sky.

Despite reunification, West Berlin still enjoyed a tremendous edge in civil amenities. So the art gallery was in Charlottenburg, not far off the Ku-damm. Posters outside proclaimed a one-woman show of both sculpture and painting by the well-known American artist Audrey Prowther.

When *El Jefe* entered, the gallery owner and the prominent female socialite hosting the show rushed up to him. He took their hands in turn.

"Herr Alvarado, how nice of you to drop in," she gushed. Etienne Alvarado was known here as a wealthy

South American devoted both to lavish entertaining and support of the arts. He had founded and headed something called the Instituto Santos Dumont.

"Business brought me here for a day or so, and I thought I'd extend my good wishes to Audrey."

The owner checked his watch. "She's due any minute now." He showed a lubricious smile. "But we both appreciate your interest. Because of your help, we've had people here from three other continents."

"Always happy to afford these small favors. But do have her come and see me."

"Oh, I will, Herr Alvarado. I most assuredly will."

Alvarado nodded his thanks and moved off to mingle. He picked up a program and one of the small stemmed glasses from a tray carried by a white-jacketed waiter. The glass was plastic, its contents German *Sekt*, and English predominant in the surrounding babble of affectations. Here and there he caught remarks through the general sound of voices:

". . . lucky enough to pick it up way back before the critics discovered her. I can't afford what she gets now, of course."

". . . drawn by its tactile appeal, just as I was."

". . . rather early and rather small, but I wouldn't part with it for a fortune."

". . . definite influence of Hans Hoffman, but hers all the same."

Just then, murmurs and the turning of heads spread in waves from a perceptual epicenter. The artist herself had arrived.

What he and the other guests saw was a woman of five-nine whose forty-plus years rested lightly enough that she might easily pass for thirty-five or so. A large, floppy hat sat askew on full, dense hair drawn straight back into a French roll. Its blondness varied in streaks from sunlight to woodsmoke.

Hers was an intimate rather than a striking beauty. It

would not stand out that much in a crowd, but tête-à-tête or vis-à-vis would act like a vortex, drawing men into her emotional centrum. It made her ideal for his uses.

Beneath a short, stylish cape, a knit dress hugged her slender waist and ample bosom and spread its pleats artfully over full hips and thighs. The physique signaled animal vigor. One could surmise she skied in winter, played tennis in summer, and had strong appetites.

Escorted by the gallery owner, she smiled and nodded her way through the gathering, exchanging a word or two here, a handshake there.

With everyone's attention on her, *El Jefe* slipped quietly out where she had entered. It was several minutes later that she joined him in the otherwise deserted business office. The conversation was brief. "I should be back in New York in a week or so," she told him. "I'll contact you by the usual means."

"And *now* can we go back to Bogotá, *Jefe?*" said Alejandro over a drink at a cafe on the Ku-damm.

"Oh, no, my friend. Not just yet. It's back to Moscow and Comrade Kravinskoi and then Odessa again."

In the Crestwood Towers, the alarm clocks were signaling the start of another day. Dwayne Chauncey shut off the noxious buzzing, eased his feet into slippers, and moved the drapery aside for a tentative look at the weather. From fourteen floors up, the Hudson looked placid and inviting rather than polluted. And the distant pinnacles of downtown Albany suggested the lure of urban life more than its dangers and frustrations.

In slippers and pajama bottoms, he entered the small kitchen, downed a glass of orange juice, then poured coffee from the Krups brewer he had programmed the night before. Breakfast was strawberry yogurt, a slice of whole-wheat toast with apple jelly, and more coffee. He carried the cup into the bathroom.

In the mirror, dark eyes, still sleep-clouded, stared

back at him out of a lean, sensitive face. Contrary to the highbrow intellectual image, his forehead was moderate.

Face-to-face with himself, fingering the stubble on the slightly sunken cheeks, he felt discomfort as well as whiskers. Ever since his wife died, he had, like electrical current, taken the path of least resistance. It had led to a life that was much less than what he felt it should be.

As the hot coffee took effect, that psychic temblor faded. He sat and set about conducting his first movement. He even hummed a bit of Brahms to go with it. Then he showered, shaved, and dressed.

Ready as he would ever be to face the world, he picked up his attaché case, turned out the lights, and rode the elevator to the garage.

Twenty-odd minutes later, he took the freeway exit for Schenectady and the GE labs. A uniformed security guard waived him through a gate. He parked in the space marked "Dr. Chauncey." Inside, another guard logged him in and handed him his security badge with his picture.

As usual, Dr. Avery Willard, who lived nearby, was already at his desk, engrossed in thought. Dwayne was reminded of their first meeting, his surprise that one of the leading thinkers in the field of electro-magnetic theory should look so pedestrian. He had a solid, almost beefy frame and taut, chipmunk cheeks beneath a low, blunt forehead. This morning, as always, the cheeks were ruddy and gleaming from the razor. Willard was over seventy now, but his ash-white hair was still thick and straight and parted on the side. Like his mustache, it was stiff and bristly.

By the time Chauncey had come on board at GE, the discovery called the Willard Effect and its principal application, the inverse magnetron, had already been tested. The device converted incident radio waves into electrical energy. If it was ever declassified, it might win a Nobel.

Willard looked up. "Oh, there you are, Dwayne. Sleep well?"

"Morning, Huck. Yes, thanks. I did. How's yourself and the Missus?" "Huck" was what Willard preferred. He was courteous and considerate as he was brilliant, and though he seldom laughed aloud, he had a puckish sense of humor and a fondness for puns.

"Dwayne, something's come up. I tried to reach you this morning, but you must have already left. They need someone to go to Washington, and . . ."

So Chauncey found himself driving back to Albany, packing, and catching a flight for National.

Five days later than expected, Dwayne finally got out of Washington. He caught the shuttle flight to La Guardia and a taxi into Manhattan. The doorman at the Upper East Side high-rise greeted him by name. "Your sister's just gone up a few minutes ago, sir."

When he reached the apartment, Gail opened the door. "Little brother!" she said, threw her arms wide, then around his neck. "You're looking fine. Come on in the kitchen. I just got home myself." He perched on a kitchen stool while she put up groceries. "You just came from Washington?"

"Right. I went for a day or two and ended up staying a week. Had to buy new shirts and underwear."

"So, what were you . . . ? Oh, never mind." She paused and rolled her eyes. "One of those things you can't talk about. Anyway, I'm glad I got here before you did. We had a pre-holiday faculty meeting."

Conversation with her was as effortless as ever. Just nod at suitable times. Abigail would do all the talking. She looked the same—tall, slender, honey-blond, very attractive for her forty-eight years. They were so different in appearance, it was often hard for strangers to believe they were brother and sister. "So how's Aaron?"

"Oh, fine. You know Aaron. Always complaining of little aches and pains and how impossible life is in New York. And he wouldn't think of living anywhere else. Say! You haven't heard: He's been invited to spend a year as a guest lecturer at Oxford. It's not final yet, but it looks likely. Think of it! A year in Britain, lots of new contacts. Good for another book."

"Sounds like a great opportunity. Another advantage in not having kids. No complications. But will they hold your job open at the college?"

"Oh, I think so. I flatter myself they couldn't find anyone with my experience in piano and music theory who doesn't already have a job he's happy with. And the salary isn't all that great. They take advantage of me because they know I'm not going anywhere as long as Aaron's at Columbia. And he'll stay till he retires. Hell, till he dies."

A key rattled in the door, and Aaron came in.

Aaron Grossbaum was a native New Yorker, an academic of the liberal persuasion, and he looked the part. He had thick, wavy hair down to his collar and thick rimless lenses—fogged now from the chill outside. He was large and fleshy, his movements ponderous. Both the hair and the neatly trimmed mustache/Vandyke combo had turned salt-and-pepper. He took Dwayne's hand and exchanged greetings before taking off his coat.

Dwayne liked Aaron, enjoyed his company, and respected his thought. He recalled the family's grim-faced shock at the news Gail was marrying a Jew. And how they had been somewhat mollified when they learned that Aaron was one of *the* Grossbaums, part of that elite circle of wealth that included the Rothschilds and Guggenheims.

Aaron and Gail had good salaries plus the income from Aaron's books. But this fashionable address, the summers abroad, the various expensive touches were all subsidized by Aaron's family money.

Aaron mixed drinks, and they settled down in the living room. He sipped his and looked at his wife. "Have you mentioned uh-h . . . ?"

"Oh . . . no." She took a deep breath. "A-h-h, Dwayne, there's someone who wants to meet you. She's . . ." Dwayne felt his stomach tighten a little as he realized a "fix-up" was coming. Gail saw his eyes roll upward and said, "Now don't just go into your usual negative reaction. All I said was she'd like to meet you. She's a prominent and successful artist. Works in both painting and sculpture. She's bright, attractive, and right in your age group."

"Damn good-looking woman," said Aaron with a theatrical leer.

"We've known her since last summer," Gail went on. "When I happened to mention you, she said she'd be very interested in meeting someone in science. She wants to know about the thought patterns of scientific research. She believes science and the arts might cross-fertilize each other." Gail leaned forward and gave him an intent frown. "And Dwayne, you can't go on hibernating year-round. Loss is traumatic, but it's time you gave life another chance."

"A Hearstian hortatory if I ever heard one." He showed a teasing smile while he waited for the pun to register on her. The worst part about it was he knew she was right. "And I'll go along with the gag. Don't I always?" He sighed. "So, this woman wants to pick my brains for her next artwork. Maybe she'll call it Volts in Revolt. Is she anyone whose name I'd recognize?"

"I should think so," said Aaron. "She's Audrey Prowther."

Chapter Eight

The Arthur Penross column read:

> *PENTAGON MISUSING MEDALS. AGAIN.*
> *The Pentagon is at it again, trying to bury its mistakes, along with those who paid with their lives.*
>
> *This columnist has learned that AWACS aircraft, those very large and very expensive jets loaded with the ultimate in electronic gadgetry, are being used secretly to monitor the activities of the Latin drug lords.*
>
> *Actually, it was only secret in the U.S. The cartel knew it all along and took exception to it, to the extent of using a missile to shoot down one of these zillion-dollar behemoths.*
>
> *The Air Force and the Pentagon are representing this tragedy as just another "operational loss," meaning an accident. They dismiss the incompetence or carelessness, or both, of whoever put that big bird and its crew up there as a tempting target,*

with no protection whatever. The families of the dead were told only that the service members had died as a result of a crash. And no bodies were recovered, indicating that the aircraft went down at sea.

Did I say no bodies? Well, no dead bodies. But there was one survivor. And who was he? Well, he just happened to be the pilot, or aircraft commander. Anyway, he was the one responsible for all those young lives. Odd, isn't it, that the man they all trusted, looked upon as a kind of surrogate father managed to save his own skin but none of his crew members?

So what did the Pentagon brass do with this guy? Court-martial? Hold a board of inquiry on his conduct? Perish the thought! No, they gave him a medal!

Champagne and cigars all around, fellahs, and didn't we do a great job papering this one over?

Well, not this time. Some righteous service member, who must of course remain nameless, just couldn't quite swallow this display of brass by the Brass.

So far, the Pentagon has declined to release the names of the dead, citing both security and "sensitivity for the bereaved families." A combination of crocodile tears and the same old shopworn rubric the Pentagon has used for decades to cover up its mistakes. But we have no qualms about invoking the Freedom of Information Act. The families deserve the truth.

Death can consign you to anonymity, but the living have no such prerogative. So we had no trouble discovering the one newly decorated for incompetence or cowardice or both is name MAJOR GUILBERT AUSTEN.

We wanted to publish that before it changed.

By next week, he could be Colonel Austen. Meanwhile, he's walking around with an Air Medal that *cost the lives of several young Americans. It must weigh on him like an albatross.*

For anyone out there who won an honest Air Medal and wants to consider turning it in, I'll have an address in a few days.

Someday, the Pentagon Brass may discover they can no longer get away with covering up their own blunders or those of their flunkies. The classic ploy of denying an act was a blunder by rewarding it will no longer wash. The dead will not stay buried. Not until justice is done.

Stay tuned.

Mystified about where he got his information as well as seething at Penross, Colonel Damon Salter knew this column meant the end of Gil Austen's assignment to Shadowbox. He called the Pentagon and said he'd recommend Austen for any plush assignment, including Air Force One.

Ehrman sat down and read the column. "The bastard knows our weak spots. We can't defend Gil without disclosing classified facts about Shadowbox."

"Gil Austen's one tough cookie," said Salter. "He'll live to see that sonofabitch Penross get his lumps."

Ehrman folded his hands and looked thoughtful. "Years ago, somebody organized a Committee to Horsewhip Drew Pearson. And compared to this bastard, Drew Pearson was a patriot and a pussycat. What we need now is a Committee to Hang Arthur Penross. By the balls."

"Gus! Gus darling, wake up! Wake up!" Michelle was shaking him, slapping him lightly on the face. He sat up in bed, his breath heaving, sweat on his brow. The bedside lamp was on, and her tigress eyes, full of concern, were fixed on him. "That must have been some nightmare."

"Yeah. Sorry. Can't figure what could've triggered it."

He swung his feet out of bed and put on the robe that was draped over a chair back.

The digital clock read 04:07 A.M. Outside, Georgetown was dead quiet, but the purr of distant traffic on the Whitehurst Freeway drifted in with the cool air that wafted the curtains. "I heard you come in, but I shut my eyes and drifted off again without seeing the clock. What time was it?"

"About one." Her face took on a look of mock outrage. "You knew I was here, and you didn't roll over and ravish me?"

"My ravishing circuits were down for maintenance. Why so late?"

"Emergency surgery starting about nine. The guy turned out to be a bleeder. Bloodstream loaded with aspirin."

He had an idea now what had triggered the nightmare. Yesterday Pete Cassidy had told him Skyhook had nearly completed shakedown and would soon be ready for the skeleton air group to begin its trial operations. His time in Washington was about to end, and he had to tell her. Soon. "Look, you might as well go back to sleep. I can't for the rest of the night, but there's no reason you shouldn't."

"That's for me to decide." She slithered out of bed and stood up.

He had finally decided her color was a deep shade of gold. In the glow of the lamp, her skin took on highlights and shadows. They had been lovers for nearly a month now, yet the revealed perfection of her body still made him catch his breath. She put on that same velvety blue robe she had worn the night of their first meeting. "Now tell me, is this dream recurrent?" The furrows on her brow deepened.

He bobbed his head. "M-m, yeah. Way back when, it was at least once a month. Nowadays it's pretty rare. Maybe three times a year."

"But that's still terrible. Why don't you—?"

"Because it's not that simple!"

She followed him down the steep stairway and into the kitchen, which, despite the age of the house, was very modern. The massive kitchen table had a top like a butcher's block and an overhead rack where utensils hung. There were two straight-back chairs.

He ran water, got out the coffee. She eased him aside and took over. "If you drink coffee, you won't sleep for sure." He plopped down on a chair. "Want to tell Dr. Mike about it?"

He got up, took several restless paces. "You don't deserve this, but I guess you have a right to it. I've never told anyone but the people who debriefed me after I escaped." He paused, took a deep breath, and said, "How much do you really know about me and Vietnam?"

"Not a whole lot. I know you shot down several MiGs." Her smile teased. "After all, I was only a kid in school then."

"Okay, okay." He made a face. "Don't rub in the age factor." He paced a few more steps. "We were the only One-Oh-Four outfit sent over to the badlands. We were there specifically to counter the MiG-21. I was just a lieutenant. Pete Cassidy was my flight commander, and Hal Maarten was the squadron CO."

He kept up the restless pacing while he spoke. "I did my hundred missions in about seven months and was eligible for rotation, but I was leery of what kind of assignment I'd get back in the ZI. And anyway, I didn't want to leave the squadron. So I volunteered to stay on and complete the year tour. I flew another twenty-seven missions. That turned out to be my unlucky number."

She listened in silence to the terse account of his bailout and capture. At first, she only gaped, but as the more gruesome events unfolded, she sank into a chair. Her hand was a little unsteady as she filled two cups with hot chocolate.

She touched and examined the small scar left by the hook. He opened his mouth and showed her the marks inside. "That spit gland under my tongue never worked quite right after that."

"Oh, my God!" Her voice was just above a whisper.

He gave her a direct look and an amused smile. "You know, I think you're turning pale."

"I feel pale." Her head wagged slowly. "I never cease to be appalled at the things men do to each other in warfare." Then she showed a sudden look of recognition. "And that's why you . . ."

"Right."

"But those Congressmen and others. If they'd known—"

"It was none of their damn business! Just the fact they wanted to kiss up to a government that supported our enemies was enough to—"

"Tsh-sh . . ." Her fingertip pressed gently on his lips. "Drink your chocolate. That's the good stuff. From Holland." She eased onto his lap, parted the robe in front, cuddled his face against her, inviting him to kiss those perfect golden breasts. He buried himself in this marvel. Then quietly they left the kitchen and went back upstairs to bed.

She encircled him with her arms and legs. Straining, groaning, grunting, wailing, heaving, they sought to merge with each other to a degree beyond the possible, yet worth the effort.

Slowly, their breathing subsided, from breaking surf to a gentle breeze through a pine forest. Afterward, snuggled together, they drifted into the sleep of the just—and the just-after.

They awoke to each other's presence, touched, stroked, joined, and renewed the ancient rhythm.

Afterward, they showered together. While they were dressing, he said, "That's the first time I've ever been able to go back to sleep after one of those nightmares."

"Doctor Mike's special treatment." She gave him an X-rated smile.

Down in the kitchen, she set about making coffee. Her look turned sober. "Is it the same dream, over and over?"

"Not exactly. Call it theme and variations."

"Okay, let's leave that alone for now. Whenever you talk about yourself, it's all professional. You never mention your marriage."

"What's to mention? It was never a real marriage. Val just wanted me for display. Like something by Dior or Givenchy. Getting me to go along with her weird politics would've been almost as good as an Oscar."

"How did you meet her?"

"A weekend party at Tahoe. That was before she became a star. Also before she got her implant of Hollywood-style political correctness. I was young and foolish and fascinated with her, and before long, we were rolling in the hay. And, as they say, the rest is history."

"Not so fast. Why do you call her politics an implant?"

"Because Val has no real idea what she thinks about anything till she hears someone say it. It's probably what makes her such a good actress. Other people's words and thoughts resonate through her, come out amplified by her personality."

He paused and let out a small, explosive breath. "The odd thing is, serious ideas hold a kind of fascination for her. They draw her like a bee to a flower. But once she gets hold of one, she won't stay with it. Dig it up to examine the roots. She just picks the bright, sweet-smelling blossom and sticks it into her intellectual lapel, like a nosegay, till it's wilted."

Michelle's mouth formed a subtle smile, and her eyebrows lifted ever so slightly. "Your way with words keeps confirming what I sensed early on." She poured coffee into mugs and brought them to the table. "Inside that adventurous engineer the world knows is something of a poet." She tasted her coffee. "So you and I have more in common than frustrated ambition. We each wound up in a lousy marriage."

"Oh? I guess I didn't realize."

"I was married to Rayford Gilliam."

Gus did a quick inventory of Gilliam's six seasons in the NFL: two-time All-Pro tight end. Career ended by a classic case of torn knee ligaments. Everything ended a few years later in a classic case of driving under the influence.

"We were already divorced when he was killed. My women friends were full of cute, risqué remarks about what my sex life must be like with, quote—that big stud. But the fact is, he took a lot of steroids." She showed a smile edged with bitterness. "I guess they helped his performance on the field, but what he gained there he lost in bed."

They went out for lunch, then spent a leisurely afternoon browsing through art galleries and driving through the Virginia countryside. By six, they were back in Georgetown. Gus mixed drinks, and they cuddled in front of the TV set.

The situation in Eritrea had worked its way into the lead news story. "Over the last twenty-four hours," said the news anchor, "the coalition calling itself the Islamic Front continued its advance on Asmara."

A map of the region appeared on the screen. The battlefront was marked off, with the territory controlled by each side.

The anchorman continued: "The Islamic Front insists that the newly discovered oil deposits must belong to an independent and Muslim Eritrea." Blotches of color indicating the oil fields appeared on the map. They were strung out north to south, a few in Sudan, most in Eritrea, including the coastal waters. "Though Eritrea was for a long time a part of Ethiopia, its people fought for decades and finally won independence from the government in Addis Ababa. During the reign of Haile Selassie, Ethiopia had strong ties with both the U.S. and Israel."

The anchorman spent perhaps another minute describing the various efforts to bring about a cease-fire. None looked promising.

At the next commercial, Michelle got up and began to pace, her body language shouting anxiety. "So what's bugging you?" he said.

She faced him. "Well, besides selling discount medical supplies and equipment, Med-Tech Exports has government contracts. We handle the medical portions of some aid programs. So I have to go to Africa. I could be gone a month or more."

He frowned. "Where, exactly?"

She shrugged. "I should find out this week."

He took a deep breath and said, "Well, since this seems to be show and tell. My days in Washington are numbered. If you're gone a month, I won't be here when you get back."

"Then how will I reach you?"

"You won't. I'll have to reach you. Where I'm going and what I'll be doing is classified burn-before-reading." He gave a sad grin.

For the span of several heartbeats there was awkward silence. Then he heard himself speaking again, though the words seemed to come from somewhere beyond. "Of course it *would* make a difference if you had the status of . . . a spouse."

She seemed to fumble with her coffee cup. Her hand took on a faint tremor. Then she put the cup down and came into his arms. "Gus!"

He smiled. "And just think of the shock Fiona's going to get."

They spent the weekend making plans as well as love: The day would be next Friday.

Monday, Michelle went to her Med-Tech office and then to the hospital and then home to her condo. One of the messages on her record-a-call was the one she had awaited with such anxiety.

* * *

The meeting took place in the Federal Building in Baltimore. Secrecy clung to this business like bad smell to portable johns. Still, meeting outside Washington seemed like owning Lutece and going out for a burger.

But Baltimore it was. And at night.

The building was dimly lit and looked deserted, but right on cue, a uniformed guard—black, about forty—was there to let her in. He made the most of the ID process, starting at her hairline and moving his gaze slowly downward to her calves. "I'm not a horse you're looking to buy!" she said. He only nodded in silence and led the way.

The office was the usual quotidian workplace of some unknown federal functionary. "Mike. Good to see you again!"

"Alex." She took the offered hand.

Alex Gossett was tall, lean, and physically hard, with a beaklike nose thrusting from between close-set blue eyes. His blond hair had retreated to expose a shiny contour of forehead and scalp. "You know Pietro here?"

Smiling, the second man extended his hand. "Pete Allegretti." He was shorter and had a Latin appearance to go with the name—olive skin and dark, wavy hair above seductive brown eyes.

Mike furrowed her brow and looked sideways at Gossett. "Am I being dealt off again, Alex?"

He made a noncommittal gesture. "Not . . . necessarily." He was already the fourth control she'd had. And while they never met alone—there was always a third party as witness—she had developed a feeling for the impending changes.

When she started, she had assumed it was the CIA, never mind the IDs that all said Defense Department. A U.S. senator had confirmed it was indeed a federal agency, all she was allowed to know at that tenderfoot stage. Even now, she knew only it was part of DoD—the

107

Pentagon. Just where it fit into the overall scheme of things was still arcane knowledge.

Gossett pulled up a government-issue chair for her, then handed her an envelope. "Airline tickets and reservations. Addis Ababa by way of Frankfurt and Rome. Open return."

She made a face. "What's this all about, Alex? I've got plans to get married next Friday."

The two men exchanged uneasy glances. Gossett frowned. "Mike, you should have let us know earlier. Your fiancé will have to be vetted and get a clean bill of health."

"Our plans were made rather suddenly. He's being sent on some assignment he says is classified burn-before-reading."

"He's military?"

"He's Gus Halstrom."

Both men relaxed. Gossett almost smiled. "No problem. Gus has clearances on his clearances. He *will* need to be briefed, though." The expression turned to a frown. "But I'm afraid Friday's out. Pete here will explain what we need you to do."

As she expected, it involved the Islamic Front invasion of Eritrea. The government in Addis Ababa was shedding its lingering Marxism like a chrysalis, seeking rapprochement with its former allies, the U.S. and Isreal. Contacts had been arranged for her to sound out the new leaders, try to discover who held the real power and their true political sentiments.

The Ethiopians were also looking to replace worn-out or obsolete hospital equipment. So the mission could involve considerable sales for Med-Tech. The company was set up to serve as her cover, but the profits it made were hers.

When she got home, there was a recorded message from Gus: "Mike, I'm pressed for time, and I can't talk on the phone. Go to my place. You'll find an envelope on the sitting room table. I love you."

Late as it was, she set out for Georgetown with a mounting sense of foreboding. Gus had said, "Go to my place," not, "Come over."

The house was dark. She let herself in, turned on some lights, made her way to the sitting room. Nothing was changed, yet she already sensed an aura of emptiness and desertion.

On the coffee table was a large manila envelope, not sealed. When she opened it, a note fell out with a set of keys. The keys to the Lamborghini.

Chapter Nine

Morning in Albany, and in the Crestwood Towers, nerves and alarm clocks jangled in unison before the relentless demands of commerce. The inmates roused themselves to face the first working day of the new year.

Dwayne Chauncey had always welcomed working days. But today, the tasks awaiting him in Schenectady had an even greater appeal. Paradoxically because they were no longer his only satisfaction. And staring at himself in the bathroom mirror no longer stirred a subliminal sense of guilt about viewing life from the sidelines.

His sister and Aaron were already congratulating themselves.

In their intellectual-academic milieu, religion was passé, but they followed the custom of gift-giving and held secular celebrations of the holiday season. And part of the function of the party they gave was to introduce him to Audrey Prowther.

No one actually claimed that sparks flew, but a consensus arose that he and Audrey were like two halves of the same creature, separated and searching for each other.

"Skyhook, Tinpan with two for recovery." Leveling from a steep descending turn, Gus eased back the throttles on the F-24A, the first production-model Scimitar. The surrounding atmosphere was neither clear nor cloudy. A sort of mist diffused the light, blurred the division of sky from the threatening gray of the north Atlantic. And somewhere close ahead was the airship, all but invisible under these conditions.

"Tinpan, we have you on the crystal ball. You're cleared to recover." The gently glowing indicators on the reflector glass of his ITD put the airship 1.7 nautical miles ahead, 3.2 degrees below the horizon, and about a half degree left. He corrected so it was dead ahead, then touched a button on the ITD control panel. Out of the featureless gray airspace ahead, flashing ruby-red pinpoints outlined the airship.

From this, he set the landing pattern. As Tinpan Flight passed over and ahead, he began a ten-second count. At the end of the count, he threw the Scimitar into a vertical bank, popped the speed brakes, and pulled the throttles to idle. Alpha Two turned three seconds later. At 180 degrees of turn, Gus rolled level, slapped the gear and flap handles to the "down" position, and resumed the turn till he was again lined up with the airship's centerline. The ruby points outlined the landing zone.

The landing mirror with its glowing meatball was a feature adopted from Navy carriers. He flew it almost to touchdown. The impact zone had a reinforced deck, but Skyhook could not afford the structural weight needed to withstand carrier-type landings. Alighting aboard had to be gentle. The mere twenty knots between the Scimitar's approach speed and that of the airship made the task simpler.

An eyeblink after touchdown, he was swallowed by the tunnel that held the flight deck. The 120-knot airstream kept the landing roll short. To economize on weight and complexity, the flight deck was always lit by the red light needed for night vision, giving an eerie cast to the surroundings.

Inside the ring of lights marking the "stop" circle, he braked to a halt and stop-cocked the throttles. A stout nylon sling lifted the Scimitar clear of the deck. The slings were attached to dollies that ran on overhead rails. Gus felt himself being trundled sideways. These rails and their supporting structure weighed considerably less than a full hangar deck strong enough to support aircraft.

During launch and/or recovery, the flight deck and its hurricane-force airstream were sealed off to personnel. Special deflector-doors opened to admit recovered aircraft to the hangar bay. There the airplane was secured with guy lines. They had just been attached to Gus's F-24 when Tinpan 2 came aboard.

With the air group being an all-officer unit, ground-crew duties were carried out by pilots. One of those hooking up the guy lines said, "The skipper asked to see you on the bridge ASAP, Colonel."

"ASAP is after I get out of all this." "All this" was the chute, the flotation vest or "Mae West," the anti-exposure "poopy" suit, and the G-suit.

On the bridge, the skipper and the others were in shirt-sleeve uniforms of Navy tan. Gus glanced out the windscreen. Nothing to be seen in all those cubic miles of air.

"From Mother Hen," Borland said, and held out a yellow teletype sheet.

Gus read the brief message: A courier was on the way to pick up him and Borland. "What do you make of it?"

Borland scowled. "I make it that, ready or not, they've got a job for us. And we don't have to look beyond the day's headlines to guess what it is." For the past two weeks, the newscasts had been full of the war in Eritrea, the Islamic Front's effort to seize the oil fields.

"I sure as hell hope you're wrong."

"Bridge, this is flight ops. The last aircraft just came aboard."

"You might as well get packed," said Borland. "Then meet me in the wardroom."

The wardroom hummed with a soft chorus of talk. Faces were turned to the TV set. Because the ship's functions were manned around the clock, the men ate on their own schedules. There was no kitchen staff, so everyone chose his own food from among the stock of frozen meals.

Gus drew himself a mug of coffee and joined Borland at the skipper's table.

"We need to get our ducks in line," Borland said. "How are things going so far?"

"No real hitches yet. Couldn't ask for a better bunch of pilots." In this trial stage, the air group had sixteen Scimitars and twenty-five pilots plus three maintenance officers. The full complement would be forty-eight aircraft, with a total of sixty pilots and maintenance officers.

"The crew's looking pretty much four-oh too. First time I've ever seen so many things done right the first time. Kind of scary." Borland's tone was tongue-in-cheek. "All the same, I think the Pentagonians might just bite off more than we can chew."

"Assuming you're right—and the more I think about it, the more I tend to agree—when they say 'operational mission,' we can't just shout 'no way' in unison."

Hank nodded. "But we do need some parameters."

"Message for the skipper and Air Group One," came a voice from the intercom unit on the table. "The courier is fifty miles out." Borland acknowledged, and they left the wardroom to collect their travel gear.

"I didn't get a chance to mention we're getting a new

crew member," Borland said as they waited behind a plexiglass barrier for the courier to come aboard. "Air Force type. Major name of Austen. He'll fill the vacancy in the cockpit crew. He should be on this courier."

He paused, frowning. "He was the AC of that AWACS hit by a missile off Colombia. Just been awarded an Air Medal for what he did there. He's the one that asshole Penross has been after. Totally unjustified, of course, but those columns could have an effect. Reports say he was grounded a month because of nightmares over the loss of his crew."

Gus knit his brow. "Any idea why Mother Hen accepted him?"

"Well, he couldn't go back to that drug-watch operation. And his boss there gave him a walk-on-water rating." He shrugged. "I guess we'll just have to wait and see."

The T-44 couriers, a military version of the Waring Merganser executive twin-jet, furnished the supply and mail link for Skyhook. They were flown on a rotational basis both by air group pilots and members of Skyhook's cockpit crew. The courier flights offered a break from the confined life aboard the airship.

Generally, the T-44 had the passenger seats removed to accommodate mail and cargo. This one arrived configured for passengers and indeed brought Major Guilbert Austen. He was about to salute Gus, who pointed to Borland. "The skipper here's your boss aboard Skyhook, Major."

Just under three hours later, they made an instrument approach to Andrews in darkness. From a dense, low-hanging overcast, they broke out into the sudden glare of the District.

Hank and his family had a home in suburban Virginia, and his wife, Melanie, was there to meet him. Gus had no real home. He had given up the house in Georgetown when he left the Pentagon.

Mike's phone didn't answer, but he had the staff car drop him at her condo anyway. His pulse rose at the sight of the lighted windows: She must have come in since he called. But the door was locked, and there was no answer to his ring.

He let himself in, found the lamps on timers and everything else in order for an extended absence. The mail was obviously being held. In the garage, the Lamborghini gathered dust alongside the Laser. The house itself had a feeling of emptiness. A small shiver of apprehension ran through him. For the first time in his life, he felt remorse at being alone.

Wednesday evening, Dwayne Chauncey was in the kitchen. The phone rang. A distant voice, husky and feminine, said, "Dwayne, darling."

"I was just thinking about you," he said. Though they had not met since the holidays, they spoke on the phone at least twice a week.

"I've been thinking a lot about you too, darling. Are you free this weekend?"

"For you I'm free anytime."

"Some friends in New York are giving a party. They're eager to meet you. Pick you up about five-thirty Friday?"

"I'll be more than ready."

They spoke for several more minutes. The prospect of seeing her again left him so giddy he burned his dinner. He scarcely tasted it anyway.

Friday, he had just finished packing when the buzzer sounded. She got off the elevator and threw her arms around him. Besides the wide-brimmed hat perched at a rakish angle on her sleek, blond hair, she wore high heels and a tailored suit that showed off her figure. Under the jacket was a form-hugging dark turtleneck.

To have this stunning creature embrace him there in the corridor, and then insist on kissing him as soon as they were inside, brought on a state of arousal he hadn't known in years. He envisioned his hormones racing like particles in an atomic accelerator.

She took in the view and the decor. "Darling, I *do* think I'll have to give you a little help with this interior." Then, with his psyche only a few degrees from meltdown, she glanced at her watch. "We should get moving. I took the liberty of making dinner reservations for nine."

Her presence beguiled him till the clustered gemstone glitter of Manhattan's towers against the dark velvet sky drew his attention outside. Next, he recognized Washington Square. They were in the Village.

Her place was a classic town house-studio on intimate terms with its neighbors. He mentioned he should call his sister and Aaron. She said there was plenty of time and phoned for a taxi.

The restaurant, which she described as "one of my favorite little neighborhood Italian places," was below ground. The soft lighting, the red-brick and wrought-iron decor, and red-checked tablecloths were predictable but pleasant. Afterward, they went to another cellar where they held hands, sipped brandy, and listened to music along with that nihilist patter Villagers like to think of as avant-garde comedy and especially their own.

It was well after midnight when the taxi arrived at her town house. He had it in mind to keep the cab and go on to Aaron and Gail's. Then he clapped a hand to his forehead: "My God! I never phoned. I guess I'd better see about a hotel room."

She smiled and told him to pay off the cab. Inside, she said, "Darling, this *is* the twenty-first century." Taking hold of his necktie, she gave a come-hither gesture and led him into the bedroom.

At around ten A.M., with their pulses and breathing rates just subsiding from the morning's encore, he said he loved her and made a straightforward proposal of marriage.

Her reply was a smile that was neither yes nor no. She

ran through the sensible clichés—exploring mutual interests, learning more about each other, getting to know each other's friends. Afterward, she rose and led him into the shower.

The party was set for the cocktail hour. They arrived suitably late. Their host, he discovered, was Sanford Draper himself. The cultivated disorder of his mass of dark, curly hair was softened just enough from that of his public image to make him real. A white-jacketed waiter presided over the bar. Others circulated bearing trays with glasses of champagne. There was a tempting array of hors d'ouvres.

Dwayne could recall movies for which Draper had done the screenplays from his own early novels. But that was all at least twenty years ago. Nowadays, he wrote sociopolitical commentary or reportage-in-depth. Or highbrow muckraking. But his reputation as a writer had been almost eclipsed by his political involvement. His opposition to the Reagan Administration had bordered on hysteria. His most printable characterization of Mr. Reagan had been: "that political hyena who dines on the dead hopes of the world's poor." His comments on the current Administration were in the same tenor.

"We've all been eager to meet the man who's so captivated our Audrey," Draper said. "I have some of her pieces here, you know. It's one of my vanities to point out that I bought her work long before the critics ever heard of her." The tone acknowledged a few reasonable vanities. His public vanities were in fact notorious.

He led Dwayne to the bar. "How about some champagne? George, pour us a couple." Dwayne noted the label: *Moet et Chandon*.

Next came a flurry of introductions. This was New York's glitterati elite. Everyone here was connected with writing, publishing, broadcasting, the arts, or the theater. Some were even more famous than Draper. Hearing their talk, Dwayne noted how their thinking all seemed to

117

mesh. And how it was closed to anything contrary to their own view of the world. He was reminded of that tongue-in-cheek office sign: "My mind is made up. Don't confuse me with facts."

Audrey moved in to reclaim him for wider display. Minutes later, he was startled to find himself face-to-face with Valerie Aubin, the movie star: "So then, Doctor Chauncey. You're Audrey's new catch. I can see why she kept us other girls away till she had a firm hold on you."

"Girls," he mused. Simple arithmetic said she had to be forty-plus. Yet she retained the sleek, glittering exterior that had made her a box-office favorite. Was it cosmetic surgery? Health spas? Or just plain superior genes? "Maybe it was the other way around," he said. "Keeping me from being dazzled by such beautiful women as yourself."

Her smile sparkled like crystal and had almost as many facets. "You're quite an artful flatterer, Doctor. So tell me about your work."

"I'm a physicist. I do advanced research in electrical and electronic phenomena."

She raised her free hand, and her face registered wonder. "Does that mean things like we used to see in the old science-horror movies? I somehow can't picture you as the mad doctor, watching dials and fiddling with controls in the dead of night while bolts of electricity crackle about."

"That's probably a credit to both of us. Most experiments in a real electrical lab would bore a moviegoer to sleep."

Her look suddenly sobered. "You know, Dwayne, it can be very tempting to focus on our own careers and forget about the good of humanity. Have you ever thought about what use your work might be put to? Say, by the Pentagon? I'm sure Audrey could tell you about this."

"You're doing just fine," Audrey said. "I'll let you

carry on while I go have a word with Sanford. Just confine yourself to his *political* education."

Valerie fluttered her lashes. "I'm a woman with normal hormones. I can't be held responsible for what may happen."

"I'll hold you both responsible."

Uneasy, Dwayne sought a change of subject. "By the way, I was in Washington recently and happened to meet your ex, Colonel Halstrom."

Her smile turned ironic. "Oh? And what's Gus up to these days? After that affair in Stockholm, I thought sure they'd can him. But it turned out the Pentagon has even more brass than I realized." She flashed a smile at her own pun. "Now I hear he's being resurrected. Or rehabilitated. Which doesn't surprise. The Gulf War and then the thing in Kosovo worked like halo polish on all the old Cold Warriors. They seem to be organizing a rerun in Eritrea."

"Well, I don't know what he's involved in, but it's so secret they joke about how it's classified burn-before-reading."

She nodded and showed a wry smile. "M-hm, I've heard that one. And it figures." She made a deft exchange of her empty glass for a full one from the tray of one of the catering staff. "The only positive testimonial I can give Gus wouldn't interest you. He's fantastic in bed."

In darkness, with gently turning screws, the *Juaquin Salazar* eased up to the dockside. Having unloaded much of her cargo from Odessa, she rode high, her Plimsoll scale exposed.

They worked without lights. Alejandro flitted and fretted: *El Jefe* frowned and nodded. "The Yankees may have no reason to suspect that this deserted island is being turned into a missile base," he said. "But their spy satellites and reconnaissance aircraft cover the whole Caribbean, and their cameras and other sensors can pick up even minimal activity." He flicked a thumb. "So we need this sky, moonless and overcast. The ship must be gone before daylight."

Chapter Ten

"Her name was Cynthia Naybors," said the voice on the phone. "Airman first class. Called Cindy by her friends." He followed with her serial number, the names of her parents, their home address.

Jotting it all down, Arthur Penross felt a certain relief. Till now, the Anvil Bravo crew roster had been a disappointment. Its members had not been the "young lives" entrusted to an incompetent and/or cowardly Major Austen, but thirty-to-forty-year-old military professionals who understood the risks. Only Cynthia Naybors fit the pattern as he wished to present it. That hers was also the only body recovered was like hitting all the green lights down Pennsylvania Avenue.

So he had sent one of his assistants, George Mercer, to check out her background. Mercer was phoning in his findings: "Monroe, Indiana's about what you'd expect. One of those tidy little cornball enclaves that grow like mushrooms out here in the flyover. Tailor-made for this story. And so is Cynthia Naybors." He recited a few particulars. "I'll have it all written up when I get back, but that should get you started."

Monroe's only paper was a small weekly, which did not carry his column. No surprise there. But the dailies in both Richmond and Indianapolis did, and they were widely read in Monroe. His words would strike their mark locally as well as nationally. Penross hung up the phone, turned to the keyboard, and set to work:

More on the sad saga of Anvil Bravo, the AWACS aircraft shot down by mysterious missiles:

As reported exclusively in this column, only the pilot, a Major Austen, survived. We have no word on how he's managing to live with himself after accepting a decoration for losing his aircraft and his crew. But our continuing investigation has brought to light some surprising facts: First, contrary to the early reports of no bodies recovered, the body of Airman First Class Cynthia Naybors, the only female crew member, was returned for burial. A funeral service was held in her home town of Monroe, Indiana.

Yet mystery continues to shroud the last flight of Anvil Bravo. We know the aircraft was patrolling the coastal waters of Colombia as part of the effort to suppress the drug trade. So presumably that's where it went down. The Pentagon, in its fanatic devotion to secrecy, will not confirm even this much.

What we do know is that the body of A/1C Naybors turned up at the U.S. Navy base at Guantanamo Bay, Cuba. The Defense Department offers no explanation for this anomaly.

What follows may be painful. It's certainly painful to write. But it's the sort of information the Pentagon must not be allowed to hide from the public: A post mortem revealed that Cynthia Naybors did not die of injuries received in a crash. She was strangled to death. Murdered. Worse, she was first subjected to unspeakable torment, including gang rape. Cynthia Naybors was your typically pretty hometown girl-next-door. She had autumn-gold curls and a pert nose with a sprinkle of freckles. She was a high school cheerleader and homecoming queen. She might have been anyone's sister, daughter, niece, or girlfriend. Now she lies in the family plot in a quiet Methodist cemetery in Monroe, Indiana, her life, along with her hopes and dreams, cut short in a most hideous fashion.

Because there is no one to speak for her now, we have decided to take up her cause. To become her advocates. It can do her no good, but it may prevent a recurrence of the kind of bungling that was the root cause of this tragedy.

So we hearby serve notice on the Pentagon that we will not stop until we get the scalps of those responsible. And our first demand is that they let us interview this feet-of-clay hero, Major Guilbert Austen. Perhaps his story will make some sense of this bizarre chain of events. In any case, it will determine the path of our investigation thereafter.

In a state of elation that resembled sexual arousal, Penross paused there and swiveled his chair to face the window. Distant figures moved over the course at Burning Tree. Though he played neither golf nor tennis, he had applied for membership there, thinking the connections would be an advantage.

His application had been summarily rejected.

Perhaps one of those distant figures was a Pentagon general who might be fired if this story worked out right. Or perhaps even an under-secretary! Woodward and Bernstein had brought down a sitting President, but that kind of opportunity came not even once in a lifetime.

* * *

"Gus, meet my brother Chip."

"Glad to know you, Gus." Chalmers "Chip" Borland had the expected hard, dry handgrip. He was a little shorter, a little darker, and a little leaner than Hank, but he had the family likeness and cinematic good looks. He was also five years older and that much earlier out of Annapolis. He had pilot's wings and six rows of ribbons on the front of his Marine Corps blouse and the twin stars of a major general on the shoulders.

"Might as well get started," he said.

Gus frowned and looked around the otherwise empty room. "Where are the others?"

"You're the others. So take a pew, and I'll get right to it." He flicked a projector switch that threw a map on the screen. Centered on the Red Sea, it took in part of the Arabian Peninsula, Sudan, Egypt, Ethiopia, the Sinai, and part of Somalia.

"The thee-ay-tah of wah, gentlemen," he said. "In the round. No backdrop, no proscenium. The continuing drah-ma of who gets the oil. Same caste of characters: industrial countries who want it, Arab governments satisfied to make money from it. The Israelis. And some Muslim fanatics who want to use it as a lever to dislodge Israel.

"Now, the geopolitical version of Murphy's Law says that when Mother Nature gives with one hand she takes with the other." Chip pressed the projector control button, and an overlay was added to the view on the screen. It showed the newly found oil deposits, a pattern of blobs along the western shore of the Red Sea. "So these deposits are mostly in Eritrea and its offshore waters. Eritrea is perhaps forty percent Muslim and voted its independence from Ethiopia some years back. Addis Ababa would grit its teeth and let the Eritreans have the oil, but not the Islamic Front. That's why they've chosen military intervention."

"The Cairo Agreements," said Hank, "were supposed to

have poured some oil on the more troubled waters over there. Not as much as Saddam dumped in the Gulf, but—"

"Middle East oil," Chip cut in, "doesn't calm troubled waters. It only fouls beaches and fuels resentment. In the wrong hands, these mega-barrels could start a conflagration that'll take a helluva lot more than Red Adair to put out."

Gus cleared his throat a little: "Is the . . . ah . . . White House worried the Cairo accords are already coming apart?"

"The Cairo Agreements are a patchwork quilt being pulled at in all directions," said Chip. "So far, the seams are holding, but several factions were eager to see them rip before the ink was dry.

"Eritrea doesn't have the resources to develop these oil fields; so they've formed a joint venture with Addis Ababa. And the Ethiopians are about to take the leap back into the Western fold plus renew their long-standing ties with Israel. And this new oil, controlled by a pro-Israeli government, would weaken the hand of the Destroy Israel faction. Hence the IF's determination to gain control."

He pressed the button again, and the view on the screen switched to a montage of various machines of war. "The IF musters a smorgasbord of weapons, mostly Russian. Missiles, tanks, artillery. For airpower, they have both Libyan and Yemeni MiGs and pilots. And lately it looks like some of the Iraqi planes and pilots that decamped to Iran during the Gulf War are showing up here. MiG-29's and French Mirages, the best Saddam had in his arsenal.

"The Ethiopians still have American F-5's, but not much in the way of parts to keep them flying. They got MiG Twenty-ones and Twenty-threes during their tango with the Soviets, but the Russians supply parts for former Soviet aircraft only for hard currency. With their cash-flow problem, the Ethiopians are keeping their operational fighters around Addis Ababa. So what's needed is a combat air presence on the scene."

"Why not send a carrier task group?" said Hank.

The general cracked a smile and gave a small, derisive snort. "You want to tell me where to find one on short notice?" The sarcasm was not softened for his brother. "You both know the situation. The Soviet Union dissolved, and we kicked Saddam's butt rather handily. Then we had eight years of a President who thought the world's just one big friendly neighborhood where we don't even have to lock our doors at night. Except, of course, for the bad guys like us who frustrate the ambitions of sundry Third World maniacs." He dropped the tone of irony. "So the carriers we have left are spread thin.

"It's very much in our interest to keep these particular oil deposits in friendly hands. And in just the last week or ten days, the situation there has gotten tense. So even if we had a carrier task group we could spare, it might not arrive in time.

"Enforcing our interests doesn't come cheap, and it will take even more time to shake any money out of Congress. Meanwhile, Skyhook looks to me like the perfect instrument: something that doesn't exist, to carry out an operation that never took place."

Gus swallowed and said, "Sir, did anyone mention the air group is less than half-strength and still in the trial and testing phase?"

"You and your pilots—in fact, everyone connected with this project—are supposed to be four-oh. The best we've got. So if you're not up to the task, then this country is in even worse trouble than I figured."

Gus swallowed again and said, "Okay, we know the Islamic Front. So who's the Islamic Rear? Who's lending material and moral support? Especially the covert variety."

"Well, Iran is the CG of Islamic fundamentalism and

no party to the Cairo Accords. In fact, Iranian support for the IF isn't covert. And both Qaddafi and the mullahs in Tehran have oil money to throw behind it." The general paused and paced and looked thoughtful. "But there's a third force involved. Something we haven't identified. It seems to have a broad base in the Third World, and it's probably being supported by drug money. And that's all I can tell you right now."

Once more, Michelle was roused from sleep by the distant sounds of artillery fire. Half awake, she tried to hide from it by seeking out Gus's hard, masculine warmth and drawing close.

She found only emptiness. With a start, she came wide awake, sat up in bed. This wasn't her condo or Gus's rented house in Georgetown, and Gus wasn't here. "Here" was Asmara, in the middle of a war zone.

Being a Pentagon agent had its hazards, but she'd gotten herself into this one. Her assignment in Addis Ababa was completed. Alex Gossett would blow his top at her for not getting on the next plane to Frankfurt. But scenes of the sick and injured, the victims of war, had moved her to volunteer. They were short of physicians, and it wasn't bad PR for anyone who wanted to do business in this country once the hostilities ended.

Meanwhile, Gus had simply disappeared, leaving her that note and his car keys. She got no mail here and had no way of reaching him.

From around the perimeter, the bombardment went on, the two sides shelling each other in the dark. She parted the curtains. Asmara under blackout looked and felt sepulchral. The horizon was lambent with muzzle flashes. Shell detonations flared in the streets while the concussion rolled over the city, rattling the windowpanes.

The glowing LED digits on her watch read 5:43. She would get no more sleep. Might as well go have a look at the patients.

B. Michelaard

In the light of the bedside lamp, the tiny room showed up drab and Spartan. Besides the single bed, it held a washstand with a mirror, a small wardrobe, and a straight-backed chair. Bathing and sanitary facilities were down the hall. She washed her face and snugged up her hair.

A short time later, wearing slacks and a light, loose-fitting jersey under a white medical smock, she entered the patient ward. White was a euphemism. The smock was dirt-smudged and bloodstained from a week's wear.

Just inside the door, she was assailed by the familiar septic smell of Third World medical practice. She stopped and got some coffee from the large metal urn. Hot baths and other amenities were scarce in Asmara, but they still had coffee.

The young Eritrean doctor on night duty came forward to greet her. She was the first woman physician he had ever met, and it amused her to note the skein of conflicting emotions she aroused. Like everyone here, he was grateful for her help. He also wanted to impress an American doctor. Such things as transplants and bypasses were not done in Asmara. He was awed that she had taken part in many.

And he scarcely knew what to make of the fact that she was American, a person of color much like himself, a skilled surgeon, and on top of it all, fluent in Amharic.

Now he greeted her with a little bow, a sort of exaggerated nod. She said good morning and started along the row, looking over the charts. He brought her up to date on each. At an empty bed, she frowned and searched her memory. The patient there was an elderly woman. "Mrs. . . . ?"

He shook his head. "We lost her. About two o'clock." He followed with a shrug.

She made a sour face. "Yes, I know. *Inshalah*." That was Arabic for "God's will," widely used here, even among non-Muslims, and she could not avoid a certain

128

note of sarcasm. She'd had it up to her crucifix with *"Inshalah."* Still, the woman had been rather old and in poor shape. It was in no way an unusual death here.

By the time they had completed the round of the ward, other day-shift doctors and nurses were appearing. Some, as she did, slept here at the hospital.

Each day brought ambulance-loads of wounded troops and sick or injured civilians. Refugees flocked into the city, straining resources. Food was running short. Their major means of supply was by ship through the port of Massawa and from there by rail, but the rail line could come under fire. Some supplies were flown in at night. During the day, the jets of the Islamic Front made it too dangerous. The Ethiopian Air Force seemed unable to challenge them.

At mid-morning, she was told "Colonel X" wanted to see her. The senior Ethiopian officers there all kept themselves anonymous like this because the Islamic Front had declared them all "war criminals" and was shooting or hanging captured officers above the level of company commander. He was her liaison contact, and she assumed he had news of her flight out.

He received her in the office of the hospital director, a spare and functional room. "Ah, Doctor St. Clair. Very nice to see you. How are you getting on here? Please, do have a seat." He indicated a chair drawn up close beside the desk.

He was a handsome devil, this Colonel X. His words and manner were unfailingly correct, yet his eyes and smile subtly teased and undressed her and told a different story.

"Better than most of the patients, I'm afraid. For me, the shortages are only a frustration. For them, it can be life or death."

He gave her a practiced look of sympathy and a delicate shrug. *"C'est la guerre.* We're bringing in all the medical supplies we can under the circumstances.

129

Indeed, I'm afraid it's going to get worse for a time. Which brings up the reason I asked you here."

He had a military map on the desk before him. Now he turned it for her to see. Lines and marks in color indicated positions and units. The front was shaped like a tadpole, with Asmara at its head. Or perhaps, she thought, like a sperm cell. The tail extended eastward along the rail line to the coast and the port of Massawa. The government still had nominal control of the railway, but it was within enemy artillery range.

"We've been holding this perimeter," he said, and went on to explain the military situation in more detail than seemed necessary. His pencil tip moved over the map to point out various features. Then his tone shifted to one of summation: "Last night, the enemy broke through around this wadi here. We were just able to regroup without major losses, but we had to sacrifice territory to save troops and materiel." His pencil traced out a new line on the map. "Unfortunately, the territory we had to give up includes the airfield." He looked at her. "So until we can manage to get it back, there can be no flights out."

Chapter Eleven

The courier flight that brought Borland and Gus back aboard Skyhook also carried cases of 20mm ammo. For the next thirty hours, every courier pilot and aircraft worked overtime. While the airship hovered just off the coast, they ran a supply shuttle of food, belted ammo, Sidewinder and Sparrow missiles, and other expendables.

To save weight, Skyhook used ingenious manual-leverage devices instead of power hoists and such. Most of the work of unloading and storing fell to Gus and his pilots.

The last T-44 brought fresh vacuum-bottle canisters of liquid helium. While the materiel was being stowed, Skyhook headed eastward for yet another rendezvous.

The added weight had reduced its free-floating altitude—the atmospheric level where it would come to rest without aerodynamic lift—to less than a thousand feet. Yet Decker cut the heat that gave the helium added lift. They would be going even lower, and these measures avoided valving off so much of the highly expensive helium.

As they approached the rendezvous point, Decker began a slow descent. The last few hundred feet actually required negative lift, using the wings to overcome the helium buoyancy. At a mere twenty knots, steering minutely by instruments of high precision, he brought Skyhook within fifty feet of the surface. When the target was almost below, he slowed to fifteen knots, just enough to maintain control and the necessary negative lift. Banking now would produce a turn opposite the normal direction, so he set the ailerons at auto-level and steered by rudder alone.

A CRT screen in the cockpit showed a tiny, blinking dot with a pattern of rings and a cross, like a gunsight. With minute changes in heading, he flew the dot into the center of the crosshairs. When the dot was centered, the copilot pressed a button.

The ship had the look of an ordinary cargo vessel. From somewhere in the darkness above, a metal dart shot down and stuck into a wooden platform. It carried a thin metal cable, which the crew detached and then hooked onto a thick, heavily insulated hose. The cable was drawn up, drawing the hose after it. Several more darts with cables came down, and each one drew up another hose. When the hoses were connected, a signal was passed, pumps were started, and liquid hydrogen was pumped from the ship to Skyhook.

"I don't know what the hell that thing is up there," said one of the men. "And we're not even supposed to guess. But if it falls on us, we'll never live to tell about it."

With the transfer complete, the hoses fell to the deck. Then the thing above appeared to rise and simply dissolve into the darkness.

* * *

With the airship taking on those additional tons of liquid hydrogen fuel, Decker went gradually from negative to neutral to positive lift. Meanwhile, liquid helium from cryogenic tanks was gasified and fed into the mylar cells. Decker again turned on the power to the filaments. By adjusting the heat within the cells, he could fine-tune both balance and buoyancy.

The Red Sea operation was code-named Sand Bar. The salient part of the ops order read: ". . . proceed to the area of the Red Sea coast of Eritrea and there carry out air operations, including combat as necessary, in support of Ethiopian forces, to prevent the capture of Eritrean territory by hostile forces." In the comm-section, a printer fed from an HF single sideband receiver came to life. The message read simply, "Mother Hen to Skyhook. Execute Sand Bar."

Primed for war, the airship headed eastward across the Atlantic. It made a landfall in darkness on the coast of Morocco and met the sunrise over the eastern slopes of the Atlas. There, another message on the HF single sideband directed them to tune in Talking Bird.

On the dorsal surface, a panel opened and a clear plastic bubble emerged from its compartment. Beneath the bubble was a dish antenna supported on jeweled bearings. It balanced and steadied itself like a surfboarder riding a wave while it aimed a narrow microwave beam into the tropical sky.

Some 24,000 miles above the Indian Ocean, in earth-synchronous orbit, Talking Bird II heard the plea for attention, one of many it got in an almost constant stream. Tiny, solar-powered servo-motors pointed a parabolic dish at the signal source and sent out an answering beam. The ship caught it and bounced it back. Together, they narrowed the beam until they were locked in mutual electronic eye contact.

Then Talking Bird's MASER sent an invisible, pencil-thin shaft directly onto the dish atop the ship. To perform this miracle of precision, each relied upon a magne-gyro, a device based on spinning magnetic fields. Its precision exceeded that of mechanical gyros by orders of magnitude.

Gus was roused from sleep by a voice on the intercom. "Message for Air Group One from Mother Hen."

When Gus came into the ready room at 0740, Commander Sam Corwin, his operations officer, was already there. " 'Morning, Colonel." Sam's thin-lipped smile showed small, porcelain-white teeth against mahogany skin.

Gus sighed and smiled back. "I don't know about good, Sam, but it sure feels like morning." They each drew coffee. Besides being roused early by that message, they had lost eight hours out of the last twenty-four from the change in time zones.

Before coming to Skyhook, Sam had been CO of a Navy carrier squadron. His quick, onyx-bright eyes and thin, pointed nose gave him a look of almost excessive alertness. In a gesture Gus had come to recognize as a partner to the smile, Sam's dark, bony hand grabbed at the tightly kinked nap on his scalp.

The other pilots began filing in. Major Elwood "Woody" Hower was the only one Gus had known before. Tall and lean, he had close-clipped blond hair and a level gaze from ice-blue eyes. In the Gulf War he had gained a certain distinction by shooting down three of Saddam's MiGs in less than a minute. Lars Kroeder was a tough-looking Marine Corps major with the flattened nose of a pugilist. Lieutenant Commander "Stosh" Stanovic was an Annapolis man in the photogenic pattern of Hank Borland. Major Garry Meighan had been ops officer in an F-16 squadron.

The rest were two-bars—Air Force, Navy, and Marine Corps. They all had outstanding flying records, including "top gun" credentials. By the nature of Pegasus, this unit was top-heavy in rank. It would serve as cadre for air groups to follow.

The coffee mugs carried colorful personalized logos with claims like "Super Stud," and "Manic Expressive." The pilots settled into their seats while Gus spoke. "Okay, we've just had word the Islamic Front has taken the airfield at Asmara. Unless the government forces can get it back, they can't hold out. They want to mount an airborne assault and are asking for fighter cover for their troop carriers. I've just messaged Mother Hen we're in position and ready. Right now, that's all I can tell you. We could get the call anytime. Or tomorrow. Or . . ." He turned his palms up. "Anyway, we're briefing now so we'll be ready. We'll get weather updates at half-hour intervals.

"Call sign Possum. Flight assignments and the usual data are on the board there. I'll lead the first section consisting of Alpha and Bravo flights, and our main task will be to get the trash carriers in to the drop zone. Sam, with Charlie and Delta, will launch thirty minutes later. That'll leave them enough fuel to cover the withdrawal. And we'll have all sixteen there at the critical time of the actual drop. Bingo fuel at the drop zone is eight hundred pounds."

There were disappointed looks. With twenty pilots and only sixteen airplanes, not every man could fly. "Except for the flight leaders, we drew names for this first mission," Sam Corwin said. "So no one should feel left out. You'll all get your chance."

Gus threw an aerial chart on the screen in front. The chart was covered by clear acetate on which he had marked in grease pencil. "Photo recon shows IF fighters operating out of two bases across the border in Sudan. This one's designated Boardwalk and the other Park Place. The airfield at Asmara is Canasta, and the one over in Yemen is Cribbage. These arcs show the radius of action for the various opposing aircraft types. Questions?"

"Any chance of communicating with these fan drivers?"

Gus showed a wry smile. "We can always hope. Part of my message to Mother Hen was a request for compatible frequencies and to make sure they have people aboard who speak English. *Mazel tov* on all the above.

"Anyway, they're supposed to have multi-channel UHF, probably the old ARC-27 or-34. Or perhaps the Soviet equivalent. So we should be able to make contact in non-scrambled mode. Here's a list of frequencies they're believed to use. If the occasion arises, one of the flight leaders can switch over, make contact, and come back. Questions?"

"What about enemy radar?"

"No known operational sets within range. ECM says that so far the only pulses they're getting from aviation-type radar come from the sets at Aden and San'a. Both well out of range."

Michelle could not avoid feeling life had lured her into a trap by taking advantage of her better nature.

Just a few weeks before, things had been shaping up like a dream. Both Med-Tech and her career as a surgeon were solid successes, and she and Gus were about to be married. Even her mission to Addis Ababa had seemed only a brief detour off that yellow brick road.

Now she found herself caught in a nightmare in a beleaguered city and apt to be taken prisoner. And the Islamic Front soldiers were known to look upon captured women the way troops had for centuries, as prizes of war. Mass rape served the dual purpose of sexual release for the troops and a calculated insult to the enemy. It was not publicized, but American service women captured during Desert Storm had been raped, some repeatedly. And given Arab rage at the U.S., laying their hands on an American woman would be like breaking into Fort Knox.

She had prepared a lethal dose and placed it in her medical bag. She held the syringe before her and stared at it. Quick death in a small glass cylinder. If the time came, could she bring herself to jab the needle into her vein and depress the plunger?

She fought back a sob, told herself the situation was not that hopeless. Colonel X was at mortal risk himself. He had mentioned prospects of getting out and taking her with him.

So far, the colonel had not so much as hinted at any favors in return for arranging her departure. If he made that proposition, she was determined to call his bluff. If it was a bluff.

There was a knock on the door. A hospital orderly told her the colonel had arrived in the director's office and was asking to see her. Spooky. Was fright making her thoughts telepathic?

"A ship with munitions and supplies has docked in Massawa," the colonel said after the usual pleasantries. "The train bringing them here should arrive soon. It will return to Massawa with the worst of the sick and wounded. I've arranged for you to go along as attending physician. From Djibouti you should get a flight to Addis Ababa." He smiled. "Djibouti is a colorful city, and it would be worth your while to see it while you're there."

"I've seen Djibouti, Colonel. What I really want to see now is Addis Ababa. And then Washington."

"Very well. I must warn you the tracks between here and Massawa could come under artillery fire."

"I'm quite aware of that, and I'd much rather take my chances with artillery shells than the troops of the Islamic Front." She paused. "And . . . ah . . . will you be going along?"

He gave her a quick little smile. "Probably not. I suggest you go and get ready. Take only what you can carry. With luck, the train will depart sometime after dark. I won't pretend we're so well organized as to say that means any particular hour."

"Very well, Colonel." She rose and then, on an

impulse, offered her hand. "I wish you well. You're a brave man."

Again that wry, deprecating little smile. "I'm a conscience-ridden man. But I thank you. I hope our paths may cross again."

She left to go and collect her few personal belongings.

Despite the airship's low visual signature, Borland made use of available cloud. They were cruising in dense stratus on a northerly heading as the air group readied for its first combat mission.

Launch Control was a windowless compartment equipped with closed-circuit monitors and manned by a pilot not scheduled to fly. The monitors showed four F-24's in transit on the overhead trolleys. With the flight deck still closed off by panels fore and aft, the aircraft were moved into position and lowered onto their landing gear.

At the touch of a finger, mechanical restraints called "straps" rose to engage the main gear struts. Aircraft in this prelaunch state were designated "in the straps." Like boas hanging from tree limbs, black power cables dropped from overhead. Each pilot reached out and plugged the cable head into a receptacle just below the canopy rail.

"Possum Alpha, Launch Control. Prepare for launch. Close and lock canopies, check safety pins withdrawn."

"Roger." Gus's voice came through the speaker. "Alpha Lead, pins and canopy." In order, Alpha Two, Three, and Four checked in.

"Opening aft flight deck panels." Far back in the tail of the airship, the panels that closed off the landing impact zone pivoted upward. "Possum Alpha, you're clear to start engines."

All eight engines whined up to idle. "Alpha Lead stabilized." The same from Two, Three, and Four.

"Opening forward panels." The forward panels were

like huge hangar doors, telescoping open with a kind of silent majesty, taking the airstream in at full flight speed. Cloud vapor poured in with it. "Alpha Flight, you're cleared for run-up." The vapor thinned and disappeared. The airship had climbed above the cloud.

Gus pushed the throttles to the stop, watched the temperature and rpm rise and stabilize on both engines. Everything was in the green, though it still felt strange to see the airspeed jump to 150 knots and then go on rising while the aircraft was apparently at rest. The added thrust of those eight engines, a total of almost forty thousand pounds, could eventually push the airship near two hundred knots. He reduced the throttles by two percent, the flight leader's concession to his wingman. "Alpha Lead launch ready." Again the other three echoed him.

"Alpha Flight, stand by for countdown." The cables and telecom leads were withdrawn. Communication was now by radio alone.

In front of each aircraft and just a little above was a light-matrix panel, like a miniature version of the electronic scoreboards in sports arenas. It could form numbers, letters, figures, almost any shape. Right now it showed a circle with eight sectors of alternate blue and orange. While Gus watched, the segments underwent rapid reversals of color. Then they began winking out at one-second intervals, starting clockwise from 12. As the last went dark, the straps popped open.

The Scimitar was already in flight and straining against the straps. When they popped open, it leaped out of the launch port. Gus raised the gear and flaps, glanced over his shoulder. Alpha Two, launched right next to him at a one-second interval, was just tucking in on his wing. On the opposite side, Three and Four moved in to complete the fingertip pattern.

He retarded throttles to ninety-two percent and began a gentle turn to port. The wide 360 brought them back abreast of Skyhook just as Bravo Flight burst out of the launch port. That timing was one of the things they had worked out over the North Atlantic.

The formation assembled in fingertip fours, with Bravo just behind and below. Half a mile astern, the airship, like some prehistoric monster returning to its primordial depths, sank back into the cloud layer.

"Possum, go flights in diamond." Each number four moved over into the "slot," directly behind the lead, giving the flight a diamond shape. Besides being the formation of choice for acrobatic maneuvers by teams like the Thunderbirds and Blue Angels, diamond was ideal for weather penetrations. Everyone flew directly on the leader. "Bravo, take separation." Woody Hower, leading Bravo, clicked the transmitter button twice, then turned his flight thirty degrees off the heading. He held that for five seconds, then turned back to parallel Alpha.

Gus took them down through the cloud, broke out near six thousand. Below, the Red Sea looked not red at all but mud-dun.

In this background of cloud and diffuse light, the Scimitar was all but invisible. Yet right after they broke out, Hower called a visual and rejoined. On the surface of each F-24 were stripes invisible to the naked eye. Through the pilots' helmet visors, they showed up in scintillating lavender.

Gus headed for the coast, some twenty miles away. "Possum, test-fire, then go tac spread." Each pilot fired a minimum burst from the 20mm. On his right, Alpha Three moved out laterally to about a thousand feet. Four took up a position a few hundred feet beyond Three. Two spread left from Gus in the same way. A thousand feet above and a little behind, Bravo Flight took on the same pattern.

Possum was in full battle trim.

For the moment there was radio silence. Only the background hiss of the radio and electronic gear, the muffled pumping of vital fluids and the sound of his own breathing came through each pilot's earphones. In the near-silence of the fighter cockpit before battle, every man was confronted with his own mortality in the sound of that rhythmic intake of oxygen.

Ahead lay the coast and the rendezvous point.

Gus knew there was no inherent reason Third World pilots could not match Americans and Europeans. James Jabara, the world's first jet ace, was an American of a Lebanese family. But the badly outnumbered Skyhook air group was expected and in fact obliged to maintain the lopsided Western advantage in air combat.

To some, it might seem hubris, but Gus felt no qualms. He had the most a fighter pilot could ask for: an airplane second to none, a team of outstanding pilots—and an unlimited license to hunt.

Chapter Twelve

She went by the name Lucy Morgan, and she was a staff
writer for *Avanti*. The hour was near midnight, and
Arthur Penross was entertaining her and lecherous
thoughts. The latter were interrupted by the telephone.
That unlisted number could be answered only in the
office. He topped off her glass of chilled Chardonnay
before excusing himself.

"Yes."

"Okay, I've finally got some skinny on this Major
Austen."

"I knew you'd come through. The Pentagon can't hide
anyone completely." He swiveled around, switched on
the desk lamp, and brought up a file on the computer.
"Okay, go."

"He's reassigned to something called Pegasus. Which
has a security classification of burn-before-reading. Officially, it doesn't exist. And for me from now on, he
doesn't either. In fact, I may have touched a wrong nerve
already. But I did pick up another little tidbit. Gus Hal-

strom's also assigned to Pegasus." There was a pregnant pause. "And this ought to be worth double the usual."

"Um-m." Penross's tone was noncommittal. "A-a-nd what—?"

"That's it. All I have. The name Pegasus. And that's all you're going to get. I'm not risking my job." The phone clicked dead.

Penross frowned, pursed his lips, then entered the name Pegasus in the file before returning to the living room and Lucy Morgan.

Distracted at finding her in nothing but panty hose, he never noticed the small plastic cube she was just returning to her purse. Despite the separation of his phone lines, that device had let her record his conversation.

The nine Antonov transports wore desert camouflage and Ethiopian markings. They flew low, in loose Vs of three. Beneath them, the pale sand and gleaming white salt flats of the Danakil desert sped by in a blur. Beyond lay the Red Sea.

In the lead aircraft, a paratroop colonel in full battle gear made his way forward. To keep his footing on the heaving deck, he did the "paratroop shuffle," a series of foot-skids keeping one foot ahead of the other. Up front, he spoke to the aircraft commander. "Major, is there any reason we're flying so low like this? Some of my troops are getting queasy from this bouncing around."

"Sir, I take it they'd rather be queasy than dead. Any higher, and we could show up on enemy radar. Those Islamic Front MiG pilots would just love to have us for targets. Anyway, we'll be over water in a minute, and the air should smooth out." The colonel gave a nod of unhappy understanding and returned to his seat.

As the shoreline passed under the nose, both pilots began scanning ahead and above. "You think they'll make contact?" said the copilot.

"We're not sure they can. Their radios are very sophisticated, made to counter jamming and interception, but may only work with each other. Anyway, I doubt if they're even here. This whole idea of the Americans giving us fighter cover is very shaky. The request had to go by shortwave to Washington. Then orders had to go from there to American forces somewhere in the region. Then they have to fly here and make an exact rendezvous." He shook his head. "Too many links in the chain. Too many potential—sonofabitch!"

A pair of odd-looking, pearl-gray fighters had just shot forward from underneath the nose. They went straight up and seemed to melt into the air. Obviously, they had swooped under the formation from behind. The excited voice of the lead pilot in the second V filled their earphones. He wanted to know if they should they scatter and attempt to save themselves. "Relax," the major transmitted. "That must be our American escort. Fighter pilots have these ways of announcing themselves."

Shortly, two of those strange fighters seemed to materialize out of the atmosphere to take up a position on each wing. And on that odd, metallic-gray surface was the familiar star and horizontal bands of blue and white of the USA. A figure inside a helmet and oxygen mask looked at them through a darkened visor. It was like the stare of some huge, alien insect.

The copilot swiveled his head, frowning. "What airplane is *that*?"

"Nothing I ever saw. Must be new since the Gulf War."

"Hello, Beanbag, this is Possum Alpha Leader."

They were both so startled that the call was repeated before the major thought to press the transmitter button and respond. "Possum Alpha, this is Beanbag Leader. I am reading you . . . ah . . . loud and clear."

"Ah, roger-roger, Beanbag. We'll be covering you en route and over the drop zone. If we meet any bandits, you may have to orbit your formation while we engage. Do you understand?"

Still a little stunned at this unexpected precision, the major said, "Roger."

"Beanbag, Possum Alpha leaving your frequency." The anonymous American pilot raised a gauntleted fist with the thumb upright. The copilot's face registered shock, then greater shock at seeing his A/C return the gesture. In most of Africa, that was obscene and insulting.

Tongues of flame burst from the four tailpipes, and the pair shot forward, then again went straight up and seemed to melt into the atmosphere. The major smiled and explained that in America that gesture signified approval and good wishes.

It had taken the SS *Moldavia* almost a week to make its way around the Arabian Peninsula and land its cargo and passengers at Port Sudan.

Alejandro, always responsible for technical arrangements but almost never told anything in advance, had questioned the need for more pilots and aircraft. "It looks to me like a case of overkill, *Jefe*. With what they have now, they have complete control of the air over the battle zone."

"Our sources tell us that Addis Ababa is on the verge of renewing close ties with both Washington and Tel Aviv," said *El Jefe*. "So, sooner or later, and probably sooner, the Americans may send one of their carriers. And the Israelis may be involved too. More combat aircraft in the hands of our friends in the Islamic Front could make a difference. And the pilots are Iraqis that went to Iran during the Gulf War. They have a claim to retribution."

After unloading at Port Sudan, the ship steamed back southward, dropping anchor the following day in the Dahlak Archipelago. By nightfall, scaffolds were hung over the sides. When the sun rose again, the ship no longer looked like a ship but resembled an island. Large tarpaulins painted and textured to look like rock and sand were draped to cover the hull. Camouflage netting masked the superstructure.

145

Beneath that netting was a large elliptical radar dish. As the sun rose, operators began tracking the Islamic Front fighters on their patrols over the battle zone or strikes on the defenses around Asmara.

To the operators, the string of fat returns near the western coast looked anomalous. Some complained of equipment malfunction. The chief controller studied the pattern for a while, noted the northward movement. "There's nothing wrong with the set! Those are troop carriers! The Ethiopians are mounting an airborne assault on the airfield at Asmara." He picked up a handset from the ship's interphone system. "Sparks, call the fighter bases. Tell the pilots they're invited to a massacre."

"Possum Alpha, this is Skyhook. The opposition has activated a crystal ball. ECM just intercepted their HF-band transmission. They have a paint on your transports, and they're calling in the bandits."

"Roger, Skyhook. Are we showing up on their crystal ball?"

"Not likely, Possum. ECM says it's an obsolescent type."

"Roger. Are the bandits airborne, or is this a scramble?"

"Possum, we show airborne bandits departing Canasta. They appear to be vectoring on the transports. Data on your Bird Dog."

"Roger, Skyhook. Alpha will vector on bandits. Bravo will cover the transports. Bravo, have 'em circle the wagons."

"A-h, roger." Woody Hower's tone was as glum as a Calvinist sermon. "Thanks a bunch for grabbing the steak and leaving us the parsley."

"That ain't necessarily so." Gus couldn't keep the amusement out of his voice. "But you know how it is, Old Chap. RHIP."

In each Scimitar cockpit, directly in the pilot's line of vision was a plate of optical-quality glass, much like the standard computing gunsight. This was the visible portion of the ITD—Integrated Target Display, called the "Bird Dog" in the brevity code. Images reflected in the glass conveyed target data. Through a collimating or infinity-focus lens, these images were always superimposed on the pilot's forward view no matter where his gaze was focused or how he moved his head.

The CMD—Combat Maneuvering Director—was a multifunction computational and warning system tied into the Bird Dog. It took input from the Scimitar's own radar and interacted with Skyhook's radar. What Gus saw at the moment was a pointer giving the direction to the nearest enemy aircraft, distance in nautical miles, and the difference in altitude from his. It directed them westward, toward Asmara.

Inland, the thick overcast that covered the sea was replaced by multiple layers of thin, shelving stratus. True airspeed was 420 knots. The Bird Dog showed a rate of closure of over eight hundred knots at an angle near head-on. From the moment the enemy appeared as distant specks in the atmosphere till they passed and were again out of sight would be less than a minute. Somewhere among those seconds was the instant to begin the pull-up and turn to get on their tails.

The Bird Dog showed multiple targets. "Skyhook, how many bandits?"

"Possum, we show twenty-four bandits at this time. In pairs and fours, strung out over about twenty miles. Enemy also appears to be scrambling from Boardwalk and Park Place."

That newly operative GCI had put out the word of fat, easy targets. Every Islamic Front pilot in the area was rushing to get in on the turkey shoot. But it posed a problem. Hitting those up front would warn all the rest and give up the element of surprise. Waiting for those in the rear could leave Bravo with too many to deal with.

The first two pairs were about thirty seconds apart. He

let them go by. "Heads up, Bravo. We're letting four bandits come your way."

"Roger, Possum Leader." There was a pause. " 'Preciate that."

The next four oncoming targets showed a lateral
spread of half a mile and the radar-guided Sparrow missile with primary kill probability. But Gus rejected the
head-on shot. Instead, he hugged the base of a stratus
layer some two thousand feet above. Against this backdrop, the Scimitars would be invisible. "Alpha Three,
move your element out for a loose-deuce." Three and
Four spread to the left to place themselves on the MiGs'
opposite side. "Alpha, douse the headlamps." That told
the pilots to turn their onboard radar to standby. The
MiGs had tail antennae to warn the pilots they were being
swept.

With the targets at about ten o'clock, Gus rolled into a
descending turn. The second element curved in on the
opposite side. "Go burner." He moved the throttles
through the detent, felt the kick of acceleration.

Plainly eager for the promised easy kills, the enemy
pilots never looked right or left. As Gus completed the first
ninety degrees, the four MiG-21's—stark, dartlike shapes
against a pearlescent backdrop of lower cloud, shot by
across the nose. The Mach-meter jumped from .98 to 1.02
as the Scimitar went supersonic. Airspeed read about 540.
That was well over six hundred true. He continued the turn
to get on their tails. "Alpha, missile volley on command."

They leveled and straightened, looking up the MiG
tailpipes at $3\frac{1}{2}$ nautical. The Bird Dog, now getting its
data entirely from Skyhook's radar, showed the heat-
seeking Sidewinder as primary. Gus put his thumb on the
weapons-selector knob, moved it to arm the first
Sidewinder. The firing tubes opened, and a growling tone
came through his earphones.

He was just moving the nose of the Scimitar around a
little to maximize the growl when it was joined by

another, more strident sound. The CMD was warning him of radar sweeping them from behind.

"Colonel X" tapped the eraser of his pencil on the desk, rolled his eyes, and fumed inwardly as he listened to the braying on the line from Addis Ababa. "Yes, Colonel," the other man said. "I'm trying to get that information for you, but our reporting channels are sometimes disrupted." The man was an officious ass. An absolute, blithering fool. Just because this was a land line was no reason to believe the enemy was not listening. There was every reason to think he was, in fact. Though they were equal in grade, the tone coming from headquarters was brusque and peremptory, as if he were an office boy instead of a line officer close to the battlefront.

The voice also delivered gratuitous advice. "Why don't you . . . ? Have you tried thus-and-so?" "It seems to me you could . . ." All on the basis of knowing almost nothing of what was going on here. If I get out of this alive and get my hands on that cretin, thought Colonel X.

"Yes, we dispatched a train for Massawa last night, Colonel," he said. "It was loaded with the worst casualties, civilian and military. We hope they can be taken down the coast by ship, and—"

The voice cut him off abruptly. It didn't give a damn about the disposition of casualties just now. It was trying to determine if the supplies and munitions sent by ship to Massawa would be handled efficiently and reach the battle zone without delay.

"We'll do our best. You have no idea of what things are like here."

The exchange went on in that vein for some minutes. On the assumption that whatever was said would be overheard by the enemy, Colonel X was deliberately vague and uncertain. The information, he thought, would be almost as damaging in this fool's hands. And all so he could complete his reports neatly.

There was one final question, a slightly sensitive matter, said the distant voice. As if that fool could recognize a sensitive matter if he sat on it and got it stuck up his butt. The American woman doctor who had gone there to help. There were inquiries about her. Washington needed reassurance she was safe and would be on her way home soon.

Colonel X paused ever so briefly before he answered. "I should think so, Colonel," he said. "I put her on that train to Massawa as attending physician. In view of the fact that the airfield's been captured and there are no flights in or out, I thought—"

Again he was interrupted by an agitated outburst. That was poor judgment, and if anything happened to her . . . etc. Furthermore, the airfield would be recaptured soon. "I can tell you—"

Colonel X broke the connection. "Yes, and tell Islamic Front headquarters while you're at it, you bloody ass!" he said aloud. Perhaps by cutting the fool off, he had avoided compromise of some sensitive information.

As for Michelle St. Clair, Colonel X let out a bitter sigh. He indeed wished he had not sent her on that train. It had seemed to be the best chance of getting her out of Asmara. To avoid telling the enemy of their own success, he had been less than truthful with that HQ type.

The enemy gunners, who up till yesterday had only been able to drop a few rounds in the vicinity of the tracks, had suddenly found the range. The train had been just chugging out of the city when shells fell with devastating effect, turned train and track alike into a shambles. For sanitary reasons, the bodies would have to be put into a mass grave.

And somewhere among them would be that of Dr. Michelle St. Clair. What a god-awful waste, he thought, of a beautiful woman.

And how the hell would they ever explain it to Washington?

Chapter Thirteen

"Alpha, fire!" Gus mashed his own firing button. Blowing smoke, the missile burst from its tube. The smoke was gone in moments; the stinging, chemical-sweet smell of burnt propellant lingered. Trails from the other missiles showed as umber streaks on the edge of his vision.

The Sidewinders went after those hot MiG tailpipes in the tight, corkscrewing motion that gave the missile its name. Gus flicked the armament switch to "guns" and the gun switch to "fire" in case of a miss.

The radar warning persisted, but it was search, not lock-on and at five-plus miles. No fighter radar could lock onto an F-24 tail-on at five miles. And Islamic Front pilots would assume any aircraft up ahead was their own.

The four Sidewinders struck within seconds of each other, the fiery billows spaced over some three thousand feet of sky. Four blobs of oily smoke writhed and plumed. Flaming debris arced out of those swirling black smudges.

"Up, up, and away, Alpha." Gus's tone was playful, sardonic as he pulled the Scimitar's nose straight up. "Burner out. Headlamps back on." They burst up through the cloud layer that had earlier given them cover. Above was only the stratospheric cirrus that diffused the sunlight.

While he was still inverted, just bringing the nose down to the horizon, the Bird Dog showed bogies at ten o'clock for five miles. As he rolled upright, he sighted the pair just completing the same maneuver.

At three miles, their silhouettes resolved into MiG-29's, once top-of-the-line for the Soviets, their equivalent of the F-15. The Bird Dog showed them a thousand feet below. "Alpha Three, you're clear to take your element and hunt targets of opportunity. These two are ours."

Alpha Three rogered. The pair of Scimitars peeled off.

The leader of this pair of MiGs was no fool. He had seen the explosions, made a correct analysis of what had happened, and anticipated the Scimitars' breakaway.

The Bird Dog showed the Sidewinder as primary but on the fringe of the envelope, kill probability only about twenty percent. He left the armament selector on "guns" and stroked the afterburners. Exultant, he closed in for a gunfight. Missiles had taken over much of modern aerial warfare, but to the true fighter pilot, dueling it out with guns was still the ultimate.

"Bravo Three has lock-on. Missile away."

"Bravo Lead has these two near the coast. Guns, Bravo Two."

"Lead, can we get these fan types to tighten up their—"

"—Nice shot, Three. Blew his ass—"

"—we've got two more at two o'clock low."

In a shallow turn, about to cross the Scimitars' noses right to left, the MiG pilots were clearly searching for whoever had just blown four of their compadres out of the air. Except the wingman was much too close for searching. Perhaps forty percent of his attention was on holding position where even ten percent was too much. Alpha Lead and Two were inside half a mile before the

MiGs finally reacted. Their wings flipped to vertical, and the burners stuck their fiery tongues out the tailpipes.

The core of the CMD was the flight-curvature/maneuvering-energy synthesizer. Gus himself had had a hand in designing it. Among other things, it gave a constant readout of the tightest available turning arc and the envelope for optimum preservation of maneuvering energy.

Right now, it was telling him the obvious: If he tried to fly a pursuit curve at this high angle-off, he'd wind up in an overshoot—outside the MiGs' flight path with no chance for a shot. The standard response was a high-speed yo-yo—break off the attack and pull up, shorten the turn radius, and convert the kinetic energy into altitude, preserving the advantage.

"Bravo Lead, it's still hard to get in a shot without risk to the troop carriers. They need to tighten up their orbit some more."

But right now, the CMD confirmed what he'd already seen—here was an opening for a "roll-off." He pulled the nose up while gradually lowering the right wing just enough to keep the MiGs in view over the canopy rail. When they were about to disappear under the nose, he steepened the pull-up to vertical and rolled further right, came over the top in what was very close to the old acrobatic cloverleaf. Earth and sky tumbled on all three axes.

With the nose inverted and about to touch the horizon, he had the MiGs near the top of his canopy and just right of center. When the nose came down through the vertical, he knew the roll-off was about to claim at least one more victim. They hung just aft of the canopy bow, the wingman still too close and now trailing behind. Gus felt the Gs increasing as he pulled the nose through hard to frame the targets in the windscreen.

Reflected in the glass was the sight reticle—two glowing concentric circles and a cross whose lines did not quite meet at the apex. The image dipped now to indicate lead on a moving target. At a range of some 1200 feet, he

B. Michelaard

flew the trailing MiG into the rings of the gunsight, let the tiny gap at the center of the cross steady over the fuselage, and touched the trigger.

The 20mm TM-61 "Vulcan" cannon with its revolving-barrel cluster had a rate of fire up to six thousand rounds per minute—a mix of high-explosive, armor-piercing, and incendiary. Thirty or so in that one-third-of-a-second burst. The MiG exploded. Gus could have easily moved the reticle to the lead aircraft and claimed it, but he mashed the transmitter and said, "Alpha Two, this one's yours if—"

"Roger, Lead! I'm on him."

But that pilot—Libyan, Iraqi, Yemeni, or whatever—evaded Alpha Two's attack, and over the next minute or so showed a high determination and considerable skill in delaying the inevitable. After they each scored hits, the MiG began streaming smoke. The smoke grew thicker, leaving an intricate abstract-art trail to mark the desperate evasive efforts.

Then the ejection seat fired; the pilot separated. The chute billowed into a canopy at the moment the MiG billowed flame.

"Alpha, fuel check," Gus transmitted.

Average remaining was about 1700 pounds. With JP, that would be close to Bingo. Burning hydrogen, they still had a cushion.

"Alpha Four, if you've got a Sidewinder ready, this one's yours."

So the second element was having good hunting too.

Determined to keep the Anvil Bravo affair on the front burner but with little in the way of new facts, Penross decided to insert the name Pegasus into a potpouri of potshots in his ongoing vendetta against the Pentagon.

On the morning after it appeared in that Penross column, Pentagon security went into the kind of convulsion military slang labels a shit-hemorrhage. Security agents

154

ferreted through files. Technicians probed computer memories while interrogators did the same with people. Official Washington was a hive alive with buzz and rumor.

By noon, a civilian DoD employee had been collared and cuffed. The authorities made a pro forma effort to suppress news of the arrest, but failed. By the end of the day, Arthur Penross found his sources drying up like desert arroyos. Some would not even take his call.

So he composed a column on the witch-hunt at the Pentagon, the return of McCarthyism, and the dire threat to the First Amendment.

"Message for Air Group One!" Gus was getting accustomed to these wee-hour intrusions. He checked the time—0421. In Washington, that was 2021—still the previous day. While he dressed, he silently groused that some duty officer was trying to stave off boredom.

The message said the Ethiopians wanted to fly a four-engine aircraft out of Asmara before the battle over the airfield renewed. It would carry a doctor and some wounded and would be flying on three engines. Proposed takeoff was 0500 Zulu. Call sign Beanbag. Would Skyhook have any problem providing escort?

Sam had reported one of the troop carriers made an emergency landing after the airfield was captured. Gus first wrote out a terse reply, then told the comm-section people to have Commander Corwin meet him in the ready room.

Time was now 0437. Takeoff in about two hours. He roused the senior maintenance officer and said they'd be launching four in two hours.

In the ready room, Sam and Gus blew their eyelids open with strong coffee and greased their stomachs with microwaved donuts. Then it came to the matter of scheduling aircrew. "We've got two warm bodies right here," Sam said. "Two more is all we need."

155

Gus frowned and smiled together. Sam grinned and tugged at the nap of his hair. "I thought it was worth a try."

Gus knew how frustrated Sam must be. He had over fifteen years as a Navy pilot, had worked his way up to command a squadron, but had yet to fire on a live enemy. During the Gulf War, he had led combat air patrols, but no Iraqi planes had even come close. And yesterday, the IF fighters were already pulling out by the time Sam got airborne.

Sam lifted an intercom handset and punched some buttons: "Congratulations. You just won the dawn patrol lottery. Get your ass down to the ready room."

Possum Alpha was in the straps at 0736 local. When the flight deck doors opened, the sky showed blood red. They were airborne before 0740, with scattered-to-broken cloud below. The air above was clear.

They climbed in tac spread on a westerly heading. Gus had the coordinates of Boardwalk, the nearest IF base, set into the Scimitar's inertial nav system. Meteorology had put the contrail level at 42,000, but that was plus-or-minus; so they leveled at forty. The two wingmen kept a steady eyeball sweep for the merest wisp of contrails. These streaks of frozen vapor were always a giveaway, but lit from below by the morning sun, they would show up like neon.

The sky was clear; the sun was behind them, and visibility was unlimited. Boardwalk and Park Place were about twenty miles apart, but from this altitude, both were visible.

These newest helmets were equipped with stubby, high-powered binoculars that could be flipped up and down. At five miles, Gus focused the 20X lenses on Boardwalk.

What he saw made his pulse jump.

Rows of aircraft were snaking along the taxiways.

While he watched, a pair began their takeoff roll. Two more moved into place. He clicked the lenses to 30X and turned his attention to Park Place. Same activity there.

"Skyhook, Possum Alpha. Be advised we have heavy activity at Boardwalk and Park Place. Launch Bravo ASAP. Put Charlie and Delta in the straps."

"Roger, Alpha. Estimating Bravo airborne in six."

Gus began a turn back toward Canasta, the airfield at Asmara, throttling back to begin a shallow descent while keeping the airspeed high. By the time he had a clear view, they were down to twenty thousand. Sam reported airborne with Bravo. Bogies kept showing up on the Bird Dog as more of those MiGs took off. "Alpha Lead going non-scrambled mode to make contact with Beanbag."

"Beanbag, this is Possum Alpha Leader." No response. He tried twice more with the same result.

The instrument panel chronometer read 0804 when a voice finally came through. "Possum Alpha, Beanbag is airborne. Reading you loud and clear."

"Roger, Beanbag. Be advised we have many bandits in the area. Recommend you go to minimum altitude and max constant power."

"Will do, Possum. Do you have us in sight?"

"Roger, Beanbag, we have you crossing the rail lines at this time."

"Possum, be advised we are maneuvering to avoid ground fire before taking up course of one-niner-zero."

Gus acknowledged and began a twisting, darting "pin-ball" descent to stay behind the Antonov and keep it in sight. With this background, its camouflage was effective.

"Possum Alpha, this is Beanbag. We have a request to use higher altitude."

Gus was puzzled. "Request, Beanbag? Whose request?"

"From American physician on board. She claims the bumpy flight is bad for wounded patients. Perhaps we could try one thousand AGL?"

In Gus's mind, a string of horrifying facts began falling into place: "She"—an American physician. "Beanbag, is this physician perhaps named Doctor Michelle St. Clair?"

"Wait one, Alpha." Then, after a short silence: "Possum Alpha, that's affirmative."

Chapter Fourteen

By leveraging the time difference, the Air France flight catered to Parisians with morning appointments in New York. It let them leave after business hours, have a French dinner over the Atlantic, and arrive in time to get a night's sleep before facing the rigors of commerce. But this evening, mechanical problems before takeoff plus strong headwinds delayed arrival till 1 after midnight New York time.

Among the passengers, only Etienne Alvarado had no luggage to claim. Carrying a garment bag and a small valise, he passed quickly through customs and passport control and was met by Audrey Prowther. "Welcome to New York," she said. "We have a car waiting."

He gave her a chiding smile. "What, no key to the city? And can you speak for the mayor and the governor?"

She mirrored the smile. "Just knowing you're here would give either of them nightmares."

Outside, each remarked how the slushy snow and vapor plumes of breath recalled their last meeting, in

B. Michelaard

Berlin. The visitor shivered and turned up his coat collar as a four-door sedan eased up to the curb. "I sometimes wonder if this climate isn't a large part of what makes Northern inhabitants such grasping, private individuals." Like his smile, the voice carried a chiding note.

He sat in the rear, Audrey in front beside the driver. "It could be seen as a short step from heavy clothing to a cloak of personal autonomy," he went on. "In the tropics, people went almost naked until the missionaries came. And attitudes there are still more communal, even after some two centuries of European influence. After all, it's difficult to maintain distance and formality with everyone's navel showing."

They were leaving the terminal area and merging into traffic. Audrey half turned in the seat and looked back at him. "I'm not sure your theory holds up, Monitor. To continue my art studies after college, I worked as an exotic dancer." Her tone placed quotation marks around the last two words. "Meaning I exposed a helluva lot more than my navel. And that didn't make me feel a bit closer to anyone."

"Oh, but of course not. You were being exploited. Reduced to an object. Both typical and symbolic of this society. The very opposite of sitting around in breechcloths sharing a meal."

The man behind the wheel was maneuvering across traffic lanes, watching the outside mirror. But he smiled and flicked his gaze once at Audrey. "Hard to picture you doing bumps and grinds."

She gave him a look of mock severity. "What are you saying? That I don't have the figure?"

"Oh, not at all! Your figure arouses a certain lust in all of us. But your creative luster has cloaked you in a certain dignity, so that—"

"So that lust gives way to luster?" Her tone was charged with humor. Then she looked back at *El Jefe*, who was known here as Monitor. "You've just come from Eritrea?"

"I have indeed. And somebody—the U.S. Navy, I suspect—has introduced some quite puzzling technology. I'm here to organize a maximum effort to uncover it."

It took Gus a moment to refocus his thoughts after the shock of learning Michelle was aboard the Antonov. Meanwhile, he continued the corkscrewing descent. At five thousand, he shallowed out, noted the Antonov had indeed climbed to about a thousand feet AGL.

As he reached three thousand, not quite all Hell but a good-sized chunk of Purgatory broke loose. A flashing light and a strident squawk in his earphones warned of both an enemy on their tails and a missile in flight. Alpha Three came through on guard channel: "Lead, we've got trouble at six."

Wracking the Scimitar into a five-G descending turn, he hit the toggle for the chaff dispenser. A small cloud of aluminum strips filled the air behind him. He switched the radio back to the primary mode. "Don't I know it! Alpha, let's all pop some chaff."

"Alpha Lead, this is Skyhook. We've intercepted opposition radio traffic. One of their FACs is calling in the fighters on Beanbag. They believe it's evacuating senior Ethiopian officers."

"Roger, Skyhook. Launch Charlie and Delta."

"Skyhook commencing launch at zero-five-one-three Zulu."

Through all this, one thought tormented Gus: The missile's target had to be the Antonov! The F-24 had a minimal radar signature, but spinning props would give a big, fat return. Straining his neck, Gus picked up the missile in flight, a white, pencil-like object with a torch eraser, tracing a graphite-smoke trail across the pale blue skirt of the welkin.

Maintaining the turn, he kept the missile in view. The dark streak of propellant smoke developed squiggles of indecision. Alpha Flight's chaff was confusing its radar. The smoke trail curved upward, went arcing over and beyond the Antonov before it self-detonated. That explosion was clearly visible from the troop carrier and must have served as an object lesson. The big multifan nosed over and leveled just above the ground.

Heading back toward Canasta, Gus had multiple targets on the Bird Dog. They were a little high, with only sky for background and well inside the Sparrow launch envelope. He locked on and fired. Alpha Three followed, then Two and Four. They got three kills and a near-miss, easily identified by the nature of the explosions.

The self-destruct function detonated the missile when it sensed a miss. Shrapnel from such a burst could still damage or destroy an aircraft. That surviving bandit headed west, trailing smoke.

"Bravo, let's take on these bandits at twelve. Fire when you have Sparrow lock-on."

Gus could almost hear the chortling in Sam Corwin's voice. After fifteen years, Sam finally had live targets in front of him and was having a ball. Charlie and Delta Flights checked in. Skyhook gave vectors. Gus called a fuel check. Alpha averaged just under two thousand pounds.

The Bird Dog showed four bandits emerging from the clutter of targets near Canasta and heading south. Somebody in the Islamic Front really wanted that troop carrier. Alpha was already too close to lock on and launch another Sparrow. Gus scanned the airspace, picked out tiny, fast-moving dots approaching. They enlarged quickly into deltas with no tails. Mirages. French-built. The most agile in the IF's fighter inventory.

"Good shooting, Bravo. Now let's split the division. Get behind this next bunch for a Sidewinder shot." In the press of combat, Sam had fallen back on Navy terminology.

Gus and Alpha were already at close quarters with the Mirages. Gunfighting range. Closing nearly head-on, Gus called for afterburners and went supersonic. The delta forms passed and went straight up. He watched and held level for three seconds.

The delay had its purpose: When he pulled the Scimitar's nose to the vertical and then beyond, Alpha was below and behind the enemy. He could keep them in sight with relative ease. The IF pilots could only crane their necks or look in their mirrors and hope for a glimpse.

The eight aircraft—four Mirages, four Scimitars— shot upward with choreographic grace. Gus began a slow spiral on a vertical axis. Its track brought him gradually toward the Mirages' six o'clock. "Alpha Three, you can try picking off their second element."

"I'm working on it."

"Ah! Stout fellow."

"Guns, Bravo. Go burner. Let's close and finish 'em off."

Gus passed through twenty thousand. Twenty-five. Still going straight up. The sky at the zenith darkened. At the crux formed by its wings and tail, the Mirage's blue-white afterburner flame was a diamond in an abstract setting displayed against a background of blue-black velvet. Gus found himself closing, the Scimitar outclimbing the Mirage. He pulled the power back to minimum burner and waited.

Slowly, the cruciform silhouette changed to a delta form against a blue-black sky as the lead Mirage came over inverted above thirty thousand. Foreshortened at first, the delta grew at one corner, revealing the needle nose and the canopy. The pitiless, impersonal glow of the Scimitar's gunsight reticle hovered over it.

That pilot would be searching the air ahead and below for the Scimitars. With a fleeting wonder if his adversary had a moment to be startled, Gus touched the trigger.

"Bravo Lead, hard starboard. Bandits four o'clock."

B. Michelaard

The thin atmosphere at this altitude would not support billowing flame or brilliant explosions. The Mirage disintegrated slowly, in a long trail of oily smoke. It got the attention of the three remaining pilots as they rolled upright. One of them let it absorb him a little too long. Alpha Three's gun spat, and then there were only two.

Those two flipped inverted and dove away, still in afterburner. Supersonic, they headed west for the Sudanese border. Psychologically, they had their tails between their legs and were not worth pursuing.

"Bravo Two, this one's yours if you're inside—"

"Got 'im, Lead. Check eight o'clock low for—"

"Delta Three, hold fire till that bandit pulls up. Stray rounds could hit the friendlies on the ground."

"Alpha Lead, this is Skyhook. Looks like more bandits going after Beanbag. Data on your Bird Dog." The figures and indicators popped up on the glass like a new video page on a computer screen. It showed Beanbag at about thirty miles and the bandits in pursuit at around twenty.

He took up a heading to close on Beanbag, lowered the nose, and called for afterburners.

"Charlie Lead, you got that pair at two o'clock low?"

"Lead has 'em, but they look like they're running."

Gus watched the rapid increase in Mach number—1.5, Mach 2, 2.5. From there it advanced more slowly—2.6, 2.7, 2.75. A yellow caution light came on. The major drawback with the synthetic airframe was its lower thermal tolerance. The leading edges were stainless steel, but the skin would distort if it got too hot from air friction. The engine inlet temps could also get too high, risking interference between the compressor's rotor and stator blades. He called for burners out and moved the throttles out of detent. The light went out as the Mach number settled back to 2.4. It declined further as they penetrated the denser levels of the atmosphere.

The Bird Dog showed two bandits now about five

miles behind Beanbag and closing, two more at five-and-a-half-to-six miles. Gus mashed the transmitter button: "Alpha Three, Second Element deal with that pair behind." Double mike click in response.

Again, he was close to the Antonov before he picked up its desert camouflage. The four bandits, each his old friend the MiG-21, were now only a mile behind Beanbag. Evidently these were the early version, with no radar-guided missiles. He had a Sparrow lock-on, but withheld fire. Too much chance it would jump from that small MiG to the big, fat return of the Antonov's whirling props. And the Sidewinder was out of its envelope.

Close and do it the old-fashioned way. With guns. "Alpha Two, guns. Lets one-on-one this leading pair." Again the responding clicks.

The slender fuselage of the MiG-21, with its delta wing and smaller delta tail, was a fitting ghost against the pale dun color of the Eritrean landscape. Gus moved the glowing, baleful eye of the gunsight to hover over it.

The 20mm shells seemed to drive it right into the earth. It spread a trail of flame and small shards for at least a mile over the desert. The other MiG instantly went into a vertical pull-up. Alpha Two fired, and flashes confirmed impacts on the metal skin. The MiG trailed smoke, continued its pull-up, and headed away toward Sudan.

"Heads up, Alpha Lead! One of these bandits just fired a heat-seeker!"

Gus rolled, corkscrewing into a thirty-degree dive, plugged in the afterburners. "Stay clear, Alpha Two."

Michelle was aboard that Antonov, and the missile's infrared sensor was homing on one of its three operating turboprops. He had to decoy that missile with something even hotter—the F-24's afterburners.

He dipped in behind the Antonov, then pulled up to the left. "Alpha Lead, that heater's chasing you now!" Gus was too busy to reply. He killed both burners, pulled the throttles back to idle, and toggled a thermite flare. It was an infrared source a heat-seeking missile couldn't ignore.

Twisting his neck, he looked back, saw the smoke trail of the missile diverging where the Scimitar had turned. It had taken the bait and was chasing the flare.

An instant's brilliant flash enveloped him. He felt a jolt. The heater had sensed a miss and self-detonated.

His first clue that something was wrong was smoke in the cockpit. Then red lights on the panel and a warning screech in his earphones.

Looking back, he saw a smoke trail. He was hit.

Chapter Fifteen

Struggling to keep her footing in the fetid, heaving, rock-and-rolling confines of the aircraft, Michelle had some wry thoughts on the perks and advantages being a disciple of Hypocrites. Not to mention the thrill of being a military target. She had just persuaded the pilot to climb into smoother air when a missile exploded nearby. The aircraft went into a steep dive, and the flight thereafter felt like shooting rapids in a dinghy.

By doing emergency surgery, she had missed the train for Massawa. When she called Colonel X to explain, he sounded like a man who'd won either the lottery or some sort of reprieve. Then he practically shanghaied her aboard this noisy, vibrating conveyance. Not that she wasn't glad to be out of Asmara by any means. Hearing what had happened to the train she would have been on nearly gave her the shakes. She had plopped the swollen appendix she'd excised into a jar of alcohol and brought it with her. She figured it would make a great conversa-

167

tion piece when she told people, "That thing saved my life."

When the copilot had beckoned her forward, she'd been curious. When he wanted to know if she was Doctor Michelle St. Clair, she was even more curious. He explained that the American pilot leading their fighter escort had wanted to know.

Which told her it could only be Gus.

As for this strange, improbable contact, her emotions were mixed. Just knowing he was nearby gave her a rush. Knowing he was doing battle with the Islamic Front set iron butterflies loose in her stomach.

Before they'd left Washington, they had, for valid official reasons, been less than candid. So these small, necessary perfidies gave their odd meeting in this remote war zone a touch of comic opera. Neither had grounds to point a finger. The best they might do was enjoy a laugh.

The flight crew was voluble in their praise of the American fighters: Two days before they had carried airborne troops for the assault to retake the airfield at Asmara. They were all concerned about having no escort. Suddenly, a pair of these same strange-looking fighters had seemed to materialize right out of the air and put on a display. Then this same American leader told them to circle the formation near the coast while he and his pilots cleared the air of the enemy.

And they did. Shot down MiGs in such numbers that the rest fled. The paratroops had jumped without an enemy aircraft in sight. The Ethiopians spoke of Gus and his pilots with a kind of awe.

The copilot was again summoning her. Annoyed, she groped and stumbled her way forward. Grinning, he stepped out and pointed out one of the side windows. Here, he said, was her chance to see a stricken enemy going down.

That was not her idea of amusement nor any reason to leave her patients. At first she saw only a thin smoke trail etched across the sky by an unseen source. Just for a moment there was a glint from a faint, silvery form that curved away and disappeared. She smiled her insincere thanks and went back to her work.

"Alpha Lead, you're hit! Trailing smoke. Looks like the starboard engine."

"You're right. It is." Gus had already stop-cocked that throttle and closed the fuel cutoff valve. That put out the warning lights and eased the vibration. The tailpipe temperature dropped from the red zone to the bottom of the scale. Airflow kept the shaft spinning, so some vibration persisted.

The smoke trail thinned and disappeared. Alpha Two came in close and looked him over. The external damage didn't seem too bad. Gus saw no real problems with recovery. They had worked out emergency procedures during training over the North Atlantic.

Then both the control and utility hydraulic pressures began falling off. Alpha Two confirmed a trickle of red fluid. Which gave a whole new tilt to the pinball machine. Jimmy Durante's famous line came to mind: What a revoltin' development!

With the loss of hydraulic fluid, the breaks could fail. The F-24's manual backup to its hydraulic fly-by-wire control system was fine for hitting a concrete runway two hundred feet wide or so and several thousand in length. But the inputs were too sluggish for the eye-of-the-needle precision needed to land aboard Skyhook. And unlike seaborne carriers, the airship was neither built to withstand crashes nor equipped to deal with the result. Pegasus doctrine was to sacrifice airplanes rather than accept a risk to Skyhook. Hank Borland had veto power over any attempt to recover a damaged aircraft. But Gus was not about to put Hank in that position.

The doctrine called for ejection and pickup by the rescue helicopter. But to be safe, he would have to eject either inside the perimeter at Asmara or somewhere out at sea. If he chose the sea, he and the copter would still need air cover, which would take aircraft off the main effort. And all that activity could lead Islamic Front pilots much too close to Skyhook.

Neither did he like the idea of throwing away an aircraft. With a new engine and some minor repairs, this bird would be good as new. The F-24 might be an economy model and the "toy airplane," but its price tag was still several times the annual income of most taxpayers.

There was an alternative—a landing in Ethiopia. He figured he had just enough fuel to reach Addis Ababa, and explained to Skyhook what he had in mind. Alpha Two moved in to accompany him. Gus waved him off, and finally had to use the only instrument that could sever the bond between leader and wingman—a direct order.

Skyhook got weather information: Addis Ababa had scattered cloud; nothing threatening en route. Landing permission and clearance were another matter. Negotiations went on over H-F single sideband. He gathered it involved Mother Hen and the U.S. embassy in Addis Ababa.

Meanwhile, he was leaving the sands and salt flats of the Danakil desert behind. The jagged horizon of the central highlands loomed ahead. In ten minutes, he had passed his point of no return and topped out near 35,000. That was optimum for the Scimitar on one engine. Spread below, the mountains of central Ethiopia looked like a rumpled GI blanket left out in the weather.

Finally Skyhook came back with a frequency on which to contact Ethiopian air traffic control.

When he made contact, he was told he was approved for landing at an Ethiopian Air Force base some twenty miles southeast of the capital. The name sounded like "Hada Mayda." The spelling turned out to be Harar Mieda.

On one of the side control panels was a small alphanumeric pad like a phone console. He punched in Harar Mieda, and a standard diagram of the letdown and instrument-approach pattern for jet aircraft appeared on the radar screen. This was another feature Gus had invented and Waring Aircraft had built into the Scimitar. The diagram showed the runway at "Hada Mayda" was One-Six-Three-Four—twelve-thousand feet long by three hundred feet wide.

When he retarded the throttle for a long, gliding descent, the fuel gauge read about 250 pounds. Though hydrogen had twice the specific energy of JP, there was a loss due to boil-off, and this increased as the tanks emptied. So he had the useful equivalent of about four hundred pounds of JP.

His continued monitoring of the gauge showed the fuel quantity dropping faster than the engine was burning it. There was a leak somewhere. A quick calculation told him he would run out of fuel before he ran out of distance to fly. He would not make "Hada Mayda."

When he shared this information with Ethiopian ATC, silence followed.

The seconds ticked by while the fuel quantity dropped.

Meanwhile, he tuned in the VOR station at Bole International, the airport serving Addis Ababa. The number-two needle on the ID-250 showed it was close to the nose.

The gauge showed 125 pounds when the voice from ATC asked for his aircraft tail number.

"Six-one-niner."

"Very well. You are designated Flight Six-One-Niner. You will use only that identifier. Please squawk one for ID." Gus flicked on the transponder, which was already in mode 1. "Six-One-Niner, you are cleared for emergency VFR descent for landing at Bole International. Contact Bole approach control at ten miles on the zero-one-zero radial. You may expect to land out of straight-in approach."

From the low cone of the VOR, he was turned over to the tower and cleared straight in. With the runway directly over the nose, he put the gear handle down, got two green and one unsafe. The fuel gauge showed just under one hundred pounds. Not enough for a go-around.

Somebody in the tower had binoculars on him. An edgy voice told him the right main was not fully extended. "Roger, tower. I'm about to deal with that." He pulled the emergency lever. Emergency extension was a one-shot deal, a high-pressure air reservoir. Once used, it precluded retraction. He had the fleeting thought they should only do so well with statements by politicians.

The right main locked into place. When he was actually on the ground and could no longer be waived off, he explained that he had hot guns and live missiles aboard. The tower said yes, they were aware of that, and handed him over to ground control.

He was met by two men in a "Follow Me" vehicle like those used on U.S. bases. It led him away from the main terminal to what appeared to be a military auxiliary on the opposite side.

The jeep led him to a hardstand, where one of the men jumped out and gave hand signals for parking. As soon as he stop-cocked the throttle, the jeep and its occupants departed.

Placing his hard hat on the bow of the windscreen, he climbed out and stretched the kinks out of his muscles. Then he opened the armament compartments, de-armed the cannon, and safetied the missiles. Finally, he went around surveying the damage. The Scimitar sat there bleeding oil and hydraulic fluid and looking resentful.

He got out of his G-suit and deposited both it and the pistol and shoulder harness in the cockpit. Along with all his checklists and charts. After that, he was left to twiddle his thumbs. Meanwhile, among the aircraft landing was a four-engine Antonov in desert camouflage.

Finally a military truck approached—olive drab, with

the usual canvas canopy over the cargo bed. An officer climbed down from beside the driver, saluted, and introduced himself as Major Something-or-other. Gus returned the salute and then shook hands, hoping he wouldn't have to pronounce the name, much less remember it.

"My regrets, Colonel, for this leperlike isolation," said the major in very clear English. Men in fatigue uniform draped what turned out to be a canvas field tent over the aircraft. "These precautions are essentially political. And temporary. Just now, my government prefers not to advertise the presence of American combat aircraft."

"No problem, Major."

"Ah, I take it your armament is all safetied?"

"Entirely."

"Then perhaps you should put your helmet there inside and close up. Keep the rain out, you know. And also it—"

Gus raised a hand. "I quite understand." The helmet not only had a U.S. emblem, but a distinctive shape. He rested it over the control stick and closed the canopy.

The major gestured. "Hop in then. Someone from your embassy should be here by now." He waved the enlisted driver into the rear and took the wheel himself. "These amazing feats at Asmara we've been hearing about. They're all done with this little aircraft?"

"Plus some smoke and mirrors."

The major nodded and smiled understanding.

Parked discreetly in the shadows near the terminal was a black, four-door Lincoln with international plates. The major dropped him there.

Not far away, ambulances and other vehicles were gathered around that Antonov he had seen landing. Gus noted stretchers being off-loaded. He thanked the major, then climbed down from the truck and turned to meet the welcoming delegation.

Delegation—a colonel plus a driver—was an overstatement. The colonel wore a Brooks Brothers suit and

173

introduced himself as Dana Hatcher, Air Attaché. The grade, Gus knew, went with the job.

They shook hands and chatted. "You won't remember me," he said, "but we shook hands once before. I was a student at the War College, and you were a guest speaker."

"Gus! *Gus!* GUS!" The voice began at *fortissimo* and rose to fire-alarm. But it was not the volume that made him snap his head around.

She was running toward him, looking disheveled. Her raven-dark hair was matted. She wore a badly stained medical smock over grubby, ill-fitting fatigues. He ran to meet her. When they were close, he could see smudges on her face, the streaks left by sweat.

And she was still the world's most beautiful creature.

Five feet away, she suddenly became self-conscious. Put one hand nervously to her face and held the other out to stop him. "Oh, no. Don't. I . . . I'm a mess." He ignored her, closed the gap, and reached for her. She accepted the inevitable and flung herself against him. He tightened his embrace till her ribs creaked from the strain. Her lips brought the taste of salt and dust.

The objective part of him said she must have gone for days without a bath. She also reeked of surgery done under conditions like those he had seen over twenty years ago in North Vietnam. It recalled meat markets that failed to get the crevices clean.

All that was mere backdrop. This was his woman. The one for whom he had decoyed that missile and would do the same again without a second thought.

She had her head on his shoulder and was fighting back tears.

In an obscure perch atop a warehouse building, a cameraman focused his lens on them and clicked several frames. He was annoyed at missing the landing of the strange

American fighter. By the time he could get here, it was out of sight, parked in the distant military section.

Yet he had no doubt it was American. The pilot had been brought in to the terminal in a truck driven by an Ethiopian officer and was met by a car from the U.S. embassy. A telephoto lens captured the details of the U.S. Air Force flying suit.

After that, the cameraman had turned a camcorder on the transport, with its wounded from Asmara. When the woman, apparently a nurse or doctor, broke into a run, his impulses said to follow her with the lens. That she led him back to the colonel was a piece of luck that just might make up for getting no shots of the aircraft.

Under the dirt and sweat from the battle zone was a dusky beauty. Might she be American too? In any case, it was clear they were lovers. With the long lens of the still camera, he caught them mouth-to-mouth. He had a nose for intrigue. Who could tell where this might lead? Or what someone might pay him?

Chapter Sixteen

Gus spent the night as a prisoner of the U.S. Embassy. It wasn't stated in so many words, but he was being sequestered from the fourth estate and the diplomatic corps.

Next day, a giant C-5 landed. The damaged F-24 was loaded aboard, and the C-5 departed, all in less than an hour. Gus returned to the airship in a T-44 Merganser. When he arrived on the bridge, Hank Borland handed him a telex sheet. "From Mother Hen." The message said the USS *Gettysburg*, CVA-99, with screening vessels, was en route from the Straits of Taiwan. Call sign Boxcar. When it cleared the Bab el Mandeb and crossed latitude 13 degrees North, the skipper would make radio contact. At that time, Operation Sand Bar would terminate.

There was no question of sharing the operation. And not only because of security. The F-24's avionics were made to work with each other and Skyhook. To the Scimitar's ITD, Navy F-14's and FA-18's or Air Force F-15's and F-16's would all look just like MiGs. In time, parts of the system

176

might be retrofitted into other aircraft, enough to make them compatible. But right now it was unique to Skyhook and the F-24.

For three more weeks, they flew combat air patrols over the battle zone. Contacts with Islamic Front fighters dwindled.

With loss of dominance in the air, the IF was driven out of artillery range of Asmara and the railroad link to Massawa. The Ethiopians set about repairing the rails.

It was 1708 Zulu—2008 local—when those on the bridge heard a voice from the speaker of the HF single sideband liaison set. "Skyhook, this is Boxcar."

Hank Borland picked up the mike himself. "Boxcar, Skyhook reading you five-square."

"Roger." There was a pause. "That you, Hank?"

"That's me, Porky. You keeping a taut ship?"

"Best I can, Hank." Again a pause. "Just where the hell are you?"

"Only God and I are allowed to know that, Porky." He paused. "Think you're ready to take over here?"

"We'll give it our best shot. You leaving?"

"Affirmative. We've pretty well pacified the locals. Word from the Wheel House is the second team should be able to handle it from here on." Hank was clearly enjoying ribbing his classmate and fellow skipper.

Sam Corwin said, "Hey, that's my old ship."

Borland transmitted, "Boxcar, there's somebody here says he knows you." He handed the mike to Sam.

"Boxcar, this is Super Sam. Anyone handy from VF-880?"

Again a pause. "That you, Sam?"

"Sure is, Harley. Say, you know what's better than a Tomcat?"

"Nothing."

"There is now. I got three scalps in one day. Five all told. Hey, I'm ace. Eat your heart out, gang."

* * *

It was mid-morning when the T-44 with Gus and Hank aboard arrived at Andrews. Hank had called home through a phone patch from the cockpit, so Melanie was there to pick him up. Gus got a staff car and driver to take him to Michelle's condo. He let himself in, put his clothing in the closet and a pitcher of martinis in the freezer. Then he fired up the Countache, drove to the hospital, and phoned her from the lobby. She answered the page from somewhere upstairs. "Hi," he said.

"Gus! Where the hell—?"

"Right down in the lobby. Can I see you?"

"O-o-h-h . . ." It was a groan of disappointment. "I'm just about to scrub. A few more minutes and I couldn't even have taken the call. Gus, darling, I wish I could've known."

"It's okay. I'll see you this evening. I should have a while here."

"Beautiful! You have your key?"

"Sure."

"Unless I call, I'll see you by six at the latest. Put your shoes under the bed and some martinis in the freezer. Gotta go now. Kiss, kiss."

"Same to you, lady." He hung up, smiling.

The sky was overcast, but the breeze off the Potomac was mild, the breath of spring. He locked up the Countache, set the alarms, then walked into Mother Hen Ops.

Hank was already there, gave him a knowing look, and said, "Better wipe that cream off your whiskers, Pussycat."

General Chip Borland arrived. "I've managed to persuade the Joint Chiefs that the senior members of the Joint Staff need to know about Pegasus. So you'll be briefing various and sundry of us over the next few days." Before he left, Chip said, "Oh, by the way. Dinner at the house tomorrow. Both of you. Informal. Drinks at seven."

Gus looked pained. Hank stepped in to help. "Gus has a fiancée here and doesn't get to see much of her."

"Bring her," said Chip. "We'll be glad to get to know her."

Gus returned to the condo a little after five, excited at the possibility that Mike might be there. But her Laser was not in the garage.

He had just stepped into the shower when he heard the automatic mechanism open and then close the garage door. He slid the glass door of the shower stall aside and stuck his head out. Her footsteps were approaching. "Gus?"

"I'm hiding," he said in a falsetto.

"If I find you, I'll ravish your tender white body." He heard her shoes fall, the rustle of her clothes coming off.

Again the falsetto: "I'm hiding. In the shower."

Moments later, nude and enthralling, she joined him. They hugged and kissed under the hot needle-spray; indulged in a steamy, soapy, slithery orgy of affection. The caress of his hands as he lathered her all over was his homage to the splendor of her figure.

"Now that we've integrated the shower," she said, "let's go integrate the mattress." This facetious expression—that they were "integrating" whatever they occupied together—was one of their ways of ridiculing racial distinctions.

Barely controlling their mutual frenzy, they dried each other. With one vigorous movement, she threw the bedclothes aside. Her golden brown perfection against the pale linen made his breath catch as she drew him down beside her.

Murmuring endearments between kisses, making small, almost incoherent sounds of ecstasy, they writhed and entwined. Soon they crossed the threshold of that special preserve of lovers everywhere.

For them, loving was a deliberate affirmation of what they brought to each other, never undertaken lightly nor terminated abruptly. The descent from the magic cresting of passion was gradual, a path they traveled together, with stops at shrines along the way. It took some time before they could speak at all, and more yet till they could talk about the real world, outside the scope of their embrace.

Later, he turned so his weight was no longer on either her or his elbows. She followed, saying, "Careful you don't break the connection, love. This ain't Ma Bell you're in bed with."

"Nobody appreciates that better than I do." He told her about the invitation he had accepted for both of them. "I hope you don't mind."

"Mind? Of course I mind. I want you all to myself for all the time you've got. But I know when you belong to Uncle Sam, even your off-duty time isn't your own. Anyway, I'll be glad to be there with you." She turned those tigress eyes on him. "But if any other woman so much as flutters her eyelids at you . . ." She made a low, growling sound.

Later yet, she rose, stepped into those gold-lacquered slippers, and wearing nothing but a smile, started for the kitchen. "I hope you made the martinis." He put on a robe and followed her.

She skewered olives and poured. The freezer had given the two stemmed glasses a coating of frost and brought the blend of gin and vermouth down to that delicious state where it poured like syrup and yielded only a tender caress on the taste buds.

She often sat around, or even did housework, in the buff. He let his gaze slide over her, and smiled. "You know, if you back into something either hot or sharp like that, it could be awkward to treat your own backside. Not to mention a bee sting or snakebite."

She raised an eyebrow along with her cocktail glass and showed a faint, sly smile as she sipped. "Might show who my real friends are."

For generations, the city of Toronto had been known as a sinkhole of social torpor and middle-class propriety.

Traveling men called it "Hogtown" and made jokes about its non-existent nightlife. And Yorkville was its most staid and proper district, home to the well-to-do. By mid-century, however, Yorkville had become drab and even a little seedy.

Beginning in the sixties, though, Toronto underwent a metamorphosis into what some proclaimed was the most livable metropolis in North America. And Yorkville became its showcase. Once-elegant town houses were restored and modernized while retaining their antique charm. Along York and Cumberland Streets, small, intimate restaurants of diverse ethnicity sprang up cheek-by-jowl with boutiques and art galleries of trendy persuasion. Craft centers and ethnic food stores nestled up to purveyors of exotic wares from around the world.

So it was a natural location for Audrey Prowther's Toronto studio. She had bought a sturdy old town house and hired an architect to adapt it to her needs. The remodeled version added an atelier with north-facing skylight. The cellar was fitted out with a kiln for firing ceramics and facilities for both acetylene and electric-arc welding.

With all this, she needed a mortgage. Through the offices of Etienne Alvarado, a bank in Singapore offered a very low interest rate but with attachments: She had to accommodate certain activities having nothing to do with figures on canvas or in clay or marble or metal. Basically, she spent every other month "in residence." But sometimes when she was not here, others were.

So, on an evening when Toronto was hit by an uncommonly heavy snowfall for March, a group of these others was gathering. Wordless, they arrived through the rear entrance, stamping the snow off their feet. She met them at the door and directed them to the elevator.

They assembled in the atelier, which took up the whole of the upper level. The flooring was hardwood parquet with an oiled finish. The sloping expanse of glass skylight was closed off now by a tight-fitting velvet draw. She taught there; so there were worktables with coarse muslin draped over sculptures in progress. Tools and equipment were neatly racked. Grouped in one corner were easels holding covered canvases.

Classroom-type desks with writing arms accommodated the visitors. Alvarado—or *El Jefe*—known to most of those present only as Monitor, was the first to step up to the lectern and speak.

"We're here for two reasons. Because there's an urgent problem of intelligence to be solved and because we suddenly have available an expert to help direct our efforts in that area. He prefers to be known as Comrade Lincoln. So at this point I'll turn the floor over to him."

The man called Comrade Lincoln rose and stubbed out his acrid-smelling cigarette. Audrey found it interesting that he adhered to the Marxist form of address. There was a time when she did too. Not merely the forms but the doctrine. Then Marxism had crumbled beneath reality.

No longer Red but with a temperament unable to fully embrace capitalism, she had shifted to "Green." She hoped to establish a genuine, politically potent Green Party in the U.S. This man they knew as Monitor had a doctrine called "Centralism" that seemed to be close to the Green view.

Comrade Lincoln did not glower or frown, yet conveyed an air of puritanical judgment. His thin-lipped mien presumed resistance, dismissed humor. Twenty years ago there had been a lot of talk about giving Marxism a human face. His was the face of Marxism as she had come to know and finally despise it. John Calvin and Cotton Mather had lived before the camera appeared, and she had never seen a portrait of either. But each, she fancied, must have looked something like this Comrade Lincoln.

He paused and paced a few steps. "It would be an advantage to our cause if the newly discovered oil deposits of the Red Sea area could be kept under Arab control. That seemed assured until the Americans somehow came to the aid of the present Ethiopian regime. Eventually, of course, all countries within the Centralist geographic band must be brought into our coalition. But that's another matter."

He covered the recent events in Eritrea. "Those on the scene have speculated that the Americans may have had a submarine aircraft carrier in the Red Sea. If so, the Pentagon managed to build, test, and deploy such a vessel without even the knowledge of most members of Congress. I can say that because we have agents on the staff of many of those members. Whatever the case, if we are to avoid further setbacks like this, we must discover just what technology they used."

He paused and simply stared at them for some seconds. "You will be well aware that this meeting violates various principles of espionage as you've learned and practiced it, some of you for decades. We in the Centralist leadership have decided to take this approach because the situation is both very urgent and very different from the former days of the East-West conflict."

Monitor rose and spoke again briefly. Each of the others, except Audrey, was called to a private interview with Comrade Lincoln. They were all gone by about midnight.

While she went around securing the doors and setting the alarms—even Yorkville was no longer immune to serious crime—she found herself thinking about Dwayne, in Albany. With spring approaching, she pictured the two of them strolling hand-in-hand amid dogwood and apple blossoms.

He had touched something very deep in her psyche with a tender magic she had thought was no longer possible. Recalling those nights together in the Village made her shiver with both pleasure and frustration. She considered phoning him, but decided against it. It would almost certainly wake him up. His sleep-clouded voice would only evoke their nights together and add to her frustration.

Chapter Seventeen

When the Soviet Union dissolved, the KGB too left the stage of history. The new Commonwealth spy agencies had to cede top billing and accept character roles in the drama of international intrigue. Meanwhile, the CIA and other Western agencies found themselves crossing the spoor of a new and unknown contestant in the game.

At Langley, this new hand at the table was assigned the code name Albigensian. A task force—a term used to avoid "committee"—was set up to deal with the problem of limning out this shadowy new presence.

The task force was headed by Milton Forrester, a senior expert in counterespionage on the D-Ops staff. His number two was Lafayette Briggs. Each had earned his cloak and dagger in some of the more colorful scuffles of the Cold War.

Since Canada had always afforded both easy entry into the U.S. and an easy base for scrutiny of U.S. affairs, the task force sent agents to Canada to take notes. Especially for shady foreign arrivals at Canadian air terminals.

In charge of this Canadian operation was one named Ingraham. By way of explaining why he had called them together, he said, "I have some shots here taken by our man in Toronto." The lights dimmed, and an image in color appeared on the large screen in front.

It was a scene of passengers exiting an Air Canada boarding ramp. Ingraham used the projector's special features to enlarge and reframe till one face nearly filled the screen and the detail began to blur in the grain of the film. Then he backed off a little. It was the next best thing to a shot with a telephoto lens. "And," he said as he adjusted the focus and the face took on a clear image, "up jumped the Devil."

Forrester and Briggs each said, "Sonofabitch!"

The face was the sort not to be forgotten, a visage where intelligence mingled with grim intensity. Here they saw a man who would do nothing by halves. The eyes were pale blue beneath a high, sloping forehead. The cheeks were hollow, the nose and facial bones prominent. The mouth was a bloodless, judgmental slash.

The eyebrows and neatly trimmed hair were whitened with age, but had the residual amber tint of the once-blond. He was obviously not young, yet he had that look of enduring, indefinite age that can mislead by as much as twenty years. He was above medium height, with a slender, wiry build. He wore a plain, well-fitted suit of dark material, and no hat.

"I'll be damned," said Forrester in a tone of wonder. "This has to be the first sighting in years. I wasn't even sure he was still alive." He and Briggs moved closer, as if to convince themselves what they were seeing was real. "But that's him, all right. May be the first time he's set foot on this continent in . . . what? Over forty years?"

"So just who the hell is he?" asked one of the younger men seated at the table. "Before my time, I guess."

"Rodney Lund," said Forrester. "And there was a time when all of us in D-Ops plus all of J. Edgar's troops were haunted by that face. I think there's still a federal warrant open on him."

"Hm-m-m, Lund . . . Wasn't he involved in the Rosenberg case?"

"That was just the tip of the iceberg. Lafe here or I, either one, could give you chapter and verse on this bastard."

"I have his file here," said Ingraham.

"I don't need a file to enlighten these youngsters," said Forrester. He paced, rubbing his palms together. "Rodney Lund." His tone conveyed a strange mixture of animosity and respect. "Alias Roland Lundberg, alias Robert Lincoln, alias Raoul Levy, alias at least half a dozen more. Born Chicago, November 1919, third of five children of Ragnar and Doris Lund.

"The father, Ragnar Lund, was brought to this country from Trondheim as a child. Served honorably in War One, was wounded and decorated in France. During the twenties, he became a sort of Joe Hill of the labor movement. Died 1933 at age forty-six. Partly from exposure to mustard gas on the Western Front. To sum up, he was a hardworking, dedicated social democrat.

"The mother, née Doris Hegstrom of Duluth, was a raging Marxist termagant. Rodney and his sister Helga were the only two of five Lund children to survive into adulthood. The mother dragged them around the country pursuing her work in what was called the Movement. So they had a very spotted formal schooling. And though he later came to speak and write very skillfully in several languages, Lund never got a high school diploma.

"In 1937, he was a volunteer with the Lincoln Brigade in the Spanish Civil War. Didn't show up in the States again till '46. His story was that he'd been in Franco's jails. We later discovered he spent War Two spying for the Soviets.

"Back in the States, he occupied himself mainly with building espionage cells in defense-sensitive industries and the scientific departments of universities doing classified research. For a long time, the FBI couldn't lay a finger on him. Then he went to a meeting with some leading Communist figures, including Gerhardt Eisler. One of those present was Matt Cvetic, a deep-cover plant for the Bureau. Lund was indicted on Cvetic's testimony, but skipped the country before he could be picked up. His name did come up again during the Rosenberg trial.

"He spent some time in Moscow or at least in Russia, then worked in Europe. Later he was sent to China as KGB liaison. When the grand schism came, the break between Moscow and Beijing, he denounced the Khrushchev regime as revisionist and threw in with Mao. After that, he became a kind of roving spymaster for Red China.

"He had grown up speaking German and Norwegian as well as English. During his travels, he became fluent in French, Spanish, Russian, Ukrainian, Swahili, and two major dialects of Chinese."

Ingraham pressed a button and threw a new image on the screen. "This is his mug shot taken by C. and I. when he arrived back in the States in '46. There's a gap of over fifty years between this and the one from Toronto, but you can see it's the same individual. Amazing, but he's over eighty now and still active."

Briggs smiled and looked over his glasses at them. "Even the most careful and experienced agent can be tripped up by his idiosyncrasies. Lund despised hats as a symbol of the bourgeois power structure. And sure enough he shows up in Toronto without a hat. Otherwise, we might not have seen the face well enough to recognize him."

Ingraham brought up a series of photos of Lund in city street scenes. "Santiago, Chile, '63. Mexico City, '65. Tokyo, '68. Santiago again, '71. Caracas, '75. Dar Es Salaam, '77. Lorenzo Marques, '78. Tananarive, '79."

"What was his cover when he operated here after War Two?"

"Oh, journalism, writing, lecturing. The Soviets fixed him up with a degree from Moscow University. He and his wife published and edited little left-slanted magazines for intellectuals. He also wrote for mainstream periodicals under various aliases."

A new slide appeared, a black and white photo of a slender, dark-haired Semitic beauty of severe dress and grooming. She stood at a lectern, and her only visible jewelry was a wedding band on the hand she had raised in gesture. Her hair was drawn back into a roll.

"Leah Lund," said Briggs. "Born Leah Halperin, New York City, August 1918. One of six children of a cantor in a Brooklyn synagogue. Graduate of CCNY, where she had a scholarship. Party member from the thirties. She met Lund in Spain, where she was supposedly a nurse and ambulance driver. After his escape to Moscow, she slipped over to Canada and joined him. This is the only picture of her beyond her college days."

"And she went to China with him?"

"At the time of Nixon's trip to China, she was interviewed in Beijing by an American journalist," said Forrester. "She was ailing then, and unconfirmed reports have it she died around 1980.

"We pretty well knew that Lund broke with the Red Chinese leadership over the purge of what was called the Gang of Four. This is our first hard evidence that he survived. It's also a lucky break. If he's involved in Albigensian, that answers the question of their ideology."

"How can you be sure?"

Briggs switched off the projector and ran a hand through his shock of stiff, ash-white hair. "Besides being an intelligence pro, Rodney Lund is an archetype of an international class dedicated to a Marxist world order. In the thirties, they swarmed to Moscow. With Khrushchev's reforms, they defected to Mao and Beijing. Now the survivors are taking their services elsewhere.

But where is elsewhere? Who's looking to take over where Lenin and Stalin and Mao left off?"

"How do I look?" Michelle turned from the bedroom mirror wearing only the two small diamonds she had just fastened through her ears.

Gus smiled. "Great but not exactly dressed for a party. I'm afraid the others don't know you that well."

"Well, if you think they're apt to be stuffy . . ." She got out lingerie.

Ready, she wore a form-fitting sheath of satin-silk brocade. It was silver-gray with a faint purplish undercaste that showed up in the folds and highlights. Gus remarked on how well it complemented her skin color.

They took the Chrysler. On the way, he told what he could about Chip and Hank and where they fit into his own work. Beneath the talk, he mulled over his anxiety: Mike was a late entry on the guest list, and hostesses were not fond of that kind of change. Chip Borland might have caught some domestic flak. Then there was the color thing. Just possibly, everyone was in for a shock. Not to mention an unpleasant evening.

Chip Borland lived in Montgomery County, near Chevy Chase, in an area of broad, tree-shaded streets, lush green lawns, and elegant houses.

Consuela Borland was a pleasant surprise. Slender and rather dark-skinned herself, she had Spanish-Carib features and a mass of raven-black hair done up in elegant waves. Her ankle-length, flowery-pattern gown hugged a figure that was definitely worth hugging.

She introduced herself as Connie, immediately exclaimed over Mike's dress, put an arm around her waist, and led the way to a patio at the rear. The two of the of them went on and on over each other's personal decor.

The patio, a twenty-foot-square of mortared flag-

189

stones, had the usual outdoor furniture plus a wet bar. It was lit by carriage lamps on seven-foot poles plus some mushroom-shaped fixtures at about thigh level that cast their light downward. Gus found the ambiance delightful.

In one corner, a steel-drum cooker emitted wisps of smoke and delicious smells. A long table was set up alfresco with eight places. Backyard cookouts in March were Greater Washington's compensation for being like a Turkish bath for three months in summer.

Connie made introductions: The Cashpools, Dan and Rhoda, looked to be in their fifties. Another pair, Lieutenant Commander Norman Lister and a Miss Leda Sandoval, were thirtysomething. Lister was a Navy physician, and "Miz" Sandoval taught English at a local junior college. Connie poured drinks. Mike struck up a line of shop talk with Lister.

Beside Levantine features, Leda Sandoval had an air of both serenity and promise. Her skin was a rich olive, her hair dark, thick, and lustrous. Lister was tall and fair-haired and tended to view the world with a knowing smirk. Gus wondered idly if he could smirk his way to first base with Leda Sandoval.

He realized she would have been invited originally to pair with him and balance the guest list. When it turned out he was bringing Mike, Lister was called on to balance the list the other way. List to starboard, list to port, corrected by Lister. He had no doubt felt the arm of the social press gang. The influence wives of general and flag ranks could exert over bachelor officers was nothing like what it once was, but it still existed.

Dan Cashpool was an engineer involved with government contracts. Lean and white-haired, with a bony face and lively blue eyes, he had a sense of humor that reduced everything to droll essentials. In a play on his own name, he called himself "Money-Puddle." "At least that's my wife's view. A bottomless well of money that will rise and engulf her if it isn't spent quickly."

Mike was telling Lister about a medical symposium to be held in Tokyo. Chinese surgeons had agreed to demonstrate the use of acupuncture in various operations. "I've been trying to get my hospital to send me, but not with much success so far. Connie, this daiquiri is delicious."

"Oh, thanks. Here, let me pour you some more. It's sort of my specialty, since I grew up with it."

"You're from Puerto Rico then?" said Gus.

"No. I was born in Cuba. My family fled when the bearded bastard took over. I was just sixteen." She smiled and gave her hair an overdone stroke. "Do you think I look my age?"

"I'd say you look ravishing for any age." He gave his eyelids an exaggerated flutter. "Of course when it comes to women, I'm an innocent. Not much good at judging age or anything else."

Leda Sandoval gave him a cool, appraising smile. "Colonel, my impression is that you're as innocent of women as a shark is of biting. I rather imagine you have a number of well-woven lines on which you invite us to hang our undies."

"Not anymore, he doesn't," said Mike with a sly smile.

Dinner was an *asado,* a Latin-American style barbecue. Marinated beef done over a slow charcoal fire in the cooker with a very spicy sauce. With it were hard rolls; crisp, raw garden vegetables; and a variety of pickles. Chip had a pony keg of beer in ice at his elbow from which he kept two large pitchers on the table filled.

Leda Sandoval complimented Mike on her diamond earrings, and Connie chimed in, saying, "Yes! Gus, your fiancée certainly has a talent for dressing well. In that outfit, she could go on stage in the Folies Bergere."

"On the other hand," Leda Sandoval said to Mike, "shouldn't you have a larger diamond? On the other hand." She wiggled her left hand and struggled not to smile at her own joke.

"We plan to take care of that while I'm here," said Gus.

191

B. Michelaard

"Right after we decided to get married," said Michelle, "we were both sent out of town. Never had time to shop for a diamond."

Coffee and dessert were served indoors. Topics of conversation rolled in like waves at the beach. Gus noticed Mike spent considerable time talking with Connie Borland, and overheard them making plans for lunch the following week. The guests all took their leave by eleven.

As they drove away, she said, "When you said we were invited here, I had some worries. Now I'm really glad we came. I have plenty of acquaintances around Washington. I think Connie could be a friend. I'd like to get to know her better."

As the Borlands' party was breaking up, Rodney Lund—alias Comrade Lincoln—was sitting in a Toronto apartment working on an intelligence puzzle. In a way, it resembled the kind in which dots were connected by lines to form a picture. By connecting a series of otherwise separate facts and events, he had a short list of those probably involved in the technological phenomenon that was his target.

Chapter Eighteen

Dwayne was waiting in the lobby when Audrey arrived. They had their usual smacky-mouth embrace before loading his bags in the trunk.

"Darling, I know you're not awfully much on parties," she said, "but I'm committed to this costume affair in the Village. I guarantee it won't be like that one on Park Avenue. These are my bohemian friends."

"Costume, you say? What do I do for—?"

"I've taken care of that." She gave him a sly smile. "Wait till you see. And don't worry about dinner. There'll be plenty there to eat and drink."

He would have preferred a quiet evening just with her, but this would be a chance to learn that much more about her life apart from his.

"We've just got time to get dressed," she said when they arrived at her town house studio. Up in the bedroom, she kicked off her shoes and backed up to him, waiting.

"Let's see. I gather something is expected of me."

"The zipper, silly." He ran the slide down, feeling a little

193

shiver at the intimacy of it, the touch of her satinlike skin.
"The bra too, darling." His hands grew a little unsteady,
but he got the hooks undone. She let blouse, slip, and
brassiere fall, gathered them into a bundle, and threw him
a provocative glance. "You'll soon get used to it."

He certainly hoped so.

The party was indeed very different. Billed as the
"Artists' and Models' Underground Ball," it was held in a
large cellar. The music was live but without amplifiers.
The guests, with their bizarre costumes and uninhibited
behavior, fulfilled his notion of Village bohemians. They
also came in many ages, sizes, shapes, and colors plus
various states of dress—or undress. Exposed female
breasts abounded.

Audrey had made both their costumes. She was a
honey bee, with battery-powered buzz and fluttering
diaphanous wings. His outfit was translucent plastic that
inflated to form a giant sperm cell. The "head" accommodated his upper body, with openings for his face and
hands. The "tail" trailed down behind him. "Believe me,
darling, it's *you*," she said.

He felt rather silly at first, but it drew so much clever
comment, he began to enjoy it. Some of the guests got
hold of marker pens and began writing lines of wit on the
plastic—things like, 'Let me tell you about my travels,'
or, 'Let's go someplace quiet and match chromosomes.'

Audrey encouraged him to dance with other girls while
she circulated. "Just confine the contact to dancing," she
added. One lively, dark-skinned girl he danced with
laughed and said, "Well, if any of us turn up pregnant,
maybe we can blame it on you."

There were bowls of punch, and from time to time,
Audrey would simply pop up at his side with two filled
paper cups. As the evening wore on, he got more and
more into the spirit of things. And vice versa.

His last—and lasting—impression was of being more

relaxed and uninhibited than he had been in years. But at some point, all impressions ended. Beyond that, he had no idea what happened.

Next, it was morning, Audrey awakened him with a kiss, then a cup of hot coffee under his nose. She said through a rather sardonic smile, "Maybe this will put some life back into the Life of the Party."

"Ooh!" He put a hand to his head. "What came over me?"

"Demon Rum, I'd say. Along with his friends Demon Whiskey, Demon Gin, and Demon Vodka."

"Was all that stuff in that punch last night?"

"No, but there was a lot of freelance booze passing around, and none of it passed you without a stop." She arched an eyebrow. "Dwayne the drunk. A side of you I hadn't seen before." Her smile teased.

"Neither have I. And I don't remember any of that."

The coffee plus some aspirin and a hot shower brought him around. Within half an hour he had shaved, and they sat down to the omelets she made. Later, while they were still sipping breakfast coffee, he looked sheepish and said, "then I guess we didn't . . . ah . . ."

"I'm afraid, you were in no shape. However . . ." She came over and settled onto his lap. In no time at all, they were heading back upstairs.

Rodney Lund's morning-after appraisal of his discoveries convinced him they were essentially valid. He rang Alvorado and arranged a meeting.

It took place in a small furnished apartment Lund rented under one of his many aliases. The furniture was plain, even a little shabby, but he had a TV set and VCR. He spread a file on the coffee table. "A central figure in this affair is an Air Force colonel named Halstrom. Rather famous as a research pilot some years ago. Perhaps you . . . ?"

"Oh, yes. I know quite a bit about Gus Halstrom. In fact, I have a score to settle with him. But that's another matter. Go on with—"

"I think it's beyond doubt he's directly involved. This video, shot by a freelance, places him in Addis Ababa at the critical time." He started the tape. It showed Halstrom getting out of the truck on the apron, returning the major's salute, being greeted by the American air attaché. The colonel's eagles and U.S. Air Force markings on the flying suit were clearly visible.

Then the frame switched to the Antonov. Michelle was at first a distant figure, then she began shouting and waving. The camera followed as she broke into a run. There was her hesitation as Gus came back into the frame, then their ardent embrace. The camera operator zoomed in on the faces.

"That's Halstrom, all right," said Alvorado.

Lund shut off the VCR, then reached into the folder and produced a Four-by-five-inch color print of Halstrom and Michelle on the apron at the airport. "Both this and the video were shot at the airport in Addis Ababa. Halstrom landed there in what appeared to be a slightly damaged aircraft. From the somewhat sketchy description, it would seem to be the new F-24 Scimitar. All the reports from the Eritrean campaign indicate it was the F-24 the Americans used there."

"And the woman?" Alvorado asked. "They obviously know each other quite well."

"An unidentified nurse or physician. I have my people looking into it. Anyway, we began by working our way backward over the recent stages of Halstrom's career. He's been connected with the F-24 since its inception as the XFL, and was about to complete the operational testing when he was suddenly reassigned to the Pentagon.

"Now, you may recall an Arthur Penross column not long ago mentioned Halstrom in connection with a supersecret project named Pegasus. Furthermore, the Pentagon essentially confirmed it for us. Right after the Penross column ran, they arrested one of their own civilian employees for leaking the information. So we can be reasonably sure that what we're looking for goes under the code name Pegasus."

Lund paused and thumbed through his notes. "Now, next among the dramatis personae is a Captain Curtis Borland, U.S. Navy. Hank to his fellow captains. Annapolis graduate and Naval aviator with a degree in nuclear engineering. Skipper of the carrier *Ronald Reagan* till something over a year ago, before Halstrom came to the Pentagon.

"Then in late summer or early fall, he and Halstrom become inseparable. They arrive and depart Andrews in an executive-type jet. When they leave, the flight plan shows Goose Bay, Labrador, as the destination. But records from Goose Bay show no corresponding arrivals."

"M-m! You have been busy," commented Alvorado.

"In this business, lost time may never be made up."

"I was referring to the fact that you established and kept up a network in the States while you didn't dare set foot there."

Lund showed the nearest thing he could to a smile. "Oh, I've been in and out of the States several times. Briefly and sub rosa, of course." He turned a page in the folder. "Now enter a third party, Major General Chalmers—Chip—Borland, USMC. Member of the Joint Staff and older brother of Hank Borland. He's also a pilot, but an early accident cut short his flying career. Since then, he's become the ideal generalist. Advanced degree in management from Johns Hopkins."

"And where does he fit into the picture?"

Lund paused in his pacing and showed a studious frown. "I'm not sure. He's a background figure, but I'm convinced he's connected with Pegasus." He leaned over and leafed through the papers in the folder. "Now we move into an area where the information may be more tenuous. Incidentally, what sort of an agent is our artistic 'Miz' Prowther?"

Alvorado gave a shrug. "M-m, clever and imaginative. No firebrand nowadays, though I'm told she once was. During her student days in the sixties and later when she studied in Europe. Probably no stomach for violence or treachery. Right now, her major contribution to our cause is that Toronto studio as a safe house. Why do you ask?"

Lund frowned. "I gave her a potentially critical assignment." He resumed his pacing. "You see, what we have here is the long arm of coincidence. She has a romantic relationship with a physicist at the GE labs. His name is Chauncey, and he may be connected with Pegasus, however remotely."

"Oh? How so?"

"It seems Prowther took Chauncey to a party to meet her friends in the artistic and literary set. One of them was Halstrom's ex-wife, Aubin. The movie queen. She's what we once called a useful idiot and passes along bits of information that are sometimes valuable. Well, it seems Chauncey mentioned meeting her former husband. He also remarked that what Halstrom was involved in was highly classified."

"M-m-hm! That would indicate their meeting wasn't by chance."

Lund nodded. "That's the way I read it."

"So, this assignment you gave her?"

"To see that Chauncey attended a certain party last night, where my people were to have at least a brief look inside his head." Lund paused in his pacing and looked thoughtful. "Interesting how often parties figure in the practice of espionage."

Chapter Nineteen

"Up betimes and to market," Gus declaimed as he carried the tray into the bedroom. He gave Mike a light slap on her tush, then knelt on the mattress, nuzzling and kissing her. She turned onto her back and purred.

"Is that the famous English diarist Samuel Pepys bringing my coffee and nibbling my ear lobe? And just how betimes is it anyway?"

"Oh, sixish. One lump or two?" He showed a sly smile. She took her coffee black and unsweetened, just as he did.

"I'll give you some lumps if you woke me at six A.M. for anything except making love." Her gaze went to the clock face, and she saw it was really a little after eight. She rose, carried the coffee into the bathroom. Gus's eyes followed the flowing animal grace of that golden body.

The market they had in mind this morning was in diamonds. Within minutes, he was all set to lay out about five yards of green for one-point-five carets of blue-white that looked like it might even glitter in the dark.

Michelle demurred. "A ring is a token, not an advertisement." They settled on a modest-sized specimen with perfect color and many facets for $1500. She chose a setting and was told it would be ready in two days.

With that, lunch was in order. They were shown to a table that overlooked the Potomac and its bridges. On the far side was the Custis-Lee Mansion, the marble-dotted slopes of Arlington, and the gray walls of the Pentagon. The sky too was mostly gray.

Over the apéritif, Gus said, "You've never explained just what you were doing in Asmara and how you got there."

"The government only sent me to Addis Ababa. Partly because I speak the language. Going to Asmara was my own idea. I saw reports of how bad things were, how much they needed doctors, and I volunteered. I'd never have gone if I had any idea things would get as tense as they did."

"That still doesn't explain what you were doing in East Africa."

She became tentative and apologetic. "Well . . . I can't tell you. But there are a couple of government guys who can. Sort of. I've arranged for it." She flashed an awkward smile. "This afternoon. At three."

"You've never explained how you came to speak the language. You weren't born there, and being an Amhar doesn't give you any leg up on knowing Amharic."

"No. Otherwise, I'd also speak some West African dialect. I'm an Amhar on one side and a Mandingo on the other. With a little French mixed in." She gave him a quick smile. "I'll tell you what. Settle back and enjoy this view, and I'll give you the story of my life."

"I can hardly wait."

She reached into her purse and took out a wallet. "First, let me show you my parents, Armand and Helene St. Clair." She opened a folder to display two satin-finish studio prints.

The man was probably well over sixty, but had that leonine masculine attraction that allows some older men not to look ridiculous escorting young movie starlets. His thick, well-groomed hair was the color of fine cigar ash. The woman might be sixty or so, but could pass for less than fifty. *And* still turn male heads. Both were clearly Caucasian.

"Stepparents, I take it." He frowned. "Armand St. Clair. Interesting. Same name as that big wheel up in Seattle. Lumber baron, industrial wizard, power in state politics."

"Yes, well, my father is that big wheel lumber baron, et cetera, et cetera. And while it's true he didn't beget me and she didn't give birth to me, in every other way they are my parents. My father's public image was pinned on him by the news media. He's really just a very astute businessman. But there was never a better set of parents. They made me the woman I am today."

"Score one for filial loyalty."

"My father's also a gifted amateur anthropologist, and traveled widely in East Africa pursuing his hobby. In Addis Ababa, he met a university professor who shared many of his interests. The two families became close friends.

"When the Dergue with their Marxism took power, the professor went into exile in Italy, where his wife died a few years later. To his daughter, the St. Clairs were Uncle Armand and Aunt Helene. After she got a degree from the Sorbonne, her Uncle Armand got her into a Ph.D. program at Berkeley and paid her tuition."

"Rather unusual for those days," he said.

"My parents are unusual people."

The waiter returned, and there was a break while they ordered lunch and the wine. Then Michelle went on. "At Berkeley, she met a young man from Haiti, and they planned to be married. The St. Clairs checked him out, found him very intelligent, gave him an Ivory Soap grading. He spoke French and Spanish like a native and English with an accent. They gave their blessing to the match and wrote to the girl's father to reassure him."

"The accent's probably what she fell for," said Gus with a teasing smile. "Those foreigners with their accents will do it every time."

"It's been said the mistake the French made in Haiti was bringing in Mandingo slaves from West Africa. As soon as France was occupied with its revolution, the Mandingos staged their own and threw the French out. The rest of the Haitians were glad to go along."

Gus sipped his Dubonnet, but his gaze was on her, not the view outside, which showed an ever more threatening sky. The wine steward brought the sauvignon blanc, which had to be tasted and left to breath.

"Well, of course Haiti was in the grip of the notorious Papa Doc. The young man, whose name was Villaneuve, was part of a secret movement to overthrow the regime. During the summer break, he went home. She later joined him, and they were married. When she came back to Berkeley for the fall term, she was pregnant. Her husband stayed on, and like many of Papa Doc's enemies, he disappeared.

"Against the advice of the St. Clairs, she went to Haiti, leaving her infant daughter in their care. Then she disappeared. The St. Clairs were appalled and wrote to the girl's father. He wrote that he was going to Haiti himself to find his daughter. And of course, he disappeared.

"Then Armand St. Clair went, raised hell, and brought in the U.S. ambassador. Still, nothing was ever found of Villeneuve, or the girl, or the professor. Armand himself was too big a fish for them to swallow. All they could do was throw him out.

"The professor was already a widower. So that left the baby. Yours truly. The St. Clairs simply took me as their own."

The waitress arrived bearing a tray bearing their

lunches. The wine was poured with due ceremony. The sky poured rain without ceremony.

"So," he said after they had each tasted the food. "At that point, you weren't even speaking English, never mind Amharic."

She fluttered her eyelids and said, "To be continued."

Gus met with Alex Gossett in the Pentagon, in an office where he'd never been. Mike dropped him off.

Gossett offered his hand. "Congratulations, Colonel. Mike's one helluva woman. Quite a catch even for a man of your status."

"The question is," said Gus, taking the hand and then taking a seat, "how the hell did you turn her into a government spook? And why?"

"Eh?" Gossett turned his palms up. "I didn't personally, and I'm not familiar with how she was recruited. Probably the usual way. An offer to sponsor some advanced training in exchange for service later on. In her case, advanced medical training." Gossett lit a cigarette and began to pace the floor. "As to why . . . well, let's just say DoD can't always rely on the CIA to act in our best interests. In certain parts of the world, the armed forces need direct but covert contact with locals. Langley is heavily influenced by Foggy Bottom, and State Department weenies seldom see things from a military standpoint."

Gus frowned. "Are you sure this is legal?"

Gossett made a wobbling motion with one hand. "In any case, we have the knowledge and approval of key members of Congress. We've kept a low profile and probably staved off a few disasters.

"As for Mike, she has certain things going for her. Right up front is being both a woman and dark-skinned. She can move around the Third World without arousing the gut reactions that attach to white males. And being a doctor is perfect cover. Actually, she does a lot of good apart from her official duty. She's a big plus for the U.S. image."

"I'm concerned about two things," Gus said. "Is it going to put her in danger? And could she be corrupted? By that I mean led gradually up the garden path of—quote—national interest into doing things she'd later regret."

Gossett sat on a corner of his desk and frowned before answering. "I wish I could give you a resounding no on both counts. The best I can do is to say either is unlikely. She got herself into that pickle in Asmara."

Gus left feeling little better about the whole affair. Neither he nor Mike spoke for a few minutes after she picked him up.

"What is Pegasus?" The voice was friendly and cajoling. It had already established Dwayne Chauncey's name and where he worked.

"Pegasus?" A slight giggle. "Never heard of him. Pegasus, pigasus, pogasus, poo. The horse that flies will do it on you." Again the giggle, louder and fuller. Chauncey was in a state of drunken merriment.

In the background, a third voice muttered, "The damn liquor. He got too buzzed before we slipped him the stuff. Now he's metabolizing the serum along with the alcohol."

"Shut the fuck up!" the interrogator hissed.

"Fuck up," echoed Dwayne. Then, imitating the imitation-Dracula accent of a TV actor selling room deodorizers, he said, "Thizz iz a gwood blaze for a fuckup."

Lund and Alvorado exchanged looks over the tape cassette. Still, they were silent, attentive.

"What do you do at GE?"

"Re-search. E-lec-tronical research." The tone was mock-pompous.

"Electronical?"

Dwayne giggled again. " 'Sa word I juss made up. Electrical and electronic. *Voilá!* E-lec-tronical."

"Okay. What do you work on in this electronical research?"

"M-m-h-m. Willard Effect."

"Willard Effect?" Roused interest showed in the voice of the interrogator. "What's that?"

"Sh-sh-sh! We're looking for a cure." The tone became mock-confidential. "Ain't you ever heard? It's enough to give you the Willards!" He went into a paroxysm of laughter. "Here, take two of these and call me in the morning. Or call me Old Two-fers."

The interrogator, a model of patience, kept on and finally elicited the word "radar." The Willard Effect had something to do with radar. But Chauncey again punned and played with it. He hit on the expression "the Oakland Radars," and again almost choked on his own laughter.

Then, in the middle of it, he suddenly remarked that he didn't feel so well, and they had to shove his head over a basin. After that, he subsided into torpor, then stupor, and they could get nothing out of him but complaints of how bad he felt and needed to sleep.

Lund reached out and stopped the tape. "Well, we didn't come up totally empty."

"Near enough, though," said Alvorado. "What's our next move?"

Lund frowned, in a pose of contemplation. "I have something for you to consider. You'll know your own people better than I do. Whether they're capable of carrying out this sort of thing."

He rose and began to pace. "We need to apply pressure. One potential pressure point is this fellow Chauncey. Some sort of blackmail. With Prowther's cooperation." He looked at Alvorado, his face asking the obvious question.

"I wouldn't count on her. I'd say she's in love with him."

205

Lund showed a slight frown, his most severe expression. But his words came out with the tone of a judge pronouncing sentence. "She no longer has the choice of putting personal considerations above the cause. She gave that up when she accepted our support. So just because Mao is dead and his successors in Beijing have given up the struggle does not mean her debt is canceled. She can still be the lever we need. Her safety for information.

"My people in Washington have discovered the identity of the woman with Halstrom in Addis Ababa. He's definitely involved with her romantically. Her name is Michelle St. Clair, and she was once something of a celebrity herself."

He took a few more restless steps, his usual preamble to getting to the crux of the matter. "She's now a surgical resident at a Washington hospital. I propose we lay hands on her. Under those conditions, our colonel might be persuaded to talk to us. An alternative but less desirable action is to seize one of those three kingpin officers themselves. Halstrom or one of the Borlands."

He continued to pace as he said. "As professional officers, they're trained to resist interrogation. The hunt for them would be intense, limiting our time. We also lack proper facilities. So results could only be obtained with drugs. Then the subject would have to be disposed of. We can't afford to leave him alive to repeat the story."

Alvorado gave a series of slow nods. "I know very little about the two Borlands, but Halstrom is a very tough customer. I'm familiar with the details of his escape from Hanoi. He had a garrote hidden in his flying suit and used it. I'd say he should be the last choice."

"Very well. Then perhaps you can begin setting up teams and making arrangements to get hold of Doctor St. Clair. Or failing that, one of those three officers."

The two senators sharing the limousine chaired the Armed Forces and Appropriations Committees respectively. The drivers were all cleared up to top secret, but the car still had the customary glass that kept whatever was said in the rear compartment confined there. There was a speaker system that let the passengers and driver communicate.

"Let's see," said Armed Forces. "This'll be your first live Pegasus briefing, won't it?"

"If you mean with slides and film clips and generals waving their pointers and all that good shit instead of just reading about it, yes," said Appropriations. "I guess the Joint Chiefs damn near had a shit-fit when Arthur Penross got hold of the name somehow. I wonder if he was right about that Major Austen."

"He was right about Austen's assignment. As for the rest, it was just one of his unresearched hatchet jobs. Hal Maarten assured me Austen's conduct was above reproach, and he deserved the medal he got."

"Someday somebody'll catch up with that asshole Penross," said Appropriations. "I just hope I'm around to see it."

The limousine pulled up to the river entrance, the one used by VIPs. They were ushered along to one of the smaller briefing rooms.

Gus was in the corridor when the pair of senators arrived. Their colleagues from the House were already there. Behind them came the CNO, Admiral Anson G. Broadwater III, the son of a son of a son of an admiral. Navy scuttlebutt had it his veins carried not blood but seawater. Some said it was piss. He walked with his gaze elevated, as if steering by the stars—or signs from the Almighty. He was trailed by three other admirals—members of the Joint Staff—plus Hank Borland, who gave Gus a discreet wave.

"Old Bilgewater," muttered Pete as they swept by, "with Winken, Blinken, and Nod."

General Harley Broome, Army Chief of Staff, "the soldier's soldier," arrived wearing his usual strictly standard uniform and carrying his own briefcase. His aide, a colonel, carried a swagger stick, and Gus had to choke down a laugh. Close behind came General John Plummer, a no-nonsense professional like those who had preceded him as Commandant of the Marine Corps.

Last was General Hal Maarten, USAF, chairman of the Joint Chiefs. He arrived alone, carrying nothing, offered a hand and a smile. "Gus, you're looking good. Lot of water under bridge since those days at Da Nang. I hear you guys did really good work in Eritrea."

"We got the job done, sir. It's all on film."

Maarten's voice lowered. "I guess Pete's told you we still hope to get you that star." He flashed a smile. "Just don't grow any horns in front of these gentlemen from Congress."

The real object here was to convince the men from Capitol Hill to fund at least one more airship like Skyhook. Hal Maarten served as MC, but Gus and Hank Borland were the meat of the act, showing how Skyhook had made the U.S. into a military magician. While the world watched, they had turned the tide of battle in a distant location; yet nobody had seen anything.

For his part of the briefing, Gus showed gun-camera film from his and other kills. He knew it wasn't all that relevant, but it titillated the latent machismo of the men from the Hill.

The briefing lasted not much over an hour. Eastbound in their limousine, the two committee chairs exchanged impressions of what they had seen. "That guy Halstrom's some kind of phenomenon," said Appropriations. "He's pushing fifty, and there he is still flying those jets and shooting down pilots half his age."

Armed Forces nodded. "At his age, most colonels are already retired. I guess the Pentagon kept him on because he's so damn good at what he does. He was up for his first star several years ago. Could have had two or three by now if it weren't for that affair in Stockholm."

"I've heard all kinds of talk. It was sort of hushed up, and even the press didn't carry a full account. Just reports that his behavior was—quote—contrary to friendly relations between the two countries."

Armed Forces smiled. "He was captured over in Vietnam, you know. Had a pretty rough time before he escaped. Sweden was openly friendly to the VC and sent aid to Hanoi. So you can't blame Halstrom for his dim view of Eric Palme's government.

"When we decided to patch things up with the Swedes, somebody in the State Department hit on the idea of sending distinguished Swedish-Americans over as special ambassadors. By then, Halstrom had made news as a research pilot. And he was married to that movie star. He even speaks Swedish. Learned it at home.

"He said no, thanks, but the Pentagon put the arm on him. He was supposed to take his wife, but they were already on the verge of a breakup. Then at his first news conference in Stockholm, he proceeded to tell the Swedes what he thought of them. I think the term he used to describe their society was cesspool. He jumped on everything from their steeply graduated taxes to their law against spanking kids.

"Twenty-four hours later, he was gone, and the State Department had egg all over its face. He was on the promotion list to BG, but some of our members wanted him boiled in oil and weren't about to confirm. So his name was withdrawn."

"Senators," came the voice of the driver through the speaker. "Message for you from the Vice President." He pressed a button and spoke into his handset. "Go ahead, sir. We're scrambled at this end."

"Gentlemen," came the voice of the Veep, dead sober and a little shaken. "The President departed Camp David about twenty minutes ago." He paused, and they heard a sigh. "I've just been informed that his helicopter has disappeared somewhere over the Catoctin Mountains. The

209

Joint Chiefs and other key personnel are being notified. Please join me at the White House."

The phone rang in the UN office of Ho Ah Ling. It was the private line only he could answer. "You've heard the news?" said the voice he recognized as Alvorado.

"No. I've been somewhat immersed in business here."

"The President's helicopter is missing. With him in it. Now is the time to move. While all the security forces are tied up with this problem."

"M-m, yes. I'll get back to you in thirty minutes."

Chapter Twenty

Evening in Albany, and once more Dwayne Chauncey was expecting Audrey Prowther. He stepped out onto the balcony and took in the view, the blue-tinted dusk over the Hudson Valley.

It made an ideal backdrop for a romantic reverie. This would be the first night she spent with him here. Tomorrow they would drive down to New York, to Fifth Avenue, and pick up the diamond they had left to be set. They would also break the news to Abigail and Aaron.

Meanwhile, the Presidential helicopter was still missing. Rain and fog hindered aerial search. Ground parties were out, but both the weather and terrain made progress slow.

His door chime sounded, which puzzled him. Audrey had her own key and could let herself in.

He noticed a large brown envelope just slipped underneath, and checked the corridor. No one in sight.

The envelope was crisp, new, and bore no markings.

He tore open the flap and dumped the contents onto the coffee table.

What he saw doubled him over like a blow to his middle.

There were three eight-by-ten glossies of Audrey in surroundings like a cellar. The first showed her tied to a chair. In the next, her arms were held, her blouse and slip badly torn. Her face showed stark terror along with a look of pleading. In the third, she was down to bra and panties, and had turned her head away. He recognized the shear, bikini-like panties that showed the outline of her pubic hair.

His voice was smothered in his throat. His tongue was suddenly dry and three sizes too large. The nausea of terror doubled him over.

Slowly he regained some control, though he still trembled. He straightened, noticed the ordinary white business envelope that had fallen out along with the pictures. It held two typewritten sheets. Hands quivering, he unfolded them and began to read:

The enclosed pictures should need no explanation. So far, nothing worse than what you see has happened to Ms. Prowther, and as long as you comply with all directions, nothing will. Only you can guarantee her safety and her release unharmed. Any attempt to communicate this to anyone else will mean her certain, slow, and painful demise.

Enclosed is a list of information we require. You will type it on plain white paper, numbering each item respectively. Any incomplete or evasive response will occasion screams from Ms. Prowther. You will be given specific instructions for delivery of your answers.

Still trembling, he put that sheet aside and looked at the other. First, he was to write everything he knew about something called Pegasus. Which was nothing outside the furor caused when Arthur Penross had printed the name in his column. Next, they demanded details of briefings or conferences involving any of three officers of the armed forces. Gus Halstrom, besides being something of a public figure, had dropped in during a session on recent developments involving the Willard Effect. They had been introduced, shaken hands, and exchanged a few words. The two named Borland, a Navy captain and a Marine general, had also been there. He understood they were brothers.

The next question was something of a shocker: They wanted to know the details of the Willard Effect and its use or application in any weapons programs. Even the term itself was highly classified. Where and how could they have gotten hold of it?

As the early shock wore off, outrage and hatred added themselves. Still distraught but slowly regaining control, he looked over the questions again. Right now, his main worry was how to convince these people of his ignorance about this thing called Pegasus. And that he had had only that one brief contact with Halstrom and the two Borlands.

He disconnected his telephone. He wanted no interruptions. Then he went to his desk, sat down at the computer, pulled up the scientific word-processing program, and began typing.

The rain pelted the windshield, the hood, and the car top as Audrey drove north out of Toronto toward the 401 freeway. It blew in dense, smokelike curtains that obscured whatever they passed over. The wipers and defrosters were just able to keep ahead of it, give her some view front and rear. She could see little to either side. The pavement ahead was a frothy blur. Water was accumulating where the drainage could not keep up.

She was finally getting out of Toronto, bound for Albany, two days after she had planned to.

B. Michelaard

Though the experience was over and she was unharmed, it had both scared the bejesus out of her and left her at the boiling point, filled with shame and rage.

Monitor had said he was sending some men around to set things up for the next meeting. Then as soon as the door was shut behind them, they dragged her into the cellar and began tearing off her clothes. She was sure she was about to be gang-raped. While two of them roughed her up, the third stood by and took flash pictures. But that was all.

They kept her shut up and out of contact for another two days. Then they left, after handing her a message from Comrade Lincoln warning her to say nothing.

She realized the photos were probably meant to blackmail Dwayne. His work involved highly technical matters at GE. She had no intent of letting him be victimized or of starting off her marriage with a betrayal. And this finished her with Monitor and all his schemes.

They could recover. She'd spend a night with Dwayne in Albany, and next weekend he could drive down to New York. Everything could still go off pretty much as they planned. It would just be delayed by a week.

She had tried to phone Dwayne, but got no answer. What had her driving in this driving rain was the message from Comrade Lincoln, his claim that the Organization had built her career and therefore owned her. Worse was his clinging to the dogma that individuals counted for nothing in the struggle for the political millennium. This was the very attitude that had soured her and many others on Marxism.

Thus preoccupied, she was functioning automatically while the tires squished and the wipers swished against the storm. The signs for various turnoffs went by, blurred by the poor visibility and her emotional tumult.

Suddenly the interchange for westbound 401 was close and coming up fast, and she was in the far lane. As she started across, there was the clattering roar of a diesel, the warning blast of air horns, and the looming bulk of a huge eighteen-wheeler right at her shoulder. Then a brief but powerful nudge broke the rear end loose.

She had always driven fast, but had never pushed the car beyond control, never induced a skid. This was the first time it would not simply go where she pointed it. Now the tires were planing. She wrenched the wheel in panic. The inevitable reactive swing caught her totally unprepared and turned into a skidding spin. She became a mere passenger, the car revolving too fast for her to follow.

As it completed its revolution, the concrete pier of an overpass loomed directly in her path.

It had now been some seventy-plus hours since Dwayne had had his reverie—and his life—shattered. In that time, he had sat at the computer well into the night, slept only briefly and poorly, and called in sick at GE. His major concern had been to convince the kidnappers of what he didn't know. To compensate and thus establish his bona fides, he had produced what Avery Willard would later label an admirably clear and concise exposition of the Willard Effect.

Pacing the apartment, he felt overwhelmed by the sheer grotesquerie of it all. He had delivered the results just as they demanded, but still had no word of Audrey. She did not answer the phone in either of her studio homes. To relieve the sense of unreality, he sought some touch with the mundane by turning on the TV to the six o'clock network news.

The major story was that the President had been found unharmed and was on his way back to Washington. A bird strike had knocked out the helicopter's communications and avionics. The pilot had wisely chosen to land in the nearest available open space and wait it out.

Now, if only Dwayne's personal crisis could come to such a happy end. Then he heard the newscaster saying,

"The art world is in shock at the death of Audrey Prowther, whose paintings and sculpture have been displayed in such well-known galleries as New York's Guggenheim. Her car apparently went out of control in heavy rain on a freeway near Toronto in the late afternoon. Police were delayed in identifying the body because it was badly burned, along with the victim's purse. Ms. Prowther was apparently on her way from Toronto to New York, where she also had a studio in Greenwich Village. No arrangements have been announced."

Without realizing how he got there, Dwayne found himself on one knee in front of the screen. His face was buried in his hands, the fingernails digging into the skin of his cheeks and forehead. He had told them all he knew, and they had still killed Audrey. He was a total loser, had betrayed his trust and still lost the woman he loved.

Then he raised his eyes to the sky outside and saw the same blue dusk he had on Friday, a lifetime ago. He sensed that she now inhabited that indigo dusk. Color was the essence of the way he remembered her.

Arriving home by taxi at the Crestwood entrance overlooking the river, the woman was shocked to see a man lying sprawled on the lawn. The sky was now dark, but the area was well lighted, and he lay there in plain sight. Irritated, she went straight in to inform the manager. After all, part of the reason people paid the scale of rent charged here was to avoid this sort of seamy occurrence.

The manager threw on a jacket and went to investigate, found a man facedown, wearing a T-shirt and trousers and socks but no shoes. Shaking the fellow to rouse him got no response, and the skin had a peculiar chill. The manager only realized the truth—that this was a corpse—when he tried to turn the body over. It had a peculiar, jellylike consistency, a bit like a water-filled bag. And the head looked distorted, like a slightly squashed melon or grapefruit.

Two uniformed police in a patrol car were first to respond. A while later, two plainclothes detectives and some technicians arrived. After a lot of measuring and photographing, the body was loaded onto a gurney and placed in an ambulance. It was only then that the manager had his first good look at it face up and said, "My God! That's Doctor Chauncey, one of our tenants. Fourteen-C."

At their request, he took them up and let them into the apartment. On the way up, he affirmed that Dwayne Chauncey had lived there alone for the past four years and was a model tenant. When asked where the doctor had his offices, he explained, "Oh, he doesn't have offices. He's a Ph.D., not an MD. Did research for GE in Schenectady."

The first thing the detectives noted on entering the apartment was the sliding glass door to the balcony standing open. It looked directly down on the spot where the body had been found. The two exchanged nods, and one said, "Probable suicide. But why?"

They got their first clue from the pictures of Audrey Prowther and the accompanying typewritten sheets. Then they found the printouts from Chauncey's word processor. The connection was clear: research at GE, probably classified, defense-related; blackmail and espionage. A matter of national security. A case for the FBI.

With the news of Audrey's death, Lund again confronted *El Jefe*, this time in rather icy tones. "It was just as well to get rid of her, but not—"

"Calm yourself. She'd become quite lukewarm, but nowadays we don't consider that grounds for termination. What happened was an accident, certainly not my order."

"There you are, gentlemen," said the Crestwood manager as he unlocked the door. "If you need me, I'll be in my office." He left without seeing the couple who were already inside.

They showed startled looks as they found themselves confronting Special Agents Rossiter and Hellman. "Who are you, and what are you doing here?" said Hellman. He was big, bulky, square-shouldered, square-jawed, with blond hair worn in a crew cut.

"Everybody gotta be someplace, Pops," said the man. His tone was in-your-face flippant. He wore a mustache/Vandyke combination and looked thirty or so. The woman was perhaps three years younger.

Rossiter, a very tall, athletic-looking black man, stepped forward showing a frown. "Don't give us any smartmouth. We're federal officers." He held out his Bureau ID folder.

The woman stepped forward. Her plain two-piece suit went with a plain severity of grooming that was perhaps carried a bit too far. "We're Dwayne's—ah, Doctor Chauncey's—friends. We came to tell him his girlfriend was killed in an accident." Her face and figure were lean to the point of being bony. Her earnest, level stare gave her the look of a schoolmarm. "It would be just terrible if he had to hear it on the news."

The two agents eyed them briefly. "You have some ID?"

She offered them a New York driver's license.

Still with enough attitude for a headwaiter, the man did the same. "So what's this all about? I can't believe Dwayne's in trouble with the law."

Hellman examined the licenses, compared the photos to the faces. "Dr. Chauncey was found dead on the ground below this balcony last night." He handed back the licenses.

Her shock looked genuine. "Dwayne . . . dead? Oh, my God!" She sank onto the couch. "He must have heard then. It must have been on the news last night." She gave them a plaintive look. "Do you think . . . I mean . . . was it suicide?"

"That's how it looks at the moment. Now, just who is—or was—this girlfriend you mentioned?"

"Oh . . . her name is Audrey Prowther. She's a well-known artist. Has anyone notified his family? His sister in New York?"

"I believe that's being taken care of." Hellman swept a deliberate gaze over them. "How did you get in here?"

"We have a key Dwayne gave us."

"I'll take it." He held out his hand, and she surrendered the key.

Rossiter saw them out the door and onto the elevator. Back inside the room, he said, "What do you think? Nice story, but—"

"Right," said Hellman. "They were searching the place. Probably for that stuff the local detectives picked up last night." He took a walkie-talkie-style radio from inside his coat, went out onto the balcony. "Hello, Crackerbox—this is Chatterbox." When a response came back, he rattled off professional descriptions of the pair coming down on the elevator and said, "Tail 'em. We'll get a cab back to the office."

"Right, Chatterbox." There was a pause. "Got a designator you'd like to use?"

Hellman frowned a moment. "Yeah. They snuck in here through a hole in our screen. Call 'em June Bugs."

Nursing a cup of coffee and a case of jet lag, Michelle sat on the deck of her parents' home while the dawn's early light crept over the Straits of Juan de Fuca below and Vancouver Island in the distance. By her body clock, it was nine A.M., but the local time was six A.M., and her mom and dad were still in bed.

With Alex Gossett's help, she had convinced the hospital authorities she needed some R&R after that experience in Africa. And spending time with her folks in their Northwest-style mansion overlooking Puget Sound was the best R&R she could think of.

They knew all about Gus, and last night she'd shown the diamond and announced the wedding was on. She

219

had even given her "grandchild" speech: "I'll get a bun in my oven or wear out a mattress trying."

Sequim, the nearest town—pronounced "Skwim" just to confuse outsiders—had no daily, but the Seattle paper was delivered here. And the sky now offered just enough light to read on the deck. On booted feet, with a parka over her robe, she crept down to the front door and got the paper off the stoop.

The robe was the same dark blue velvet she had worn that first night she met Gus, and she associated it with him. Wearing it let her imagine the feel of his arms around her. Just to test what kind of guy he was, she had put it on that night over nothing but her birthday suit, offering him an apparent chance to take advantage of her.

He had come through with a perfect score as a gentleman. That and his "I love you" note had convinced her he was the man she'd been waiting for.

Back on the deck with her coffee freshened, she scanned the headlines, read a few of the front-page stories, went through the op-ed columnists, checked on her favorite comics. Then an inside column head caught her eye. Curious, she noted the dateline was Washington, D.C.:

GENERAL MISSING FOR SECOND DAY
Authorities still have no solid clues in the strange disappearance of Marine Major General Chalmers Borland, of the Joint Staff. His wife, Consuela, called police when her husband failed to return home or call her by eight o'clock. Her call to his office in the Pentagon confirmed that he had left there as usual about six P.M. Montgomery County (Maryland) sheriff's officers later discovered the general's car abandoned on an isolated stretch of road just a few miles from his home. The car was undamaged, had plenty of fuel, and nothing mechanically wrong. There was no evidence of violence or

any indication of what might have happened.

The FBI has entered the case, which is considered a possible kidnapping, though no ransom demand or other message has been received. However, General Borland comes from a family of considerable wealth, which may be seen as a motive.

Heart pounding, Mike went to the kitchen phone and dialed Connie's number.

Chapter Twenty-one

In his UN office, Ho Ah Ling was fretting. The people interrogating General Borland were not trained for the task, while the general was clearly well trained in resistance. Even with pentathol, they were getting nothing.

If he could just be there in person, he might do better. He did have a little experience. But his work for the Chinese UN delegation gave him no plausible excuse for an extended visit to Baltimore. Unlike the previous Administration, the President and staff were so security-conscious they bordered on being hostile, imposing severe restrictions on all Chinese diplomats.

It appeared then that to get information out of the general, they would first have to get the general out of the country, away from the FBI search. Lund's U.S. organization had wide capabilities, but was not set up to conduct interrogations. In the Far East, he had men and facilities good enough to extract classical poetry from a clam.

At a safe house near Baltimore, the general had first

been injected with an hallucinatory drug, then placed on a water bed in total darkness. The subject, once released from such a nightmare of disorientation, would often babble happily on about any desired subject.

General Borland had emerged full of hostility and had to be subdued.

After that, they had tried pentathol, supplied by Lund. But only a trained chemo-psychotherapist or chemo-interrogator really had the skill to extract precise information against resistance. With each injection, Borland would hyperventilate and force himself into a semi-coma. Whenever he was awake and being questioned, he would sing bawdy Marine Corps songs or recite scatological limericks at the top of his voice to drown out that of the interrogator. Physical abuse did not subdue him, and they were limited in that by the danger of injuring or killing him before he talked.

Ho made the decision to call Lund.

Despite her ordeal, Connie sounded composed when she answered the phone. "Oh, Mike! It's good to hear from you." She paused, heaved a sigh. "I had to call Pilar, our daughter, and tell her before she could hear it on the news or see it in the papers."

"Connie, I'm so sorry I was gone when this happened, that I wasn't there to . . . to do whatever I could. I'm out in Seattle with my folks. I just saw the news in the local paper. Have you heard . . . anything?"

"Nothing. The FBI's here around the clock, with a tap on the phone and all sorts of electronic gadgetry. You know Chip's involved in the same project with Gus and Hank." It was half question, half statement.

"I didn't, but I suspected."

"I don't know what the connection is, but it's there. Chip and Hank have never been able to talk much about their work. But Mellanie and I have never known the brothers to be so tight-lipped as this." All at once, she let out a sob. "That's why I have to think he was grabbed for what he knows. This supersecret project. It could've been Gus or Hank, but Chip was the one available because he drives to work. Why else would this guy be here from the Pentagon? His name is Gossett."

That gave Mike something of a jolt, hearing Alex was involved.

She thought: She didn't want to leave just yet. Life in Seattle was so relaxing after that ordeal in Asmara. And she hadn't seen much of her parents for almost a year. But friendship was a two-way thoroughfare, and Connie needed her. "Look, Connie, I'll be back as soon as I can get a flight out. I'll—"

"Oh . . . Mike, that's not necessary. I'll be—"

"Just hang in there. I'll see you soon. Bye."

She went back out on the deck, but her coffee was cold, and the sunrise had somehow lost its luster. She suddenly wondered what kind of light and weather Gus was seeing. Most of all, she wondered if there was another situation like that in the Red Sea. An unknown and unreported event where both sides shot to kill.

Facing Special Agent Hellman across a lean and clean desk in the Hoover Building, Gossett also confronted his own subconscious bias: Hellman might look like a Papa Bear—or a Bears linebacker—but he came across sly as a fox in the briar patch of investigative nuances.

"So far," Hellman was saying, "any connection between General Borland's disappearance and the suicide of Doctor Dwayne Chauncey looks rather tenuous, but my gut tells me it's there. We started running names through our computer, and it was like flushing termites out of old, rotten woodwork. Some go back to the radicals of the sixties.

"First, there's the late Audrey Prowther herself. Way back when, she was up to her artsy ass in what was called the New Left. Later, she decamped to Europe, and we pretty much lost track of her. Since then, her views seem to have mellowed enough so she could be elected to Congress from—say, Berkeley or almost anywhere in Massachusetts.

"Some of the others actually had outstanding federal warrants, but we made no arrests. And our surveillance was really revealing. Their pavement work is right out of Moscow Center under Andropov."

"So how does all this relate to General Borland?"

"I'm coming to that. Some information from your office tied the general in with Chauncey, our scientist-suicide in Albany. Chauncey's work involved something called the Willard Effect. The general is somehow involved in this project called Pegasus, and whoever kidnapped Prowther wanted to know about both the Willard Effect and Pegasus."

Gossett felt familiar twin surges—anxiety and stomach acid. Just then a female voice on the intercom said, "Crumm's here, sir."

"Send him in," Hellman responded. Then to Gossett: "This is one of the agents on the case. Let's hope he's got something positive."

"Disaster," Crumm said as soon as the door was shut. He was rather nondescript—medium height, weight, and coloring. Ideal for a shadow.

Hellman's face took on a hard set in which open-mindedness struggled against reproach. "What happened?"

"I was tailing that couple code-named June Bug, and they went into a Big Boy. I took a seat across the room just to see if they made any contact." He made a helpless, disgusted gesture. "Then—would you believe it—this guy I went to college with—haven't seen him in two or three years. By shear bad luck, he pops into the place and spots me. Van, he says. Long time no see. You still with the FBI? That was in Baltimore, and they probably heard it down in Annapolis."

"And that spooked the June Bugs," said Hellman in a flat tone.

"They took off like scalded cats, and outside they split up. I remembered June Bug male was wanted on that old warrant, so I collared and booked him on it. I figured it just might make 'em think that's all he's wanted for."

"If you arrange to let this guy out on bail," said Gossett, "it might reinforce that impression. Plus lead us to something bigger."

"Could be worth a try," said Hellman. He reached for the phone. "Who was the judge and the U.S. attorney?"

When the phone rang, Ho thought it might be word from Toronto. Instead a familiar voice said, "Mr. Ho, this is George. There's been a jump in those commodities we discussed yesterday. My suppliers can't deliver at the price I mentioned. Perhaps we could meet and discuss it."

"Very well. The usual place in half an hour." Ho hung up wondering what had gone wrong. "George" was actually Vietnamese, Nhu Than Nguoc, one of Lund's networks, and that message signaled an emergency.

The "usual place" was the lobby of the UN building. There was the usual greeting, during which they checked each other's backs for surveillance. With Ho was a tall man who wore dark glasses and an Uncle Sam goatee and was introduced as "Mr. Lincoln."

They took a cab and rode in silence to Ho's apartment. Inside, Ho made a quick security sweep. Returning to the living room, he found Mr. Lincoln had removed his dark glasses and goatee.

"Fooled you, didn't I?" said Rodney Lund.

Ho grinned and grasped Lund's hand. "But aren't you taking a risk?"

"Small and calculated. And for good reason."

Ho turned to George. "So what's happened?"

Nhu related how the couple in Baltimore had discovered by pure chance they were under FBI surveillance. "They were responsible for logistics at the safe house, bought the groceries, paid the rent and utilities. Their

226

names are on the lease. Not real names, of course, but the FBI has probably broken their cover by now."

"We should get General Borland out of there at once," said Ho.

"That's already been done." Seeing Ho exhale in relief, Nhu said, "But wait. It gets worse. They decided to make the move after dark and injected the general with a tranquilizer. The dose was supposed to let him walk, so he wouldn't have to be carried. Evidently, it wasn't enough. He feigned stupor till he was outside, then he started shouting and tried to break free and had to be subdued."

Nhu pleaded the press of business and excused himself. When he was gone, Ho looked with a sigh at Lund and said, "What went wrong? Why are we—?"

"You mean why, now, after the century we all thought would usher in the Marxist millennium, is Marxism in shambles all over the globe? So that I've now thrown the shank end of a life devoted to Marxism into working for a relatively obscure new revolutionary star?"

He paused, took a few restless steps. "Because this man known to the world as Etienne Alvorado is the first one with the vision to see we were fighting the wrong battle all along. Lenin, Stalin, Mao, Ho Chi Minh, and the others all made the same basic mistake. I followed them, devoted myself to them, so I now must look back on a life that was mostly wasted."

"Wasted?! A harsh judgment on all you've accomplished."

"The simple truth, old friend. We were fighting on one side of what was really only a civil war within Eurocentric industrial society." He took to pacing as he spoke. "And I was too immersed in the tactics and techniques of that war to see the natural conflict was not between East and West but between the temperate zones and the tropics. What the Americans and Europeans are pleased to call the Third World.

"So, while I was scoring small victories in that war, one man had the insight to know those who have grown up under and absorbed the exploitative, competitive social climate of North Temperate Zone industrialism can never adapt and live under a communal society."

He paused and faced Ho. "Even the Russian workers and the Chinese farmers, those who would have most benefited under a Marxist society, rejected it. Fought it, and subtly undermined it."

"So where does this leave us now, Comrade?"

"It leaves us with the task of forging a new nation called Centralia, unlike any that have gone before it." Lund resumed his pacing. "Communal life is more natural to the tropics. I spent a lot of time there, working for Moscow and later Beijing, and I slowly came to realize it. But Alvorado grasped it long before."

"I'll admit," said Ho, "that your *El Jefe* is impressive, magnetic. But he seems to have abandoned Vietnam to pursue his own advancement."

"Not his own but the concept of Centralia. He needed a bigger power base. And Vietnam was also poisoned by temperate zone attitudes. First through French colonialism and then dependence on Moscow. Since leaving, he's made a start at not only the new nation of Centralia but a whole new concept of nationhood. Much of what you see around the world, wherever the northern industrialists are turned back, he's behind it.

"In the short time we have, I can give you no more than a glimpse of it. But I'm convinced he's our best hope. He's rescued me from despair and restored my motivation."

"I've believed and followed you for a good many years," Ho said. "I see no reason to change now."

Lund put on his dark glasses, stood before a mirror to stick on his goatee. Unsmiling, with his left hand on the door handle, he offered the other. "I won't live to see the triumph of Centralia. But you well might." He opened the door. "I have to get back to Toronto tonight. You'll hear from me soon."

Audrey Prowther had no close family, no one to come and tidy up her affairs. Her death went largely unnoticed outside her circle of friends and the art world. The bank holding the mortgage on her Toronto town house-studio was in Singapore and had ties to the Centralia Corporation. For the present, the studio remained a safe house for Lund's *apparat*.

So it was there that Lund again met with Alvorado. "Ho was one of the agents I trained in China some years ago," he said by way of explanation. "He broke with Beijing when I did, but I persuaded him to stay in place and work for me covertly. He was the ideal one to put in overall control of the abduction."

"But now something's gone wrong?"

"Not really. We had hoped to interrogate this Borland and learn the secret of Pegasus on the spot. But I have only amateurs available in that kind of work, and he's proving a tough nut to crack."

Alvorado frowned. "So how long will it take?"

"No longer than it takes to have one of your ships call at New York or Baltimore. We'll spirit the general aboard and be off. In fact, if we can get the right people together, they can conduct the interrogation on board and dispose of the body at sea."

Alvorado nodded his approval.

Chapter Twenty-two

Between them, Officers Daggett and McCready showed the same color scheme as their black-and-white cruiser. Responding to the reported disturbance at the Albigensian safe house in Baltimore, they found it deserted. Daggett, the black half of the pair, noted the signs of a hurried departure. "They had something to hide, that's for sure. And it doesn't take an Einstein to figure out what."

"Our major growth industry," said McCready. The two had been teammates in high school, classmates in the police academy, and partners ever since. They argued and bitched like a married couple, but could practically read each other's thoughts.

Sergeant Bell, shift head at the precinct, first accepted their evaluation of the house as a drug pad and minor distribution center. But the witness's statement made references to "the hostage." He shuffled through the latest circulars and came up with an FBI report on the missing Pentagon general. " 'Smatter, you guys don' read yer bulletins?" he said to the pair. "You think I'm jus' talkin' to hear myself when I say check them bulletins?"

With that, the FBI was notified.

Ingraham sat in his office at Langley and pondered this fresh and rather startling communication from the FBI: In Baltimore, a man struggling and shouting for the police had been dragged from a house and forced into an automobile, which had then driven away. And a witness certified as sane and sober stated the man fit the basic description of General Borland.

Ingraham's thoughts went back to some recent events. First, Rodney Lund had shown up in Toronto, not only still alive but no doubt still up to his id in espionage and subversion. Operatives never changed their ways, only their masters.

Then there was the suicide of Doctor Dwayne Chauncey, the scientist at GE somehow involved with Pegasus, the supersecret Pentagon project. Toronto had also seen the demise of the late Audrey Prowther, Chauncey's fiancée and self-proclaimed artist-in-residence to the world's downtrodden. She had once been one of that radical band who looked to Mao and his Little Red Book to save the world from Yankee imperialism. That was back when Lund was swinging a big bamboo in Beijing.

Which brought up the name Ho Ah Ling, known to have trained under Lund in China. Ho was now operating with the cover of Beijing's UN trade rep. And since secret U.S. technology was no longer being traded to China for campaign contributions, his real function was to procure it by means both overt and covert.

Lund and Ho were known to operate together when Lund was still loyal to Beijing. Was Albigensian currently funding this corrosive combo? One thing Ingraham felt sure of: If Ho was involved in the kidnapping, it was not on behalf of the People's Republic. Beijing had too little to gain and too much at stake to risk indulging in this kind of hugger-mugger.

Because the Borland kidnapping and the Chauncey espionage-cum-suicide were somehow connected, the Bureau had assigned them to one man. Name of Hellman. Ingraham checked the number and reached for the phone.

Like most Bureau men, Hellman had little use for the CIA and their tweedy, sherry-sipping, British-derived ways. And this Ingraham was the epitome of that school. He even affected a British accent. Yet what he said made sense. He had a set of facts and had marshaled them to make a point: This Ho Ah Ling needed checking out, and the first order of business was a search warrant. Hellman reached for the phone.

The sun had settled behind the Jersey Palisades, leaving a chill over Gotham's steel and concrete canyons. Shops and stores were ushering patrons out. The bars and lounges beckoned them to the solace of soft lights and flowing booze.

Arriving in the Bureau field office where the team of agents had assembled, an assistant U.S. attorney waived a large brown envelope and said, "Got it. Any word from the stakeout?"

"Thimble still hasn't turned up." Thimble was the code name for Ho.

"Good. Let's go have a look inside." He handed over the warrant. "And by the way, the Attorney General agreed to let that Pentagon agent—what's his name? Gossett, I think. Anyway, he gets to examine all papers and written material first. He'll meet us there. We're to collect whatever looks like military information and turn it over to him unread."

One of the agents broke into a chuckle. "How're we supposed to know if it's military information without reading it? It's like that old joke we had when I was in the service. How some things were so secret they were classified burn-before-reading."

They drove uptown and parked about a block from the apartment building. As they approached, the team chief used his walkie-talkie: "Any sign of Thimble?"

"Negative. No one's entered or left since we got here."

"Okay, we've got the judge's paper, and we're going in. Give us a squawk if you see anyone coming."

Gossett met them in the lobby. The building super, a spare, elderly woman, looked shaken at the mere sight of the court order and Bureau IDs. She let them into the apartment and readily agreed to say nothing.

Four of them went in and began a methodical search, careful not to disturb things. But that need to be careful soon vanished. Certain typewritten sheets held very suspicious questions and answers. Gossett identified General Borland's voice on tape cassettes. The subject matter was Pegasus and related military hardware. "Plenty of evidence there to deport Ho," said the agent in charge. "And prosecute any of his buddies who don't have diplomatic immunity."

A radio beeped. "You're about to have company," said a voice from the black box. "Thread's just entered the building. He's waiting for the elevator." Thread was the code designator for Deng Su, Ho's amanuensis.

A few minutes later, Deng opened the door with his key and entered. He was Asian, about five-four and 145 pounds, but his reaction on seeing them was to launch himself feet-first in a quick, silent, martial-arts attack. It was clear as Absolut Vodka he was trained as more than a secretary.

One of the agents was caught by surprise and forced to dive for cover. Gossett, trained in this sort of thing, moved in. They parried and traded blows, knocking over furniture and smashing frangible objects. Then one of the others managed to get behind Thread and bring a pistol butt down smartly on his head. When he came around, he found himself manacled to a straight-backed chair by the wrists and ankles.

"Damn you, what are you doing here?" he shouted. "You have no right to search here. The resident of this apartment is a member of the UN delegation of the People's Republic of China. He has diplomatic immunity."

"You're right," said the agent in charge. "*He* has immunity, and so does his office in the UN Building. But this is a private dwelling with no diplomatic status. It's subject to federal, state, and local laws just like any other." He showed his ID folder and the search warrant. "Now, unless you want to be arrested and deported, I suggest you leave immediately. If you agree, I'll release you."

The little man glowered at them, then recovered his composure and said, "Very well. But you will regret this. You *and* your government."

Once the secretary was descending on the elevator, the team chief spoke into his radio: "Thread's just leaving. Put a tail on him."

Ho was more than shocked when he learned the federal authorities had searched his apartment. How could he have missed the signs they were closing in? He silently castigated himself for being so lax as to leave the tapes and transcripts there.

Important as this operation was, even more was involved. Once Beijing learned he'd been doubled, he'd disappear and never be seen or heard of again.

Survival was not yet his main concern; he could always get false papers and go underground. But without diplomatic cover, he would lose much of his usefulness to the Centralist movement. Lund would turn a harsh face and even harsher words upon him. He dreaded the mere thought of their next meeting.

Meanwhile, he had to warn those in Toronto of the

near-debacle here, then perform a few miracles to repair the damage. And none of his normal communications could be trusted.

He took a devious route to the waterfront. Whole chapters of the pavement artists' manual went into throwing off any tail.

He normally encoded messages using a master codebook he kept in the safe in his UN office. Now he had only the much simpler code he carried with him on sheets of rice paper. Just the use of this would tell those in Toronto that the New York operation had been blown.

Finished with its misadventure in the Red Sea, the S. S. *Moldavia* had docked in Manhattan to await the captive General Borland. About ten minutes after Ho went aboard, the ship's transmitter began sending on a common ship-to-shore frequency in the HF band.

The signals were picked up by an antenna atop a building in Manhattan, identified as code, and sent by wire to McClean, Virginia, to be fed to a giant computer.

This was the NSA's code-breaking center. The machine and its operators had penetrated far more sophisticated ciphers than Ho's simple portable model. When the reply came from Toronto, in less than an hour, the code was different but similar in pattern, characteristic of simple one-time pads. The McLean machine dealt with it even more summarily than it had the first.

The code-breaking function was performed for all federal agencies. Copies of the original and the reply were on Ingraham's desk when he arrived next morning.

After studying both messages, he said to his assistant, "There's some tie-in between the Borland kidnapping and the guy who jumped off the balcony in Schenectady. And I have strong suspicions the Albigensians are involved in both." He paused and frowned. "Let's see, Gossett is DoD's man on the case. See if you can get him for me."

B. Michelaard

In his office in the Pentagon, Gossett picked up the phone himself. An unknown voice asked him to please hold, then another, all too well known, said, "Good morning, Mary Sunshine."

"I hope this isn't social. I'm up to my ass in alligators."

"Not at all, dear boy. Let's scramble."

There was a delay while each man pressed a button on his phone console. "Okay, you read?"

"Yes, quite. And now to business. I hold in my hand a printout of a certain coded message from New York to Toronto, intercepted yesterday in the gloaming. Also a reply from Toronto about an hour later." He gave the identifying NSA file numbers. "You have your copies yet?"

"Mm, no."

"Alas, distribution gets no better on the banks of the Potomac. Anyway, there's a certain China Bird who's got a hot package he wants to export. All signs point to the label as General Borland. I gather the Bureau put a rather heavy foot on Ho's operation yesterday but failed to turn up the general."

"Right. No question they're the ones who grabbed him. Whoever *they* are. I was in on the search and saw the evidence." Gossett paused. "So what's your interest?"

"Our interest is precisely the *they,* dear boy. We think it's a new opposition that's somehow sprung up in the Third World and is looking to fill the vacuum left by the implosion of the KGB."

"Well, first priority has to be getting General Borland back unharmed and above all uninterrogated. At least by any experts. I'd say he's been able to resist so far, but we both know that with enough time and the right facilities you can get information out of anybody."

"My dear Alex, we are of one mind in this matter. I had more or less divined what you've just told me, and I thought we might scratch each other's itch. With your

236

cooperation, we could retrieve the general and snuff two birds with one snuffer. To turn a phrase."

"Yes, you do have a way with words." Gosset's tone dripped irony.

"These new players in the game seem to have set up shop in Toronto for the nonce, so we'd probably have the event venued there. Avoid any embarrassing complications."

"Sounds to me like a way to guarantee complications. A member of the Chinese UN delegation turns up deceased of unnatural causes on Canadian territory. Tempers flare between Beijing and Ottawa. And meanwhile there stands Uncle Sam like a cat with feathers on its whiskers saying he has no idea what happened to the canary. And you think Ottawa isn't going to be pissed?"

"You do have a lurid imagination. Our scenario would leave Beijing with no grounds for complaint without admitting their man was an agent. It would all be done with our usual finesse."

"That's what worries me." Gossett couldn't resist that small dig. "However, to respond to your inquiry, this is way above my head. You'll have to talk to my Director. Correction, your Director will have to talk to mine. However, I'd expect a go-ahead."

The facility that had picked up Ho's message to Lund had directional capability. By cross-referencing, the operators located the source of the signals at the berth occupied by the SS *Moldavia*. Again, Hellman had U.S. attorneys and federal judges working overtime on a warrant to search the ship. He also had to enlist the aid of U.S. Customs and the Port Authority police since they had primary jurisdiction.

When everything was ready, a motorcade approached the docks with sirens blaring. Dozens of agents swarmed up the gangplanks, interrupting cargo-loading.

B. Michelaard

Among the search party were men familiar with this class of vessel. They knew all the obscure places where things could be hidden. The search was thorough and left no hatch cover unturned. Yet when it was over, they had to report to a very chagrined Hellman that there was no trace of the missing General Borland or the elusive Ho Ah Ling.

Even as Ho left the docks, he was formulating a new plan: Chinese surgeons would be demonstrating the surgical use of acupuncture at a medical symposium about to convene in Tokyo. As a trade representative, he had been active in promoting and publicizing this event in North America, getting U.S. and Canadian surgeons to attend.

Now, he decided, General Chip Borland was about to become a candidate for acupuncture.

Chapter Twenty-three

As part of the search for General Borland, Alex Gossett spent the day overworking both his head and the phone lines. When he finally left the Pentagon, he was startled to discover the sky was dark. The clock and the sun had raced while he had run on a treadmill.

Divorced some years ago, he now kept a bachelor pad near Annandale in suburban Virginia. During the half-hour drive, he went on tugging at the problem like a raccoon at a garbage can, but once home, he decided to rest his brain before it overheated.

He poured three fingers of scotch, added ice and a dash of soda, kicked off his shoes, and sat there in the dark with his feet up. Limply, he pondered whether to go out for dinner or throw something together in his own kitchen. Neither held much appeal.

The phone interrupted these desultory thoughts. "Yeah." His own voice sounded hoarse.

"Gracious, my dear fellow, you do keep late hours. I've

B. Michelaard

been trying this number since just after six. And you sound a mere shell of your normal self."

He was in no mood for Ingraham's Brit-style line of patter, and was about to give him the vocal scorched-earth treatment. But a pause and swallow of scotch brought milder counsel. "I was in the comm center till late. So what can I do for you?"

"It's what I can do for you, old chap. But first, let me ask—you did get your copies of those intercepts?" Gossett affirmed he had. "Well, I think when they're read aright, they tell us where a certain rendezvous is to take place."

Gossett straightened in his seat, and before he realized what he was saying, said, "Where?"

"Oh, come now, Alex. Not over an unscrambled phone. Not in this town. The overwork must be getting to you."

Gossett sighed. "Right. So . . . ?"

"Meet me at the Cappuccino. Say, twenty minutes? I'll buy you a drink. You sound like you need it."

"I'll have to make myself presentable. Then there could be traffic. Say half an hour."

"Fine. I'll be in the bar."

While he showered, shaved, and dressed, Gossett's thoughts were plagued by Ingraham. The fact that the damned Brit accent and Oxford manner happened to be genuine made them no less annoying. Nor did they keep Ingraham from being a genuine Yankee, born in the USA. He had simply spent his growing-up years in Britain, where his father had represented an American company. Somehow, the young Ingraham had gotten into one of the better English prep schools and from there into Oxford. It was a story he'd been known to recount at the drop of an eyelid.

Driving away from the apartment, Alex checked his watch. Going on ten. At this hour, even the Cappuccino should have some empty seats, which could solve his dinner problem. A steak and a tossed green salad with a mug of imported German beer made a suddenly tempting prospect. And he might have cause to celebrate.

Traffic wasn't bad. In just over twenty minutes, he pulled up under the porte cochere and surrendered keys and car to the valet attendant.

The Cappuccino was only a few years old, but already among the favorites of the fat-cat lobbyists who used topless showgirls and bottomless expense accounts as tools of their trade. Along with meals at places like the Cappuccino.

Image congruity was not a serious or even familiar concept around the Capital, so despite the Italian name, the interior was the usual designer's version of English Tudor. Gas log fires flickered beneath copper hoods. The "leaded" windows were plastic, but the floors were real quarry tile. There was antiqued brick and rough-finished wood and red leatherette. To mute the sounds, fake baronial banners hung from the walls and ceiling beams.

Entering the bar, Alex spotted Ingraham alone in a booth, where a waitress was just arriving with a martini. He caught her before she left, ordered a scotch, then slid into the seat opposite.

For the first few minutes, they made small talk. When the waitress brought Gossett's drink, Ingraham raised a hand. "Allow me, please." He laid some bills on her tray.

Gossett glanced around and said, "Odd place for this kind of exchange. Now, what's this amazing discovery?"

"Not really." Ingraham raised a cautionary finger. "One moment, however." From inside his sport coat, he took what looked like a small transistor radio, extended its telescoping antenna. When he switched it on, soft music was heard. "Now we can talk with reasonable safety. My little toy here will ward off any evil spirits with parabolic mikes and other electronic snoopery."

"So talk," Gossett said.

"Anent the suicide of Doctor Dwayne Chauncey. The key element here would seem to be Prowther. Girlfriend,

241

fiancée, or whatever. A woman with something of a political past, and once a dedicated Maoist. The Bureau has a file on her dating way back. Ours covers the time she spent in Europe. Why she ended up medium-rare on a Toronto freeway is still a mystery. It may even have been a genuine accident." While he spoke, he was packing the bowl of a large, curved-stem briar.

"So what's the connection with General Borland?"

"All in good time." Ingraham sipped his martini and glanced over the room. "During Prowther's time in Europe, her politics apparently mellowed from Maoist to Green, but she was still in touch with her old friends. And we think some of them may be part of this new opposition we've been trying to get a handle on. Hard-core Marxists who filtered out of China and the Soviet Union and set up shop together in the Third World. Chauncey was involved, albeit indirectly, in this thing called Pegasus. They kidnapped Prowther to make him tell what he knew."

"All very fascinating," said Gossett. "But I still don't see—"

"Patience, dear fellow. We're almost home." Ingraham flicked his lighter and spoke around the pipe stem as he drew flame into the bowl. "Prowther's Toronto studio is a plush town house four stories high with a mortgage to match. We managed to trace the same to a Singapore bank known to deal with the rougher elements in the Third World plus launder money for drug cartels. On her death, the title reverted to them."

He was looking intently across the table. "Am I making sense now, Alex? The *studio*. The place named in the message as the rendezvous. Apparently one of their safe houses. And they'd have time to bring in an expert interrogator."

Gossett jerked upright in his seat. "Sonova—!"

"Exactly. I thought you'd agree. You'll also recall the statement that Ho's contact would be someone he'd recognize. We think we know who that someone is. Old-line Marxist named Rodney Lund. Dates back before you and I were in knee pants. As soon as I made the connection, I put the place under surveillance. We can recover the general, intercept Ho Ah Ling. And who knows what birds might fall into our net."

Gossett smiled and sipped his drink. "I never wore knee pants."

Ingraham's expression turned ironic. "Oh, that's right. In this country, the privileges and symbols of adulthood come first. The duties and responsibilities later. Or not at all." He returned the device to his inner pocket before finishing off his martini. Then he got to his feet and clapped Gossett on the shoulder. "Relax, Alex. Enjoy your dinner. This'll all go off as slick as greased owl shit." Still puffing the pipe, he walked out without looking back.

Rodney Lund had spent the day cloistered in the studio, trying to understand some small facet of Chauncey's paper. As darkness fell, he was still baffled by these pages of math, which might as well be hieroglyphics. Were they a genuine exposition of the Willard effect or just scientific gobbledygook cooked up by Chauncey for Prowther's release? Equally frustrating were the transcripts of General Borland's interrogation. They yielded only what was known—Chip Borland was one tough Marine.

Chauncey—with his tongue loosened by drugs but his brain giddy from alcohol—had said the Willard effect had something to do with radar. And the air battles over Eritrea and the Red Sea suggested a stealth device, made to foil radar.

If these abstruse equations were genuine, they could be unbuttoned by Centralist scientists and engineers. But that would yield only technology, not the actual weapons system. So, in practical terms, General Borland was still their best hope in solving the Pegasus puzzle. The *Moldavia* at sea had seemed ideal for this operation.

But Ho's message on the ship's transmitter showed the FBI was close on his heels. The fallback was to hold the interrogation here, and the reply had told Ho to bring the general to the studio. Less than an hour later, a raid on the ship had nearly caught Ho in the dragnet.

So the messages had been intercepted, the code broken. Not surprising. The studio itself was probably blown. He was still here only because he was expecting a critical message—Ho's plan and requirements for moving the general to the Far East.

They had been watching the place in shifts for two days, fighting off ennui. Now one of them spoke into a hand transceiver. "Spud Three here. Somebody's just leaving the place. Sneaking out the back way."

"Description?"

Spud Three peered through a starscope at the receding figure. "Male. Tall and slender. Trench coat with no hat. White hair. I can only see his back, but that much fits the description of Stetson." "Stetson" was their code name for Lund, a backhanded reference to his view of hats.

"Spud Four, close in under that street lamp at the corner. Verify the face. Give us one beep for positive, two for negative."

When Lund emerged from the alley, a man apparently studying a city map by the light of the street lamp gave a start, then a fearful, almost hostile stare. He edged away, looking nervous, keeping his gaze on Lund, who nodded, delivered a jaunty, "Good evening," and kept moving.

"Evening," the man grunted in a tone of drunken suspicion. He reached up and pressed once on a button on his collar mike.

There was a faint, twanging sound. Lund jerked a little, continued a few staggering steps while his body twitched in small spasms, then collapsed. For several seconds, he lay there quivering and jerking, went rigid a moment, then limp. Dark-clad figures converged on him. Two of them carried "stun guns." One was reeling in the wires through which the device delivered its paralyzing shock.

The brief glow of a pocket flashlight lit the subject's face. "That's our man. Let's get him in the car." The limp figure was lifted and moved into the rear seat, positioned between two of them. The car drove away, joined by one parked nearby and another that emerged from the alley.

"Help me get his arm out of this sleeve," said one of the two in the rear with Lund.

The man next to the driver spoke into a handheld mike: "Potato Patch, be advised Spud has retrieved the Stetson."

"Spud, this is the Patch. Proceed as planned." There was a pause. "And good work."

"Wait a minute," came a mutter from the rear, where a hypodermic was poised near Lund's arm. "I'm not getting any pulse." He moved his fingers to the neck, to the carotid artery.

"Kind of a humdrum way to report we just got us the notorious and legendary Rodney Lund," said the driver.

"What we got," said a voice from the rear, "is a dead body."

The call from Alex Gossett wakened Michelle from a sound sleep. "Pack your bags," he said. "You're on your way to that acupuncture demonstration in Tokyo."

Today was her return flight to Washington, so her bags were already packed. What's the catch?" she managed despite her sleep-clouded brain.

"The catch is we think that's how they're moving General Borland out of the country. Somebody got hold of a message to that effect. Pacific and Orient Airways flight One-Oh-One. New York to Tokyo via Chicago, Seattle, and Anchorage. Three days a week. The next one's tomorrow. Be on it and keep your eyes open."

She sat up and huffed in annoyance. "Alex, are you deliberately trying to foul up my wedding plans?"

She heard his soft chuckle. "Nothing of the kind. But

you know Borland personally. And as a physician, you've got a logical reason to be on that flight. So you're my first choice. That's all I can tell you. Your reservation's been made. Pick up your ticket at the P&O Airways counter."

When P&O Airways 101 arrived at Sea-Tac Airport, a chauffeur-driven Mercedes was waiting at the terminal. The locals all recognized that Armand St. Clair and his wife Helene were either meeting their daughter Michelle or dropping her off.

With boarding for the continuation of POA 101 announced, Helene St. Clair said, "Now Mike, darling, you will stop again on your way back?" She had a relatively unlined face and a trim, athletic figure that could have passed for twenty years less than her actual sixty-three. "And do try not to have one of those quickie weddings. All your friends will want to meet your young man, who's so famous."

Michelle's full mouth curved into a smile. "Keep in mind my *young man* is a colonel well up in his forties. And in some quarters he's still thought of as not so much famous as notorious. As for the wedding, a quickie may be all we can manage. Anyway, I've had my white-gown wedding." She put her arms out, embraced and kissed her mother. "Bye Moms. It's been too short but great all the same." Then she turned to her father.

Armand St. Clair was a bear of a man, and engulfed Michelle in a bear hug while she kissed his cheek. He had a dense, stiff shock of ash-white hair and the complexion that went with life outdoors. "This colonel of yours sounds like my kind of man, but I just don't like turning my baby over to somebody I've never met."

She grinned at him. "Dad, your baby's thirty-six years old. She's been falling and skinning her knees and getting up on her own for quite a few years now." She hugged him back. "Love you, Woolly-Bear."

Last call for Flight 101 was announced. She turned,

passed through the detectors, gave a final wave, then hurried along, among the last to board. Soon after she was seated, the doors were closed, the engines started, and the plane taxied.

She was not the only surgeon on board bound for Tokyo and the symposium. She got recognizing waves from those she had known and worked with.

Cocktails were served and then dinner. Afterward, she read until the head stew announced they were thirty minutes out of Anchorage and on time. She decided to visit the rest room before the seat-belt sign came on.

As she passed toward the rear, she noticed for the first time a man whose face was swathed in bandages. He was surrounded by what appeared to be another group of doctors, none of them known to her. Evidently taking their own patient to Tokyo.

The aircraft was a wide-body, with two aisles. The center section had four seats across. Those on the outside had three each. The man with the bandaged face was in the middle seat on the outside section. As she passed along the aisle, he suddenly reached out and clutched her by the arm, pulled her toward him.

She was startled and then frightened, tried to pull away, but his grip was powerful. He put his head close to her, and she heard him say, "Mike ! It's me! Chip Borland! I liked your silver dress the night you came to dinner."

Chapter Twenty-four

"I can't believe it! Rodney Lund right in our grasp." Forrester made a fist as he spoke. "Then you pull off a cowboy operation, and we end up with nothing but a body to dispose of and bills to pay!" Behind him, Lafayette Briggs paced and frowned.

Ingraham sat there doing his best to look composed and confident. "Your pardon, Milt," he said. "But this was no cowboy operation. It was run according to Hoyle and the Marquis of Queensbury. We could've had the Good Housekeeping seal."

"Then why have we got an empty file"—Forrester dangled a manila folder—"and a *corpus* which is definitely non-delectable?"

"Unforseeables. From Lund's meager medical profile, our medical plus a contract consultant recommended stun guns over chemical darts. We had no way of knowing he had a pacemaker."

"A simple knock over the head too low-tech for you?"

Ingraham smiled. "Now *that's* real cowboy. *And* too

risky. What does one tell the chance passerby? And too hard a knock can be fatal or induce memory loss. We took all that into account."

Briggs paused in his pacing. "We did get a few positives. Lund was carrying sensitive papers. A decoded message about General Borland. Plus the account by that GE scientist about something called the Willard effect. The Pentagon has it classified burn-before-reading."

Forrester grunted. "Great. At least the Pentagon's happy. Their supersecret toy is back under wraps."

"Not until we get General Borland back," said Ingraham. "They tried to interrogate him but didn't get anything because it was done by amateurs. I'm sure their plan was to bring their experts to that studio in Toronto and have him interrogated there."

Forrester sighed, leaned back. "The question is: Was it Albigensian?"

"No doubt in my mind," said Ingraham. "Lund was a Marxist fanatic. With the Soviet Union dissolved and Red China faded to pink, this was his last, best hope."

"This," said Briggs with a deep frown. "But we're still like the blind men feeling the elephant. We still don't have the size and shape of this. Much less its geographic centrum."

Hearing the bandaged man, Mike was stunned. Before she could react, the man in the aisle seat-stood up and pulled the other's grip loose. "I'm sorry," he said. "My cousin's not himself. We're taking him to Tokyo to see if they can help him there." He was tall, with dark hair and an affluent look. Her physician's eye put his age as at least mid-forties, but noted he could pass for several years younger.

She sought out an attendant and said she needed to send a message to Anchorage.

"Yes, well, that'll be up to the captain." The girl took an intercom handset from its cradle and spoke into it.

After a brief exchange, she hung up. "He'll be here in a minute."

Captain Alphonse Morgeau came across as a self-consciously handsome man. His uniform was finely tailored and the gray in his hair carefully limited to the temples. Mike put his age at mid-fifties, surmising that exercise, saunas, skin emollients, and massage were staving off the ravages of time.

He was trim and fit-looking, but below medium height and evidently sensitive. In the confines of the galley, she towered over him. He avoided having to look up by standing beside instead of in front of her.

When she gave her name, he showed a smile of recognition. "Oh, yes, the Olympic skater. I'm very glad to know you."

"The disqualified *former* Olympic skater," she corrected, and saw the man's eyebrows go up. She showed him the folder that identified her as a federal agent while being suitably vague about the agency. Then she filled him in.

He listened carefully, then asked, "Are you sure about this man? I'd hate to have a nasty incident over a case of mistaken identity."

"I know the general personally. His wife and I are friends. He grabbed me and said something only he could know about me."

Again, he took her hand. "Thanks for bringing this to our attention. I'll explain the situation to the authorities in Anchorage. After that, it'll be in their hands." He touched his cap and departed.

Moments later, Mike and the attendant confronted the muzzle of a silenced revolver. It was held by the dark-haired man who had intervened in the general's attempt to speak with her. Behind him was a second—blond, shorter, but about the same age—who also carried a pistol.

Several thoughts raced through Mike's head: How had

they gotten guns aboard? Were they real, or just realistic fakes?

Mentally, she labeled the pair Calvin and Hobbes. The tall, dark-haired one who seemed to be in charge had his gaze fixed on her. "Now, just what stories have you been telling the captain?"

"None of your damned business," she snapped. His hand with the gun drew back. She threw an arm up to protect herself, and a fist in the midriff knocked the breath and voice out of her. She bent over and struggled against nausea.

The attendant's face puckered with fear and shock, and her eyes were tearful. "Oh, God! Stop it, please! She told him that kidnapped Pentagon general is on board. She says she knows him." She looked pleading. "Look, please. All I did was—"

"Shut up!" said "Calvin." There was a short silence while he appeared to weigh alternatives. "All right, we're all going to walk out of here and up forward." He looked at the attendant. "I'll shoot the first one who makes trouble. And you'd better hope nothing goes wrong so we can let you walk off this plane alive." He gestured with his head. "Now move."

The attendant went first, followed by Calvin. Hobbes got behind Michelle and urged her along. That punch in the middle still had her gasping. When they reached her seat, he muttered, "Sit down and stay there."

The rest of the flight passed without visible incident. The two men went up forward and did not return, but another quietly took the seat next to General Borland.

The airplane descended through shelving stratus and dimming light. There was the usual reminder to fasten seat belts. They broke out of the overcast over Cook's Inlet, with the lights of Anchorage glowing up ahead. The announcement that they would soon be landing was followed by a second message: "Ladies and gentlemen, due to circumstances beyond our control, Pacific and Orient Flight One-Oh-One will be delayed in Anchorage. We ask that all passengers please leave the aircraft at the air terminal. Be sure to take your personal belongings. You will receive further information regarding the continuation to Tokyo. Thank you for your cooperation."

With the passengers gone, Ho Ah Ling sat there, thinking almost feverishly, while trying to avoid one particular thought—that events were conspiring against him. Lund had taught always to have a backup plan, but he was feeling overwhelmed by the number of failed backups. And Lund was not there to help, gone missing under ominous circumstances.

Ho's only piece of good luck had been to leave the *Moldavia* before U.S. authorities raided and searched the vessel. His one pleasant surprise was the extent of Lund's network. Someone among the service crews at Seattle-Tacoma airport had gotten pistols aboard. That salvaged the operation from the sheer bad luck of having that woman aboard. Then he recalled what Lund had said about luck. The more he thought about it, the more he was inclined to believe she was a federal agent.

The situation remained tense. He considered various possibilities, and one began to emerge as the most promising.

Conspicuous among the milling pilots and flight attendants in POA Ops was a knot of uniformed police plus others whose civilian clothes plainly said "law enforcement." They conversed in low, tense voices.

As Michelle approached, one of them—a lean, wiry man of medium height and wearing glasses—introduced himself: "Granger, ma'am. U.S. Marshal." His clothing and complexion lent him an air of being at home in the out-of-doors. The two with him he introduced as Stoller and Whitehead, FBI agents.

"Michelle St. Clair, DoD." They exchanged ID displays. "We had information that General Borland might be aboard," Granger said.

They peppered her with questions about what happened after the general spoke to her. At the part where Calvin and Hobbes threatened them with guns, the questions grew detailed and probing. A forensic artist was summoned and produced a picture of Calvin from Mike's description. As the face took form on the page, the two FBI men began trading glances. Finally, one said, "Well, I'll be damned. Right out of the woodwork. And after all these years."

"Clifton Burr," said the other. "Firebrand campus radical of the sixties. One-time head of the Student Revolutionary Movement. Disappeared in seventy-two. Still wanted on a federal warrant for bombing a university lab that had Pentagon research contracts." Mike recalled the name.

"So when do you expect to have General Borland free?"

Their mouths tightened, and their feet shifted uneasily. "We don't know. Right now, the hijackers are holding the flight crew and demanding the airplane be refueled."

"I need to report to my . . . supervisor. Tell him we've located General Borland." She didn't want to say "control" to these people.

While they caucused, she sought out a phone and called the contact number for Gossett. She got a recorded message and left one. Then she rang Connie, who cried and laughed at once and hardly made sense. Gradually, she calmed down so Mike could relate the details.

After hanging up, Mike went to look outside. The POA aircraft, its metal skin gleaming under flood lamps, had become the focus of a tense drama. The baggage was being unloaded, and refueling hoses were connected. The news media had arrived with all their gear, but the cameras and reporters were being held back, along with the general public.

She tried to read a medical journal, but it was no good. She couldn't concentrate, could only pace and stew internally.

Then her attention was grabbed by a series of popping and crackling sounds, muffled but recognizable as gunfire. Along with the others, she hurried toward the windows to see what was happening, but police and airline officials kept everyone back. A short while later, Granger again appeared and beckoned to her.

He introduced her to a big, lean, ruddy-faced police commander named Porter. "May I ask what your medical specialty is, Doctor?" said Porter.

"I'm a thoracic and general surgeon."

He looked hopeful. "Any experience with gunshots?"

"Quite a bit."

"We've got a case of what appears to be a ricochet somewhere in the upper chest. Lightweight frangible slug, twenty-five-caliber. Not near the heart. Perhaps you could advise us . . ."

"Wouldn't it be easier to move the patient to a hospital? You could—" She noted his awkward look. A sudden chill invaded her midsection. "Something tells me it's General Borland."

"Well . . . ah . . . 'Fraid so. We broke in, but they held one of the stews with a pistol to her head, so our men had to back off. The general's still aboard the aircraft, and they're asking for a doctor. Demanding, in fact."

That chill took a tighter grip on her viscera. The last time she volunteered, she'd come close to being killed or taken as a prize of war.

But this was Chip Borland. He was her assigned responsibility. And she couldn't call Connie "friend," yet turn her back on Chip. She heard herself saying, "Then make the arrangements for me to go aboard. And I'll need medical supplies and instruments. Sutures, sterile dressings, blood plasma. I'll make out a list."

Porter looked at Granger and the others. "I'll leave the arrangements to you gentlemen while I get started on those supplies."

The wait was not long. Before she had time to regret her action, Granger was back. "If you'll come along, you can go aboard now."

"Get me a large pair of shears. I'll need them to cut the clothing away from the wound."

As soon as she entered the aircraft, she was grabbed, the scissors taken from her. "So, it's you," said the man identified as Clifton Burr. "Sort of poetic justice since you're the cause of all this trouble." He made her spread her legs and lean against a bulkhead while he did a very thorough search, showing no reticence about her female parts.

"I won't try to dispute the twisted logic in that statement," she said. "But if you've had your jollies now, could I see my patient? And I'll need those shears."

The odor and sting of tear gas hung in the air. She found General Borland lying across a four-seat center section. The wrapping had been removed from his head. His shirt was blood-soaked, and the seat cushion was damp with blood.

Quickly, almost roughly, she cut away the clothing to expose the wounds. Her examination told her he was in shock from substantial blood loss. The entry wound was a small, neat puncture, not the keyhole shape typical of ricochets. But the exit showed haggled flesh and extensive trauma. The light, frangible, high-velocity bullet had probably struck a rib and shattered, the largest fragment making an exit through the intra-costal space. The rest could be anywhere. The saliva was blood-tinged; so the lung had sustained some trauma but not collapsed.

"He's in serious condition," she said. "We'll have to get him to a hospital."

"That's not possible."

255

"Then you just may have a dead man on your hands. I won't say on your conscience, because I know you don't have any."

"Two dead men, Doctor." He pointed to the corpse of "Hobbes," which she had not noticed before. "The pigs killed one of ours when they tried to shoot their way in here. Anyway, you and the general both go with us. And if he dies, we'll hold you responsible."

Chapter Twenty-five

One last time, Melissa Carrell, in the guise of Lucinda Morgan, pressed the button below the brass plate inscribed *Penross* in antique script. After tonight, Lucy Morgan would disappear forever.

The closed-circuit camera scanned her with electro-mechanical suspicion. Then the concierge lock buzzed, and she pulled the door open.

Her excitement rose with the elevator, albeit tinged with regret. This would be her last romp with Arthur Penross. One of the better rolls in the hay she'd had with "subjects" of her "profiles." She'd been playing Penross like a fiddle, and tonight was the grand finale.

His smile and expectant look spelled relief: He had no suspicions. She'd be glad to give her best in return for doing her worst.

"Pigs," Michelle mused as she knelt beside the wounded general. Clifton Burr had referred to the police as the pigs. His mind-set was congealed circa 1969. "Get a blanket over him," she said, looking up at Burr. "And a cushion to prop up his feet." She sneezed from the lingering tear-gas fumes. "And for God's sake ventilate this place. He's having enough trouble breathing."

"The pilot assures us the ventilation system will have the fumes out shortly." Burr too had sniffles and watery eyes.

She pointed at the overhead panels and said, "Oxygen." One of the stews dropped a mask out of its compartment. Mike placed it over the general's face and continued her examination. "Tell the authorities I'll have a further list of supplies I'll need."

"Write it out, and we'll deliver it," said Burr.

"I'll dictate. I can't spare the time to write. Let me make one more plea to have this patient moved to a hospital. Otherwise, I really can't be responsible."

"As I've already made clear, Doctor, you *are* responsible."

"More of your twisted logic."

"You American doctors are lost without all those machines. In most of the world, there are no hospitals in reach of the poor. Yet somehow the doctors manage."

"I know more than you might think about medical practice in those places, and their survival rate is a fraction of ours. If you wreck your car, you take it where they have the proper tools and equipment to do the repairs. It only makes sense to give the human body the same advantage."

"And we're only trying to get the wealthy nations to share their means so the poorer ones can have more hospitals and such."

"Only poverty can be shared by force. Wealth has to be created, through effort and ingenuity. So instead of playing Robin Hood, you'd do better to convince them to put in a full day's work. But then nothing so prosaic would make you feel like their anointed savior, would it?"

He seemed about to argue with her, but she was all

business again. "Now, why don't you make yourself useful and try to expedite those medical supplies." She noticed the cigarette and lighter he had taken out. "And don't smoke near this oxygen or my patient."

He put them away and went toward the cockpit.

She got two of the plastic sacks that contained eating utensils and taped them over the wounds as an air seal, to prevent sucking and pneumothorax. Beyond that, she could do little besides monitor his condition.

The first supplies were delivered shortly, and she gave Borland an antibiotic to ward off infection. Then she got a pint of plasma going on an IV. An attendant improvised a way to suspend the bottle with a coat hanger.

At 11:00 P.M. in New York, 8:00 P.M. in California, the major networks all preempted normal programming for live coverage of the hijacking.

Since the Red Sea affair, TV news had become a kind of mild addiction aboard Skyhook, and most of the men not on duty were already in the wardroom, Gus and Borland at their usual table. "Good evening," said the anchorman. "In a somewhat bizarre chain of events, Marine General Chalmers 'Chip' Borland, the kidnapped Pentagon staff officer, today turned up in a drugged state aboard a Pacific and Orient Airways jetliner bound for the Far East, apparently being spirited out of the country.

"The discovery triggered the hijacking of the aircraft by armed men among the passengers. Our correspondent is on the scene, and we now take you live via satellite to Anchorage, Alaska."

Around the wardroom there was a stir and an almost involuntary turning of heads to glance at Hank Borland. The local correspondent appeared on-screen against the background of the POA airliner. "The first to identify General Borland was Dr. Michelle St. Clair, another one-time public personality and a personal friend of Mrs. Borland. Now a surgical resident at a Washington hospital, Doctor St. Clair was a center of controversy some years ago when she was disqualified as a member of the U.S. Olympic figure-skating team."

Moments later came the second shock—the news of Chip's wound and Mike's return aboard to administer to him. They showed film of her going up the boarding stairs and entering the airplane.

Hank looked at Gus and muttered in an unsteady voice, "That woman of yours sure has her nerve. God bless her."

When the last of the supplies were delivered, Mike could finally give an injection to counter the effects of shock and blood loss. Then she and one of the stews, a former nurse who offered to assist, scrubbed and donned surgical gloves, masks, and gowns. After numbing the area with a local, Mike located and removed some of the bullet fragments.

Working intently, she lost track of time. She heard the doors being shut and the engines started.

She cauterized and began suturing the wounds.

So far, the general had remained comatose, or nearly so. Now his vitals began to improve. He stirred and made faint sounds. The strong stimulant plus the plasma seemed to be overcoming both the shock and the drugs that had kept him in a subdued state. As she was taping the dressing in place, his eyelids fluttered open. Then he pulled the oxygen mask down. "Jesus, what happened? Where the hell are we?" His voice was faint and husky.

She cautioned him, touching a finger first to her own lips, then to his. In a soft, steady voice with her mouth close to his ear, she oriented him to time, place, and circumstances.

"Mm, yeah. I remember being grabbed out of my car. Then the cellar of a house." He followed her cue and spoke in a whisper. "They kept sticking me with needles. I almost got away once, but they shoved me into a car. Since then, everything's pretty much of a fog. Then I recognized you coming down the aisle. I thought, my God! That's Gus's fiancée." He frowned. "How'd you—?"

"Tsh! tsh! tsh!" Again she cut him off with a finger to his lips. "I'd rather not have that known right now. They've had you chemically pacified. I suspect the kind of drugs used to keep people quiet in nursing homes. You've been mostly just alert and aware enough to walk and eat and sit upright."

The call on Arthur Penross's private line came at a most awkward moment. He and "Lucy Morgan" were locked in passion's embrace. Yet even in flagrante delicto, he interrupted his pelvic thrusts and, between heaving breaths, muttered, "Oh, damn!"

She tightened the grip of her arms and legs and hissed, "Never mind! Finish what you've started!"

Meanwhile, his answering machine invited the caller to leave a name and number and promised a prompt return. After the beep, a man's voice said he had just gotten hold of some sensitive documents for a limited time. He asked for a meeting in half an hour.

Moments later, Penross was seized by quivering, seismic groans, and surflike sighs. Then he sagged into inertia like a beached whale. Finally, he moved to disengage, but Lucy clung with all four limbs. His efforts to free himself against her resistance set her giggling, renewed their pelvic motion, and were rewarded with an orgasmic lagniappe. Then she too succumbed to languor and let him roll off her.

He rose and went into the bath. She heard the shower run briefly. He came out and dressed. At the bedroom door, he paused and said with a smile, "I shouldn't be more than an hour. Don't go 'way."

When he was gone, she took her time and a shower too, knowing he wouldn't be back before dawn.

During her earlier visits, she had played on his ego, gotten him to reveal some of the details of his computer system, while being careful not to generate suspicion. After a minute or so at the keyboard, she chose one of his several phone lines and dialed a number.

When it was answered, she said, "Okay, we'll talk on this line. Here's the number to dial for his modem." She read it off. In about half a minute, the computer responded. She began working the keyboard while periodically giving advice or instructions over the phone. After almost an hour of false starts and experimental moves, she abruptly said, "Bingo! That's it. We're in. I'm leaving now. You can crank up the vacuum. See you in about twenty minutes."

She wrote Penross a note of regret.

For Michelle, the situation had settled into nerve-wracking tension-cum-boredom. The interior lights were dimmed, and the hijackers took turns dozing. Her aggressive measures in treating the general were complete. What remained was monitoring his condition. With her supplies spread on the floor, she was down on her hands and knees a lot.

That was how she happened to see the pistol.

It was underneath the seats near the dead man. It must have fallen from his hand and somehow gotten pushed out of sight.

Furtively, afraid of being discovered at any moment, she slid it along the carpet under the seats.

She had had some training and familiarization with weapons and identified this as a Browning automatic, unfired: The muzzle carried no whiff of cordite. The clip was full.

Sooner or later, they would come looking for it. She would be searched. Thoroughly. So would everything. One place was probably safe. She unzipped the general's fly, meanwhile whispering an explanation into his ear. Together, they worked the gun into his shorts till it rested just below his buttocks. Then she pulled the blanket up around him.

Silent as a ghost and nearly as invisible, Skyhook slipped its moorings and rose in darkness. At five hundred feet, the pilot brought in the power. The huge electrogenic propulsion units emitted a deep-toned, pervasive sound, like a distant waterfall. It spilled down the slopes, spread over the Mojave, and like water, was absorbed without trace.

This was Dead Man's Mesa, on the eastern edge of the Sierras. To Gus, the whole area was doubly familiar: Some fifty miles south was George AFB, on the western rim of the Mojave. He had arrived at George fresh out of fighter gunnery school. The wing had assigned him to a squadron, and the squadron had assigned him to B Flight. That was the key event in his career: The flight commander was Pete Cassidy. A few months later, he and Cassidy and all those others had taken their F-104's to Da Nang.

Near enough to see was Muroc Dry Lake and the lights of the Flight Test Center at Edwards. There, years later, he had gone through the Flight Test School, then helped probe the limits of manned flight, and built his reputation as a research pilot.

The message from Mother Hen had come while they watched the newscast from Anchorage. It withdrew Skyhook from Exercise Pol Roger and directed the airship on a course that took them southward.

Part of Pol Roger was to be Skyhook's first operational drop of paratroops. The provision for paratroops was a long pod attached to the belly. It accommodated fifty men and had its own sanitary and messing facilities. When the message came, the pod was attached though empty, and they took off with it in place.

They had passed San Diego when the second message

arrived. Gus and Hank retired to Hank's day cabin to go over the text.

It covered the events at Anchorage and added that the POA aircraft, still under control of the hijackers, was on a southerly course paralleling the coast. Destination was thought to be somewhere in the cocaine-producing area of South America.

Skyhook was to take up a direct course for a point ten miles off the coast of Colombia and wait there.

Pete Cassidy himself arrived in Mother Hen ops and took an active role in decision-making. One of the colonels led him over to a large video screen mounted faceup, like a tabletop. It showed a map of the west coast of North America and the adjacent Pacific. "This shows the track of P&O 101 so far," he said. A bright line extended about a hundred miles southeastward from Anchorage and roughly paralleled the coast of North America. "We managed to attach both a radio beacon and a radar transponder to the belly of that aircraft. So we're having no trouble tracking them."

"Battery-powered?" Cassidy said, showing a frown.

"Only as a backup, sir. It's powered through the nav light circuit."

"Any indications where they may be headed?" said Cassidy.

"Intelligence figured two main possibilities: the Far East, or some location in the cocaine country of South America. So it's looking like the second. We've sent Skyhook ahead on the projected track with a lead of about nineteen hundred nautical. It should be there waiting when the airliner reaches the coastal waters of Colombia."

Cassidy was still pondering all this when they were interrupted. "Call for you, General. Your office. Colonel Boulding."

Cassidy went to the glassed-in dais that overlooked the ops center and picked up a receiver. "Yes, Barney?"

"Sir, it's from the Red Queen. She sounds excited. Can you take it now? If so, we should scramble."

He pressed a button on the console. "Okay, scrambled. Put her on."

"Hello, Pete?"

"Fiona? What's up?"

"I think we've just nailed Arthur Penross. You're gonna love it."

Chapter Twenty-six

"Melissa, my dear, you've given the term pay dirt a whole new meaning. Or rather made it a double entendre." Fiona Freeland watched pages scroll by on the computer screen. "Getting us into his hard drive was super, but working out his labeling system was the real key. We're absolutely plundering his files."

The midnight electricity was burning in the *Avanti* editorial offices. "We worked our way backward till the stuff was too old to be interesting. Now it's all there in our own memory banks and as good as gone from his. And would I love to be there when Penross discovers our little virus."

"Where'd you manage to—?"

"Tut-tut, my dear. Your old Aunt Fiona has a right to a few secrets yet." Her look turned lascivious—grotesque on that ravaged face: "And just think how you got to amuse yourself while pulling off our little coup. I'd have a medal struck in honor of your more persuasive parts, but some narrow-minded people might see it as porno.

Then again, how many girls can get paid for doing it without being labeled you-know-whats."

"I don't get paid for doing it. I get paid to unlock doors. Doing it with the men involved when I happen to feel like it is just one of the perks."

Mike was sitting on the floor drowsing when she was yanked to her feet by Clifton Burr. "All right, where is it?" His voice was calm, menacing.

"Where is what?" She managed to look befuddled and vacuous. Not difficult as things stood.

He hit her in the face, forehand and backhand. The blows caught her totally off guard. Her ears rang a little, and her cheeks felt what seemed to be the imprint of each of his fingers.

"Now, I'll ask you one more time, where is it?"

She met his eyes, forced herself to look into his face and look frightened, which again was not difficult. "You've lost your marbles! I'm doing just what you demanded. How should I—?"

"Take off your clothes."

"I'll be damned! Find yourself a copy of *Playboy*."

"Or we'll do it for you." His voice was deadly calm.

With swift, perfunctory movements and a look of resigned disdain, she began unbuttoning. He seized, felt, and threw aside each item as she removed it. When she was down to basics, she turned her back to him, hooked her thumbs into the waistband of her panty hose, and without hesitation pushed it down to her thighs. "Have a look if you care to."

He threw the slip back at her. "Cover yourself, you black bitch!"

But the search was not over. He jerked the general's blanket off, looked, and felt around in the spaces between the seat cushions. "That's a good way to send him into shock," she said. Her voice was sharp, with no hint of a quaver, but her heart was thumping so hard she was afraid the tremors in her breasts might give her away.

They went through her medical kit and supplies and her purse. By the time she was dressed, they had moved the search elsewhere. When she finally heaved a sigh and again slumped to the floor next to the general, his hand slid out and gave her a squeeze on the shoulder.

She had confronted her captors where they held the advantage, and she had won. Her tremors of fright and the fragile sense of her own mortality were replaced by a new confidence.

The outrage against her privacy was sublimated. She felt a new assurance she would survive to feel Gus's embrace again. So far, she had not allowed herself more than fleeting thoughts of him. Too much potential for despair.

In darkness, Skyhook cruised a southeasterly heading that would lead them across the Mexican border near Yuma, Arizona.

Anticipating problems, Gus did not bother going to bed. Lying on his bunk in his flying suit, he slept only fitfully. About 0400, he strapped on his boots, shaved quickly, and went up to the bridge.

There was early-morning light around them and water below. The chronometer read twelve minutes after the hour. His watch, still on Pacific time, read 0412. But while he dozed, they had flown toward the sun and met the dawn. The altimeter read over ten thousand feet. That gave a true airspeed of about two hundred knots. Skyhook was well above the max altitude attainable on buoyancy alone.

The Navy commander who had the watch filled him in: During darkness, they had flown down the Rio Grande Valley and coasted out at just about Tampico. Right now they were over the Gulf, with the Yucatan Peninsula some three hundred-plus nautical miles to the east and Veracruz off the right wing at about a hundred. They should make landfall near Tabasco in less than an hour. From there, they would fly over Guatemala, parts of Honduras, and El Salvador, Nicaragua, and Costa Rica. They had covered about half of the approximately three-thousand-nautical-mile total, and should reach the Pacific coast of Panama near midday.

"And that hijacked airliner?" Gus said.

"Still paralleling the coast."

Gus stepped into the CIC. While he was talking with the duty controllers, the intercom announced another top-priority, "eyes only" message for him and Hank Borland.

Again, they met in Hank's day cabin. The message directed shooting out the airliner's engines one at a time as a way to induce the hijackers to give up. Shooting out all four engines might be necessary as a last resort. Every effort would be made to have a rescue ship on the scene if it came down at sea.

Borland shook his head. "Real can of worms."

"More like snakes," Gus said.

Hank sighed and gave him a level gaze. "They're asking more than they have a right to. Do they know in the Pentagon about you and Mike?"

"Would it make any difference?" Gus stood up. "I'd better go get things organized." He rang up flight operations and told them to get two birds combat loaded and on the line. He specified loading the guns with armor-piercing and ordinary tracer rounds only. No HE. The intent was to shut down the airliner's engines, not blow them up. Then he went back into CIC to check on the progress of POA 101.

The hours before getting airborne would always be a blur in his memory. As the time drew near, his years spent with airplanes and the immutables of flight took over and sleepwalked him through the preflight and launch. He was doing this personally. If any of the dozen or so things that could go wrong did and Michelle died as a result, he would not have to live with the memory that he had sent someone else.

Airborne, he was suddenly in full touch with his surroundings. To delay coming to grips with the terrible decisions ahead, his mind focused on the minutiae of reality. Each detail—the instrument readings, the cloud formations, the wash-day blue of the Pacific below, the shadow caste in the misty atmosphere by the two aircraft as the wingman took up position some eight hundred feet on his right—etched itself into his retinal memory.

This was his milieu, the earth's gaseous envelope, in which he had spent much of his adult life. In some ways, he felt more at home here than he did in the world of men and cities. Yet now the chill it laid on his spirit and its icy hand on his gut were cold as the stratosphere where he flew.

POA 101 showed on both Skyhook's radar and his own—a fat, inviting target. Ferocious as ever, the Bird Dog offered continuous primary and secondary means of destroying it.

The F-24's most fuel-efficient climb was supersonic without afterburners. He let the Mach meter rise to 1.15, raised the nose to hold it there. The speed also gave him a healthy overtake on the airliner. At ten miles, it emerged as a scintillating speck against deep indigo.

Well before they leveled, it loomed as a large shape in the view through the reflector glass of the Bird Dog, which showed the range now as 1.5 nautical and the Sidewinder as the weapon of choice. He throttled back and leveled out looking down the leading edge of its right wing, then moved in till he could see the details of the P&O logo on the vertical tail.

"Gentlemen," the SecDef, Harlan Walsh, was saying. "The currently operating Pegasus airship plus those projected to be built give us—in their uncompromised state—the capability to project American military power nearly anywhere in the world with unprecedented stealth and swiftness." He spoke in measured, scholarly tones that carried total conviction. Along with Pete Cassidy, he represented the Pentagon's view.

The Vice President had been hauled out of bed by a call from the White House, told he was needed to chair a meeting. It turned out to be in Mother Hen Operations. He knew about the Pegasus project and Mother Hen, but had never been here before.

"I quite appreciate that, Mr. Secretary." The CIA director lifted one eyebrow as he responded to Walsh's statement. His tone and manner—cold, urbane, patrician—were his trademark in official Washington. "My colleagues and I all do." He gave a languid gesture at that advisory body—or bodyguard—he had brought with him: the D/Ops, the AD for Counter-Intel, and three technical experts: Briggs, Forrester, and Ingraham.

Pete Cassidy was quick to second Walsh: "The cutbacks of the nineties all but gutted our capabilities. These petty Third World tyrants are springing up like weeds, and nowadays, we barely have the conventional forces to deal with just one at any one time. Without some means of pissing on a brushfire while it's still a brushfire, we'll find ourselves facing a real conflagration with no hydrant in sight. With Pegasus, we can land troops, support them with tactical air, launch cruise missiles. But if it becomes known that these airships even exist, then their effectiveness could be cut at least in half."

"These brushfires, General," said the Company's AD for Counter-Intel. "These Third World disturbances. What if we could put our finger on the cause? On the central figure behind most of these schemes?"

Cassidy raised his hands and showed the expression of a man offered a good deal on some low-tide property. "Fu Manchu! Doctor No! Professor Moriarty!"

"No, General. Albigensian," said the Director. "That's our code name. We've got a file on it as thick as the D.C.

271

phone book." He showed a small, deprecating smile. "It's a bit of whimsy on our part. The original Albigensian was a Christian heresy that arose in southern France and sought a return to pre-feudal Christian purity. This one arose in Moscow, spread to Beijing, and sought a return to the ways of Stalin and Mao. So it was branded a Communist heresy. Even before Gorbachev started talking *glasnost* and *perestroika* and Deng suppressed the Gang of Four, our Albigensians were taking up their cudgels in the name of Marxist purity.

"Some set up cells inside their own Communist Parties. Others burrowed into the Third World. They've built a sophisticated financial network in which drug traffic is one of the major sources of funds. Plus a considerable power base in the Third World—politicians and bureaucrats who are either bought, intimidated, or genuine converts. They've established connections with the new worldwide organized crime networks. We've seen a small but definite shift in policies that show their influence.

"They've also built up a network of spies, saboteurs, and assassins. We're about ninety-nine-percent sure Albigensian was responsible for that missile attack on your AWACS aircraft."

"That's all fascinating," said Gossett, there as part of the DoD legation. "But the immediate problem is they've got General Borland aboard that airliner and could be interrogating him right now. If they land anywhere out of our control, then the secret's as good as blown."

"Not necessarily, Alex old chap," said Ingraham. "The man in control is our old friend, Ho Ah Ling. He's been hit by a series of setbacks and forced to improvise, and by now must be close to panic. They have no idea they're being followed, so they're probably running for the surest refuge. With the airliner heading south and a maximum range that just takes in Valparaiso, there's a strong suggestion their destination is someplace in the area of

Colombia or Peru. The heart of cocaine country. We believe Albigensian Central has to be there."

"Still someone else's territory," said Hal Maarten. "To pursue them in from the coast, we'd have to get permission through diplomatic channels or violate local sovereignty. At sea, we can shoot out one engine at a time til the hijackers either give up or the airplane is forced to ditch. Either way, we can have our people on the scene. Rescue General Borland and the others and deal with the hijackers however it's convenient."

But Ingraham persisted: "If we follow P&O 101, find where it lands, your marvelous airship could help save its own security. Go in there undetected and pounce on the Albigensian leadership right in its lair."

"Alejandro, this is for Kabul. And bring me the message files from North America and Europe. Then tell the chef we'll have breakfast. We'll need some nourishment to deal with this continuing tense situation."

"As you wish, *Jefe*." Alejandro took the sealed form and delivered it to communications, where it would be opened and coded for transmission. There, he was given another envelope, also sealed, to take back to *El Jefe*.

This was how *El Jefe* spent most of his time at Casa Elena, receiving reports, issuing advice and directives. He was in almost constant radio contact with his various cells and operatives worldwide. On occasion, he even bought time on communications satellites, using the cover of the Centralia Corporation.

This morning, he was also awaiting news of P&O 101—the "tense situation" he had mentioned. Rodney Lund must now be presumed dead, and Ho's network destroyed. Yet General Borland could still be their key to the mysterious Pegasus Project. And having sustained such losses. *El Jefe* was prepared to go to extremes to have P&O 101 land at the Curracabamba airfield. Since taking over the property of the former mining company, he had had the runway extended and reinforced. He had ordered the receiving party to be there at least an hour before the ETA of 101.

The weather was also some concern. Late summer storms darkened much of the horizon.

His real concern, however, was the Pentagon. The Americans were sure to make some effort to divert that airliner, so he had taken measures to assure delivery: Once P&O 101 was picked up on radar, he could reach out and gather it in, like a poker pot. And Uncle Sam might discover that his mysterious adversary had some very effective teeth.

El Jefe's smile beamed irony. The company that had once mined copper and chemicals at Curracabamba had built, besides the mines and runway, a terrible reputation for exploiting its workers. The airstrip that had served as an instrument of private profit was now being used for a very different purpose.

Chapter Twenty-seven

As a copilot many years before, Captain Al Morgeau had been hijacked to Havana. He'd never forgotten and was prepared in case it ever happened again. And while he was pondering how he might get the chance to act, an unfamiliar but definitely American voice came through his earphones: "P&O 101, this is Hardshell Alpha. How do you read?"

"I read you loud and clear, Hardshell." The voice was coming over one of their UHF channels.

"One-Oh-One, you're directed to land at either Howard or Albrook air base in Panama. Stand by to copy navigational and approach clearance."

"I'd be happy to, Hardshell, but I'm afraid any deviation from our present course will get me or my crew members shot."

"Roger your situation, One-Oh-One. Have your hijackers given you a destination?"

"Affirmative, Hardshell. An airstrip somewhere near the border of Colombia and Ecuador."

"One-Oh-One, tell your hijackers to look out either side. We have orders to shoot out your engines one by one."

For Michelle, the hours after that search were an anticlimax, eroding some of her newly won confidence. Which she realized was just as well. In that hyper state, she might have done something foolhardy. Now, as Morgeau passed the word over the PA, they all moved to the windows.

Just beyond the wing tip was one of those odd-shaped silver-gray fighters she had seen during the Red Sea affair. Could Gus possibly . . . ? No. Coincidence would only stretch so far. Anyway, just the sight of the U.S. emblem was like hearing the bugle and seeing the cavalry charging over the hill to rescue the wagon train. Her confidence in living to see him rose another notch.

Thin smoke trailed from a small opening low in the fighter's nose. Then she understood: That pair had been sent to make sure General Borland did not fall into the wrong hands.

"*Jefe*! We have radar contact!"

Alvorado left his desk and came into the communications center, where they were getting the reports. The modest-sized room was jammed with state-of-the-art electronic equipment. "What distance are they?" The radar station perched on a peak some thirty miles distant. The control center was on the airstrip at Curracabamba. Here he had both radio and phone links with the center.

"Just inside the two-hundred-nautical-mile limit of our radar, *Jefe*," said one of the men wearing headsets.

"Have they made radio contact?"

The man shook his head. "We tried raising them on the one HF wavelength known to be used by Pacific and Orient and got no reply."

El Jefe turned to the man in charge of the comm center and said, "Call *Commandante* Volkov at Curracabamba.

Tell him to intercept our prize and escort it in. My orders." Then he clapped Alejandro on the shoulder. "By damn, if the Yankees have any plans to interfere, we'll show them we've now got teeth and claws."

"P&O One-Oh-One, tell your hijackers that unless you turn for Panama in one minute, I'll be forced to fire on you."

After some delay, the captain's voice came back. "They say no dice. I think they don't believe you."

It was what Gus had feared most, the end of his options.

Since this was essentially a close-range stationary target, the gunsight would remain caged, and the shot would be more like strafing than aerial gunnery. Because of the gap between a pilot's line of sight and the axis of his gun barrels, the two must be harmonized. In the Scimitar, the gap was small; so its TM-61 cannon was bore-sighted at two-thousand feet, meaning the line of the gun barrel and that of the fixed gunsight reticle met at that distance.

Here at 43,000, the trajectory would be near its flattest, meaning the shells would cross at almost the same distance. The sight could be depressed to bring that convergence in as close as five hundred feet. He worked out these minutiae to calculate an aiming point where the damage would be confined to a small area of the engine.

The diameter of the engine pod was close to eight feet. The gap at the center of the cross in the sight reticle was two mils—two feet for each thousand feet of range. So he moved back till it spanned a quarter of the engine pod— and found just the problem he had expected: In the turbulence of the jet exhaust and the vortex off the wing tip, the Scimitar danced and bobbed. Accurate fire was impossible.

He would have to fire from below, in a slight pull-up. He dropped below the turbulence, tried a few test pull-ups, then flipped the cannon control switch to "fire."

There was only a fleeting moment while the outboard engine pod hung there inside the rings of the sight reticle, but that was enough. He touched off a minimum burst. Flame belched from the engine and bannered for perhaps a hundred feet. Then the airliner yawed as the pilot cut the throttle. The flames died quickly, but lead-gray smoke continued to stream from the tailpipe.

"See if that will convince your hijackers, 101."

"I don't know about them, but it sure as hell convinced me."

Gus could see faces at the windows. Then the wings banked to port, and he allowed himself a tentative feeling of relief. They were finally seeing reason—or reality. He followed, hanging close to the big plane's wing tip and conforming to its turn.

Too soon then, the wings tilted the other way as it came back to the original heading. "I thought they'd see reason, Hardshell," came the captain's voice. "All it got me was a gun stuck in my ear." In a lighter note then: "They sure as hell gave you a call sign that fits."

Gus had to admire a man who could keep his sense of humor in a situation like this. "Alpha Two," he transmitted, "that port outboard is yours." He explained the sight depression and other details.

"Roger." The wingman followed Gus's example, tried a few dry runs before firing. Again there was flame and smoke, and the fire took longer to subdue this time.

He was still waiting for a response when the controller came on in unscrambled mode, a note of urgency in his voice. "Hardshell Alpha, this is Skyhook. Bogies approaching, bearing one-one-five magnetic for fifty, angels four-five, true airspeed about four-fifty. Data on your ITD."

Gus frowned under his oxygen mask and visor. That was higher-performance aircraft than any of the locals were known to have. Something at least in the F-4 category. And already more than a hundred nautical out to sea. Not a routine training mission. "How many, Skyhook?"

"They're still at extreme range for my crystal ball, so we can't be sure of the numbers, but it looks like at least eight."

"Skyhook, scramble Bravo. And see if Mother Hen has a clue about who might be operating aircraft in that performance category." It seemed unlikely, in fact damn near impossible, but those bogies were looking like a reception committee, fighters sent out to escort the airliner in.

On three engines, P&O 101 had begun losing altitude. With two knocked out, the loss was more rapid. "Alpha, go tac spread, commencing climb. UHF back to scrambled mode."

There were no contrails at 43,000 and probably none at forty-five. Here in the tropics, the contrail level might be above fifty thousand. Gus wanted at least as much altitude as the approaching aircraft, but kept a close watch for any sign of those telltale white streamers.

At the Scimitar's best subsonic climb speed, they had to weave to stay behind 101. "Alpha, the bogies' search radar indicates MiG-29. Also confirm the number as twelve. Bogies now three-eight nautical and closing." There was a pause. "Alpha, radio traffic indicates a GCI vectoring bogies in on Jumbo." "Jumbo" was the designator for P&O 101.

MiG-29's under GCI control? Gus had a sudden queasy feeling. He swore at himself for not having at least two backup aircraft launch-ready, but the situation had hardly seemed to call for it. Bravo would take some fifteen minutes to get airborne, more to get here. Air battles seldom lasted that long. In 1940, during the Battle of Britain, ten minutes was about average. In the Gulf War, three to five was typical. It was looking like the two of them would have to deal with the situation at six-to-one odds.

"Alpha, the bogies have acquired Jumbo on their scopes. Radio traffic indicates they're here to escort Jumbo to a landing. Mother Hen reports negative data on late-model fighters this area."

"Alpha, let's douse the headlamps." The MiG-29 would warn its pilot if he was being swept by weapons-type radar. Alpha could use the input from Skyhook's radar and still keep the element of surprise. Against odds of six to one, he was looking for any advantage he could get.

"Alpha, bogies' radio traffic in English. Stand by for a patch."

Skyhook's monitors constantly scanned the spectrum and picked up radio traffic, all bands, all frequencies. The "patch" was a direct connection, letting them eavesdrop on the enemy.

The enemy? At this point, international law and the Rules of Engagement gave him no grounds to treat these intruders as enemy.

". . . Iyam seeink smoke, Centralia Control. Stand by and Iyam contacting him." There was a pause. "Hallo, Paceefic and Oriental Wan-Oh-Wan. Here is speaking Centralia Force."

Gus listened with only half an ear to the P&O captain's reply. His thoughts were on the transmission he had just heard. That was English spoken with a Russian accent. Russians flying MiGs out of South American bases? And under GCI control? What the hell was going on?

When the strange foreign-accented voice came over the company's UHF channel, Al Morgeau had his hands full with the aircraft and his mind occupied with the hijackers. As he shut down the number-one engine and moved to suppress the fire, he realized he would have to take a risk. The opportunity he had hoped for was not going to happen.

His attempt to make a turn for Panama after the first engine was shot out had brought two of the hijackers into the cockpit to menace him with their guns. They were still there when the second burst of fire took out the number-one engine. "He's just shot out another engine," he said. "If you don't let me turn now, we'll all end up in the ocean down there."

"Pah-ceefic Wan-Oh-Wan, here is speaking Centralia Force."

"*Now* who the hell is getting into the act?" Morgeau growled. There was no one to hear but the copilot, on the interphone. "Centralia . . . whatever, here is speaking P&O 101."

"Wan-Oh-Wan, we are here for escorting you. You are trailing smoke from outboard engines. You are perhaps havink trobble?"

"Nothing we can't deal with."

At this point, the hijacker on the flight deck overheard enough to rouse his attention. "Is that Centralia calling? Let me talk to them."

It took a minute or so to rig a microphone—the hand-held type with a push-to-talk button—and a set of earphones. "Hello, this is the Centralia team aboard P&O 101."

"Hallo, Centralia Team. Here is speaking Centralia Force. What is tr-r-oble with two smokink engines?"

"Some American fighters are trying to force us to change course for Panama by shooting out the engines. I guess you scared 'em away."

Just then, another of the hijackers burst into the compartment. "Hey, come and see. We've got a reception committee of our own fighters. Chased those Americans off like shooing flies."

Morgeau could look over his left shoulder and see, off the left wing tip, a fighter very different from the U.S. Air Force pair. He couldn't identify the type. Most peculiar of all, it had no national markings.

The hijacker in the cockpit bent forward to look out the windscreen. "Do you see them?"

What Morgeau saw was his chance. The best he was likely to get. "Up ahead." He pointed forward. Then, speaking into the interphone in the tone he used order the gear or flaps raised or lowered, "Stand by with the flashlight, Stan." There was nothing ahead but air and clouds. He was relying on the inability of non-flyers to see other aircraft at a distance. Plus the natural human impulse to follow a pointing finger. Sure enough, the man bent farther to look out the windscreen, lowering his pistol slightly. Morgeau's left hand came up holding a small aerosol can, and his finger triggered the spray nozzle. "Flashlight, Stan."

The spray of chemical MACE left the hijacker immobilized. In the next moment, the copilot swung the large, heavy flashlight in a vicious arc to the back of his skull. The man slumped, and the pistol fell from his grip, but the copilot, in a frenzy of released frustration, hammered away.

"Enough!" said Morgeau. "I'll call for another one to come up. But first get this one out of the way." The copilot bent and picked up the hijacker's 9mm. Then he and the flight engineer heaved the limp form onto the crew's rest bunk. When the next one opened the door, in response to Morgeau's summons, a 9mm round caught him full in the chest; a second tore his throat out. He was clinically dead by the time he hit the floor. The flight engineer pounced on his pistol.

The two shots made Michelle jump as if she'd grabbed a live wire.

Burr and the Chinese had been looking out the window. They were startled but recovered quickly, drew pistols, and hurried forward.

Michelle was still standing there transfixed when she felt cold metal pressed into her hand. The Browning automatic.

Chip Borland had anticipated her need.

Without a backward glance, she ran forward, her gaze

fixed on Burr and the Chinese. Ducking behind a row of seats, she leveled the pistol with her arm resting on the seat back, and shouted, "Stop right there!" Just in time, she remembered to move the safety catch to "off."

Burr whirled to face her. His face was livid, his lips taut as he leveled the pistol. "You bitch, I knew I should—"

In sheer reaction, Michelle squeezing the trigger. The Browning jerked in her hand. Still without thinking, she steadied it and fired again.

She saw him stagger. Blood poured from his mouth as he fell to his knees. For a few seconds, he quivered and struggled to lift himself, then collapsed and lay there facedown.

At that moment, two shots from the crew compartment knocked Burr's companion off his feet.

As if in a dream, guided by learned responses, she lowered the pistol and walked toward the crumpled figure of Clifton Burr. Fearing the worst, she felt the carotid artery and got no pulse. With a convulsive effort, she turned him onto his back. The pupils were dilating and the corneal surfaces already taking on the glaze of death. She moved quickly to the other man, the Asian, and repeated the exam, with the same result.

She was a surgeon, a healer, and she had just shot a man dead. Her mind rebelled at the thought. No matter the justification, both in law and morality, she felt shaken and depressed and out of her skin.

All she could do was get a grip on herself and go on coping.

Meanwhile, the copilot was grinning and cavorting. "That's it," he yelled. "All four of 'em. We're back in control." Then he looked at her. "Say, you're one helluva woman. You plugged that guy twice right in the chest with about an eight-inch spread." He paused and sobered when he saw her face. "Uh-h . . . maybe you could have a look at this one up here. See if he's still alive. I cracked him over the head pretty hard."

She followed him into the crew compartment and bent over the man on the bunk. The dilated pupils, the mucouslike cerebro-spinal fluid oozing from his ears were unmistakable signs. She had no need to check for a pulse. "No, he's dead too. What the hell did you hit him with?"

"Just my flashlight." He flicked the switch, gave it a shake. "Damned thing won't light now."

"I shouldn't wonder." She turned to cover the body with a blanket.

Chapter Twenty-eight

When the P&O captain first announced they had regained control, Gus thought it might be a ploy on the part of the hijackers. "I'd rather not try for Panama on two engines, Hardshell. Quito is the nearest airport with proper facilities. We'd appreciate an escort in case anything goes wrong."

That convinced him the claim was for real. He wanted badly to confirm that Mike was all right, but the opposition would overhear any transmission in the unscrambled mode.

Almost at once, that Russian-accented voice came on again. "Paceefic Wan-Oh-Wan, Centralia Force is now escort. Follow us, or we are leavink you to sharks."

Gus took no notice of 101's reply. "Skyhook, you copy that? Clear case of a threat to a registered U.S. air carrier in international airspace. The rules of engagement say we can use 'em for target practice."

"Target data on your Bird Dog, Alpha."

One-oh-one was now below thirty thousand. Three

four-ship flights had emerged from the airspace ahead and swarmed around the airliner. Four were indeed MiG-29's. The rest were MiG-23's—simplistic Mach 2-plus flying hot rods, still dangerous in the hands of skilled pilots.

Gus waited till the MiGs settled into escorting positions, then pulled the helmet binoculars down and selected 50X, the max power. Rubber bushings on the lens shrouds let him brace them against the canopy and hold one of the MiGs steady in the frame. He moved it to another and then a third. They had no national markings.

The F-24 carried two Sparrows and two Sidewinders. A surprise missile attack could take out as many as four of the opposition and reduce the odds to four to one. After that, it would be a hard-maneuvering fight at close quarters and high G-loads where only guns were reliable.

The channel was cluttered with voices attempting to speak English. Apparently, the four MiG-29's were flown by former Red Air Force pilots and the 23's by a mixed bag from the Third World. What brought them together here and under what aegis was more than he could ponder at the moment.

And they talked too much. Again and again, the leader tried to suppress the chatter. That was a major problem with Third-Worlders as fighter pilots. They could not restrain their mouths.

The MiGs had settled into a loose V with 101 at the apex and the 29's on either side. "Alpha, we'll pick off the two outside pairs. Stealth-launch Sparrows and follow up with Sidewinders."

Again, Alpha Two needed only a double click to acknowledge. He had not transmitted a word during this mission. That was true radio discipline.

"Stealth launching" was a technique Gus and others had worked out during the Gulf War. Properly executed, it all but assured a kill. The pilot of the target aircraft had no warning the missile was after him till moments before impact. But it took skill and precise timing, especially when used together with a Sidewinder.

Gus rolled inverted, dropped the nose into a thirty-degree dive, then rolled upright. The F-24 quickly went supersonic. The Bird Dog, still taking its information from Skyhook, showed the range as seven miles and the Sparrow as primary. Gus chose the blip corresponding to his target, and set it in the Bird Dog's memory. Still without looking inside, he armed the number-one Sparrow. At six miles, he leveled about one-thousand feet below the target. At five miles, he eased the nose up, centered the MiG in the sight reticle, and pressed the missile firing button on the stick. In a burst of flame and smoke and noise, the Sparrow was away, held steady on course by its gyros.

Immediately, he selected the number-one Sidewinder, turned to frame the second MiG in the windscreen. Almost holding his breath, he waited for any sign the enemy had spotted the flash and smoke of the Sparrow launch. Not a twitch. A growl in his earphones told him the Sidewinder could see the hot tailpipe ahead and was eager to give chase.

The countdown on the Sparrow's time-to-impact showed in the Bird Dog reflector glass. At forty seconds, Gus flicked the Scimitar's own radar from standby to active. Taking its cue from the Bird Dog memory, the moveable dish antenna sought out that particular MiG and locked onto it. At that moment, Gus pressed the Sidewinder firing button. Belching flame and smoke like a dragon, the second missile went after its quarry.

As the F-24's radar locked on, the pilot of the outside MiG reacted.

His reaction was fatal.

Instead of a hard pull-up, a split-S, a hard turn—any maneuver that might have taken him out of the path of the missile—he rolled into a left vertical bank and then reversed, trying to make visual contact.

What he got was physical contact.

That steep bank and reversal kept the MiG almost in place. The Sparrow sensed proximity and detonated. In the thin air, the MiG smeared a long, flame-accented stroke of oily black across the sky. Out of it popped a compact-looking object, which then separated into two. That slow disintegration had given the pilot time to eject.

Far out on his left periphery, Gus caught a similar sluggish, elongated fireball. "Scratch one." Alpha Two's first transmission since launch. Meanwhile, the MiGs' channel had erupted with chatter. The MiG-23 pilots had lapsed into their native tongues. The Russian leader kept snarling, "Shaw-tup," and trying to get a coherent report.

Still without looking inside, Gus uncaged the sight. Supersonic, he closed on the target from six o'clock low, ready in case the Sidewinder should miss. His thumb was poised on the gun button when the missile flew up the MiG's tailpipe.

That pilot had no chance to eject. The aircraft dissolved into a dirty fireball. Blazing shards arced away from the furnace core, trailing smoke and banners of flame. Gus had to pull up to be sure of clearing the debris. "Scratch two," Alpha Two reported.

"Roger. That's four down."

The chatter continued. One terse command in Russian cut through.

The next moment, the four MiG-29's abruptly arced upward in unison, leaving the 23's still loosely escorting the airliner. Hurriedly, Gus selected the second Sidewinder, let it growl its recognition of another MiG tailpipe, and launched. With the propellant smoke still hitting the windscreen, he pulled up hard to follow the four MiG-29's.

Gus's once-considerable proficiency in Russian had gone rusty, so he had to concentrate on what he had heard: orders to switch to their guard channel. "Skyhook, four of our bandits have just switched channels. See if—"

"We've got 'em, Hardshell. Patch coming through."

Sergei Ivanovitch Volkov had been a leading fighter tactician in the Red Air Force. And its youngest colonel. When the Berlin Wall came down, he was commanding a fighter wing in the German Democratic Republic—"East Germany." His wing of MiG-29's was among the first withdrawn to Russia. After the Soviet Union disintegrated, he was offered a lower command in the new commonwealth, with grade of lieutenant colonel.

Then came the offer from the man who called himself *El Jefe*.

Unlike the impoverished republics, the mysterious *El Jefe* practically sweated money. He was buying up Soviet-built aircraft by the dozen and looking for experienced pilots to fly them. Volkov would head a new air force in the salubrious climes of South America, with the title of "commandante."

The salary was several times the pay of even a Soviet colonel. The living was marvelous, including the company of comely young women the color of light-brown sugar. Too late, Volkov realized this *El Jefe* was playing some very dangerous political games.

This simple mission was supposed to offer the newer pilots some experience. He had no confidence in their combat skills, but he felt sure the "Centralia Force" could brush aside any likely opposition. Certain features on these latest MiG-29's had come too late to benefit the former Red Air Force.

He was already regretting his decision. The mission was turning out anything but simple.

Four of those Third-Worlders had just gotten themselves blown out of the air, and the others were clogging the primary channel with their chatter. Just as he managed to get Red Flight, his Russian pilots, over to the backup channel, another MiG-23 exploded, hit by a missile. But at least he could now hear the controller.

Meanwhile, they were facing an unseen opposition of unknown numbers. He felt sure of only one thing—these were Americans.

"At first it was seeming there was only pair of USA fighters, witch fled at approach of Centralia Force," said Tschernichev. "Probably from Panama; so fuel must be gettink low. Wood'n hef much flyink time left."

As Volkov's deputy, Tschernichev was dressed for flying. A remoted radarscope let them see the situation just as the controllers saw it, and a speaker carried the voices of controllers and pilots.

When the smooth course of the operation had suddenly turned rough, *El Jefe* had helicoptered over to Curracabamba to see first-hand what was happening. There was vocal clutter and tactical confusion on the primary channel. Plus somber news—hits from missiles fired by an unseen enemy. Recalling events in Eritrea, he was gripped with a haunting sense of déjà vu. And P&O 101, with the prize of General Borland aboard, might yet slip out of his grasp.

"One-Oh-One was trailing smoke and flying on two engines when Commandante Volkov made contact?" said *El Jefe*.

"Correct, sir. Other two engines shot out by USA fighters. Then transmeeshun by pilot of airliner to USA fighters say crew has recovered control of aircraft. He is askink escort to Quito. No reply from American leader. And no real evidence of USA fighters on radar." He waved a hand at the scope. "Volkov is arriving on scene with Central Force. Telling Wan-Oh-Wan pilot he is now escort.

"For wile is having relative silence." Tschernichev's tone and manner made it plain what he thought of the non-Russian pilots' poor radio discipline. "Then suddenly confusion is heppenink. Pilots all talking at once.

Forgetting use Eenglish. Talk of meesile hexplosions and pilot-eject. Volkov is takink his flight first to emergency channel, then to secondary channel."

The radio speaker could carry only one channel at a time. So they could tune in either Volkov and his four or the MiG-23 pilots. And for some reason, all they were getting of either was snatches.

"Welcome to realities of warfare, *Jefe*," said Tschernichev with a sardonic tone and faint, wry smile. He picked up the direct line to the radar control station. "Hallo, here is Tschernichev. Wot is trobble? We are getting only broken transmeeshuns . . . Eh? . . . Hmm! . . . Hokay." He rang off. "They are havink same problem. Eenterference. Pilots not getting their transmeeshuns either."

"Could it be the weather?" asked *El Jefe*. He referred to the thunderstorms and dark clouds that could be seen in the distance.

Tschernichev frowned. "Not likely. UHF not much subject to hatmospheeric disturbance."

In Skyhook's CIC, Sam Corwin acknowledged the launch of Bravo. After that first taste of combat in Operation Sand Bar, he had wanted to lead Bravo Flight so badly he could taste it. The live enemy out there might be the last of his career. But he knew where his duty lay, so he sat with his gaze fixed on the airship's Bird Dog.

Skyhook's Bird Dog was the big brother of those in the F-24's. It combined information from radar and other sources on all airborne objects within radar range. It could also detect and furnish considerable data on surface ships as well. The results were displayed on an eight-foot circular screen. The key data—altitude, true airspeed, ground speed, heading, track, friend-or-foe, type aircraft, and weapons aboard—were shown by combinations of colors and symbols.

The Bird Dog was only the visible part of Skyhook's Integrated Targeting and Battle Control System, the

ITBCS, called the Wizard. It could make comparisons, calculations, and projections to help focus or simplify tactical decisions. It also sent the coded target information to the airborne fighters for display on their Bird Dogs.

The CIC aboard Skyhook was a rectangle about the size of the living-dining room area in a typical American home. The screen took up one end. The controller work stations and seats were in three tiers facing it. At the rear and elevated a few more feet was the combat command station. Each of its four positions had an elaborate comm console, and Sam Corwin occupied one of these.

The clear voices coming from one speaker were those of Gus and Alpha Two, an Air Force captain named Thoringer. Two other speakers emitted only staccato sounds. Skyhook's ECM was playing games with the enemy's communications.

Still, Gus and his wingman had their hands full against six MiGs.

". . . Lead, heater launch, ten o'clock."

"I've got it. Popping a flare. Roll and dive." Sam was impressed the opposition had heat-seekers that need not see the target's tailpipe before launch. That was as good as the latest Sidewinder.

"That one's going for the flare, Lead. But here comes another one!"

"Pop a flare, Two. Hard pull-up. Those are smart missiles. They're going for the leading-edge friction . . ."

"Lead, you see my flare?"

"Roger, Two."

"That missile's still heading for you, Lead. It's not taking the bait!" Thoringer's tone had a taut edge.

"It's after you now. Pop some chaff and max the Gs. I'll cover."

Sam looked at the Bird Dog screen. Bravo had about a hundred nautical miles to cover and seemed to be creeping. "Tell Bravo to go gate." Sam's order meant plug in the afterburners.

There was a long and ominous silence. After about a minute, Alpha Lead's and then Alpha Two's IFF return suddenly disappeared from the screen. At once, the controller tried to raise them on the radio. There was no response.

Chapter Twenty-nine

Major Gil Austen felt destiny had brought him back here. Somewhere in the hundred square miles of ocean spread below was the final resting place of Anvil Bravo. And somewhere beyond the coast was the haunt of those who had destroyed it.

This assignment had taken him out of reach of that bastard Penross. Meaning there were no newspapers, so he didn't have to know what that asshole was writing about him. Still, it chapped his backside that an East Coast weenie could get away with that kind of crap. But the demands of security kept the "all-powerful" Pentagon bound and gagged.

Once they took care of this matter, he just might arrange to have a serious talk with that lying bastard. Preferably in a dark alley.

In Centralia flight operations at Curracabamba, the radio interference had suddenly cleared, though the weather had gotten no better.

As Tschernichev listened, absorbed, to the rapid-fire Russian *El Jefe* demanded to know what was going on. "Volkov and his pilots are disagreeing on how many Americans they have hit. Seeing flames from meessile hexplosion but no debris. Also question of how many they are engaging. USA fighters givink near zero radar return. Also werry hard to see. Panax missile system was latest Soviet dewelopment. Using enemy radio signals when radar return is not strong enough."

Sam Corwin and the duty controllers were in a state of shock. The tales of Gus Halstrom's wizardry in the air were a legend, not only throughout the American services but in NATO. Yet he and his wingman had just disappeared while engaging Russian pilots of this mysterious Centralia Force.

"Lost all contact, Commander," said the chief controller. "Radio, IFF, and Bird Dog. We killed the jamming on the enemy radio frequencies, and first thing we heard was the opposing pilots speculating on how many aircraft their missiles had hit." He paused and cleared his throat. "It wasn't a total loss, sir. Alpha took out at least six. Not bad against that kind of odds."

Corwin only nodded acknowledgment. Both his mind and his gaze were focused on the situation: P&O 101 was still heading for Quito, apparently unmolested. And Hardshell Bravo was still heading for the scene of the action.

By the time Bravo arrived, the action was gone. Of the twelve MiGs, only two remained—heading eastward. He gave the recall order.

For some minutes, a tense and dismal atmosphere hung over CIC; then two IFF markers suddenly appeared on the screen at about fifty nautical. Both Sam and the controllers were puzzling over this when Halstrom's voice came through the radio speakers: "Skyhook, Alpha to recover. We have minimum fuel and battle damage."

* * *

Fewer than half the twelve Centralia MiGs returned to the airdrome at Curracabamba. Fewer yet actually landed. One of the MiG-23 pilots flew into a mountainside attempting an instrument approach. Two of the missing were MiG-29's. Yet with such catastrophic losses, they had not brought the airliner back. *El Jefe* had sharp words for Volkov.

Volkov, already seething with frustration, was in no mood to be lectured by an amateur. Flight operations was cleared of all but him. *El Jefe*, Tschernichev, and the ubiquitous Alejandro. "You are forcing us to fly with these"—he waved a finger to indicate the absent third Worlders—"incompetents. Chattering on radio like monkeys. Also having brains of monkeys." He paused and made a bitter face. "No, that is insult to monkeys. Never looking behind, so right at beginning, they are loozing four aircraft to meessiles."

El Jefe realized his mistake in criticizing Volkov, at least in the present circumstances. "How many American fighters were there?"

Volkov paced and threw his hands in the air. "Deefficult say. Maybe six or eight. Their aircraft werry smawl. Also werry deefficult to see against cloud background. And giving werry poor radar return. Without Panax meesile system, we are in much trouble. Without radar return, Panax homes on awailable radiation. During battle, American leader is figuring this out, shutting down all transmitting equipment."

He interrupted his pacing to stare out through the large-pane windows. Dark thunderclouds still loomed in the distance. Out on the flight line, tugs were hooking onto the nosewheels, towing the MiGs into hangars for repairs. Even the tail of his own showed hits from 20mms.

A faint smile that was both wry and amused shaped his lips. "I theenk maybe we are meeting Gus Halstrom.

Among NATO pilots, he is legend. I shake his hand once at Paris air show. And always I am hopink to match myself against him." He turned and looked at the others. "Today, I think I am doing it. Was werry interesting."

El Jefe's look suddenly brightened. "If what you say is true, Commandante, it was more than interesting. It supports our late comrade Rodney Lund." He sighed and took a few restless steps. "The concept of fate, some mysterious force influencing human life, is of course non-scientific rot. An old folk superstition. Yet it almost seems this Halstrom and I are drawn to each other by fate."

Back aboard Skyhook, Gus and Thoringer were besieged with questions.

"Those MiGs were shooting some pretty smart missiles," Gus declared. "The heaters were going for the leading-edge friction. They fired at us from well ahead of nine and three o'clock."

They all understood: The early heat-seeking missiles could only sense the high infrared of engines and tailpipes, so they had to be fired from somewhere behind the target. In the eighties, both the U.S. and the Soviets had begun developing missiles that could pick up the lesser heat generated by air friction on the leading edges of wings and such.

"So you used the leading-edge coolers?" Sam offered.

Gus nodded. "With some interesting results." To counter the newer missiles' ability to sense leading-edge friction, Waring Aircraft had incorporated one of Gus's ideas into the F-24: The heat of friction was dispelled by fuel ducted inside the leading edges. Liquid hydrogen could actually cause frost, but it then "boiled off" and had to be vented.

"When that vented hydrogen hits the hot gases from the tailpipes, it produces quite a fireball. Lot like missile impact. It's what made the opposition think they were scoring hits. Could turn out to be useful."

"But why the sudden radio silence?" asked Bingham, the chief controller. "The parrots both strangled, the CMDs turned to standby."

"They've got a missile that homes on any of those," said Thoringer. "The colonel signaled me into close formation and used the hand-signal code. Told me to turn off everything and stay off the radio. That meant giving up the Sparrows entirely. We could've used the Sidewinders, but the way things worked out, we did pretty well with the guns."

"Specially considering we had no HE rounds. I had the guns loaded with AP and plain tracer ball to keep damage to 101's engines to a minimum."

"Pretty well?" said Sam Corwin said with a mixture of praise and dismay. It was plain he hated to hear about what he had missed.

"There were four MiG-29's, flown by Russians," Gus explained. "The other eight were MiG-23's with a mixed bag of Third World pilots. Couldn't keep their mouths from clogging the channel. The head Russian took his four over to a backup channel. ECM followed that.

"One of those Third-Worlders fired a missile that near-miss-detonated on one of the 29's." Gus couldn't avoid a grin. "That really pissed off the head Russian. He threatened to shoot them all down himself, then told them to go home. We spent a lot of time dodging missiles. But we managed to get in close and scratch two with the guns."

His face turned grim and dead serious. "That new missile must be the Panax that was under development by the Soviets some years ago." He paused. "Now, what's the story on P&O 101?"

"Last we heard, it had made contact with Quito approach control."

Within minutes of 101's arrival at Quito, newscasts were carrying the story. They noted it made an emergency landing with smoke trailing from two of the engines. The aircraft was isolated and access tightly restricted. Follow-up reports told of the hijackers' bodies being removed.

El Jefe called for maps of Quito and the surrounding territory and an immediate inventory of forces available. "Our comrades brought the prize many thousands of miles through great hazards and difficulties," he said. "Surely we can bring it the mere hundred kilometers or so remaining.

"I assume this General Borland will be taken to a hospital before being flown out. Find out where. Put every available agent on it. I want progress reports every half hour. Meanwhile, we can start working up an operations plan." He looked at Alejandro, who was always there in the background. "Now hand me that road map of Equador."

They had been at work for less than an hour when one of the staff members reported, "we have it, *Jefe*! A private clinic on the outskirts of the city. Patronized by the wealthier families. Small but well equipped. Has facilities for surgery and intensive care. Right here." His pencil point touched the location on a map. "We should have photographs in an hour."

"In not more than an hour," said *El Jefe*. "And I want videotape of the approaches and surrounding area. We go tonight. They could fly him out as early as tomorrow."

Michelle was at General Borland's bedside when the gunfire erupted. Her gut reactions told her it was trouble. The hammer of automatic weapons came closer and grew louder, reminding her of Asmara. Then it shook the very walls and corridors inside the clinic. The near-silence that followed seemed deafening. Next came urgent voices, the sound of running feet.

When the general was brought here to the Clinica San Luis, she and the chief of surgery had operated and removed the remaining bullet fragments. The patient had come through in good shape. The traces on the monitor screen were all reassuring.

B. Michelaard

The U.S. ambassador and his staff had been effusive in their praise. They put her up in a hotel, where she had gone to bed, exhausted. While she slept, messages of thanks had arrived from the Secretary of the Navy and the Commandant of the Marine Corps. SecDef Harlan Walsh stated he was nominating her for a Presidential medal.

At that point, she would have been completely justified in turning the general over to the clinic. But Chip Borland had become her patient, and she would not leave him till he was on a plane to the States.

So there she stood when the troops in jungle-pattern fatigues burst in. A short, stocky man with Indian features was in command. He gestured at the general and said, "You will prepare this man to be moved immediately." His English was accented but clear.

"This man has just had surgery. He cannot be moved." It was only a stalling tactic. In the pocket of her fresh, white medical smock was a small cassette recorder. They were used by doctors here at the clinic in lieu of writing out daily orders for patients. Casually, she moved her hand down and switched it on.

The stocky officer gave her a humorless smile. "You mean he cannot be moved safely. Whether he lives or dies, he goes with us." His expression turned harsh. "Now!" They had come well prepared, she noted. Two more men wheeled a gurney into the room.

She began disconnecting the monitor leads. "Where are you taking him?"

The officer only looked at her carefully. "You are Doctor Michelle St. Clair. You will also come with us."

She made a sour face, and her tone dripped irony. "Now how was it I knew you were going to say that?"

The heavily sedated general was lifted onto the gurney. While the men had their attention on this, she clicked off the cassette player, slipped it out of her pocket, and left it on the bedside table.

* * *

Six Marines from the embassy staff and two local police-men had died defending the clinic, but one of the Marines lived long enough to gasp out a rough account: The attackers—at least thirty, perhaps as many as fifty—were trained fighters, well armed and dressed in jungle fatigues and berets. They had carried away their dead and wounded, amounting to over a dozen. The defense had been determined.

That Marine's account plus Michelle's cassette tape showed this had been a well-planned abduction.

An Ecuadorian police official, commander of the two dead police, called a friend at the U.S. embassy and offered his help: He pointed out a certain area that spanned the border between Peru and Equador. "It's called Curracabamba. The main feature is a worked-out phosphate mine. There are also veins of copper that were deep-mined. The mining company built a fair-sized run-way, and much of the product was flown out.

"For some years now, this area has been off limits. Anyone who ventured inside was apt to disappear. We assumed it was involved in the drug traffic and tried to raid it. But someone high up in my government has been protecting whoever is there.

"More recently, there have been reports of jet aircraft flying from the company's old airfield and military exer-cises by troops with modern weapons. The whole area is honeycombed with mine tunnels and shafts. No telling what use they've been put to."

His pencil tip pointed to a location not far from the abandoned mine. "Right here is another suspicious site. A large and elaborate country estate. A famous architect designed it for the president of the mining company, who named it Casa Elena, for his wife. Then quite suddenly, he disappeared, and she sold the place and left. Argentina or Spain. Only the drug lords or someone associated with them have that kind of power."

He straightened and looked at them. "Gentlemen, I am

deeply concerned over the prospect of such sophisticated weaponry in the hands of private warlords, whether they're in the drug trade or not. It's almost as if they intend to carve out a nation of their own."

For once, the Pentagon moved swiftly. Minutes after the message from the embassy telling of the kidnapping, Operation Spring Harvest was under way. The embassy was designated the on-site command post, staffed by the attachés.

With Skyhook on the scene, Mother Hen became the operating arm of DoD in Spring Harvest. The embassy was given the call sign Harvester and an HF channel for direct radio contact with Skyhook. Their first message gave the information about Curracabamba, including a description of Casa Elena.

Mother Hen directed Skyhook to the lower slopes of the Andes. Follow-up messages gave the essentials of what had happened. It took Hank Borland all the cultivated aplomb and self-discipline of his years as a Naval officer to carry on as usual. No mention was made of Michelle, and Gus had no reason to think she was still involved.

The basic plan was to identify the location where General Borland was being held, then drop paratroopers from the pod attached to the belly of the airship. There were Special Forces troops in Panama ideal for the job. The air group would furnish air cover and support as required.

Buried in clouds and darkness, Skyhook hovered over Curracabamba. Its infrared scanners, ground-mapping radar, sound detectors, and other sophisticated gear tracked the convoy's movement. The pattern was consistent with the return of the raiding force. The highly sensitive equipment could even identify the vehicle types—trucks, jeeps, motorcycles.

They headed for the abandoned mining operation,

except for a few, including an apparent ambulance, that
split off for Casa Elena.

The severe weather that had hovered and threatened
for the past twenty-four hours now began to advance.
Skyhook was forced to retreat and lie off the coast till
sunrise.

When the new day broke, storm clouds still loomed.
Gil Austen was at the controls. Despite Gil's late arrival,
Decker had declared him the best of the cockpit crew,
with an uncanny feel for this flying leviathan.

The storm clouds formed a kind of loose picket line.
Austen probed along it, looking for the best opening.

A wide gap appeared, a kind of saddle formation with
only lower cloud. Beyond were the verdant humps and
ridges of foothills. Beyond those loomed the shadowy
massif of the Andes. Bright shafts of sunlight, the sort
depicted by artists, radiated from that five-mile space
between vertical columns of cloud. Austen headed Skyhook into it.

Rising spirits on the bridge matched the climb toward
that broad aperture. The sight reminded Gus of the closing scene from *Das Rheingold*, Wotan leading the Gothic
pantheon into the gleaming promise of Valhalla.

The trouble struck without warning.

A strange, sharp crack-and-crunch, and abruptly the
airsteam was hosing in their faces through holes in the
plexiglass screen. Loose papers swirled like autumn
leaves. One of the watch crew was knocked to the deck, a
nasty gash on his forehead. The strident "br-a-a-t, br-a-
a-t" of a warning klaxon jarred their ears, and red lights
flashed. Gus sensed a drop in thrust, noted Austen had
pulled all eight throttles to idle.

The duty met officer stared at the chunks of ice on the
deck. "Jeezus! Clear-air hail." He picked one up and
stared at it in fascination.

It was a rare and dangerous phenomenon: The powerful vertical currents inside thunderstorms lifted water

303

drops above the freezing level, where they turned to ice and fell as hail. But sometimes they acted like bingo counters, falling and being lifted over and over by air currents, taking on new ice each time. Those on the airship's deck were the size of baseballs. A really violent updraft could carry these chunks up where the jet stream might fling them for miles.

The officer of the watch switched off the alarm. "Damage reports," he demanded on the bullhorn just as Hank Borland rushed out of his day cabin still buttoning his shirt. "Medic to the bridge. We have a casualty."

"Ground-mapping radar out," reported the flight engineer.

"Weather radar out," came Eversham's voice from the met section. Minor in the normal scheme of things, both items were critical at the moment. Between them, those two radars were needed to avoid flying into a severe weather cell, with more hail. Or into a cloud with a granite core.

Yet there was a more severe and immediate danger—holes the hail must have made in the skin. The airstream could get in through these and rip off ever larger chunks till the ship was destroyed.

This was clearly why the quick-thinking Austen had cut the power abruptly. Airspeed was down to sixty knots and dropping. On the other hand, they had been flying well above buoyancy, which might not by itself support them in the manner to which they had become accustomed. Meaning somewhere above the surrounding terrain.

To minimize the surface damage, Austen was maintaining just enough airspeed for control. The flight engineer and copilot were feverishly gasifying helium and feeding it into the cells. The heating elements were turned up to maximum.

Gus thought of the hangared aircraft: They were guyed and secured, but those guy lines were designed to counter the airship's normal sedate maneuvers. The prospects for Skyhook in the next several minutes were anything but sedate.

Gus imagined he could feel the ghosts of the *Akron* and the *Macon* staring down at them.

Chapter Thirty

It was near daybreak when Arthur Penross returned to find a note from Lucy Morgan but no Lucy.

He set the radio alarm, filled and programmed the coffeemaker, lay down for a few Zs, and awoke to a cultivated radio voice urging him to try the newest Eggo Waffles. It continued with the latest developments in the saga of P&O 101—recovery of control by the crew, the landing at Quito.

Penross poured coffee, carried it into his office, and began ringing up his contacts. Some still refused to talk to him. Others spoke of intense subsurface activity in official Washington. A covey of high-powered entities— the Joint Chiefs, the SecDef, the Veep, the CIA Director—was said to be in conclave in connection with the hijacking.

Beating the telephonic bushes, he failed to flush the quarry.

His computer files were indexed and cross-referenced

to show up diverse connections. He decided to scan the headings for any that might shed light on the situation.

Seconds after he called up the first, he knew something was drastically wrong. The lines of text began slipping down the screen like running paint. One by one, the pages scrolled up and melted away. He recognized a computer virus, but the computer would not respond to his commands. The pages kept on self-destructing. In panic, he hit the off switch, then sat there cursing Lucy Morgan, the horse she rode in on, and her ancestors back even unto three and four generations.

Finally, he got a partial grip on himself, reached for the phone, and dialed. His breathing was rapid and shallow

When Zachman, the software expert, answered his phone, he heard a voice he could barely identify. Between raving and sobbing, it repeated "that bitch" and "ruined." Then, after a pause for a long, deep breath, screamed out, "Get over here! Right now!"

Zachman hung up. He took that sort of abuse from no one. He silenced the resumed ringing and stirred his coffee while he reflected: It would be worthwhile to go over and take care of Pennross's problem. Not to mention seeing Arthur Penross stripped of that cold composure of which he made such a fetish.

Wounded, blind, cloud-shrouded, and mountain-ringed, Skyhook fell through the atmosphere. To those on board, the loss of both weight and control brought on a queasy feeling. On the bridge, the tense silence was like a tableau, the men in frozen postures, barely breathing. Hank Borland's resonant tones ordered everyone to strap into a seat.

All eyes and thoughts focused on two critical readouts: the radar altimeter, which showed how much air there was between them and the earth, and the level of buoyancy. They were like the devil and the angels: The first defined the threat, the second the hope of salvation.

The altitude—height above sea level—showed a steady decline. The radar altimeter undulated, sometimes by hundreds of feet, outlining the terrain below. But the trend was downward. The gap between them and the earth was shrinking at an alarming rate.

Maximum buoyancy was seldom used. The pilot would set the buoyancy at some moderate level and rely on wing lift to attain altitudes above it. Without propulsion, the ship would normally descend in a gentle controlled glide to its free-floating altitude.

Here, the haven of air density where the atmosphere would support Skyhook was pierced by mountain peaks. Not the towering white sharks' teeth of the Andes, but solid earth nevertheless. These would demolish the airship, bare the secrets of Pegasus to the world, and terminate the project. Not to mention everyone aboard.

The flight engineer was working furiously, gasifying liquid helium and feeding it into the cells, raising the level of buoyancy. Heated to some 250 degrees Fahrenheit by electric filaments, the helium more than doubled its lifting capacity.

Yet Skyhook continued its fall.

Suddenly then, Austen brought in the power on all eight engines and raised the nose to keep the airspeed just at minimum control. As Skyhook assumed a steeper nose-up attitude than ever before, Gus again thought of the Scimitars suspended in the hangar bays. His sphincter gave an involuntary pucker.

But Austen's technique was effective. Pressure on their buttocks signaled a decrease in the rate of descent. Meanwhile, the gap between the altitude and the buoyancy level had narrowed to less than five hundred feet.

For what seemed all day, they hung there like that, the wings at an angle just below stall, the engines churning out full power.

The radar altimeter slowed its alarming trend, steadied briefly, then began to show an increase. They had cleared a ridge or peak of some sort. Breaks in the cloud revealed patches of meadow and forest below.

Finally, the gas bags inflated enough for the buoyancy to meet the altitude.

Austen eased the power back and gently lowered the nose to level flight. There were sighs, then a rumble of approval, then a small cheer for Gil Austen. They had just witnessed what was both an inspired response to emergency and a first-rate, first-ever feat of airmanship.

A break in the clouds revealed a broad, though apparently uncultivated, valley with a river running through it.

"Ground-mapping radar restored," came a report from Engineering. "We've hooked up to a spare antenna. We'll have the weather radar back in a few minutes."

Hank Borland unsnapped his seat belt and rose. "Gil, that was one helluva piece of flying. You may just have to find room on your chest for another Air Medal if not a DFC. Now, activate the vapor shield." He paused to look up at the flight instrument readouts and showed a sour smile. "Too bad those don't tell us a thing about hail damage to the skin."

"Only one real way to find out," Gus said. He was already on his feet. "Crank up the air ponies."

"Be careful out there," Hank said. "You're on instruments in that security blanket, and I never did trust the stability of those damn little things." The vapor shield was the artificial cloud that hid the ship from any of those rare conditions of light and background that could make it show up. Small surface vents emitted a dense, chemically induced vapor.

The air ponies, tiny one-man helicopters, were the rotary-wing equivalent of super-lights. The operator sat astride a saddlelike frame—hence the name air pony— under a plexiglass cover that shielded him from the direct downdraft of the twin lifting rotors that spun on separate shafts, making the customary tail rotor unnecessary. For starting, an external auxiliary motor spun the blades up fast enough to force air through the tiny jet engines on each blade, the pony's source of power. It could also be started, just once, without the auxiliary power, by small solid-fuel rockets that did the same thing.

Four ponies were carried aboard, and Gus was one of the few checked out on them. So he and three others saddled up, fired up, and air-taxied aft to the tail section where the huge aft panels stood open. They took flight from what was the touchdown area for the F-24's.

Hail damage would be located on a grid, reported by radio, and noted on a chart by the engineering section.

The damage turned out to be minor. Evidently a freak cluster of hail had hit the nose, knocked out the ground-mapping and weather radar antennae, made holes in just the windscreen and a few nearby surface panels. Repair would amount to replacing the two antennae and radomes plus the damaged surface panels and the plexiglass on the bridge.

As Gus rounded the tip of one of the giant triangular wings, the vapor was stirred and parted by the draft of the rotors. He had a sudden view of the landscape below.

At once his eye was caught by what had to be Casa Elena. This was the huge estate designated "Roundhouse" in the ops plan. The most likely place for their mysterious enemies to have taken General Borland.

The house was built in the abstract geometric "modernist" style, with a towering cathedral roof and large areas of glass. It was set amid tennis courts, a huge free-form swimming pool, and a nine-hole golf course. He also recognized a glassed-in botanical garden, horse stables, and a diesel-driven power plant. The whole thing was situated on a lagoon or oxbow lake and connected by a man-made channel to Lake Curracabamba.

He pressed the transmitter button: "Skyhook, Pony

One here. I think I've spotted the Roundhouse. I'm squawking two and going in for a closer look." The "squawk" was the transponder code that let the GCI controllers identify any aircraft.

"Pony One . . ." The voice of Hank Borland. "Suggest you wait for reinforcements. Don't poke the hornets' nest without a Flit gun handy."

"Don't worry, I'll be cautious."

He descended in a wide arc, leveled at treetop height, and began circling the house at a distance of about half a mile, using the roof peak as a guide. Now and then, he came to a hover for a clear view.

The helmet binoculars let him observe details. He reported whatever seemed significant, and the controller aboard Skyhook acknowledged, though reception was poor. To preserve stealth, the pony's transmitter was very low-power.

The air pony was designed only for brief flights, and the fuel was already down by half. He decided to have a look from one more angle.

That look changed everything.

Rising slowly from behind a copse of conifers, he saw an upper level deck or terrace, plus—for the first time—people, a man and a dark-skinned woman apparently seated at a table having coffee.

And suddenly there was also something familiar about the woman. He clicked the control gnarl, kept raising the magnification while struggling to keep the scene framed with the pony bobbing in the air currents. At 12X, he centered on the woman—and confirmed what had been only a gnawing fear: Michelle!

It fit the weird pattern of this whole affair: She had been attending Chip Borland aboard the airplane. She must have stayed with him in Quito.

And been captured with him.

Just then, with his mind in shock and his emotions in

turmoil, he heard, over the sound of the rotor blades, vehicle engines nearby and getting nearer.

Waiting for Zachman, Arthur Penross sat in his office with three TV sets, each tuned to the morning show on one of the major networks. And for the second time that morning, he got a severe shock.

"Controversial muckraking columnist Arthur Penross," the newscaster said to begin the story, "known for his exposés of other peoples' dirty laundry, today had some of his own soiled linen hauled out for public viewing. The editors and news staff of the magazine *Avanti* claim to have gotten hold of some of Penross's files. And if their claim is authentic, then Penross, far from being the crusader of his public posture, played his stories for maximum effect.

"Indeed, it appears he often wrote a story from two or more angles before deciding which to go with. One example given is his recent vendetta against Major Guilbert Austen, the pilot of a C-141 who survived when his aircraft and the crew were all lost. Those at *Avanti* claim to have discovered alternate texts that would have depicted Austen as a hero and the victim of Pentagon bungling."

Having sat there scarcely breathing while the newscaster dismantled his professional standing, Penross took in a great gulp of air. That bitch Lucy Morgan! She had done this to him!

The helmet Gus wore was made to seal out noise. When the O2 mask was merely hanging loose, the way he wore it on the air pony, sound crept in through the gap between the cheekbones and the earphone pads. What came in now was the roar of the off-road vehicles that suddenly appeared, laboring across the uneven terrain, knocking over saplings and pushing their way through underbrush.

They also mounted heavy machine guns on swivels.

312

Each had a man in front beside the driver, plus another in the rear to handle the weapon. They wore infantry-style helmets and camouflage fatigues and carried side arms. Those in the front passenger seats also had sleeve insignia indicating NCO grade.

The air pony was not a high-performance machine. If he tried to make a dash for it now, those guns would turn it into junk and him into hamburger. In the two to three seconds while all this registered, he lowered the collective, settling behind the trees. And the moment it touched, he killed the engines.

In what seemed a minor miracle, he had gone undetected. But the lead vehicle was drawing closer while the men's gazes swept the terrain.

Chapter Thirty-one

General Borland had recovered consciousness and was doing well. From a purely medical standpoint, Michelle was pleased. Now she had to explain what had happened.

He gave her a rueful little smile and a slight shake of his head. "You'd be justified in wishing you'd never seen me," he said in reply.

Gus recognized the NCO-grade insignia as Cuban. With the pony's engines cut, he pulled the collective to maximum, making the blades slap the air at full high pitch. That slowed the rotors enough to let him brake the shafts to a complete halt. With nothing moving, he might not be seen.

Even armed, he'd be in trouble. With no weapon, he could only retreat. The pony's IFF was still on "squawk two." Just as he removed the helmet and slid off the saddle, he thought to turn on the continuous carrier-wave. For as long as the battery lasted, the UHF would send out continuous beeps on his last known channel. It was low-power, but Skyhook was close and might pick it up.

On the vehicles came, in that slow, grinding, inexorable way. The men in their steel helmets and combat fatigues looked sinister. Then one of the NCOs looked directly at him.

Somehow, the man's vision never penetrated the shadows. It passed over, and the vehicles passed on, bouncing and jolting.

They passed out of sight, but he decided against starting up and taking off right away. Better to wait for darkness—or at least twilight. And he had to do something about Mike.

Zigzagging, using available cover, he moved toward the house. After some twenty minutes, he again caught sight of that glassed-in A-frame and the deck overlooking the swimming pool. Mike and the man were no longer there.

Realizing he might be seen by anyone using binoculars, he moved to get back into cover. As he stepped backward, keeping his gaze on the house, his foot came down on something springy.

There was a dull mechanical sound. Then pain! Shock! Fright! Something god-awful had him by the ankle.

He looked down and saw he was caught in the jaws of a steel trap.

General Borland shut his mouth abruptly at the approach of footsteps. The door swung open, and the man called *El Jefe* came in. "Ah! I see our patient is coming around and looking fit." He had put on a cheery smile and tone for the occasion. "You've done well, Doctor. Now we have another patient who needs your attention. If you'll come along with me, please." The "please" was mere form. For all his cheery manner, the tone was peremptory.

The clinic, the same one where General Borland had

315

B. Michelaard

been brought, had four examining tables and a stock of medicines as complete as a typical American pharmacy. No surprise there. She'd wager more than a shekel *El Jefe*'s money came from the drug traffic.

El Jefe led, partly blocking her view. A guard in jungle camouflage, with a holstered pistol, stood to one side. The new patient, a man of considerable size, lay on one of the examining tables, his feet toward her. He had a nasty-looking injury just above the ankle. The boots he must have been wearing were on the floor nearby.

With her next breath came the shock of her life.

"Gus! Oh, my God!"

He raised himself on one elbow. She rushed forward and threw her arms around him. With his free arm, he returned her embrace but said nothing. His mask of pain showed he was stifling the urge to groan—or perhaps even scream. She looked at *El Jefe* and said, "What the hell caused this?"

El Jefe showed a faint, mocking smile. "I rather thought you two knew each other. As for the injury, to use a common North American expression, he put his foot in it."

"Animal trap," Gus managed between clenched teeth. He tried to smile, but it came off as more of a rictus.

"What kind of barbarians *are* you!?" she shouted.

El Jefe's look segued from mocking smile to phony shock. "Merely basic measures against unwanted intrusion."

She scrubbed and set to work. The only thing to do. "Find someone who knows this pharmacy," she snapped. "I'll need drugs."

The words were barely out when a wizened, gray-haired, compulsively neat-looking little man appeared. His spotless white pharmacist's jacket was the old-fashioned kind with a high collar and buttons across the shoulder. In accented but clear English, he introduced himself as Señor Cavalante. They had a little difficulty with drug

316

names between English and Spanish, but once he understood, he quickly produced whatever she asked for.

She injected a local anesthetic, then cleaned and cauterized the wounds. Where the teeth of the trap had struck, the flesh was bruised and haggled. In places, they had penetrated to the bone. The more she worked, the more she seethed inside.

Gus awoke to find his injury bandaged, the pain a dull ache. And he was now in an ordinary bedroom. "Ordinary" considering this was a luxurious South American estate. The decor was modernist-elegant. The wallpaper had an abstract design with colors and textures including shiny, foil-like strips. The huge, round bed stood on an elevated dais. On the ceiling above it was a large mirror. The drapes were full-length and partly open. He judged the time as late afternoon.

His boots were on the floor near the bed, and he still wore his flying suit. Oddly, his elaborate personal chronometer was also still on his wrist. The time showed 0736. He checked Zulu—Greenwich time—and that jibed—eight hours ahead of Pacific. He checked the date, and sure enough it had advanced by one day. Had someone tampered with the watch to confuse him? Or had he—?

Just then, Michelle came in carrying a TV tray with a bowl of soup. She put it down, then climbed onto the bed with him. They kissed and snuggled and were on the way to getting excited when she cleared her throat and sat up. "Here, eat your soup while it's hot."

"Soup is a poor second to what I had in mind. What time is it?"

She looked at her watch. "Almost seven-forty."

"It's really morning? I've been—?"

"Yes. I gave you something to make sure you slept about twelve hours."

He sat up, picked up the spoon, and began eating. The

soup was thick and delicious, beef stock with pieces of meat, vegetables, and a seasoning he had never tasted before.

He had just finished when two guards in that Castro-style uniform entered. One announced in heavily accented English that the two of them had been summoned by *El Jefe*. Gus put on his boots.

They were led to a gym. Perhaps a dozen men, all in martial-arts attire, were engaged in various exercises. One in particular wore a black belt and was defending against four others ringed around him. Gus had had enough training in this sort of thing to recognize a true expert. The man's hands and feet had thick carapaces of callused skin. He seemed to anticipate the attacks, move to block the kicks and fists aimed at him, and respond with counterblows. When that routine was finished, they held up boards and chunks of tile, which he shattered. Drawing closer, Gus recognized him as the one called *El Jefe*.

Finished, *El Jefe* picked up a towel and began dabbing the sweat from his neck and face as he came toward Gus and Michelle. And Gus realized he had seen this face somewhere before.

Another man entered. He carried a roll of paper under one arm and wore a uniform like a stage costume, riding breeches and cavalry boots. A pistol and holster were slung on a Sam Browne belt. The cap had a peak modeled on the St. Louis arch. The blouse was festooned with gold-braided epaulettes with stars. It all looked like something out of Viennese operetta. Or a Charlie Chaplin movie. Gus couldn't avoid laughing.

Yet something sinister also registered in his visual memory. The one called *El Jefe*, said, "Yes, Colonel, we've met before. In a very different setting. Hanoi, 1972. I was known then as Major Minh. And Trang here was only a captain."

Trang! Of course. The one who had strung him up on

318

that meat hook! He had grown older and fatter, but the arrogance and cruelty were still there in his face.

Minh seemed to have aged little. Gus recalled that smooth, expressionless face. And the air of quiet menace it projected. "You must be somewhat disappointed in your country today," Gus said. "The way it's rejected most of the doctrines of Marx and Mao and even Uncle Ho."

"Vietnam was never *my country,* Colonel. I served it then because it served my purpose. You may recall I said the tropical nations must unite to avoid becoming mere satellites. For the past twenty-odd years, I've been laying the groundwork for that union.

"We've now gotten beyond the groundwork. In every capital between the tropics, there are people loyal to me. They influence current policy and lay the foundation for the future." He paused, turned. "But enough of reminiscing, Colonel. Trang has a message for you."

Grinning, Trang stepped forward. "You only colonel." He gave that snorting, inane little laugh Gus had heard over twenty years ago. "I major gen'ral now."

"Must be the boots," said Gus. "I never had a fancy pair of boots like that. Those the same ones you had in seventy-four?"

Trang frowned, then turned officious, unrolled the paper he had carried under his arm, and held it up before him like a town crier delivering a proclamation: "Gustavus Adolphus Halstrom, you tried and convicted *in absentia* in people's court for murder of one Hugh Bronquist, U.S. citizen and resident of Evanston, Illinois."

Gus gave a momentary frown, then said, "Ah! So that was his name. He deserved what he got. And your so-called people's court is an irrelevant anachronism. It has no jurisdiction here."

"Gus . . . ?" Mike's look was troubled. "What are they talking about?"

"Oh? Your lover here never told you he once strangled a man in cold blood?"

319

"They had this turncoat American actor who was a dead ringer for me. When they couldn't persuade me to make anti-American broadcasts, he was all set to step in. When the sonofabitch came to look me over, I killed him, changed clothes with him, and walked out. He was with this peacenik tour group, so I just joined them. Once we were airborne, I disabled the flight crew and flew the airplane to Bangkok. That's the story of my *mysterious* escape from Hanoi. Anyway, that all happened over twenty years ago, and their so-called people's court is irrelevant."

"Confirms the evidence of your conviction," said Minh. "QED."

"It was war," said Gus. "And everything I did was sanctioned by the Geneva Conventions."

"You will find here, Colonel," said Minh in cold, flat tones, "that your Geneva Conventions are irrelevant. A tool of capitalism, constructed by capitalists. And the sentence of the court is life at compensatory labor. You will atone for this murder and your decades of crimes against humanity by working for the ultimate success of the true people's revolution."

"You're raving," Gus said.

Minh showed a kind of satisfied smirk. "See if I'm raving when I tell you we've discovered the secret of what you call Pegasus." Gus noted how Minh was observing him, and checked any impulse to react. Still smirking, Minh gestured, and someone handed him an old copy of *Popular Mechanics* plus what looked like one of those *Time-Life* special interest volumes. He opened the *P-M* and held it up so Gus could see the double-page spread.

It was a pictorial cutaway of one of the Navy's dirigible aircraft carriers of the thirties. He next opened the *Time-Life* volume, one of a series on flight. This one covered lighter-than-air craft, and it too had a segment about the former Navy dirigibles, with full-page pictures.

"I think these sum up what Pegasus is all about,

Colonel. A modern revival of a sixty-plus-year-old concept. You and your pilots have been flying from a very high-tech, updated dirigible-aircraft carrier. That's how you were able to arrive at the Red Sea so quickly and operate there with such stealth. That, together with your presence here, by whatever odd circumstance, also convinces me this airship must be lurking about our airspace. Even though it doesn't show up on our radar."

"You're still raving."

"No more than General Borland was when we interviewed him. Men do not rave under truth serum." Again, Gus had to keep a tight rein on his reactions—anger, hatred for this smooth-talking bastard who had everything going his way.

At this, Michelle flared up. "You had no right to administer drugs to my patient without consulting me!"

"*Your* patient?"Minh again showed that cynical amusement. "My dear Doctor, you're in need of a reality check. He's *our* prisoner. Just as you are."

Finally confident he could keep his tongue and passions in check, Gus let himself speak. "You have me, and you seem to be finished with the general. You might as well let the two of them go."

"Ah! The gallant gesture." Minh chuckled with amusement. "How American, like the old Hollywood movies. And how stupid! Do you really think I'd call a taxi to run them in to Quito?"

His face resumed its smirk even while he began to pace, and he took on a lecturing manner. "Like you, General Borland has spent his career as part of the American effort to delay and deter the course of history. The United States has made itself a criminal nation by acting to frustrate the progress of mankind toward a communal society.

"Of course, we could just shoot the pair of you. That was the justice meted out in the early days of Mao's revolution. But compensatory labor is more exemplary. A body in an unmarked grave is soon forgotten. The irony of American officers working to overcome their own past will demonstrate how our revolution deals with its enemies."

Gus did a little smirking of his own. "Well, in case you hadn't noticed, humanity has been bringing in votes of no confidence on your communal society. Which has pretty well demonstrated its inability to produce prosperity."

Waving the rolled-up magazine like a pointer or swagger stick, Minh again lectured: "The United States conducted economic aggression against the socialist countries. As it still does against Cuba. Including that carnival-show array of gew-gaws and gadgets you call prosperity. It makes teaching socialism like trying to get children to do their lessons with a circus across the street."

"Yes, I can see how distracting it must be to watch your neighbor cut trees with a chain saw while you do it with an ax. Or move dirt with a bulldozer when you've only got shovels. And light his house with electricity where you use kerosene." His tone dripped irony. "No doubt about it, prosperity seduces people. Work of the Devil, I suppose."

He let his gaze stray around, to indicate the house and estate. "But I can see what a sacrifice you're making. Gathering all this prosperity unto yourself so others won't be corrupted. Pretty much like the Politburo did in Moscow."

Minh's face turned as cloudy as the peaks of the Andes. "I thought you might be educable, Colonel. But in spite of your brilliance as an engineer, you have the inherent stupidity that goes with your caste of mind. You're quite hopeless, so I leave you to begin your labors." He turned and started for the door.

"Wait," Gus said. "There's still no real reason to keep Doctor St. Clair. She can't have seen or heard that much. She's—"

"As I would expect, you fail to understand that our

322

movement, like Islam and early Christianity, is militant. Each of them holds that life belongs not to the individual but an abstract creator. Hence the injunction against suicide. So we hold that each person belongs not to himself but humanity as a whole. Doctor St. Clair will remain with us. We can always use a good doctor, and in time she could come to see the error of her past life." He showed a mocking smile. "We might even find her a suitable mate. Incorporate the obvious high quality of her genes into our movement."

Chapter Thirty-two

Gus found himself in quarters like a monk's cell, one of a row of cubicles opening onto a narrow corridor. It held a cot, a washstand, and a wall rack for clothing. Shower and toilet facilities were communal.

His injured leg was still sore, but he could strap on the boot and walk. It was his psyche that was troubled. He was a prisoner of a shrewd, sadistic madman and tormented by the twin specters of the compromise of Pegasus and the threat hanging over Michelle.

Next morning, he was rousted out by two of Minh's minions. The hour was uncertain, since his wrist chronometer had now been expropriated.

He still wore his flying suit, though both Minh and Trang had assured him that this time they would come up with work clothes to fit.

He was led to a large dining hall where men sat eating at long tables. He was herded through the line where dull-eyed servers wearing Quechua Indian features and grubby kitchen whites ladled out steaming-hot glop in various shades of dismal. The only thing he recognized was beans.

Soon afterward, a group of what he recognized as North Americans went through the line and settled nearby. Nearly everyone here wore either the Cuban uniforms or native costume, yet these men, an even dozen, were in Mao jackets. He also noted their generally frail appearance, as if they had been left weakened by disease.

At first they showed him only passing curiosity. Then gradually, a hostile stir animated their conversation. Meanwhile, some of their faces began to emerge from anonymity. Suddenly the truth burst upon him: These were his fellow prisoners from Hanoi, over twenty years ago!

Michelle sat in her room reflecting on her circumstances. Minh's remark about finding her a suitable mate had lit a blue-white flame of rage. She had shot Clifton Burr out of necessity and then suffered remorse. Right now, she would gladly pull the trigger on this one who was called *El Jefe*.

Maria, her combination jailer and *duenna,* gave the usual brusque knock, then entered unbidden. The door could be locked only from the outside, so there was no easy way to prevent this outrage. Maria was Indian—stolid, dumpy, ageless, and sexless. If she spoke anything beyond Spanish or the local Indian dialect, she kept it to herself. What she did not trouble to hide was her hostility toward Michelle, North Americans in general, and indeed all who did not share *El Jefe*'s vision of the future.

She gave the usual peremptory jerk of her head to convey that Michelle was to come with her.

"You're Halstrom, aren't you?" Gus faced them with his arms folded and his buttocks resting against a table, in a room remarkably like a drafting or engineering facility in the U.S.

"We have a right to know if you're the one who killed

325

that fellow back in seventy-four, then escaped and left us to take the heat."

"Yeah," a third voice from somewhere back in the group. "We were all interrogated. Some of us beaten. They were convinced we helped you."

"I did what every prisoner of war is both entitled and obliged to," Gus said. "What the Code of Conduct requires. I escaped when the opportunity arose. And the guy I killed had it coming. He was a—"

He was drowned out by a chorus of threats and abuse. "Let's get one thing clear," said the spokesman. "We have a life here. Not much of a life, but more than just an existence. And it didn't come easy. So don't get any ideas about doing it again. We've all agreed there's to be no escape. Nobody skips out and leaves the rest of us holding the bag."

Again the angry chorus seconded his words. Gus waited till he could be heard. "I have every intention of breaking out of here." He stood erect then, to emphasize both how he towered over them and the robust, muscular nature of his physique compared to theirs. "And, if I have to kill all of you to do it . . ."

There was an exchange of stunned looks that quickly segued back into hostility. "There are a lot more of us. You can't stay awake around the clock. We may just get you first."

Gus smiled. "At least, we know where we stand."

The dour Maria led Michelle to the clinic. Entering, they passed through a room where perhaps a dozen people waited. The place echoed with coughs, sneezes, and wheezes; the crying of the young, the soft moaning of the old, the stoic silence of the macho.

She protested: She was a surgeon, not qualified to diagnose and treat general ailments. Nevertheless, she was required to don a white medical smock and stethoscope and spend the day doing just that.

Señor Cavalante, with no FDA to exercise oversight, kept only a rough account of the drugs he stocked and dispensed. His major concern was reordering an item before it ran out. So she easily concealed a lethal dose in her purse. Just as in Asmara, she was prepared to take her own life as the ultimate way of opting out of *El Jefe*'s plan.

That evening, on the way back to her room, *El Jefe* intercepted them and dismissed Maria. "I thought you might like a tour of what will be your home." By her expression—or lack of it—she made it plain she did not accept that idea. "And it *can* be a home. *Or* a prison. The choice is up to you. To accept the place and the future we offer here or continue to act and be treated like a prisoner."

He led the way. It occurred to her that knowing the house and grounds would be very useful when the time came for escape. So she made careful mental notes of the layout. Most of all, the various exits.

A very large, cathedral-like room called the *sala grande* had a tile floor and was thick with live plants. On one side, a glass outer wall towered three stories and afforded a marvelous view of the lake and the distant Andes. What caught her attention most, however, was the vast aquarium whose top was some eight feet above the floor. Inside, she sensed the gliding motion of shadowy forms.

He explained that he kept specimens of the continent's best known aquatic predators, then paused to hold a brief exchange on an interphone speaker. Soon two men in laborer's dress entered on the upper level, a banquette or balcony atop the aquarium. Each one carried an object in a jute sack. From the grunts and squeals, she realized they were live objects and began to feel a certain foreboding. The men lifted a section of the flooring on that upper level, dumped the objects in.

They were piglets, some fifteen to twenty pounds each. For a few moments, they swam and struggled, looking for some escape. Then darting, silvery forms swarmed. Blood clouded the water, and the struggles subsided. Michelle looked on in fascinated horror long enough to realize these were piranha devouring the piglets live. Then she turned away in disgust, her stomach churning.

"It *is* rather shocking at first," he said. "But you'll get used to it, perhaps even come to enjoy the spectacle."

"I assure you," she said through clenched teeth, "that I shall do neither!"

Next morning, instead of Maria, her escort was that malevolent clown Trang in his stage uniform. On the way, he babbled on in his pidgin-English. When she did not respond, he said, "You must teach yoo'se'f to like us. Much better fo' you."

The route led through the *sala grande*. Outside, an overcast covered everything, and the colors of the land-scape were muted. Judging from the dim light, it was still rather early.

Then, in a kind of surreal scene, men in parachutes descended out of that overcast. More appeared every sec-ond. There seemed dozens. She stared in wonderment.

Trang was even more stunned. With eyes and mouth gaping, he sleepwalked toward the window. And while he was mentally immobilized, she recovered and saw this was her salvation: Those were paratroops sent to rescue General Borland!

Almost unbidden, her hand flew out and plucked Trang's pistol from its holster.

That brought him out of his trance. Snarling, he turned. But instead of knocking the weapon aside, he grabbed the barrel and pulled, in a contemptuous gesture, as if he were simply taking it from a child. With his other hand, he struck her across the face, then clutched at her throat. She pushed the muzzle against his midriff and pulled the trigger.

The effect was startling. Momentarily, his already rotund abdomen ballooned; blood erupted from his nose and mouth, and he collapsed. Pressure more than bullet passage caused massive internal hemorrhage and tissue damage.

The muffled shot had probably not been heard. The body was too heavy to move quickly or far, but she dragged it over the tile into cover among the large potted plants. With the pistol in her purse, she went in search of Gus.

The distant rattle of automatic weapons fire signaled that Spring Harvest had begun. Gus was instantly alert.

So were the two armed men who stood guard over the lab. The Hanoi prisoners looked up and stirred uneasily, but remained at their work. One of the guards sent the other to learn what was happening.

The one remaining carried his AK-47 slung. When he turned to peer down the corridor, Gus saw his chance. Sensing a threat, the man tried to unsling the weapon. Gus's leg—the injured one—shot out in a kick blow. It knocked the guard against the wall and the weapon from his grip. Gus seized it and slammed the butt against his head. The guard fell and never twitched.

Now the others were astir. "What the hell are you doing?" one of them shouted.

Before Gus could answer, the second guard reentered. Gus leveled the Kalashnikov and pulled the trigger. It burped and bucked in his grip. Chunks of both the guard and the plaster spattered.

With his pulse racing, but with a calm exterior, Gus moved to collect the man's weapon. Meanwhile, he swung the other muzzle to cover the others.

"Oh, my God!" The voice was almost plaintive. "You've done it again. Come here and ruined things for us! We'll all be—"

B. Michelaard

"You jackass! This is your chance get out of here and back to the States. That shooting you hear means American troops."

"And what would we do back in the States?" Another near-plaintive voice. "We'd be strangers. Our wives will all be remarried, our kids grown up without knowing us. Everything changed."

"So you'd rather rot away in this hole, working like trained seals for that insane bastard who wants to pick up where Stalin and Mao left off? Building nuclear missiles that might someday be fired at the States? That is what you're doing, you know. I've seen enough. And you've all worked with plutonium too. That's what's got you so wasted."

He waited for his words to sink in. "I knew it," came a voice. "I told you guys that was plutonium, but you—"

"Oh, shut up! He's just trying to—"

"Then how did Schroeder and Sanborn die? Remember? I said that was radiation poisoning, not typhus like they told us."

"I think the die is cast," said yet another voice. "If he's right—and he probably is—Minh can't take the chance of seeing us repatriated."

"Smart thought," said Gus. "Now get your butts moving before they get here."

With the hesitancy of sheep or cattle being herded into a chute, they edged toward the door—and freedom, a concept they hadn't entertained in years.

Chapter Thirty-three

Leaving the *sala grande,* Michelle heard bursts of automatic fire from outside. Her surest way to freedom now was to go out and wave till the paratroops saw her. But she wanted to be sure Gus too was free.

Finding him would be a mean proposition. At the clinic entrance was a passage extending beyond, into what seemed a separate wing, not part of the original. A good place to start.

She found the clinic deserted. The corridor here had no flooring or parget. In the cold light of overhead fluorescent fixtures, the quotidian sterility of concrete floor and walls of concrete block felt sinister. She suppressed a shudder and hurried on. At first there were only blank walls; then the corridor made a right angle, and she passed what must be doors to small rooms. Side corridors offered the same prospect. Finally, she went through a large, swinging double door.

Beyond, she came to offices with desks and files; others with those large, tilt-adjustable drawing tables used by architects and engineers. This too was deserted. Yet another door opened onto a laboratory with equipment and instruments.

Opposite were tandem doors with frosted glass, and beyond that what seemed to be daylight. Hurrying over, she was brought up just short of it by a pool of blood, still moist except at the edges. The wall above was blood-spattered and bullet-pocked.

"What are you doing here!"

The voice of *El Jefe* was soft but full of menace.

Gus herded the captives into the open, emphasized they must stand quite still and raise their hands when they met U.S. troops. For himself, he counted on the markings on his flying suit, including the U.S. flag on the shoulder. And the troops should know he was here.

Skyhook must have flown to Panama, loaded them into the troop-carrier pod, and flown back, all in a matter of hours. It was downright fortuitous the pod was already in place because of the exercise.

He also thought of those steel traps. Hundreds could be scattered over the grounds, a serious threat to both the captives and the paratroops. For now, he could only warn the captives and hope for the best.

Then, while the firing advanced toward the mansion, he went back inside to search for Michelle.

Carrying an AK-47, he ran through empty corridors, opening doors, calling her name. Finally, he came to a cathedral-like room with a glass wall three stories high, a Sea World-size aquarium, and enough greenery for an arboretum. There was a rush of booted feet, and he was facing a dozen or so Uzis. He dropped the weapon and raised his hands.

"Colonel Halstrom?" A paratroop captain in full battle gear came forward and saluted.

"Right." Gus returned the salute. "Have you located General Borland or Doctor St. Clair?"

"Not yet, sir. We just got inside." From his front pocket, he produced an envelope. "For you, sir." While Gus opened and read the message, the captain got on his walkie-talkie. "Hello, Sandusky, this is Cat's Paw Charlie. Be advised we have just delivered the package to Pony One." A voice from the radio acknowledged.

The message read, "Return aboard ASAP. Orders from Mother Hen." It was signed, "Skipper."

That plus the captain's strong insinuation he'd only be in the way dissuaded Gus from joining the search. "Don't worry, Colonel. If they're here, we'll find 'em."

"By the way, did you run across any steel traps?" Gus was curious.

"Dozens of 'em, sir. But we were warned in advance. Our mine detectors sniffed 'em out, and we sprung 'em." He paused. "All the same, be careful where you step. Can't say for sure we found 'em all." Another pause. "That little one-man copter yours, sir?"

"Sure is. Where'd you—?"

"Sitting there in a grove of trees transmitting signals. We carried it up here." He jerked a thumb. "It's outside."

"You find any Americans in Mao jackets wandering around?"

"We had some reports about stray Americans. I think they've all been rounded up. Hard to tell what their status is."

"Well, treat 'em gently. They're Vietnam POWs. I know it sounds crazy, but it's a fact. Contact your command post and see they're cared for and moved to safety."

"Yes, sir. We can do that."

Gus hesitated. "Now, could you spare me a couple grenades?" The captain frowned, considering. Gus figured what persuaded him was his own paratroop badge below the pilot's wings on his flying suit. Army men tended to vest a certain confidence in anyone who had completed that course at Fort Benning. A bag of grenades was turned up and two of them handed over. "Thanks, Captain. Carry on."

To orient himself, he mounted the stairs to look out the windows at the level atop the aquarium. The floor there had removable sections, and one had in fact been lifted out of its place, leaving a hole roughly three feet square. He could see into the murky greenish water below, and realized it was connected with that channel and the oxbow lake outside, the one he had noted from the air.

A slice of the lake and the diesel generators were visible. And there right next to them sat the air pony.

Finding it was one thing. Getting airborne and back to the airship still presented a problem. The fuel had been pretty low when he landed. The battery would be run down, and there was no auxiliary power here. His one chance was the one-time emergency start.

The diesels were housed in a large shed with a fuel tank above. Diesel fuel was similar to jet fuel, so he decided to try to draw some.

As if it were made just for him, a length of garden hose and hand pump, apparently for fueling tractors and such, protruded from a hole in the metal cover of the tank. U.S. troops showed up and were eager to help. They climbed onto the roof of the shed and pumped while he filled the pony's tank.

Afterward, they gathered around and watched, intrigued by the notion that such a toylike machine could actually carry a man aloft. He took a deep breath and hit the emergency starter button.

The rockets fired and spun the rotors. So far, so good. But would they create enough juice for the run-down battery to spark the ignition? His triumphant "Ha-ha-a-a!" was drowned by the rocket exhaust and then the whine and roar of turbines as the engines fired up. He gave a thumbs-up. The men fell back from the rotor wash, and he got airborne.

Some twenty minutes later, he eased the pony through

a temporary gap blown in Skyhook's vapor shroud. The ruby lights rimming the huge maw of the recovery port loomed out of the blend of natural and artificial vapor. He air-taxied up the flight deck to the nose section.

Excitement had given him an adrenaline rush. Now he realized how swollen and painful the leg still was. He limped his way to the flight surgeon. As the dressings were peeled off, he was reminded that Mike had put them on. It emphasized her status—still missing.

On the bridge, a smiling Hank Borland said, "Well, I guess your little inspection flight turned into quite an adventure."

"Enough to write a book about." He paused, doing a mental gearshift over Hank's obvious good mood. "Any word from the troops at Casa Elena?"

"Just had a report. Came through Harvester. They found Chip. He's okay. Surprised the people in the clinic where they had him." Hank hesitated, swallowed. "And Gus, we owe his life to Mike. We'll never be able to thank or repay . . ." His voice trailed off. "So whatever has to be done to get her back . . ." Again, he left the sentence hanging. "No word of her yet, but they're still looking."

Mother Hen wanted to know everything Gus had learned at Casa Elena. He told them, winding up with his estimate of Minh's objective: a Marxist regime spanning the tropics as a base for the continued pursuit of world revolution. He added that back in '72, Minh had shown him a '60 class ring from Ohio University.

All this really shook someone's tree in the Pentagon. He was tied up in the comm center answering questions he suspected came from the CIA and/or DIA.

The exchange went on and on—in an on-and-off pattern. Gus worried about Mike, and slept poorly. Eventually, a voice from Mother Hen said, "We're transmitting a picture, a computer-aged photograph. We believe this is

Minh or *El Jefe* or whatever he calls himself as he'd look today." The picture came up on the video monitor.

For a moment, Gus stared, fascinated. "That's our man," he said. "In living color."

"Good. That's all for now."

A few hours later, a comm center printer began spitting out a fresh message: Minh/*El Jefe* was born Joseph Simpson, in 1939, on a North Dakota reservation. His father, Howard Simpson, aka Walking Bear, had won a scholarship to the Sorbonne. In Paris, he'd married a fellow student, a Vietnamese named Minh. Howard Simpson had volunteered for service in War II, was commissioned a lieutenant of infantry, and died in action in the Ardennes in 1944. In 1946, the mother, by then a dedicated Marxist, took her son to Hanoi. Later, he'd earned an AB from Ohio University, then an advanced degree from the Sorbonne.

The next Harvester message stated that the defenders, who'd put up little resistance, were nearly all Cubans farmed out by Castro. A thorough search had turned up no trace of Doctor St. Clair.

What Gus had learned during his brief captivity—that Minh probably had a modest arsenal of nuclear-tipped IRBMs—made a radical change in the color of things. Mother Hen messaged that the President and the Joint Chiefs would rejoice greatly if the complex at Curracabamba was destroyed. But with no appearance of U.S. involvement. If possible, it was to look like an accidental explosion.

Part of Skyhook's armament was cruise missiles. To impress a few still-wavering key members of Congress, several advanced models of those used during the Gulf War had been brought aboard for that exercise in California. Something added in the way of targeting was a tiny homing transmitter to be planted by infiltrators. It let the missile follow an indirect course and double back on its target.

Gus and Hank sat down together and worked out a plan.

It included Gus's infiltrating Casa Elena in search of Michelle.

So the comm officer with the worried frown found Hank there just after sunrise. "Sir, I've got this message from Mother Hen for Air Group One, and I can't seem to find Colonel Halstrom."

"Message them back he's on a reconnaissance flight." Hank turned to stare out the windscreen and said to himself, "We're not really lying; we're just stretching the truth."

A frontal system moving through the area brought gusty winds that rocked and pitched the airship. Hank decided to take shelter in the lee of one of the larger foothills where natural cloud would afford cover.

Gus found himself fighting those same rough conditions as the air pony slithered through the half light of dawn.

Photo intelligence plus all other sources indicated the mine excavations honeycombing Curracabamba as the hiding place of the missiles and their support systems. The adits of the old mineshafts and tunnels still stood open, vulnerable points in the complex. Using maps supplied by the former mining company, he and Hank had selected several that seemed the most likely.

Throughout Spring Harvest, Major Gil Austen was putting in extra time, and would be in the ship's cockpit for the next four hours. Word had gotten around that this was the location where he had lost his aircraft and crew, and Decker was indulging him.

Gus located the chosen mine adits and placed one just inside each. This was not the sort of function for the Sky-hook CAG. If things went wrong, his butt would be hanging out in the breeze of bad judgment. He could forget about any more of Pete Cassidy's favor or any thought of a BG's star and a key role in the expansion of Pegasus.

But Michelle was now the most important thing in his life, far beyond whatever might be left of his career. Life without her would be less than half a life. And to know he had failed to seize even the slimmest chance to save her was more than he could live with.

He circled Casa Elena at rooftop level, confident the wind and the roar of the diesel generators would drown out the relatively low volume of sound from the pony.

By necessity, he had come in something of a hurry, managing to get hold of a few hand tools that might be useful. He still had those two grenades he had bummed from the paratroops plus his pilot's personal side arm.

A complete circuit showed no easy entry. The doors and windows were all shut. He needed the advantage of stealth, so he couldn't just smash a window.

Something caught his notice then, a dish antenna, which had not been there before. It was a lot like those used for satellite TV reception. Its high elevation was consistent with the latitude here near the equator. That dish was aimed at a satellite in earth-synchronous orbit.

It was mounted on a vertical wooden chase at the apex of the roof. The chimneylike chase extended some ten feet above the ridge poles and obviously carried the antenna leads. It might also afford a means of entry. That rough air made the binoculars too unsteady to see much detail.

The steep pitch of the roof meant the pony could not simply straddle a ridgepole. He could only hook the landing gear over it from the upwind side. With the collective in negative lift, both the wind and the idling rotors helped hold the pony in place.

Getting off and making his way along the ridge, he clung to that sharp crest the way a non-swimmer clings to a life preserver. His injured leg made it no easier.

The antenna was attached to a supporting metal shaft by a universal joint and controlled by an electric motor through worm-drives. The shaft was secured to the chase by U-clamps. The antenna lead had a quick-disconnect. It gave him an idea: He loosened several of the screws that held the U-clamps. The wind did the rest and tore the antenna off.

Airborne again, he came to a hover at some distance and waited. In a few minutes, two men in workman's coveralls emerged atop the chase. They lowered a segment of steel ladder, descended to examine the wood where the screws had pulled out, held a brief exchange, and went back inside.

He stared, almost holding his breath: They had left the ladder in place.

Chapter Thirty-four

Michelle was thinking that twice now her nobler impulses had led her to an abyss and threatened to push her over the edge.

In Eritrea, things had looked bleak; here they looked hopeless. She was a prisoner in an underground labyrinth. As the paratroops closed in, Minh and his inner circle escaped in elevators disguised as closets.

He had discovered Trang's body and followed her trail. When she'd tried to get the pistol out of her purse, he'd hit her across the face in cold fury. "You'll pay for that, you murdering bitch!"

That fury had perhaps had a plus side: He'd taken the pistol, but had not discovered the needle and syringe. More and more, she clung to that lethal drug as her last line of defense.

His threat of retribution hung over her, but so far she had only been called upon to exercise her medical skills on behalf of the company in these catacombs. She had soon realized they were not down here just to hide. Their comings and goings had an urgent and—she feared—a sinister purpose.

After the two men disappeared down the chase, Gus again alit on the roof and made his way along the ridge-pole. He climbed the ladder, and inside found an open steel hatch cover to a narrow vertical shaft with a steel ladder.

He descended without seeing anyone, found himself in a loft—a superstructure of steel trusses traversed by cat-walks. The light was minimal and came from below.

He was on one of those catwalks, and set out to see where it led.

The figure seemed to arise out of nowhere. One moment Gus was seeing only the geometric shapes of structural steel; then a human form emerged. There was a faint click, and a light came on nearby, a small bulb, but enough for Gus to see clearly the man in workman's clothing.

And for the man to see him.

The instant their eyes locked, Gus went for his holster. But on the way, his hand brushed against the tool belt and his mind against a better idea. Without thought, he had the screwdriver in his grip, the blade forward. Like a machine under digital programming, his forearm drove forward to strike and back to withdraw. The blade and shank penetrated just below the notch of the sternum.

With a faint gurgling sound, the man staggered back-wards. Gus reached to grab the shirt, but the torso twisted away, tottered, and pitched headlong over some unseen drop-off.

Aghast, Gus edged forward, found another ladder. His victim had fallen all the way to the floor below.

"You will come with us, Doctor."

Mike's pulse leaped. Was this her summons to face retribution?

No. She was told to bring her medical kit. A man was injured. "We don't even want to move him ourselves," said one of the pair.

She had no kit as such. She could only throw items that might be useful into one of those airline bags and tell Señor Cavalante to stand by. The clinic in this underground stronghold had the same supplies and equipment as the one above, albeit fewer beds.

She did not take her purse. If the time came for that lethal dose, she felt sure she would have some notice.

Apparently Minh had decided she was a dangerous character. One man led the way; the other walked behind and carried a pistol.

They entered an area where she had not yet been and came to a large door, like those found in public buildings. Her escort pulled it open and motioned her in.

"Control room" was the term that came to her. Men in white lab smocks sat at CRT screens, operating keyboard consoles. Rows of colored lights on panels winked in baffling, fascinating sequence. It recalled telecasts of launches from Cape Canaveral.

"Over here." Men wearing workmen's clothes and worried frowns stood around another lying crumpled at the base of a steel ladder. It seemed obvious he had fallen; nevertheless, she asked what happened.

They muttered in Spanish and shrugged. Then one said in English, "Must have lost his footing. It's dangerous up there."

Overhead was a shadowy loft of steel trusses. She too looked up, checking the distance he had fallen.

Up in the shadows, a face was just ducking out of sight. And for the second time in the last several minutes, her pulse leaped.

Gus!

From his hidden perch, Gus heard Mike pronounce the man dead of a broken neck. He had drawn back to avoid her gaze lest her reaction give him away. Yet he hoped now that she had seen him.

Everything here confirmed his judgment: Minh had ballistic missiles with nuclear warheads, and this was a countdown for a launch.

He didn't have to think twice about the target—or targets. And he was now not merely the first line of defense, but the last. He had to do battle in an arena where he was an amateur.

And he had to win. Or die trying.

Mike had the body covered quickly, before anyone could notice the minor external bleeding from that small but fatally deep puncture wound in the V of the rib cage. Gus must have been forced to stab him to keep him quiet. Hard to say if the victim was already dead when the fall crushed two cervical vertebrae and severed his spine.

She had known Gus would never abandon her, yet there seemed so little he could do. But he was here, and that lethal dose was looking a little less needed.

She felt obligated to ease his task, try to contact him. The clinic offered little enough to do. The rate of sickness and injury down here was nothing like that among the workers and soldiers she saw up on the surface. Though on call, she was idle.

After sitting there some time and letting out a few bored sighs, she casually picked up her purse and told Señor Cavalante she'd be in her room, which was more like a cell for a cloistered nun.

She had come down by an elevator whose upper entry was disguised. So the bottom must be guarded. Any stairways or ladders were probably watched too, but she had to make the effort.

Cautiously, she approached the elevator. No one in sight. So it was probably deactivated. Still, it was worth a try.

At her touch, the door slid silently open. With her

pulse doing a lively canter, she stepped inside and pressed the upper button. The door closed, and the car began to rise.

Knowing Mike was unharmed was a relief, but it brought Gus no closer to getting her out or preventing the launch of those missiles.

He had thought of throwing his two grenades into the electronic entrails of that control room. But that would use up his one chance and only delay the launch, not prevent it.

He decided to refuel while he thought about the problem. Like a moth, he flitted from the roof of the mansion over to the shed housing the diesel-powered generators. He had to get the siphon started from the roof, then move the pony to the ground below. Getting fuel into the tank involved spilling quite a bit.

The idea flickered through his mind: Could siphoning all the fuel out and stopping the generators stop the countdown?

No. The filler pipe that curved over the edge of the tank and through the cover was a five-inch tube of galvanized steel. The lower end was in the ground, connected to a pump inside a buried supply tank right about under his feet. Clamped to the pipe was a steel conduit carrying electricity to the pump, which would be cycled on and off by a float valve. To exhaust a huge underground tank with a garden hose might take a week.

But that led to another thought.

He took off and hovered along the edge of the water till he located the filler neck for the underground tank. The lagoon connecting the lake with the mansion and the aquarium was man-made. Shallow-draft barges would be brought up the river and maneuvered to unload diesel fuel.

The filler cap was secured by a nut like the one on a fire hydrant.

Back to the shed. And there, on an empty oil drum behind the roaring diesels, he found the massive wrench that fit.

A pebble dropped into the open filler pipe produced a small, satisfying "plop" several feet down.

Decision time: He had no idea how long before launch. His plan would start his own bomb ticking. No recall and no delay.

Could he get Mike out in that time? He wasn't even sure how much time it was. Twenty minutes? Thirty? An hour?

An hour would be too long. By then, the missiles could be in flight. No matter. It was his best chance. Perhaps his only chance.

He took a grenade from his belt and thick, strong rubber bands from his pocket. He placed a rubber band over the fuse handle, withdrew the pin while still holding the handle down. Slowly, carefully he relaxed his grip, ready to fling the grenade out into the lake.

The rubber held the handle down. He dropped the grenade into the open filler pipe, heard it splash into the fuel.

Now the bomb was set and ticking: Rubber, unless specially treated, would soften and deteriorate in contact with most forms of petroleum. Gasoline was the quickest. How long would diesel fuel take? In any case, when the rubber band gave way, the handle would pop open. Ten seconds later, Hell on earth. Or at least this part of the earth. Anyone who hadn't left by then never would.

He had a brief but unknown time in which to penetrate that underground maze, find Mike, and get out. The shaft on the roof was not the way. It led only to the loft and the control room.

He lifted off and again began to orbit the mansion. In half a circuit, he was looking at himself and the pony reflected in a vast expanse of glass: the huge room with the aquarium, where he had met the paratroops. He set the pony down on the paved patio outside the glass wall and left the engines idling.

No time to waste or spare now. And no one to hear breaking glass. But no need. The first door he tried was unlocked.

With the sky heavily overcast, the light inside was dim despite all that glass. The plants made the place dark and spooky, almost junglelike. He moved slowly, senses touchy as a seismograph.

The sudden rapid footsteps sounded like a stampede.

Gus whirled, took cover behind one of the massive potted shrubs. His hand groped for the pistol. With the muzzle leveled, he waited for the figure to emerge from the shadows and greenery. His finger tightened, awaiting a clear shot.

"Mike!"

"Gus!" His gut froze at what he had almost done.

Then time dissolved; place dissolved. Reality itself shrank to a single luminous fact: He had done it. He had found her.

Against lottery-size odds and mega improbabilities, he had found her—whole, well, and retrievable.

Which was why the mocking voice from among the ferns and fronds nearby did not fully register at once. "A touching scene, *mes enfants*," Minh said as he came forward. "It pains me to have to intrude."

Chapter Thirty-five

"And in local news here in Washington, a well-known syndicated columnist has been charged with assault. Earlier today, Arthur Penross entered the offices of the magazine *Avanti* and attacked Melissa Carrell, a reporter and staff writer. Her male colleagues intervened and held him till police arrived. He is free on bond pending arraignment. Meanwhile, the judge has issued a restraining order forbidding him to go near Miss Carrell."

After a moment's mental paralysis, Gus went for the pistol, but Minh was quick as a mongoose. His kick sent it skittering out of Gus's hand and out of sight among the shrubbery. The second blow, an instant later, knocked Gus into the shrubs with it. He took the blow on his arm, which was nearly paralyzed, but he saved his ribs.

Minh turned to Michelle, who fled to the mezzanine. Gus picked himself up, dashed up the other stairway, teeth clenched against the pain in his leg. By the time he gained the top, Mike was in Minh's grasp. Her purse fell to the floor.

Gus aimed a blow at Minh's neck, putting everything into it. Minh evaded, took the blow behind the ear. Yet he grunted, let go of Michelle, turned to face Gus. "Very well, Colonel. This will be a fight for survival. With Doctor St. Claire an added prize. The loser will be food for the fish."

"Mike, get out of here!" Gus said. "There's no one to stop you. They're all down in that hole. It's your best chance."

Minh showed a faint smile that bordered on a smirk.

Then he attacked.

Gus found himself pummeled by frightening, painful blows. Frightening because they were held back. Minh danced away, balancing catlike on the balls of his feet. "This encounter is a paradigm, Colonel," he said. "Your Eurocentric culture is waning. Its concept of the primacy of the individual is being replaced by the Tropical view. Mankind as a part of nature and each person a part of the whole."

Plainly enjoying himself, Minh added an occasional feint to his words, flicked out a fist or a foot to make Gus dodge or retreat.

Gus ignored Minh's socio-babble and focused on the problem: He had done enough martial arts himself to know that the typical karate blow develops its full force as the arm or leg is extended. To be safely parried, it must be turned aside or arrested while the limb is still flexed.

His best hope was to get in close, crowd Minh, even grab wrists or body. Somehow he had to get past that deadly, bone-cracking perimeter.

Which was a bit like the mice's plan to put a bell on the cat.

The answer came as a kind of reaction, without thought. They were still near the balustrade, at the edge of this mezzanine level. He grabbed one of the potted plants and hurled it at Minh's head. As Minh ducked and threw up a guard, Gus rushed and was all over him.

Minh solved the strategy at once and tried to retreat, but Gus crowded him, grasping, punching at the midriff.

In a few minutes, they were both breathing hard. Gus was somewhat stronger, Minh greatly more adept. Reality told Gus he could hold out longer this way, but in the end would still lose.

"Ee-youw! You bitch! I should've . . ." Minh whirled, reacting to the stick of Mike's hypo needle in his neck. As she depressed the plunger, he tore free, sending the syringe skittering across the floor in fragments.

Instantly, Gus drove his fist into Minh's ribs, felt a crunch.

For the first time, Minh lost his air of supreme confidence. He registered shock and pain, then determined hatred. Crowding him again, concentrating on body blows, Gus knew his enemy was no longer holding anything back. If Minh once got set and delivered a maximum blow, the fight would end abruptly.

Then Gus realized that crisp timing and perfect balance were fading. Whatever was in that syringe was having an effect.

Falling back, Minh hit the loose section of flooring that still lay beside the opening, tumbled backward. His skull made a sharp contact with the parquet flooring. Gus added a kick to the head, then turned and grabbed Mike's hand. "Let's get out of here."

They ran for the stair. With the ebb of adrenaline, his leg began to feel it was still in that steel trap. The rest of his body felt worked over with a ball-peen hammer.

She cast a sideways glance at him. "By tomorrow, you may look like plum pudding."

After several trials and wriggling efforts, she managed to squeeze in behind him on the air pony. He added the throttle and raised the collective. "Good thing you're not any heavier," he said.

He sensed peripheral motion. The plate-glass door of the *sala grande* swung open. With a look of mad tenacity, Minh came reeling toward them, drugged but determined.

Gus twisted the throttle to full power. Minh lunged, grabbed the left landing gear, and hung on.

For hour-long seconds, everything hung in the balance of forces—weight, lift, thrust.

Then slowly, the pony eased forward. Gus let it follow the slope of the stone steps downward, gathering a little speed. Minh's feet bumped along, but he kept his grip.

The forward speed increased. Easing the cyclic back, Gus called on the rotors to pass a little more air and gain a few feet of altitude. His gaze sought some object on which Minh could be "scraped off." But there was only grassy lawn and shrubs.

Finally, they were fully airborne, Minh's two feet dangling some three feet above the earth. Gus recalled the diesel generators: That shed would do nicely as a "scraping" object.

Rounding the end of the mansion, he spotted the lake, flew over the lagoons. But the pony was still not high enough to clear the generators.

Turning aside, still gaining altitude by the inch, he recalled the aquatic tanks in the sala grande were open to the lagoons.

Which gave him another idea.

Lining up on the nearest, he slowed, eased down toward the water, felt the drag as Minh's feet got wet. He came to a hover with the water up to Minh's chest. This partial floatation reduced the effect of Minh's weight, gave a little more control.

Minh kicked and jerked, trying to tilt the pony out of equilibrium. Gus plied the cyclic, maintaining it. The motion set up a waving and splashing in the lagoon.

The surface was riffled by the downwash from the rotors.

Then there was a roiling in the depths.

Minh's bellow of pain and terror merged with Mike's horrified scream. She put her hands to her face as blood tinged the water.

Suddenly free of Minh's grasp, the pony lifted. Gus turned to clear the lagoon, then came to a hover.

A five-foot circle of bloodied froth marked the place where Minh's pet piranha were putting an end to the mad design called Centralia.

That desperate fight had so consumed Gus's thoughts he had forgotten about the missiles and the countdown. He pressed a button to transmit a UHF carrier wave. It was the signal to Gil Austen that he was clear to launch the cruise missiles.

Just then came a heavy rumbling from somewhere on the far side of the mansion. He flew a wide circle, let the airspeed build. As it got more air through the rotors, the pony climbed better, and soon cleared the roof.

"Holy Jesus!" Gus heard himself exclaim.

His time bomb had finally ticked down.

The mansion jiggled on its foundations. The earth itself heaved, as if giving birth to some gigantic homunculus.

Then it erupted.

Flame geysered. Smoke mushroomed. The pillar of fire exceeded Biblical proportions. The earth divided. The fissure split the lagoon, belched flame, and looked seismic. The water itself seemed on fire. Steam billowed, obscuring the view.

Gus stared, fascinated. Then he realized Mike was screaming and pounding his shoulders. "Get us out of here!" It did seem prudent.

The course led them toward the mine shafts. He hoped to find a way through the gaps between the

351

clouds and the mountains, to reach either the coast or Quito.

What he came upon was a chilling sight.

A gleaming fifty-foot shaft stood upright on its launch pad next to a slender gantry. As they stared, fascinated, the gantry pivoted away, disconnecting the umbilical. In the distance, he could see perhaps half a dozen more in a similar prelaunch state.

He recognized the thin fog beneath the nozzles as the prelude to ignition. Then wavering flames grew rapidly into monstrous torches. But the blue-white blaze was not deflected by concrete. There was the empty space of an underground silo beneath. The deafening thunder penetrated even his helmet and padded earphones. It shook the earth and the atmosphere. They felt it in their limbs and viscera.

These were missiles with live warheads targeted at the Continental U.S. Minh was about to reach back from beyond death and have his vengeance. And Gus could only stare in frustration.

A flicker of motion tugged at the edge of his field of vision. The object's near-sonic speed made it ghostlike, a shadow flitting over the landscape. Before he could focus on it, he was left with only a swirl of dust at the mine adit—the pressure wave from the missile reflecting off the mouth of the tunnel.

Again, prudence advised a reversal of course. But he delayed, unable tear his gaze away.

The ballistic missile had just begun to lift when the earth once more began trembling. This time, he turned and headed away at full throttle.

A sunburst explosion made the landscape glow, blew a hole in the overcast, and filled his view in the mirror: One of those cruise missiles had found a really tender spot, ruptured fuel lines and/or storage tanks. Stores of binary rocket fuel—LOX and cryogenic hydrogen—had joined and ignited spontaneously. The result was volcanic.

352

That flame front rushing toward them looked like the surface of the sun. The heat would have burned exposed skin. Yet he knew the worst was yet to come.

Because the terrain itself would retard the rush of air and break up the shock wave, the greatest safety lay near the ground.

Yet getting there involved the risk of being caught in the most severe region, below the Mach Y-stem: As the shock wave spread through the atmosphere, it bounced off the ground below. This reflected wave traveled faster through the heated air behind the burst till it caught up and reenforced the initial wave. They joined in a Y-shaped configuration.

He went into a max descent, leveled just above the treetops. "Cover your ears and yell as loud as you can," he shouted. Then he fastened the oxygen mask on tight. The pursuing flame front slowed, climaxed just short of devouring them, and abated. Mike was clinging to him, muttering softly. He realized she was praying. "Yell!" he repeated.

The next instant, they were swallowed by a cataclysm.

The jolt from the shock wave felt like the punch of a thousand fists, all at once, all over the body. The noise was a thunderclap's embrace. The air pony rocked and jolted. Despite the seal of the helmet and earphones, his ears rang. "You okay?" he yelled at Mike. She gave him a nod and a weak smile.

They were sinking. That shock wave had flamed out one or more of the mini-jets. The pony was overloaded and flying on reduced power. As trees loomed ahead, he hit the emergency start. They clipped the tops, and a bit of branch lodged on the strut. More trees loomed across their path. Beyond lay a clearing.

The starter rockets gave the pony a modest boost. He got the nose and the cyclic up just enough to clear the trees. Beyond, they again sank below the treetops. Then the dead engine—or engines—lit off at full throttle. The surge of power propelled them toward a wall of trees that ringed the clearing. Trees filled his view ahead. He pulled back on the cyclic and held his breath.

A slice of sky appeared at the top. Again the landing gear clipped some upper branches, but they were free and climbing.

He turned the pony for a look back at this holocaust. That fireball had risen about a thousand feet and looked like a miniature nuclear burst.

Then something else caught his eye.

The fifty-foot shaft of the missile was tumbling end-over-end. The blast had tilted it beyond the limits of gyros and gimble rings. It was over a mile away now, but they could still hear the thunder of the rocket exhaust. And the twenty-foot torch at its tail made him think of a flaming baton tossed by a juggler. It arced over and began falling. The explosion when it struck was a mere firecracker compared to what had gone before.

And that was the only one to make it off the launch pad. The others had been destroyed by the gigantic explosion of the fuel stores.

The course reversal had led them back toward the estate. All that was left of the mansion was the foundation outline. A huge crater marked what had been the buried fuel tank, including the shed and its huge diesel generators. The lake had rushed in to fill all the cavities.

Miles away, in the cockpit of Skyhook, Gil Austen saw the gigantic billow of flames, the pencil-shaped missile rise and then tumble.

Straightening, half rising from his seat, he lifted his arms and shook his fists above his head. His animal bellow of triumph segued into something entirely different. He sank back into the seat, dropped his chin to his chest, and sat there sobbing gently.

The men on the bridge understood. The ghosts of Anvil Bravo were finally laid to rest.

HALSTROM NOMINATED AS BRIGADIER

Washington (AP)—Colonel Gus Halstrom, jet ace and noted research pilot, first made the Air Force promotion list to brigadier general several years ago. Today, the Pentagon announced he has again been nominated for that grade.

Actual promotion to general or flag rank requires Senate approval. After the controversial incident in Stockholm, it appeared impossible to get approval through the Senate, and Halstrom's name was withdrawn. This time around, his key role in the success of a sensitive and highly secret project is expected to tip the balance in his favor.

PHYSICIAN AND SKATER DOCTOR MICHELLE ST. CLAIR HONORED WITH PRESIDENTIAL MEDAL

Washington (AP)—Doctor Michelle St. Clair, daughter of Armand and Helene St. Clair of Seattle and once an Olympic figure-skating hopeful, today received the Citizen's Presidential Medal, the highest honor given to civilians for service to the United States and/or fellow citizens. In a ceremony conducted on the South Lawn of the White House and witnessed by the President, Marine Major General Chalmers "Chip" Borland hung the medal with its ribbon around the neck of a smiling Doctor St. Clair and then bestowed the customary "double-barreled" kiss on each cheek while her parents and Borland's wife, Connie, a close friend of Doctor St. Clair, looked on. Also present were Doctor St. Clair's fiancé, Colonel Gus Halstrom, Washington hotesss Fiona Freeland, and perhaps a dozen other friends and well-wishers.

The ceremony is thought to be unique in that General Borland was the direct beneficiary of Doctor St. Clair's heroic efforts. She knowingly walked into a dangerous situation aboard the hijacked P&O Flight 101 at Anchorage to treat the general for a gunshot wound. Her actions did not end there, but security prevents disclosure of further details.

NUPTIALS FOR FIGHTER ACE
AND PHYSICIAN-SKATER

Colonel Gus Halstrom, just named to become a brigadier general, today will marry Doctor Michelle St. Clair, one-time figure-skating champion and now a surgical resident at Gramercy Hospital. Doctor St. Clair, who won a national championship and was considered a strong contender for Olympic gold, would have been the first black woman to compete for the U.S. in Olympic figure skating. She was disqualified for a technical violation of then-stringent amateur rules.

The pair will exchange vows before the Reverend Severus Ward of Holy Trinity Episcopal Church. Best man is Air Force Chief of Staff General Pete Cassidy, a long-time friend of the groom. This is the second marriage for each. Halstrom's first wife was movie star Valerie Aubin. Doctor St. Clair was married to the late All-Pro tight end Rayford Gilliam.

"I'll get to the bottom of this thing yet!" Fiona was holding court and a glass of champagne, upstaging the bride and groom with her usual five-star chutzpah. After all, she was the hostess and was paying for all this.

The delay in their wedding plans, to let Gus's injuries heal and Mike's parents fly in from Seattle, created just the opening Fiona knew how to exploit. Like a five-hundred-pound canary, she took over and staged the reception at the Army-Navy Club, where she had a survivor's membership. "I mean, it's simply not done. No one gets away with a serious love affair on my turf, right under my nose."

Michelle showed a smile whose mixture of innocence and deviltry might be worth a Tony award. "So, if I give birth to a full-term baby in about seven months, that'll really put your harp out of tune." She held Gus's hand and smiled up at him.

The newlyweds were already in their travel clothes. Out front, the Countache awaited. Their honeymoon luggage had been sent ahead. The Lamborghini had no trunk space.

With her monologue completed, Fiona sidled up to the pair. "See that pathetic-looking character in black tie over there? That's Arthur Penross, the *former* nationally syndicated columnist."

"Oh?! What's he—?"

"Covering the wedding. For one of the local papers. And how are the mighty fallen!" She fluttered her eyelids and gave Gus a look that said she knew more than she was telling.

"In that case, I may just make his day. And certainly someone else's."

As Gus approached, Penross said, "Oh, Colonel! I've been hoping to have a few words with you. Could we—?"

"Afraid I haven't time. But there is someone else here you've been wanting to talk to." He led the way. "This is Major Gil Austen, the man whose feet of clay you were so eager to expose. Gil, this is Arthur Penross, one of your favorite columnists."

Gus faced the red-faced former pundit. "Incidentally, tapes of the radio traffic from the Anvil Bravo affair show Major Austen stayed at the controls so his crew could all bail out safely. Which meant he damn near didn't make it himself. The irony is that's what saved him. He came down some distance from the others. They were either picked up by the bad guys or machine-gunned in the water."

To Gus, the look on Penross's face was almost worth all the agony he had gone through at Casa Elena.

He caught Michelle by the hand and made for the door. "Come on, babe. Let's blow this joint."

THE
JAKARTA
PLOT
R. KARL LARGENT

The heads of state of the world's most powerful nations—the United States, Russia, Japan, Great Britain, Germany, and France—are meeting in Jakarta, on the island of Java, to issue a joint declaration to the Chinese government. China must stop its nuclear testing or face the strictest sanctions of the World Economic Council. But a powerful group of Communist terrorists—with the backing of the Chinese government—attack the hotel in which the meeting is taking place and hold the world leaders—including the Vice President of the United States—hostage. The terrorists have an ultimatum: The WEC must abandon its policy of interference in the Third World . . . or one by one the hostages will die.

___4568-0 $5.99 US/$6.99 CAN

THE SEA

R. KARL LARGENT

At the bottom of the Sargasso Sea lies a sunken German U-Boat filled with Nazi gold. For more than half a century the treasure, worth untold millions of dollars, has been waiting—always out of reach. Now Elliott Wages has been hired to join a salvage mission to retrieve the gold, but it isn't long before he realizes that there's quite a bit he hasn't been told—and not everyone wants the mission to succeed. The impenetrable darkness of the Sargasso hides secret agendas and unbelievable dangers—some natural, other man-made. But before this mission is over, Elliott Wages will learn firsthand all the deadly secrets cloaked in the inky blackness.

___4495-1 $5.99 US/$6.99 CAN

Dorchester Publishing Co., Inc.
P.O. Box 6640
Wayne, PA 19087-8640

Please add $1.75 for shipping and handling for the first book and $.50 for each book thereafter. NY, NYC, and PA residents, please add appropriate sales tax. No cash, stamps, or C.O.D.s. All orders shipped within 6 weeks via postal service book rate. Canadian orders require $2.00 extra postage and must be paid in U.S. dollars through a U.S. banking facility.

Name_____
Address_____
City_____State_____Zip_____
I have enclosed $_____ in payment for the checked book(s).
Payment <u>must</u> accompany all orders. ❑ Please send a free catalog.
     CHECK OUT OUR WEBSITE! www.dorchesterpub.com

THE MILLENNIUM PROJECT

JOSEPH MASSUCCI

At the stroke of midnight, December 31, 1999, the microprocessors controlling America's top-secret strategic defense satellite network will fail, rendering the network useless and the country vulnerable to attack. As experts scramble to defeat the problem, a mad genius and his army of militants stand ready to commit the ultimate crime.

___4460-9 $5.99 US/$6.99 CAN

Dorchester Publishing Co., Inc.
P.O. Box 6640
Wayne, PA 19087-8640

Please add $1.75 for shipping and handling for the first book and $.50 for each book thereafter. NY, NYC, and PA residents, please add appropriate sales tax. No cash, stamps, or C.O.D.s. All orders shipped within 6 weeks via postal service book rate. Canadian orders require $2.00 extra postage and must be paid in U.S. dollars through a U.S. banking facility.

Name_____
Address_____
City_____State_____Zip_____
I have enclosed $_____ in payment for the checked book(s).
Payment <u>must</u> accompany all orders. ❑ Please send a free catalog.

WAR BREAKER
JIM DeFELICE

"A book that grabs you hard and won't let go!"
—Den Ing, Bestselling Author of
The Ransom of Black Stealth One

Two nations always on the verge of deadly conflict, Pakistan and India are heading toward a bloody war. And when the fighting begins, Russia and China are certain to enter the battle on opposite sides.

The Pakistanis have a secret weapon courtesy of the CIA: upgraded and modified B-50s. Armed with nuclear warheads, the planes can be launched as war breakers to stem the tide of an otherwise unstoppable invasion.

The CIA has to get the B-50s back. But the only man who can pull off the mission is Michael O'Connell—an embittered operative who was kicked out of the agency for knowing too much about the unsanctioned delivery of the bombers. And if O'Connell fails, nobody can save the world from utter annihilation.

_4043-3 $6.99 US/$7.99 CAN

LADY OF ICE AND FIRE
COLIN ALEXANDER

Colin Alexander writes "a lean and solid thriller!"
—Publishers Weekly

With international detente fast becoming the status quo, a whole new field of spying opens up: industrial espionage. And even though tensions are easing between the East and the West, the same Cold war rules and stakes still apply: world domination at any cost, both in dollars and deaths. Well aware of the new predators, George Jeffers fears that his biotech studies may be sought after by foreign agents. Then his partner disappears with the results of their experiments, and the eminent scientist finds himself the target in a game of deadly intrigue. Jeffers then races against time to prevent the unleashing of a secret that could shake the world to its very foundations.

_4072-7 $5.50 US/$6.50 CAN

T.J. McFADDEN
LANDING PARTY

The Navy destroyer USS Kimmel is in its seventh month of a six-month deployment when they receive orders for one final mission—retrieve a hijacked Libyan helicopter containing a CIA agent and a defecting Libyan Major who knows where a group of Americans is being held hostage. Simple enough. But when the Kimmel arrives in the Mediterranean, they find the helicopter shot down, the Major dead, and the agent floating alone in the sea. The agent knows where the hostages are being held, but he also knows that if the situation is not resolved within seventy-two hours, the hostages will be killed. Now everything hinges on the Kimmel and its exhausted crew. Can they put together a landing party, armed only with equipment in the ship's armory, locate, rescue, and retrieve the hostages— all before the clock ticks down? They have no choice. And the hostages have no other hope.

___4627-X $5.50 US/$6.50 CAN

Dorchester Publishing Co., Inc.
P.O. Box 6640
Wayne, PA 19087-8640

Please add $1.75 for shipping and handling for the first book and $.50 for each book thereafter. NY, NYC, and PA residents, please add appropriate sales tax. No cash, stamps, or C.O.D.s. All orders shipped within 6 weeks via postal service book rate. Canadian orders require $2.00 extra postage and must be paid in U.S. dollars through a U.S. banking facility.

Name_____
Address_____
City_____State_____Zip_____
I have enclosed $_____ in payment for the checked book(s).
Payment <u>must</u> accompany all orders. ❏ Please send a free catalog.
        CHECK OUT OUR WEBSITE! www.dorchesterpub.com

SILENT DOOMSDAY

ROBERT PAYTON MOORE

The U.S. military has developed a new technology so effective it will render modern weapons of destruction totally useless. But the dream turns deadly when a mole in the lab leaks the technology to a Libyan despot with dreams of a unified Middle East under his iron rule, with no country able to stand between him and his terrifying goal. Suddenly the U.S. is confronted with their own super-weapon, and a total, all-out war to save the world from a silent doomsday.

___4395-5 $5.99 US/$6.99 CAN